***Praise for* John Gilstrap**
and his thrillers

SCORPION STRIKE

"Relentlessly paced as well as brilliantly told and constructed, this is as good as thrillers get."
—***The Providence Journal***

"A sizzling beach read for military action fans . . . the perfect summer read for thriller fans."
—***Publishers Weekly* (starred review)**

"The series deserves attention from anyone who enjoys plot-driven thrillers. . . . Grave is, as always, a solid series lead."
—***Booklist***

"This Jonathan Grave installment is pure John Gilstrap . . . on steroids!"
—**BookReporter.com**

"Grave, Boxers, and the rest of the gang are all back in *Scorpion Strike*, another action-packed thriller from John Gilstrap that'll have readers on the edges of their seats."
—**The Real Book Spy**

FINAL TARGET

"Fast-paced and well-plotted."
—***Booklist***

"Exciting ... es will

FINAL TARGET

"A superbly crafted thriller that will leave you craving more! *Final Target* is a nonstop, action-packed thrill ride."

—***TopShelf Magazine***

"Fans of Jeffery Deaver and Harlan Coben will find lots to love in the novel's action, suspense, political intrigue, twists, and deceptions."

—**Woman Around Town**

FRIENDLY FIRE

"If you only read one book this summer, make sure it's *Friendly Fire*, and be ready to be strapped in for the ride of your life."

—***Suspense Magazine***

"A blistering thriller that grabs your attention and doesn't let go for a second!"

—**The Real Book Spy**

NICK OF TIME

"A page-turning thriller with strong characters, exciting action, and a big heart."

—**Heather Graham**

AGAINST ALL ENEMIES

WINNER OF THE INTERNATIONAL THRILLER WRITERS AWARD FOR BEST PAPERBACK ORIGINAL

"Any John Gilstrap novel packs the punch of a rocket-propelled grenade—on steroids! Gilstrap grabs the reader's attention in a literary vise grip. A damn good read."

—**BookReporter.com**

"Tense, clever. . . . Series enthusiasts are bound to enjoy this new thriller."
—*Library Journal*

END GAME
AN AMAZON EDITORS' FAVORITE BOOK OF THE YEAR
"Gilstrap's new Jonathan Grave thriller is his best novel to date—even considering his enviable bibliography. *End Game* starts off explosively and keeps on rolling."
—Joe Hartlaub, BookReporter.com

DAMAGE CONTROL
"Powerful and explosive, an unforgettable journey into the dark side of the human soul. Gilstrap is a master of action and drama. If you like Vince Flynn and Brad Thor, you'll love John Gilstrap."
—Gayle Lynds

"Rousing. . . . Readers will anxiously await the next installment."
—***Publishers Weekly***

"It's easy to see why John Gilstrap is the go-to guy among thriller writers when it comes to weapons, ammunition, and explosives. His expertise is uncontested."
—John Ramsey Miller

"The best page-turning thriller I've grabbed in ages. There is no place you can put this book down."
—Beth Kanell, Kingdom Books, Vermont

"A page-turning, near-perfect thriller, with engaging and believable characters . . . unputdownable!"
—***Top Mystery Novels***

DAMAGE CONTROL

"Takes you full force right away and doesn't let go. The action is nonstop. Gilstrap knows his technology and weaponry. *Damage Control* will blow you away."

—Suspense Magazine

THREAT WARNING

"*Threat Warning* is a character-driven work where the vehicle has four on the floor and horsepower to burn. From beginning to end, it is dripping with excitement."

—Joe Hartlaub, BookReporter.com

"*Threat Warning* reconfirms Gilstrap as a master of jaw-dropping action and heart-squeezing suspense."

—Austin Camacho, *The Big Thrill*

HOSTAGE ZERO

"Jonathan Grave, my favorite freelance peacemaker, problem-solver, and tough-guy hero, is back—and in particularly fine form. *Hostage Zero* is classic Gilstrap: the people are utterly real, the action's foot to the floor, and the writing's fluid as a well-oiled machine gun. A tour de force!"

—Jeffery Deaver

"This addictively readable thriller marries a breakneck pace to a complex, multilayered plot. . . . A roller coaster ride of adrenaline-inducing plot twists leads to a riveting and highly satisfying conclusion. Exceptional characterization and an intricate, flawlessly crafted story line make this an absolute must read for thriller fans."

—*Publishers Weekly* (starred review)

NO MERCY

"*No Mercy* grabs hold of you on page one and doesn't let go. Gilstrap's new series is terrific. It will leave you breathless. I can't wait to see what Jonathan Grave is up to next."

—**Harlan Coben**

"John Gilstrap is one of the finest thriller writers on the planet. *No Mercy* showcases his work at its finest—taut, action-packed, and impossible to put down!"

—**Tess Gerritsen**

"A great hero, a pulse-pounding story—and the launch of a really exciting series."

—**Joseph Finder**

"An entertaining, fast-paced tale of violence and revenge."

—***Publishers Weekly***

"No other writer is better able to combine in a single novel both rocket-paced suspense and heartfelt looks at family and the human spirit. And what a pleasure to meet Jonathan Grave, a hero for our time . . . and for all time."

—**Jeffery Deaver**

AT ALL COSTS

"Riveting . . . combines a great plot and realistic, likable characters with look-over-your-shoulder tension. A page-turner."

—***Kansas City Star***

AT ALL COSTS

"Gilstrap builds tension . . . until the last page, a hallmark of great thriller writers. I almost called the paramedics before I finished *At All Costs*."

—Tulsa World

"Gilstrap has ingeniously twisted his simple premise six ways from Sunday."

—Kirkus Reviews

"Not-to-be-missed."

—Rocky Mountain News

NATHAN'S RUN

"Gilstrap pushes every thriller button . . . a nail-biting denouement and strong characters."

—San Francisco Chronicle

"Gilstrap has a shot at being the next John Grisham . . . one of the best books of the year."

—Rocky Mountain News

"Emotionally charged . . . one of the year's best."

—Chicago Tribune

"Brilliantly calculated. . . . With the skill of a veteran pulp master, Gilstrap weaves a yarn that demands to be read in one sitting."

***—Publishers Weekly* (starred review)**

"Like a roller coaster, the story races along on well-oiled wheels to an undeniably pulse-pounding conclusion."

***—Kirkus Reviews* (starred review)**

Also by John Gilstrap

Scorpion Strike

Final Target

Nick of Time

Friendly Fire

Against All Enemies

End Game

Soft Targets

High Treason

Damage Control

Threat Warning

Hostage Zero

No Mercy

Six Minutes to Freedom (with Kurt Muse)

Scott Free

Even Steven

At All Costs

Nathan's Run

JOHN
GILSTRAP

TOTAL MAYHEM

A Jonathan Grave Thriller

PINNACLE BOOKS
Kensington Publishing Corp.
www.kensingtonbooks.com

PINNACLE BOOKS are published by

Kensington Publishing Corp.
119 West 40th Street
New York, NY 10018

First printing: July 2019

10 9 8 7 6 5 4 3 2 1

ISBN-13: 978-0-7860-3982-1
ISBN-10: 0-7860-3982-5

Printed in the United States of America

Electronic edition:

ISBN-13: 978-0-7860-3983-8 (e-book)
ISBN-10: 0-7860-3983-3 (e-book)

To Benjamin Charles Branch.
Welcome to the scrum, kid!

Chapter One

Tom Darone had seen a lot of people die in his day, but not like this. The lady in the blue coat—the first to go down—made a barking sound and then folded in on herself. Tom's first thought was that she'd suffered a seizure, or maybe a stroke. She sat two spaces down from him in the bleachers and one row closer to the football field. Her emergency happened at the same second when Number 19 of the Custer Cavalrymen intercepted a pass at the end zone, robbing the Hooker Hornets of a go-ahead touchdown.

In all the excitement, nobody saw her collapse. Then her husband noticed. "Anita?" he said as he stooped to help her.

Then the crowd erupted with a new kind of cheer.

People pointed, and Tom followed their fingers to see that a player had collapsed on the field. Was that blood?

Then two more players fell. A chunk of helmet erupted in a gruesome spray from a fourth.

The lights went out. In an instant, the field went

from the artificial daylight brightness that is unique to nighttime football to true darkness.

Anita's husband shouted, "Oh, my God, she's been shot! Help me!"

A ripple of four spectators to Tom's right fell side by side among yelps of pain.

The field was under attack.

Tom watched with a strange sense of detachment as the panic hit. Home now only two months from his sixth deployment to the Sandbox, and six weeks into his new status as an unemployed vet, the reality of the moment crystalized in an instant. The first survival challenge would be to avoid being trampled in the stampede.

The panic around him didn't blossom or bloom. It erupted. Those who'd been hit—and the people who loved them—hunkered down, while everyone else fled. In a single instant, hundreds of people decided that survival trumped everything. A few were so overwhelmed by the enormity of the swirling action that they simply shut down, but they were the minority. Most people ran. They had no obvious destination, and they had no apparent plan. Most didn't even know where the exits were, so they followed the people ahead of them on the assumption that strangers were smarter than they were.

The mayhem grew to critical proportions in mere seconds. Tom realized in a rush that he was in the epicenter of the kill zone. As the sea of spectators pushed and tumbled past each other—and as bullets continued to find their marks—Tom dropped to his stomach into the foot-trough of the bleachers and rolled to his right. As he dropped into the matrix of the metal support structure, his boot found a foothold, and then so did his hands.

From there, it was like climbing down a ladder designed by a funhouse architect. Nothing was level, and no edge was smooth, but at least the spacing was even and predictable. And gravity was on his side.

Above him, the screaming continued, along with the horrid percussive sounds of bullet impacts. The entire structure of the bleachers trembled as the human tsunami created its own earthquake, and Tom was struck with another critical concern. Structures like bleachers were not designed for this kind of dynamic load. If the structure collapsed with him under it, his body would likely not be found for weeks.

As he dropped the last few feet to the ground, his feet crunched on gravel and litter. Above and around him, others were beginning to follow his lead and scrambled down the scaffold-like support structure.

Now what? Exiting to the field was out because that clearly was part of the shooter's target picture. A fence ran the length of the bleachers along the back, but he remembered from his own days as a football player—could it really have been only nine years ago?—that there was a way to sneak in, unless the never-ambitious maintenance crew had finally gotten around to fixing it. The hole had been there since Tom's oldest brother had played ten years before him. And as far as he knew, there'd been no turnover in the maintenance staff.

Tom pressed himself up against the fence as he moved toward the center of the bleachers. In the reduced light, he hoped that when he came upon the opening—

There it was, right at knee level, a section of chain

link that had been pulled back. If he could have seen better, he was certain that he'd find the ground still littered with empty beer cans that displayed the whole reason for the opening to be there in the first place. These days, kids got expelled for such things, but could teenagers have changed that much over the years?

Tom bent at the waist and squirted into the open, where the horrors continued. Out here the darkness was less absolute, with partial illumination spilling in from towering lights from the BMW dealership on the other side of Spring Hollow Way. In the dim light, he tried to ignore the aimless running and screaming. He was getting the hell out of here, and that meant making a beeline toward the driveway and the street beyond.

Ten yards from the fence, everything changed.

A cop lay dead next to the door of his cruiser, his windshield a shredded mass of broken glass. Blood poured from wounds in his head and shoulders. To the right, parked immediately behind the first cruiser, a second cruiser sat similarly shredded, its officer slumped behind the wheel.

Tom Darone's battlefield instincts kicked in.

This was no random shooting. This was a coordinated attack, and at less than a minute into it, the bad guys were winning big. They'd targeted the school's power plant to bring darkness and chaos, and then they'd taken out the armed element of their opposing force. This was going to be a slaughter.

But where was the shooter?

The bullet holes in the cruiser answered his question. The rounds had all entered from the front of the vehicle—from the west, the scoreboard end of the field.

The shooter wouldn't be there. A carefully choreographed assault like this included a viable escape plan, and a rickety spiral ladder from the ass end of the scoreboard wasn't it.

The screaming of the crowd had crossed the pain threshold, and football fans were still falling.

So, where was the sound of the gunshots?

Jesus, he's got a suppressor.

Where the *hell* was he?

Had to be high ground. In Nebraska.

The water tower!

Two minutes into the slaughter now, Tom knew where the shooter had to be. It was the right compass point, and it was the right height. The red light that sat atop the bulbous structure had been winking to him all along.

What was that, an eight hundred-yard shot? Barely even a challenge if the shooter had the right gun and a thimbleful of training.

Tom had slid his butt into the first cruiser's driver's seat before he realized what he intended to do. Really, by process of elimination alone, it wasn't a hard decision. Staying here was untenable. Running away, knowing what he knew, was a choice he could never live with. So, that meant taking the fight to the shooter.

He needed a gun. He rolled back out of the cruiser and stooped to the dead officer's side, forcing himself not to look at the dead man's eyes. He pulled the cop's body toward him so he could access the holster on his hip. It was a leather job with a thumb break, and it cradled a midsize Glock. He guessed it to be either a 19 or a 23, and as the weapon slid free from its holster, Tom lifted two more snap closures on the cop's Sam Browne belt and helped himself to a couple of spare mags. If he'd read his gun-related websites properly, the three magazines gave him something like forty-five rounds to bring to whatever fight lay ahead.

The cop's name was Feitner, according to the plate pinned over the right breast pocket.

Officer Feitner had died with his engine running. Tom slid behind the wheel, dropped the transmission into gear, and started nudging fleeing spectators out of the way with his bumper. The spider-webbed windshield made it nearly impossible to see where he was going, but in times like these, the pedestrians were 60 percent liable for their own safety, and they needed to jump out of the way. He'd made that number up, of course, but so far, he hadn't run over anything that sounded like a person. He avoided using the horn to keep from drawing attention to himself.

The clock was ticking.

The gunman—whoever he was—was going to be less than happy to see the police vehicle he thought he'd killed up and living again. Tom was fully aware that he was personally the most valuable target for the shooter to shoot. He was rolling the dice that the sniper had gotten distracted and moved on to other targets. And what the hell? If he was wrong, he'd probably never know it.

The Indian Spear municipal water tank sat atop six tall supports, rising from the lot adjacent to the football field. Tonight, it occurred to Tom that it bore a striking resemblance to the Martian creatures from *The War of the Worlds*, and it posed every bit as terrible a menace. A chain-link fence separated the two properties, and as he closed the distance, he jammed the gas pedal to the floor. If a spectator got in his way now, there'd be another victim to add to the list.

The speedometer had just crossed fifty mph when the cruiser slammed through the fence. The deceleration forces were more than Tom had anticipated, and when the air bag deployed, it startled the crap out of him.

The cruiser was done, and fifty yards still separated him from the shooter's platform. Tom gathered the pistol and spare mags in his right hand, and with his left, pulled the handle for the driver's door and pushed with his shoulder. The fence had wrapped itself around the cruiser's body, pushing back against his efforts to force the door open. Every push resulted in a rebound, but after four tries, the opening was big enough to allow him to tumble out onto the twisted tangle of steel mesh.

He paused on his way out.

A shotgun stood tall to his right on the bench seat, but it was locked into place, and Tom didn't know how to unlock it.

"Way to go," he grumbled. "Bringing a pistol to a rifle fight."

Woulda coulda shoulda.

From ahead and above, he could hear the outgoing fire now. It wasn't the kind of booming he expected from a rifle, but rather quiet, percussive snaps, and there was no muzzle flash.

Suppressor.

The wrecked chain link felt spongy under his feet as he rolled out of the cruiser's door, and it clattered loudly as he scrambled on his hands and knees to what used to be the top of the fence and the water tower property beyond. He'd made too much noise and now presented too excellent a target to spend any time dawdling.

He didn't know who the hell the shooter was or why he'd decided to murder people, but unless someone stopped him, the murdering would continue. Tom could not let that happen.

As he sprinted across the grass toward the massive legs of the tower, he realized with a start that the lights here were still on. They were security lights, designed to provide enough illumination to make vandals think twice about graffiti or other forms of mischief. Not bright by any means, but bright enough to reveal a man sprinting across the ground.

As he ran, Tom focused his attention exclusively on the base of the ladder. He'd done his own mischief on this property back when he was a kid, so he knew the ladder didn't even reach all the way to the ground. It stopped about ten feet short to keep people in general—and kids in particular—from getting access. He wondered if the town fathers had ever considered the possibility that the tower might become a sniper's perch when they made the ladder hard to climb.

Tom wasn't at all surprised to find a stout hardware-style A-frame ladder at the base of the tower. It stood at the bottom of the access ladder, clearly put there by the shooter. Tom stopped at the A-frame long enough to stuff the Glock trigger-deep into the waistband at the front of his jeans, and then he started to climb.

Aware that this was the most impulsive, stupidest thing he had ever done, he kept climbing because at this point, he didn't know what else to do. This attack was still only a couple of minutes old. He'd come this far, and people were still dying. How could he turn back now? Even if he did, how would he ever live with himself?

"Six tours in Hell," he mumbled, "all so you could get yourself killed at home."

The ladder was a straight shot—no turns or landings—until he got to within twenty feet from the top. There, it ended at a six-foot-square landing from which a caged ladder rose vertically to a three-by-three-foot opened trap door in the expanded metal walkway that surrounded the belly of the water tank. He started the final climb.

Tom's plan—if you could even call it that—was to make his way around the circular tank to the eastern side, the side that faced the stadium, and pop the shooter. The scuttle hole in the floor of the walkway lay on the southern side of the tank, so once he was up on the expanded metal, he'd work his way around to the right, and after a quarter of a circle—

Wait. Where were the gunshots? Since he'd first been able to detect the sound of the suppressed rifle, the pace of fire had been steady. Not hurried, but relentless. Now, he didn't hear any shooting at all.

"Oh, shit," he hissed. *He's done.*

And this ladder was his escape route.

Shit, shit, shit.

Tom was ten feet off the landing when he saw the movement through the openings in the expanded metal. Whoever it was, he was moving quickly, anxious to get out of here.

Should have waited for him on the ground.

He had exactly one chance. If he could catch the shooter unaware, as he was transitioning from the platform to the ladder, he'd have a shot. It wasn't much of a chance, but it was a chance, dammit.

He had only a few seconds. No time to climb back down to the landing, and if he dropped, he'd make too much noise. This, right here, was his Alamo. This was where he was going to have his gunfight, hanging on to the ladder with his left arm while he Matt Dilloned one-handed shots at the figure who appeared in the opening.

Leaning out from the vertical ladder, Tom drew the Glock from his waistband. He hadn't brought it up all the way when the silhouette appeared in the opening. The silhouette was no more than an inkblot against the night sky. And the inkblot had a rifle.

Tom fired without aiming. He couldn't see his sights in the darkness, anyway. The Glock bucked in his hand twice. Four times. Six. The noise and muzzle flashes were his entire world. Eight. Ten.

Then, for just half an instant, he felt a heavy impact at the top of his breastbone, followed by a searing heat that consumed everything.

And then he felt nothing.

Chapter Two

The little village of Fisherman's Cove sat along Virginia's Northern Neck, a largely ignored east-west peninsula of land that was bordered by the Potomac River on the north and the Rappahannock River on the south. Real estate agents had the audacity to call it a suburb of Washington, DC, but such claims were borderline criminal. It was a two-hour one-way commute on a good day and five or six hours on a bad one. At a time when urban sprawl was consuming Northern Virginia at a rate of thousands of acres per year, Fisherman's Cove was a throwback to older times. The downtown, such as it was, still thrived with the kind of businesses that catered to local residents and fishermen, and zoning regulators' ears were well tuned to a populace that had zero interest in malls and big box stores.

Jonathan Grave had been born in Fisherman's Cove, and except for his college years and his decades of deployment to most of the world's shitholes, it was the only home he had ever known. Now that he'd left the Army and its Special Forces in his rearview mirror, it was the home of his future. As far as he was concerned, there was no finer spot on the planet.

He'd just finished his four-mile run and now stood on the near edge of the town's marina, drinking in the beauty of the October morning. The sun hadn't risen more than a hand's width over the horizon, and it lit the water with a light that made the fog on the surface look alive.

"By God, I believe you're breathing hard, Dig," said a familiar voice from behind.

Jonathan turned and smiled at Doug Kramer, Fisherman's Cove's chief of police, who was approaching up Water Street. Built as if the love child of a bullet and a fireplug, Kramer was one of those guys the charts would say was fat, but it was the kind of fat that would break your fist if you punched it.

"Next time, I'll give you a call and we can race," Jonathan said.

"Only if it's to the pasta table," Kramer said. "Haven't seen you in a while. Buy you a cup of coffee?" He nodded toward Jimmy's Tavern, a hundred yards to the east.

They started walking. "Business good?" Doug asked.

Jonathan felt his poker face fall into place. "Pretty good. Clients keep calling, and the ones we've got keep re-upping. We've even hired a couple of new investigators in the last few months." His answer referred to the official part of his company, Security Solutions, the side that provided private investigation services for some of the world's most recognizable corporate names. There was another side to the business, though—a covert side—that few people knew about it. Sometimes, Jonathan got a sense that Doug Kramer knew more than he should.

"How's *your* business doing?" Jonathan asked, turning the conversation around.

"Mine's always been a growth industry," Doug replied. "Burglaries are up, and there's been a spike in assaults."

Jonathan recoiled. "Really? This town always seems so bucolic to me."

"Well, this part of town is," Doug said. "I guess it helps to have the police department in the middle of everything on Church Street. But when you get a mile or two out of town, the place gets less romantic. The folks in the country are hurting."

This news bothered Jonathan. In the grand scheme, Fisherman's Cove was more rural than urban, and he'd always admired the ability of its residents to eke out solid livings through their farms and their fishing boats. "Hurting how?" he asked.

"Hurting like everybody," Doug said. "You look bothered."

"I *am* bothered. This is my home. Those people, whoever they are, are my neighbors."

Kramer threw out a dismissive puff of air through his lips. "Every town has its underbelly, Dig. You can't give a handout to all of them." After a beat, he chuckled. "Okay, maybe *you* can afford to give them all a handout, but it wouldn't be smart, and they wouldn't appreciate it."

Jonathan Grave was the only billionaire to his knowledge within a hundred miles, give or take. As much as his wealth embarrassed him and as hard as he tried to give it away to charitable causes, there was a practical cap to such things. As it was, he was the primary benefactor for Resurrection House, a school for the children of incarcerated parents, which sat a little farther up Church Street on the plot of land that had served as Jonathan's childhood home. He'd deeded that, plus the mansion that sat on it, to St. Katherine's Catholic Church for one dollar, on the condition that the residential school would be founded and maintained in perpetuity.

As a criminal's kid himself, he understood how easily the sins of the father and mother can poison the lives of their progeny.

He struggled to keep his philanthropy private, but secrecy was tough in a small town. Again, it seemed that Kramer knew things that Jonathan would rather he not.

Kramer continued, "Most of the stuff in the hinterlands is domestic crap. Drunk parents and kids wailing on each other. The fact that the harvests are all done and the cold weather is on the way has 'em laying in more alcohol than usual, I guess. Lots of drugs, too. Opiates, mostly. These aren't the folks you interact with very often."

When they got to Jimmy's, Kramer pulled the glass door open for Jonathan. Known locally for its fresh seafood and killer barbecue—and a bartender with a heavy hand—it was strictly a bacon-and-eggs place in the morning. Jonathan led the way into the underlit interior and headed straight to the bar, where paper cups were stacked like an inverted Christmas tree next to a stainless-steel urn of coffee. He poured two cups and handed one to the chief.

"Still take your coffee like candy?" Jonathan teased. He added a little cream and a sugar packet to his own and stepped out of the way.

Kramer added a glug of cream and four sugars to his brew. "They tell me that real sugar is better for me than the fake stuff," he said.

A woman's voice yelled from beyond the bar, "Help yourself to a table. I'll be out in two shakes." That would be Irma, the day manager and only waitress. Aged somewhere between sixty and ninety, she had a voice that made Whoopi Goldberg sound like a soprano and a service ethic that was built around the philosophy that customers should do what they were told.

They took seats near the window, overlooking the boat slips at the marina.

"Still hate the water?" Kramer asked.

"I don't hate the water," Jonathan said. "I hate being in or on the water. But I love looking at it." It had been a signature element of his life since childhood. Since then, he'd logged countless hours afloat, but more times than not, it was in unfriendly places where drowning was the least of his concerns, and probably the preferred way to die. If only to change the subject, he asked, "JoeDog been spending her time with you the last few days?" Joe was the once-stray black Labrador retriever that was exempt from leash laws and slept pretty much wherever she wanted, though Doug's and Jonathan's pads seemed to be her favorites.

"She was there last night, but took off as soon as I opened the door this morning. Maybe she's got a boyfriend."

"Well, hello, handsome," Irma shouted as she emerged from behind the bar. She wiped her hands on a towel as she approached. Skinny as a pillar, she nonetheless sported a world-class wattle under her neck that filled the void left by her open-collared white-ish blouse. Cigarette smoke clung to her like putrid perfume.

"Why, Irma," Doug said. "You have the hots for me."

"Not you, flatfoot," she said. "I mean the sweaty guy sitting across from you. Haven't seen you in a while, Digger. Been off saving the world or some such?"

Jesus, did she know, too? "Doing my part, I suppose."

"Want the usual, Chief?" she asked Kramer. Apparently, small talk was over. "Three eggs, sausage patties, side of pancakes?"

"Sounds good."

"Lord almighty, Doug," Jonathan said. "There's a thing now called nutrition. Heard of it?"

"Leave him alone," Irma said. "Meals like that pay for the free coffee. I suppose you're gonna want some egg white and bean sprout shit, right?"

Jonathan laughed.

"I expect a man to eat like a man in my place. I don't care how broad your shoulders are or how flat your gut is. So, what do you want with your eggs, yolks and all?"

"I'll have eggs and toast," Jonathan said.

Irma kept looking at him.

"And bacon?"

She nodded and turned back toward the kitchen. "Have 'em out in a jiffy."

"I only want one egg," Jonathan called after her.

"Too bad," Irma said without turning. "And if you don't want me to bring you five, you'll quit pokin' me."

Kramer pulled on his coffee. "I don't care how tough you think you are. Irma could take you out."

"One-punch fight," Jonathan agreed. "You were talking about our crime wave."

Kramer rolled his eyes at the phrase. "I'll tell you what, though. People are freaking the hell out over these terror attacks. They want to know what I plan on doing to keep it from happening here."

Jonathan scoffed. "Just play the odds," he said.

"They hit six high school football games simultaneously!"

"I'm not downplaying the awfulness of it," Jonathan said. "In fact, I don't see what could be worse for the national psyche. And all of them in Middle America, where people think they're safe. But still, the chances of the bad guys picking our town are pretty miniscule."

"You know that, and I know that," Kramer said, "but from the parents' point of view, Angler High School faces exactly the same risk as any of those other schools that were attacked."

"Statistics don't work like that, Doug. By that logic, everybody has an even chance of getting struck by any unfortunate thing that can happen."

"I actually looked this up," Kramer said. "As of whenever the last survey was taken, there were, like, twenty-three thousand public high schools in America, and over seven thousand private ones. That's thirty thousand, overall. Of which ours is only one."

Jonathan cocked his head. He wasn't sure where the chief was going with this.

"What I'm saying," Doug said, "is it's stupid for everybody to be wrapped so tight, but given the wall-to-wall coverage—"

"You've got to do something."

"Exactly." He punctuated his word with a forefinger

pointed at Jonathan's nose, then sipped his coffee again. "You asked how my business was going."

"So I did." Jonathan likewise sipped. "Well? What's your plan?"

"I have no idea. Nobody wants to cancel Friday night football, and it's not practical—maybe not even possible—to lock everything down whenever there's a game."

"Plus, there's the precedent," Jonathan agreed. "For all anyone knows, those attacks were a one-off. And if that's the case, it was pretty much the perfect act of terror. Nobody's been caught, right?"

"Not so far as I know. The shooters just evaporated."

"And if there's another incident in the planning, there's no guarantee that it will be another high school. Or even a school at all. It's pretty much impossible to protect against snipers for an extended period."

Kramer cradled his cup in both hands. "One lady actually told me that if it was the president who was at risk, we could make something happen."

"True enough," Jonathan said. "All you need is a couple hundred people devoted to every community member."

The absurdity of it made both of them laugh. Then Kramer turned serious. "You've been up against snipers before, haven't you?"

Jonathan's days in the Unit were a secret to no one. "Only in a military environment, and most of those times we had countersnipers deployed. In a civilian environment, there's no practical defense."

Kramer reared back. "So, we just let ourselves be victims?"

Jonathan considered before answering. "For the first shot? Yeah. That's the bad guy's call. The shooter always has the upper hand for the first shot. Now, you can have plans in place to take cover and fire back, but without advance intel, the first shot is his."

Kramer fell silent, contemplative.

"This can't be a surprise to you," Jonathan said.

Kramer inhaled deeply through his nose. "No, it's not a surprise. I guess I was hoping you'd have some advanced, wizardly solutions."

"I can help with training responders," Jonathan offered. "In fact, I'd be happy to." His cell phone buzzed in the pocket of his shorts. "Excuse me." As he produced the phone, he checked the caller ID and smiled. "It's Dom." He pressed the connect button. "Morning, Padre. I'm having breakfast at Jimmy's with Doug Kramer. Want to join us?"

Dom D'Angelo had been Jonathan's roommate all through college and now was the pastor of St. Kate's, just up the hill from Jimmy's. "Love to, but I can't," Dom said. "And you have to leave."

Jonathan scowled. "Where am I going?"

"To Location Bravo," Dom said. "Just got off the phone with Wolverine. She said she needs to see you as soon as you can get there."

Jonathan resisted the urge to cast a glance at Kramer. Wolverine was Jonathan's name for Irene Rivers, the director of the FBI. His head swam with questions, but now was not the time. Not here. "Okay, then," he said.

"Just you," Dom added. "She was very specific about that. She doesn't want to draw attention with a crowd. And no, I have no idea what this is about."

After a quick good-bye, Jonathan clicked off and stood. “Duty calls, I’m afraid.” He pulled a small wad of bills out of his pocket and peeled off a ten. “Tell Irma I’m good for the rest if this doesn’t cover it.”

Among the panoply of Catholic cathedrals throughout the world, Jonathan Grave always thought that the Cathedral of St. Matthew the Apostle on Rhode Island Avenue in Washington, DC, was an architectural lightweight. The Episcopalians got the high ground—literally—a few miles away, and they pulled a real coup when they grabbed the name Washington National Cathedral. When people thought of the DC equivalent of New York’s St. Patrick’s Cathedral, the National Cathedral was what they envisioned. Jonathan found the dull redbrick edifice of Saint Matthew’s to be entirely uninspiring.

Once the doors opened, however, the God Palace competition was on, and the Catholics could beat the Episcopalians walking away. The mosaic work throughout St. Matthew’s reminded Jonathan of St. Mark’s Cathedral in Venice, Italy.

Not that any of that mattered today.

As Jonathan stepped through the huge doors from the chilly morning sunlight into the dankness of the narthex, he waited a few seconds for his eyes to adjust. He scanned for the towering men he’d come to think of as the Tweedle brothers—Dee and Dum—and he found them just where he’d anticipated, flanking the entry to Our Lady’s Chapel, an enclave built into the cathedral’s northern wall in honor of the Virgin Mary. His appointment would be waiting for him there.

Jonathan knew this spot as Location Bravo, one of five preordained sites where Wolverine could meet with people and harbor no fear of being overheard.

As FBI director, Irene had access to all manner of SCIFs—sensitive compartmented information facilities—at government offices, but none were as secure as Location Bravo, because only a handful of people in the world knew that it existed. DC was a town built around information and deception. Just because a SCIF protected a conversation from being overheard by foreign actors didn't mean that it wasn't overheard by the sponsoring agencies' own paranoid security teams. Everybody listened to everybody else in Washington.

Using funds that were largely unaccounted for, Wolverine had commissioned the project to make the chapel secure several years ago, while the entire cathedral was being renovated. She'd used her own contractors, posing as regular workers, to install jamming transmitters that rendered all electronic equipment useless, and she had the space swept and recertified on a regular cycle that she'd never shared with Jonathan.

Jonathan smiled as he approached the Tweedles and gave a little finger wave, this time using four more fingers than he often did. "Morning, gents," he said. "I presume the boss is in her usual spot?"

They glared at him. In unison. It occurred to him that they looked like Christmas Nutcrackers, but dressed in ill-fitting business suits.

"Are you armed?" Dum asked.

"Yep," Jonathan said. "As always. High on my right hip. A Colt Commander. Sweet shooter, too. Thanks for asking."

He continued past the security team and smiled when he heard Dee ask Dum, "Why do you always give him that kind of power?" At least these two were better than some of the others Irene had dragged around in the past. Apparently, the cream of the federal law enforcement crop does not aspire to standing security details.

Irene Rivers sat upright in an uncomfortable-looking cane-backed chair in front of the chapel's altar, her head bowed. Her back was turned to him, and from this angle, he thought he might have caught her in a moment of prayer. But then, as he got closer, he saw the folder full of papers on her lap and the cheap government-issued pen in her hand.

"Good morning, Wolfie," he said as he approached.

She didn't look up. "Pull up a chair," she said. "I just need to finish this note and pray my assistant will be able to read my handwriting."

"If only someone hadn't turned the place into a Faraday cage," Jonathan quipped as he planted himself in the chair three down on her left. "You could send an email." He turned sideways and tucked his right calf under his left thigh.

"It's the price we must pay for privacy," she said. She clicked her pen and closed the cover of the manila folder. "Welcome to the snake pit."

Jonathan waited for her to get to the point.

"I need your help, Dig."

"I figured as much. Dom made you sound agitated." Because of the nature of their relationship, Jonathan and Irene always contacted each other through Father Dom. Given her position, every person she visited and every phone call she made were legally discoverable to anyone with a subpoena and an agenda. But even the FBI director got to be off the record when she spoke to her priest.

"Agitated is the wrong word," Irene said. "I'll give you pissed. And very concerned."

"Sounds like somebody downrange is going to have a bad day."

"Your lips to God's ear," she said. "What do you know about the Black Friday shootings?"

"Just what I've heard on the infotainment pages." Jonathan had long ago lost faith in what passed for news these days.

"Is that all?" Irene pressed. "Just public access? Nothing from your own rumor mill?"

His shields came up. For years—for a career—Jonathan had been a part of the Unit, the very tip of Uncle Sam's spear, and, of course, he'd kept in touch with the other players. But what he knew and from whom was none of Wolverine's business.

Irene rolled her eyes. "Oh, for crying out loud, Dig, I don't need sources and methods. I just need to know if there are rumblings out there. I promise that after you answer, I'll tell you why I need to know."

"I'm not trying to be obtuse," Jonathan said. "There's always a ton of chatter about a lot of things. Give me a clue what you're looking for."

"Anything about who the shooters might be."

Jonathan leaned forward. "I need more than that," he said. "The big winners are Islamists, but they're always the easy pick."

Irene's scowl deepened.

"Look, Wolfie," Jonathan said, "I sense that you're turning yourself inside out trying not to tell me something. Just let it out." He'd rarely seen her this uncomfortable. The Irene Rivers he knew was a between-the-eyes kind of gal.

"Fair enough. I have reason to believe that you might know at least one of the shooters."

He hid behind his best poker face, waiting for the rest.

"I say that because we have a guy in custody who told us that."

"Who is he?"

"Not yet," she said.

"You have a guy in custody who says he knows me? By name? How the hell did that even come up in conversation?"

"Well, not you, specifically," she hedged. "Not by name, anyway, but he indicated that your old teammates have turned terrorist."

"Bullshit."

"I thought you'd say that. And remember, you're in church. Watch your language."

"God's been listening to me cuss for a long time," Jonathan said. "I don't think he pays attention to the venue. Now, if I'm being accused, I have a right to know—" A piece fell into place. "Wait a second. I heard one of your minions on television just this morning saying that you had no suspects and no one in custody."

Irene looked away. "Yeah, well, we kind of lied about that."

"Why?"

"Because there's a lot we don't want the bad guys to know."

"Okay, but now *I* know," Jonathan said. "What's his name?"

"Logan Masterson."

Jonathan tasted the name, got nothing. "Don't know him. Look, Wolfie, you need to start dealing off the top of the deck. What aren't you telling me?"

She prepared herself with a deep breath. "You remember that Stepahin business a while back?"

"All too well," Jonathan said. "But you can't tell me he's back. I saw his brain on the pavement."

"No, he's still dead, as far as I know. But you remember the prison program I told you about?"

Jonathan felt a flutter in his stomach. "The secret ones? The *illegal* ones? You told me you shut that program down."

"We did," Irene said. "The program is dead. But the facilities are still there. On Black Friday, Masterson was one of the shooters at the Nebraska incident. I should say at least one of them. A Good Samaritan was able to wing him. By the time he woke, up, we had him."

Jonathan's bullshit bell clanged. "You skipped a part. You say you have him, but nobody knows you have him. That's a hard detail to hide."

Irene cocked her head. All of this was making her progressively more uncomfortable. "The administration wants justice on this one," she said, "so when we found out there was a suspected shooter in custody, we took control immediately and made him disappear."

"What about the locals? Aren't they going to reveal the secret?"

"We swore them to secrecy. National security and

all that. If they do, we'll just deny it. Everybody trusts the FBI." She smiled and winked on that last part.

"I'm going to guess that there's no arrest warrant for him?"

Irene laughed. She didn't even honor the question with an answer.

"You'll never be able to prosecute," Jonathan said.

"Don't try to out-lawyer the lawyer," Irene said. "We're not interested in prosecuting him."

Jonathan reared back at that one. "What, you're just gonna kill him?"

"Haven't really thought that far out," Irene said. "In the near term, we're going to make him miserable and squeeze him for information."

"You're going to torture him."

"The FBI does not torture people," Irene said, but Jonathan couldn't tell if she was being ironic.

He let it go. "Okay, so why did you summon me?"

"Masterson said that Black Friday was part of a larger plan and that the key players were all Special Forces types. All American."

"Well, I'm not a part of the plot, if that was what—"

"Oh, God no. Never thought that for a second. I want you to talk to him."

"Why me? Don't you have, like, thirty thousand people working for you?"

"Discoverability," she said. "We're breaking more than a few laws here. I can't trust sworn agents to take care of details like this. The entire population of people who know about Masterson is fewer than twenty."

"Plus someone in the White House? You mentioned that *the administration* wanted justice on this."

"I have exactly one trusted source in the White

House," Irene said. "You have no need to know his or her name, but they're trustworthy and they tell me things. President Darmond is unhinged over all this. There's a lot of pressure on my people to come up with answers. If we go the normal habeas corpus route with Masterson, he'll lawyer up, the press will get involved, and we'll all go into damage control mode. That will slow things tremendously."

"So, you're just going to torture a guy off the books?"

"The FBI does not torture people." There was that weird tone again.

"Well, neither do I," Jonathan said. "I hate that shit."

"I want information, Dig. I need details that will get us out in front of this, and I don't care how I get it."

Jonathan wanted to stand and pace, but resisted. "Look, Wolfie, this is just not the kind of work I do."

"Talk to him. That's all I'm asking."

"And what's the next step after that?" Jonathan pressed. "Say I get a juicy tidbit. Where do we go from there? You can't use it. It'll be fruit from the poisonous tree."

"If you get that far, I'll take it from there," Irene said.

Jonathan had never been adept at saying no to Irene Rivers, but he would have taken about any excuse right then. "How are we going to get past the guards at the secret prison, wherever the hell that is?"

"We?"

"I haven't said yes yet, but if I can't work with my team, it's a hard no. Not negotiable."

Irene's eyes took on a sparkle, and a tiny smile began to grow.

Jonathan scowled. "Did I just walk into a trap?"

Irene reached into her bag and produced four boxes, each about the size of a paperback novel and bearing the official seal of the FBI. "Welcome to the Federal Bureau of Investigation," she said. "You'll find badges and credentials for you, Big Guy, Gunslinger, and Mother Hen. The identities will hold up to all but the most rigorous background check, at which point your identity disappears, anyway."

Then she handed him a thumb drive. "Don't lose this," she explained, "and destroy it when you're done. It's all the background on your aliases."

Jonathan took the boxes and turned them over in his hands. "You're going to want us to track down what we find, aren't you?"

"I am," she said. "My entire agency will be focused on the Constitutional methods of investigation, while you wander the back roads." She stood. The meeting was over.

"I didn't say yes yet," Jonathan said.

"Yes, you did. I wish I could be there when you tell your team."

Chapter Three

"Why did you lie to her?"

The question took Jonathan off guard, and the fact that it came from Boxers, his longtime friend and right hand, startled him. "Excuse me?"

Boxers' real name was Brian Van de Muelebroecke, and he was built like a sequoia. "To Wolverine," he said. "Why did you lie about knowing Logan Masterson?" He and Jonathan had served in the Unit together and had been a fighting team for many years.

Jonathan looked to the rest of his team. Gail Bonneville and Venice (Ven-EE-chay) Alexander stared back at him from their positions around the massive teak conference table in the War Room, the operations command center for the covert side of Security Solutions. "Do y'all know what he's talking about?"

Venice and Gail exchanged glances. "Should we?" Gail asked.

"We served with him, Dig," Boxers insisted. "Not for long. I think it was Scarlet Tendril, that snatch-and-grab outside of Kandahar, toward the end. He looked like Opie Taylor, down to the freckles and red hair."

Jonathan scoured his brain for something but couldn't pull it up.

"He liked the shooting way too much."

"Holy shit," Gail said through a laugh. "That's coming from *you*?" Boxers had a well-earned reputation for being exceptionally lethal.

Boxers feigned insult but laughed in spite of it. "Yeah, well, that tells you something, doesn't it?" He looked back to Jonathan. "You remember Scarlet Tendril, right? Some kingpin—"

Jonathan snapped his fingers. "Got it. He posed for pictures with the bodies."

"Bingo."

"Good Lord," Venice said with a wince.

"Yeah, exactly," Jonathan said. "That got him transferred to a different squadron."

"Got him kicked out," Boxers corrected. "Nobody wanted him. Sicko."

"Mass-murder-level sicko?" Gail asked.

"So it would seem," Jonathan said. "Ven, I don't suppose you've been able to pull up any pictures of this guy?"

"Right now," she said. The lights in the War Room dimmed as the projector in the ceiling descended and the 106-inch screen at the far end of the rectangular room revealed itself from a bank of shelves. The image of a stone-faced soldier appeared. He wore the black beret of an Army Ranger, and yes, he looked remarkably like Opie Taylor of the old *Andy Griffith Show*.

"That's the guy," Boxers said.

"Makes me sick to see him in that uniform," Jonathan grumbled.

"Will somebody tell me why I need FBI credentials and a badge?" Venice said. "I don't work in the field."

"Great way to talk yourself out of speeding tickets," Gail said.

"I don't like it," Venice said. "And what's with the new name? Constance DuBois? Sounds like a character from a James Agee play."

"I'll pretend I know what that means," Jonathan said.

"I drew Gerarda Culp," Gail said. "Is this Wolverine being funny?"

"You're asking that to Cornelius Bonner," Jonathan said. "I'd go by Jerri if I were you."

"Got it, Corny."

"I think we'll make it Neil," Jonathan said. "What about you, Big Guy? What name did you draw?"

Boxers grumped, "Just because she runs the Feebs doesn't mean we can't beat her up."

"Come on," Jonathan prodded. He already knew what it was, but he'd been dying to hear Boxers say it.

"Xavier Contata."

The War Room erupted in laughter.

"I *know* I can beat you people up," Boxers said.

"I'm thinking Professor X," Gail said.

"How about Zave?" Venice offered. "You can name your autobiography *Save Zave*."

As much as Jonathan enjoyed the moment, his read on Boxers was that it was time to back off. It was one thing if Jonathan rode his ass like a horse, but he'd earned the right. The ladies, maybe not so much. "Okay, back to the task at hand," he said. "Madame Director said she was going to send us some files."

"We got them," Venice confirmed. "But I've got to tell you they're hard to look at."

"What are they?"

Venice tapped the keys at her command center. A world-class tamer of electrons, she could do with a computer keyboard what Mozart could do with a piano. The screen filled with a mosaic of images.

"I've only scanned these briefly," Venice said, "but I warn you that there's a lot of gore."

"Crime scene photos?" Boxers asked.

"I believe so," Venice said. "Of all of the Black Friday incidents."

"Five high schools?" Gail asked.

"Six," Jonathan corrected. "Total of one hundred thirty-seven dead, over a hundred wounded, many of those crush injuries during the escapes."

"I can't imagine the horror," Gail said.

Jonathan cast a glance to Boxers, who flicked an eyebrow. Oh, they could imagine. That, and a lot worse, because they had seen it all.

Venice hit a button, and for the next twenty-five minutes, they looked at horrific photos of the dead. The photos followed the same pattern: the establishing shot from a distance, and then the same gruesome victim from ever-closer distances, and then from additional angles. Jonathan didn't pay attention to the personal details of names and ages, because he didn't want to know. He didn't *need* to know. His job required focus on the tactics deployed, not on the mechanisms of death. The local homicide detectives would take care of that.

After only a few minutes, Venice clacked more keys,

spun around in her chair, and stood. "I can't watch these anymore," she said. "Call me when it's done. I've got the timer set for four seconds per image. Note the number in the upper corner if there's something you'll want me to bring up again." As she got to the War Room door, she said, "I might have to go home and take a shower."

Many, but not all the victims were children, perhaps fewer than half. If Jonathan guessed right, the oldest was easily in her seventies, the youngest under ten. Truly, it was awful.

Rivers of blood.

"Are you noting the marksmanship?" Boxers asked.

"I am," Jonathan said.

"Head shots and upper torsos," Gail said. "Pretty high caliber. For sure five-five-six or better. Maybe seven-six-two." The 5.56-millimeter round was arguably the most popular caliber in the world, certainly in the United States, and it was the staple of the AR15 rifle, also the most popular platform in America. The 7.62-millimeter round was a common choice for snipers and game hunters, and it was also readily available on an AR platform.

"Single shots," Jonathan said. "Aimed shots. This is not spray and slay. These shooters are good."

"From as far back as nine hundred fifty meters, if the news reports are right," Boxers said. "Adds credibility to Wolverine's theory. These shooters are marksmen."

"I think we need to look for trends," Gail said. "Other than the marksmanship and the sheer tonnage of bodies, we need to find commonalities between all these different scenes."

"The cops," Jonathan said. The images continued to churn.

"What about them?" Boxers asked.

"They're one hundred percent kill ratio," Jonathan explained. "There's not a lot of security at games like that, and when you get way the hell out into Butt-scratch, I don't know how much security they can actually provide, but our attackers didn't take any chances. Every cop at every game was killed in the initial volleys."

"Are you sure?" Gail asked. "I mean, there are a lot of dead cops, but how can you say for sure that it was a hundred percent kill ratio?"

Jonathan held up his smartphone. "As soon as I thought I saw the pattern, I texted Wolfie. She confirmed."

"And here I thought you were bored and playing a game," Boxers said. He pointed to the screen. "Either of you know how to turn that shit off? I'm tired of looking at them."

Jonathan reached to the phone on the table and pressed the intercom. "Hey, Ven, we're ready to watch a different show. Can you come back to the War Room, please?"

Fifteen seconds later, she was there. "You really don't know how to turn off a PowerPoint presentation?"

Boxers held up his hands and splayed his fingers. "You really want these sausages messing with your keyboard?"

"You're not the only one in the room," she said as she made the screen go dark.

Jonathan said, "Well, I pay your salary, so . . ." He sold it with a smile. "One hundred percent of security forces killed. What does that tell us?"

"It tells us that they know what they're doing," Boxers said.

"Tell me I don't hear admiration in your tone," Venice said.

"Admiration's the wrong word," Boxers replied. "That infers approval. Maybe *recognition* is a better word. I recognize that they knew what they were doing."

Jonathan explained, "The hardest part of any large-scale hit-and-run op like this is the running part. Any asshole with a gun can sneak in undetected and take his shot. It takes a higher level of planning to spray bullets and then get out."

"Okay, how would you do it?" Gail asked. "I mean, if you were the shooter—if this was an op you were planning, how would you do it?"

Venice squirmed in her seat. "Oh, my God, I'm not comfortable with this."

"You've got to think like your enemy to get to know him," Jonathan said. "Ven, can you pull up the establishing shot of the Nebraska site, the aerial one?"

"Why Nebraska?" Gail asked. "As opposed to one of the others?"

Jonathan said, "Because that's where Logan Masterson was one of the shooters. He's the one we're going to get a chance to talk to."

The screen switched to a honeycomb of tiny images, a digital proof sheet of what they'd already seen.

Venice clicked on one, and it filled the screen. "Here," she said.

The image changed to an overhead shot that might just as easily have been printed from one of the commercial satellite websites. The gray, flat roof of the school itself dominated the upper left side of the image, and the football stadium occupied most of the rest. Parallel banks of bleachers flanked an oval track. A water tank could be seen in the lower part of the photo. Little arrows and numbers indicated evidence markers.

"I need to see it for real," Jonathan said. "We need to visit the school."

"I don't understand," Gail said. "Why?

Jonathan stood. "I figure we get one chance to talk to this guy. If I were him, I'd just shut down and say nothing. The second-best choice would be to lie my ass off to misdirect people from the truth. The more I know, the more I've seen, the less manipulatable I'll be. I'd like you to come along. I can use all the observation power I can get."

Gail bobbled her head as she thought it through and said, "Sure, why not? Big Guy, too?"

"I always go," Boxers said.

Jonathan winked. "Somebody has to drive the plane."

Indian Spear, Nebraska, population 5,500, sat almost exactly in the geographic center of the state, about 190 miles west of Lincoln. Jonathan didn't know what industry kept it thriving, but there was no denying the charm of the place. As in so many Midwestern towns, a one-block-square patch of real estate defined the center of activity, with dozens of businesses lining the perimeter of the square and a bandstand gazebo in the center of the square itself. There was nothing touristy about any of it, though if a filmmaker wanted a location for quintessential Middle America, this place would do perfectly. At a glance, Jonathan saw a hardware store, a grocery, a barbershop, two cafés, and a string of Somebody & Somebody storefronts that he could only assume were law firms.

Jonathan guessed that two weeks ago, this little burg would have been the dream of many Americans who wanted to simplify their lives and return to the basic values of God and community. But that dream had been shattered, and the collective grief felt palpable as Boxers piloted the rented Suburban through the streets. Black bunting draped every door and archway. Flags hung at half-staff, and of the few people walking the streets, none smiled.

"In a town this size, everybody lost somebody," Boxers said.

"I can't imagine the emptiness," Gail said. "How will they ever stop mourning?"

"When they find out the bastards who did this are stopped or dead," Jonathan said.

Acts of terror were more than physical acts of violence, more than death and destruction. They were acts of psychological warfare. People who lived in New York and Chicago and Washington, DC, lived with a constant expectation of violence. They didn't dwell on it, but there was an awareness among residents that they existed as juicy targets for jihadists and assholes with a cause. It was baked into the social contract.

Consequently, public safety organizations had established protocols to mitigate the physical, medical, and psychological aftermath of terror attacks. In places like Indian Spear, where the PTA meetings and fire department bingo events were populated by the same folks who attended meetings of the Board of Supervisors and the church social, those mechanisms didn't exist. In a place like this, everyone was family.

And large-scale violence stripped them of a kind of innocence. It wasn't that small-town people didn't see hardships and suffering—three-quarters of every Army division in the world consisted of men and women from towns such as this—but rather that long-held presumptions of safety were shattered. It was hard to tell your children that going to a shopping mall or to a movie theater was dangerous after it had never been so.

This was why Jonathan wanted to visit Indian Spear in the first place. Having spent so much of his life in harm's way, doing awful things to people who inflicted even greater awfulness on others, it was too easy for him to surrender to the cynicism.

"You okay, Dig?" Boxers asked. "You look . . . far away."

"I'm fine," he said. "I'm right here. The very opposite of far away."

"You getting your hate up?"

"Yes, I am."

"What does that mean?" Gail asked.

"Just what it sounds like," Jonathan said. "If things go the way I hope they do, we're taking a big fight to some very dangerous people."

"Hate drives passion," Boxers added.

"It also blinds reason," Gail said.

Jonathan waved that off. "Not with me. *Anger* blinds reason, not hatred. Hatred provides focus. Keeps me inspired to finish what I start."

"So, let's start," Big Guy said. "What's the first step?"

"Let's go to the high school."

George Armstrong Custer High School seemed to divide Indian Spear between the residential and industrial centers. While it officially sat in the 1200 block of 7th Avenue on its eastern border, it occupied an enormous footprint that spanned all the way to 11th Avenue on the west and ate up the equivalent of ten blocks north and south.

"Venice puts the school population at just over eight hundred students," Gail said from the backseat.

"From a population of five thousand," Jonathan mused aloud. "Must have kids bused in from the county."

"Thus spreading the trauma even farther," Gail said.

"There's the football stadium," Boxers said, pointing through the windshield. It was an enormous complex, far larger that the footprint of the school building.

"Drive to the other end," Jonathan said. "Let's get as close as we can to the water tower."

The fence surrounding the school was clearly designed to mark territory, not to keep people out. An easy hop would take you from the street onto school grounds.

"Looks like the place is back to normal operations," Boxers observed. "No evidence markers or police tape."

"I think it's good to bring normalcy back to children as soon as possible," Gail said.

Jonathan wasn't sure that he agreed, but he kept his thoughts to himself. Normalcy bred complacency, and that was what allowed this awfulness to happen in the first place.

Boxers parked the Suburban at the far western end of the field, where the chain-link fence for the stadium joined with the chain-link fence for the water tower. Jonathan planted his hands on the top rail of the fence, pushed himself up, and then swung his feet. Gail was next, and he resisted the urge to help her over. Chivalry was fine on date nights, but not at work. For Boxers, the climb was more like a big step.

Ahead and to the left, a fifteen-foot section of fence appeared to have been trampled by something. It lay far over on its side, nearly touching the ground on the water tower's property.

"I wonder if panicked people did that," Jonathan mused aloud.

"I'm guessing vehicle," Boxers said. He pointed to tire tracks in the dirt.

"Maybe the emergency responders," Gail said. "Now that we're here, what, exactly, are we looking for?"

"Just general observations," Jonathan said. "I'm hoping we'll know what's important when we see it." He craned his neck to look up. "Y'all ready to climb?"

"I think I'll find my observation inspiration down here," Boxers said. "See that cage around the ladder way at the top?" He pointed.

"Yeah."

"I'm just eyeballin' but I'm not a hundred percent sure I wouldn't get stuck in that."

Jonathan and Gail both laughed.

"And I'm not giving you two the satisfaction," Big Guy finished.

Truth be told, Jonathan thought he'd made a good point. He turned to Gail. "You?"

"I've been feeling better every day," she said. "But the thought of a straight vertical climb like that without someone chasing me, makes me hurt." Several years ago, Gail had been badly injured during an op, and it had been a long slog for her to return to work. It hadn't been that long since she tossed her cane away.

"See what you can see, then," Jonathan said. "I'll be down in a few." He looked to Big Guy. "Give me a leg up to that first rung?"

Boxers made a stirrup with his hands and when Jonathan got his foot set, Big Guy damn near launched Jonathan onto the ladder.

"Sorry," Boxers said through a chuckle. "I keep forgetting how tiny and tender you are."

Jonathan went to work. The climb wasn't difficult so much as it was awkward. And, for the first thirty feet or so, scary. Gravity was an unrelenting bitch. A misstep would mean a fall, and the higher he climbed, the more devastating the consequences of the impact.

When he reached the landing, just a couple dozen feet below the walkway that surrounded the tower, he paused and offered up a small prayer. He knew from the reports that Irene had sent him that this was the spot where the Good Samaritan had died and from which he had inflicted the wound that got Jonathan's team wrapped up in this in the first place.

"You done good," he whispered. "Whoever you are, however you're remembered, at this spot on that night, you done good." He started climbing again.

Finally, he reached the top, and he pulled himself up through the hatch in the floor of the walkway. Bits of police line tape still clung to the rail, tiny tails of granny knots vibrating in the breeze. As he stood to his full height, Jonathan white-knuckled the railing. Notwithstanding countless parachute jumps in all kinds of crappy conditions, he'd never been comfortable with heights. Being in an enclosure was fine, and free falling was fine—the parachute made that fall not really a fall at all, but rather a flight—but standing ninety feet above the ground, with only a rusty guardrail between him and his maker, he felt . . . *vulnerable.*

The view was a sniper's wet dream. At this elevation, with the sky as clear as it was, he could see to the curvature of the Earth—five, maybe six miles. The entire stadium played out before him. He could see every seat in the bleachers and even into the vendors' stands. Jonathan noted the places where the police vehicles had been stationed on both the northern and southern edges of the field, and there again, the shooter had unrestricted fields of fire.

Sadly, the flip side of that observation was that the entire stadium had an unrestricted view of the shooter. Perhaps the bright lights would have restricted visibility to some degree, but if someone had thought to look that way—or if the police had thought to secure the area in anticipation of a terror attack—none of this would have happened. But why would they have even considered securing the high ground? Nightmares like this never happened in places like Indian Spear.

"Agent Bonner!" He recognized Gail's voice, but it took him a second or two to remember that he had an alias. Neil Bonner.

He looked over the edge to see Boxers and Gail standing next to a police patrol car.

"This gentleman needs to speak with you," Gail called.

Chapter Four

When Jonathan's feet were on the solid gravelly ground again, he turned to see a young cop in a beige-on-beige uniform standing between Boxers and Gail, his face a mask of practiced sternness. The star on the front of his white felt cowboy hat matched the star over the pocket of his shirt.

Jonathan wiped his palms on the thighs of his jeans and extended his hand. "Afternoon, Officer," he said. "Neil Bonner, FBI." As the cop returned his grip, Jonathan produced his creds case from his back pocket and badged him.

"It's Deputy," the cop said. Not yet thirty years old, he had an athletic look about him. Jonathan guessed track or swimming. "Deputy Schaeffer. Can I ask what you're doing here?"

Jonathan returned the badge to his pocket. "Chasing down details," he said. "You've met my colleagues?"

"You freak people out when you crawl around up there. Nobody told me you guys were coming back."

"Maybe the sheriff got it," Jonathan offered.

"Don't have one of those anymore." Schaeffer's cheeks reddened. "He was killed in the attack."

"I'm sorry."

Schaeffer folded his arms across his chest. "Surprised you didn't already know that. The last team you sent was all over it. Sent wreaths and everything."

Jonathan saw Gail's eyes arch.

"Welcome to Uncle Sam," Jonathan said. "We try to give the impression of organization, but sometimes the reality is just ugly."

"We lost all the other deputies, too," Schaeffer said. "I'm all that's left."

"Jesus," Jonathan said. His sympathy was real. "I can't imagine."

The deputy's posture remained rock solid. He wasn't yet buying what Jonathan was selling. "So, you see, since I'm the only remaining deputy, if y'all had called, I'd have been the one you talked to."

"Then, I'm sorry again," Jonathan said. "Clearly, we dropped the ball."

"Why are you here?"

Deputy Schaeffer was not one to be distracted by small talk. Jonathan decided to take a shot at the offensive. "Why do you look so pissed?"

"I'm not pissed," Schaeffer said. "It's been a very long two weeks. Between you guys and the media, this town needs a break. We need to get back to something that looks like normal. We've gotten a dozen calls in the last twenty minutes, and people are worried about everything from you being more shooters to you being vandals trying to desecrate hallowed ground."

"We should have called," Jonathan conceded.

"You still haven't told me why you're here."

"I'm following up on details."

"What details?"

"Federal details." That came from Gail, a.k.a. Gerarda Culp.

"The hell does that mean?"

"It means that there are multiple investigations going on," Gail said. "We're not trying to cause you any trouble, and we certainly don't want to raise the stress levels in town."

"We thought we were being subtler than I suppose we actually were," Jonathan said. He stopped himself from apologizing for a fourth time, just on principle. "But since we're here, would you mind answering a few questions?"

"Ask them, and I'll let you know." The deputy still hadn't moved.

"Is there someplace we can go to sit for a while—"

"I'm good with what we've got right here. I'm losing patience."

Jonathan walked to the deputy's cruiser and hitched a thigh on left front fender. "Old war injuries," he said. "My back starts to hurt if I stand too long." He knew from past experience with police officers that it was a sin to put his butt on the vehicle, but if Schaeffer was going to be an asshat, Jonathan figured he might as well give him cause. "So, what is the scuttlebutt around town about the shootings? Who do your constituents suspect?"

"It's not a question I ask."

"But you impress me as a good cop," Jonathan said. "That means you're a good listener. You've got coffee shops, online chatter, comments in the grocery line. What are people saying?"

Schaeffer hesitated for a few seconds, and then something about him seemed to relax. He was tired of being a badass. "Terrorists, I suppose. About the only thing that would make sense."

"Well, of course," Jonathan said. "Sort of by definition, right? I mean anyone who could do such a thing has to be a terrorist. Of what variety? Do you have Antifa issues around here? White supremacists?"

"Yes to both," Schaeffer said. He relaxed even more and leaned his butt against the cruiser's hood, just above the grill. "But I don't think it makes sense for it to be them. The attackers killed whites and blacks. A couple of Orientals, too. About the only common denominator I can find among the victims is that they was all Christian."

"Which means what to you?" Jonathan was nearly certain where this was going, but he wanted to hear it from the deputy.

"Had to be Islam, right? I mean them assholes been terrorizing the world for decades."

"You said *attackers*," Jonathan said, leaning on the word. "As in, more than one. Are you certain of that?"

"The only thing I'm certain about anymore, Agent Bonner, is my name. And sometimes, I wonder about that. The world is changing in ways I don't understand and at a speed I can't comprehend. But given the number of dead, I don't see how one man could do that without help."

"And you're certain they were men?"

"Aren't they always? What are you driving at?"

It was time for Jonathan to test drive his team's cover story. "There are inconsistencies in the testimony and evidence," he said. "Not just here, but with all the other shooting sites." He nodded at Gail. "What Agent Culp wasn't telling you a minute ago was that we're not really part of the original investigation. We're a different team, on a different but related investigation."

"To find out what?"

"That's the part I can't tell you." *Because I haven't made that part up yet.*

"That explains why you don't know things," Schaeffer said.

Jonathan made a rocking motion with his hand. A noncommittal gesture designed to ramp up the sense of mystery.

"Or, you know things and pretend to be ignorant," Schaeffer said.

"That's closer. So, I'll ask you to forgive the doubling up on information. I presume your colleagues were all killed in the initial part of the attack?"

"I presume that, too. I wasn't here that night." Schaeffer's voice caught in his throat at that statement. "My wife is pregnant, and she had some issues that night. Some bleeding. I stayed home to be with her."

"What kind of evidence did you recover from the scene?" Jonathan asked.

"Me personally?" Schaeffer responded. "Very little. By the time I heard about it, the shooting was over, and we were in full crisis mode. I was swamped with sorting the living from the dead and getting people to hospitals. Then we had to coordinate the reunion of families."

"So, how long you figure it was before evidence collection started?" Jonathan asked.

"As long as it took for the State Police to get here. But then you guys arrived just a few minutes after that and took over. So, I'd guess that it was maybe an hour, hour and a half before we really started to treat this like a crime scene. And by then . . ." His voice trailed off.

"Things were pretty much trashed," Jonathan said for him.

"Trashed is as good a word as any," Schaeffer agreed.

"Any weapons recovered?"

"Not from the shooters, no."

"But from someone else?" Gail asked.

"From one of our deputies. Deputy Feitner. A Good Samaritan, a guy named Tom Darone, got his hands on Feitner's Glock and tried to assault the shooter on the tower. Never made it. The terrorist got him before he could make contact."

"The Samaritan was killed?"

Schaeffer pointed up the ladder. "Just up there, a little below where you were."

"Did you know the guy? Darone, I mean?"

"Not really. In a town this size, I kinda know pretty much everybody, but I can't say we were friends. Is that important?"

"I don't know," Jonathan said. "I'm just asking the questions that pop into my mind."

"Uh-huh."

Something changed in Schaeffer. Something in his

eyes. Jonathan had a sense that the deputy had offered up a test, and Jonathan had somehow failed. "Something wrong, Deputy?"

Schaeffer pushed away from the car and took a few steps closer to Gail and Boxers. When he pivoted back toward Jonathan, he planted his fists on his Sam Browne belt. "I'm wondering when you're going to get around to what you're actually here to talk about."

"This isn't it?"

Schaeffer just stared back.

Jonathan scanned his colleagues for a clue and got nothing. "I'm sorry, Deputy, you're going to have to give me a hint."

"No, you give *me* a hint," Schaeffer shot back. He clearly was losing his temper. "Better still, why don't you give me an answer."

Over the years, Jonathan had learned that as one party of a conversation starts to spin up with anger, his best counter was to settle himself and project calm. "Okay, if that's the case, instead of a hint, ask the question I'm supposed to answer. I'm not sandbagging you here, Deputy. I honestly don't—"

"Where's the terrorist you guys whisked out of here?"

Jonathan held his poker face. If Schaeffer had a rhetorical knife to throw, he'd get to it.

"I haven't told anyone, you know," the deputy said. "Yet."

Part of the mission given to Jonathan by Irene Rivers was to suss out what the locals knew about Masterson's abduction. Jonathan knew there would be a delicate balance to learning information without revealing any. He decided to play it with more silence.

"That's it?" Schaeffer said. "You're just going to stonewall?"

"I'm not stonewalling," Jonathan said. "I'm trying to figure out how to do this."

"So, you're aware that we had a terrorist in custody?"

"I can't answer questions yet," Jonathan said. "Not until you fill out the edges of what you know."

Schaeffer explained, "By the time I got here, the shooting was over, like I said. All that was left was the bedlam and the bleeding. Took us forever to get enough ambulances here. In fact, probably half of the injured were transported by private vehicles. Sometime after the state boys had been relieved by you feds, we were in the middle of the secondary search when I got the idea to check the area of the water tower."

"Why hadn't you done that before?" Gail asked. "Wasn't that the obvious place where the shots were coming from?"

"They weren't coming from anywhere anymore," Schaeffer said. "We were in full rescue and recovery mode. Truthfully, when I got here, it never occurred to me to even try to find a shooter."

"Because your friends and neighbors were dying," Boxers said, his first words in a long time.

"Exactly. We were probably close to an hour into it all when I heard people shouting from the water tower. When I got there, I saw Tom Darone's body on the landing. I climbed the ladder to check on him, and, of course, he was dead, shot through the chest and the top of his head. And, of course, that rang a bell because it meant someone had to be higher up than him on the tower. I climbed the rest of the way to the top, and there was the shooter. The guy was dressed out like he was going to war."

"What does that mean?" Jonathan asked.

"That means he was kitted up like he was going to Iraq. He had an assault pack on his back, and he was wearing a plate carrier. His clothes were all black. He looked like a professional."

"And he was hit?" Boxers asked.

"A lucky shot," Schaeffer said. "I don't know how many shots were fired in total, but before Tom took one to the head, he got one off that zipped under the shooter's vest. Entered at his groin and lodged somewhere in his gut."

Jonathan squirmed and winced.

"Not that part of his groin," Schaeffer clarified. "At the crease where pubes meet the leg."

"Pity," Gail said. She looked startled, as if surprised that she'd spoken her thoughts aloud.

Schaeffer smiled for the first time. "I can't imagine he'll have much use for his boy parts for a while." He seemed to be waiting for a response on that, and when he didn't get it, he elaborated. "The feds were pretty rough with him when they took custody."

"How did they get custody?" Jonathan asked.

"How do you not know?"

"Pretend I don't," Jonathan said. "Humor me."

"I don't know how they got word," Schaeffer said, "but I was still up there with the guy when they arrived and took over. They pushed me out of the way and said they had control."

"You didn't push back?" Boxers asked.

"Why would I want to? I was already drowning in a nightmare. Why the hell would I want to make the waters any deeper?"

"How did they take him away?" Gail asked.

"They shoved him into a government car and disappeared."

"Why hasn't there been anything in the news about that?" Jonathan asked.

Schaeffer's eyes darkened again. "Why do you think?"

"That's specifically what we're here to find out," Gail lied. But she did it well.

"I'm guessing threats," Boxers said.

Schaeffer snapped a forefinger at Big Guy. "Bingo. They hadn't been down the road three minutes before a leader type badged me and asked who else had seen the shooter. I told him nobody, as far as I knew. Then he hit me with some national security bullshit line and told me that if he ever read about any of this in the paper, he would see to it that my life would be ruined forever."

"Those were his words?" Jonathan asked.

"Ruined forever," Schaeffer repeated. "They still resonate in my head. As if somehow I turned into a bad guy."

"And after that?"

"Nothing. Haven't heard a word from them, haven't spoke a word to anyone else. Until now." Another change in demeanor, this time to something like timidity. "Unless this was my loyalty test right here."

"No," Jonathan said. "We're not here to test your loyalty."

"What *are* you here for, then?"

Jonathan inhaled noisily. He owed this guy something, but he wasn't sure how to go about it. "We're here to gather background," he said. "That's as close to the truth as I can tell you."

"Is the shooter still alive?"

Jonathan looked to Boxers, who gave a subtle shake of his head. He thought it was a bad idea to share.

"As far as I know, yes," Jonathan said. "And I truly appreciate your candor."

"To hell with my candor. What about a little justice?"

"We're working on that."

"Do you have any idea how much it would mean to my community if they knew that you had somebody in custody? If they knew that the asshole who did this didn't just get away?"

"It would mean a lot," Gail said. "But to tell them would ruin a bigger investigation. You can't do that."

"Watch me," Schaeffer said. "I owe a shit ton more to my neighbors than I do to any greater investigation."

"I get the emotion," Jonathan said. "I really do. I cannot imagine how awful these past two weeks have been for you or how difficult the next year or five or twenty are going to be. Maybe things never get back to normal. But for now, we need to urge you to be a team player."

"Whose team?"

"The good guys."

"Are you really the good guys?"

There was an honesty about the question that took Jonathan off guard. "I guarantee that we are," he said.

Schaeffer seemed to sense the subtext. “What about the guys who were here that night?”

Boxers’ headshake grew dramatically.

“We need time,” Jonathan said. “That’s all I can give you. The rest is above my paygrade.”

Chapter Five

It had been a long time since Venice had allowed a man into her life and even longer since she'd allowed one into her bed. Derek Halstrom was special. Gentle and kind and smarter than just about anyone she knew, he brought a tender intensity to lovemaking that she'd never experienced.

Lovemaking. Not just sex. Real, caring mutual exploration and ecstasy, though neither of them had dared to call their relationship what it was. Once the *L*-bomb was dropped, there was no going back, so why take the risk?

As she watched him dress at 3:00 A.M. so he could be clear of the house before Mama or Roman woke up and then make the eighty-plus-mile commute to Fort Meade, it all felt so undignified.

"I'm sorry it has to be like this, Derek," she whispered as he pulled up his very brief blue briefs.

"I know," he said. Muscles rippled on his wiry frame as he worked his arms into his purple shirt. A puckered scar marred his otherwise perfect midsection. She'd asked him about that, but he'd dodged the question. "You need to convince your boss to hire me. Then, when I sneak out, I only have to go a short distance."

He pulled his carefully folded suit pants from the chair where he'd placed them four hours ago.

Official records showed Derek to be a data analyst or some such for the National Security Agency, where he tracked down secrets. But in his spare time, he was feared by the Hackersphere as TickTock2, one of the most brilliant hackers Venice had ever met. She'd caught him one time with his cyber-knickers gathered at his ankles and challenged him on it. Then he'd struck back. He'd been able to figure out what, exactly, the covert side of Security Solutions did for its clients. When the dust had settled on the tit for tat, each could out the other as felons.

Back then, when they first met, she'd never have believed that their relationship would evolve into what it had become. Truth be told, Venice thought he'd be an enormous asset to the company, but Digger was a hard sell.

"Give it time," she said. "He'll come around one day."

He buckled and zipped. "He doesn't approve of my sense of style, does he?" Derek's sartorial esthetic ran toward ultramodern, with suit trousers and jackets that were studiously too short. If he wore socks at all with his always out-there dress shoes, they were of a color and pattern that had little relation to the rest of his ensemble.

"I think you look hot as fire," Venice said. "At least you *have* a sense of style. That's hard to find in a cyberstalker. But Digger is what you might call old-school."

"You know it's illegal to use appearance as a reason not to hire someone." He sold that with just the right smile.

Venice laughed. "You might want to leave a farewell note before you file that lawsuit," she said.

He put on his shoes. Nope, no socks. "Does your mother know that we're . . . spending time together?"

"Her name is Mama," Venice said.

"Even to me?"

"To everyone," Venice said. "If she knows—and I think she does, because she knows everything that goes on here—she hasn't said anything about it."

"Shall we tell her?"

"Not at this hour," Venice said. "I think we should wait until there's something real to tell her. The good news for you is that Oscar Thompkins knows."

"Who's Oscar Thompkins?"

"He's in charge of the mansion's security team," Venice said.

Derek smiled. "Good to know I won't get shot in the hallway. One day, we need to discuss why this place rivals the White House for physical security."

"We had some trouble a few years ago," Venice explained. "Two of the students were actually kidnapped from the dormitory."

"Oh, my God!"

"Yeah, that was a scary time. The story had a reasonably happy ending, but it changed our thinking in a big way."

Derek slung his suit jacket around his shoulders and shoved his arms into the sleeves. "Resurrection House is for criminals' kids, right?"

"Exactly," Venice said. "We realized that every one

of those poor boys and girls has some kind of a price on their heads, if only as a means to hurt their parents."

"But why all the security here in the mansion?"

Venice chuckled. "When Jonathan Grave starts on a security binge, he just keeps going."

"Who pays for it all?"

"I've never asked," Venice said. "I figure it's none of my business, but the smart money says it comes out of Digger's pocket."

"Holy shit."

"Yeah, a little bit." She sat taller in the bed as Derek approached for his good-bye kiss.

"We need to do this again," he said.

She smiled. "Soon."

"Busy tonight?"

"I have to help Roman with a history project," she said. Roman was her only child, and he was having a tough time navigating his first year as a teenager. "It's not enough to write a paper anymore. You have to do a diorama with it, too."

"He doesn't go to school here, does he?"

Venice bristled at his tone. "This is a perfectly fine school," she said. "Our teachers do great work here."

Derek cocked an eyebrow.

"No, Roman goes to Northern Neck Academy. But it's only because of the transient nature of Rez House's student population, not because of any quality issues." Maybe this one cut a little close to home since Mama was the de facto mother to all the students, and the administration had recently been beaten up pretty badly by state accreditors.

Derek kissed her. "Duty calls," he said. "From a long, long ways away." He winked.

After the door latched behind him, Venice lay back into her pillows and wondered if, in fact, he was the one. If Derek Halstrom—no less than TickTock2 himself—might be the one to make her little family feel whole again.

She was reaching for the bed stand light when a yell pierced the otherwise silent house.

"Zulu, Zulu, Zulu!" someone hollered. The adolescent squeak was unmistakable. The voice belonged to Roman, and *Zulu* was the established family emergency code word.

Venice threw her covers off and wrapped herself in a robe as she rushed to the door. Someone had already turned on the lights, and as she emerged into the second-floor hallway, everything crystalized in a glance.

Roman stood at the bottom of the stairs, wearing only a pair of boxer shorts, a carton of crackers clutched to his bare chest. He continued to yell.

Three steps above him, Derek waved his hands in the air to bring back sanity and serenity.

"Roman, stop!" Venice yelled.

To her left, Mama Alexander emerged from her bedroom, thoroughly sleep-fogged.

"Who the hell is he?" Roman yelled, pointing. "And what is he doing here now?"

Venice felt heat rise in her face. Roman knew perfectly well who Derek was. The point of this display had everything to do with his second question.

"Watch your mouth, young man," Mama said. Nothing brought her around quite like the deployment of a bad word.

Down in the foyer, beyond Derek, Venice saw the security team gathering, weapons at the ready.

"No!" Venice said. "Oscar, I'm sorry, but this is a false alarm. Roman, you know better."

"Why is he here?" the boy demanded. Then, to Derek, "What are you doing to my mom?"

"Roman!" Venice couldn't believe the rudeness. Wasn't sure how she would handle the humiliation.

Down in the foyer, the four assembled guards sort of folded in on themselves, clearly wishing that they could be anywhere else.

Derek said, "No, I get it. Look, Roman, I'm sorry—"

"Don't," Venice said. "You don't owe him an explanation, and if anyone owes an apology to anyone, it's Roman apologizing to you." She made a point of looking straight at her son. "I'll see you tonight, Derek."

Derek looked fairly terrified. "Um, maybe—"

"I'll see you *tonight*. After Roman and I have finished with his history project."

Silence hung in the air like a dense fog as everyone waited for something to happen.

Finally, Derek moved first. "Excuse me," he said, and he squeezed past Roman.

"You don't belong here," the boy said as he passed. "You are not my father."

Venice cast a look at Mama. "You can't tell me this surprises you," Mama said. "Interestin' days ahead." She disappeared into her room.

Venice kept her spot at the top of the stairs. "Go to bed, Roman," she said. "We can talk about this in the morning."

The defiant stare was the latest of his teenaged gifts. He kept his eyes locked on his mother as he climbed the steps. On the landing, he said. "It *is* morning. And *he* doesn't belong here." Then he padded down to his room. The door slam shook the whole structure.

"Interesting days indeed," Venice mumbled.

To Jonathan's eye, southern South Dakota could easily have been mistaken for northern Nebraska. Farmland stretched forever, in all directions. Or maybe it was prairie. Truth be told, he wasn't sure he knew the difference. On this midautumn day, there wasn't much color to the grasses and crops. Rolled bales of hay seemed to be the primary architectural elements, and he found the landscape quite beautiful. "When people think of the American heartland—of American plenty—this is what they think of," he said to the others in the rented Suburban.

"Looks like a lot of nothin' to me," Boxers said from the driver's seat.

"When the snow starts falling, there'll be a lot more of that nothingness to go around," Gail said from the backseat.

They'd passed a road sign a few minutes ago that announced that they were approaching the town of Bateman, ten miles ahead, due north. According to the coordinates sent to Jonathan's GPS, they'd drive up on their destination within the next few minutes.

"We're looking for a white farmhouse with green shutters," Jonathan said. "It'll be set about a mile off the road on the right. The end of the driveway is supposed to be marked with a tall white birdhouse." Out here, as in the hinterlands surrounding Fisherman's Cove, street addresses were different than in the city.

Rural route numbers were still the current state of mail technology.

Boxers pointed through the windshield. "Isn't that a birdhouse?"

"Bird condo is more like it," Jonathan said. The birdhouse sat atop a fifteen-foot six-by-six-inch pole. Its multilevel three-foot-square design reminded Jonathan of the old New Jersey resort hotels, the kind you'd find in places like Cape May.

"Those are some spoiled rotten birds," Gail said.

"I'd guess spoiled rotten cameras," Boxers countered. "And, since they were built with Homeland Security money, I'm guessing they're high-end cameras, too." He slowed. "I presume we're going in?" He didn't wait for an answer, and Jonathan didn't offer one.

"I'm surprised there's no fence," Gail said. "Not even a chain across the driveway."

"I guess when you're running an illegal secret prison, you want to draw as little attention to it as possible," Jonathan said.

"This is so disturbing," Gail said. "The very fact that we have secret illegal prisons . . ."

"You've got to remember the level of paranoia in the immediate aftermath of Nine-Eleven," Jonathan said. "People were scared shitless, and they wanted answers. They wanted assurances that they'd be able to sleep safely at night."

"But secret *prisons*?" Gail pressed. "They didn't want *that*."

"Weren't you with the FBI when Nine-Eleven happened?" Boxers asked.

"I was," she replied.

"Then you have to remember the pressure," Jonathan said.

"I remember the hysteria. I remember the paranoia, but I don't remember suspending the Constitution."

"We *all* cut a lot of corners back then," Jonathan said. "Due process took a big hit everywhere. We talk a big game when it comes to the rights of the innocent, but when it comes down to us versus them, we pick and choose our preferred sections of the Constitution. It comes down to the government to keep the panic from running out of control."

"You sound like you approve," Gail said.

"Your law professors must be really proud of you," Boxers teased.

"The social contract is a fragile thing, Big Guy," Gail said.

"Exactly," Jonathan said, but in support of a different point. "When the public is scared, they want action. Washington was trying to keep a revolution at bay. It fell to the likes of Irene Rivers to sort it out. We got help from the Pakis and others to help us deal with the foreign nationals."

"Through black site prisons," Gail said. "The ones that we were forced to shut down in shame."

"The ones we acknowledged and shut down in pretend shame," Boxers corrected.

"We had domestic threats that needed to be taken care of," Jonathan said, "so we opened some black sites of our own."

"How did they get agents to go along with that?" Gail wondered aloud. "I'll stipulate that you could get a handful of agents to throw their oaths to the gutter, but you're talking a lot more than that."

"Hundreds, I would guess," Jonathan said. "Which is why they didn't use career agents."

"Contractors?" Gail asked.

"Bingo. If the money's right, you can talk anyone into anything."

"My God, your cynicism knows no bounds, does it?" Gail leaned forward so she could get a better angle to glare at Jonathan. "Were you one of the selected contractors?"

"Not me," he replied. "I was still doing wet work for Uncle."

"But you were aware."

"I heard rumors."

"And what did you think at the time?"

"War is ugly."

"Oh, please don't patronize me."

"Do you really see Digger as the patronizing element in this conversation?" Boxers asked. He clearly was losing patience.

"None of that matters now," Jonathan said. "What was, was. The domestic sites were closed down as Uncle got a better feel for the magnitude of what we were facing."

"And as the international sites filled up," Gail pressed.

"There's that, yes," Jonathan agreed. "As far as I know, the domestic black site program shut down. But it seems that the sites themselves still exist."

"How many?"

"I have no idea," Jonathan said. "At least one, it would seem. And it's at the end of this driveway."

"Hey, Boss, we're not alone anymore," Boxers said, pointing ahead. An all-terrain four-wheeler approached them head-on, manned by three heavily armed men in jungle camo. "Badasses at twelve o'clock."

"Stop the truck and let them come to us," Jonathan said. "And remember we're on the same team."

"Do they know that?" Gail asked.

"Probably not. At least not yet."

"I don't like it when people point guns as me," Boxers said.

"Doesn't look like their fingers are on the bang switch yet," Jonathan said. "And they're not really pointing them at us." In fact, their muzzles all pointed skyward.

The four-wheeler stopped as well, leaving a thirty-foot gap between them. The soldier look-alikes peeled off of their riding positions and formed a loose sort of skirmish line. The guy who'd been riding shotgun brought a megaphone up to his lips and said something.

Jonathan cracked his window to let the sound in. "Did you hear what he said?"

"I think it was something about coming in for dinner and drinks," Boxers said. "But I could be wrong."

Jonathan opened his window the rest of the way and shouted, "We're friendlies. We need to chat."

The guy with the megaphone said, "Turn around."

"We're FBI," Jonathan shouted. He pulled his badge holder from his front pocket and stuck his hand through the window to flash the gold shield. "I guess we need to start wearing these puppies on our belts," he mumbled to the others.

"I'm afraid it will burn my flesh," Boxers grumbled.

"Get out and approach our vehicle," Four-wheeler said.

"Anybody see a downside to that?" Jonathan asked.

"Other than me hating being told what to do?" Boxers asked.

"It *is* their playground," Gail said. "They get to set the rules."

"Agreed," Jonathan said. "Plus, I always like the *holy shit* look people get when they see Big Guy for the first time." He yelled, "On our way out."

"Are you armed?"

"Of course," Jonathan said.

"Dipshit," Boxers grumbled.

"Just don't make us jumpy," Four-wheeler said. Finally, there was a lightness of tone that showed he might not be an asshole.

"Y'all know the drill," Jonathan said. "Keep your hands visible and move slowly. And try not to block the warmth of the sun from the Earth." That last part elicited a finger from Boxers.

They opened their doors simultaneously and stepped out onto the gravel. Once he was standing straight, Jonathan clipped his badge to his belt, next to the buckle, and closed his door. The two other doors closed more or less in unison. Jonathan set the pace. He kept his arms down, with his fingers spread like jazz hands as he walked at a casual stroll toward the other team.

"You can stop there," Four-wheeler said when they were still fifteen feet away. "Now, state your business."

"We're here to interview Logan Masterson," Jonathan said.

The other team exchanged significant looks. "I don't know what you're talking about," their spokesman said.

"Way to play a bluff," Boxers mocked.

Another of the guards stiffened. "Watch your attitude."

Boxers laughed. "Okay, now I'm really, really afraid of you."

"Is this really necessary?" Gail asked. Her voice dripped with disdain.

"No, it's not," Jonathan said. "Stand down, Agent Contata." He turned back to the spokesman for the guards. "I'm Agent Neil Bonner. I appreciate your stonewalling, but I really don't have time for it. We need to speak with your house guest."

The leader looked to his cohorts, and they looked back at him. This clearly was not a conversation they expected to have. "What's the pass code?" he asked after turning back to face Jonathan.

"You start," he said. That was the beginning of the pass code.

"Green cheese is moldy," the leader said.

"It'll make you healthy if you eat it," Jonathan replied. "But it needs a nice chianti."

And that was it. All four of the defenders let their rifles fall against their slings. "Mount up and follow us," the leader said.

The rest of the drive took less than three minutes. "You kept a good poker face thorough that ridiculous pass phrase exchange," Gail said.

"And to think I haven't been practicing my lines," Jonathan said. For pass phrases to work, they had to be random enough to be unguessable, yet sensible enough to be memorable. Often, those two requirements led to ridiculous exchanges.

The road ended at a substantial chain-link fence and

attended gate. After a brief chat between the commander of the four-wheeler and the attending guard, the gate pulled open, left to right, with the assistance of an electric motor. As the four-wheeler pulled through, the attending guard wandered up to Boxers' door and made a spinning motion with his forefinger, indicating that he wanted the driver to open his window.

"Afternoon, folks," the guard said. "Leave your vehicle out here. Park it anywhere. It's not like we get a lot of visitors."

Boxers backed the Suburban up a few yards, executed a T-turn so it was facing out, and pulled it a few feet off the driveway.

"Okay, sports fans," Jonathan said. "Let's see what we see."

"What will success look like?" Gail asked as she opened her door. "What's a home run?"

"Damned interesting question," Jonathan replied. "Ask me when we're done."

Jonathan led the way through the gate to join the guard staff, who seemed anxious now to talk. The leader stepped forward and offered his hand. "I'm Ray," he said. "No need for last names."

"Because they're not real, anyway, right?" Jonathan said with a smile.

"You got it," Ray said. "I was wondering when you boys—and girls, sorry—were going to come and pick this guy up."

"So, we're the first?"

"Since I've been here, yes. That's about a week and a half."

"Have you been talking to him?"

"We have orders not to."

"Orders from whom?" Jonathan pressed.

"From on high. My bosses. They don't have real names, either."

From off to the side, one of the other guards said, "But their cash is very real."

"Tell me what I should expect," Jonathan said.

Ray pulled at the stubble on his chin. "I don't know what to tell you. Our orders are to watch him in the monitors, keep him fed, and call a doc if he goes south. None of us has ever said a word to him."

Jonathan heard Gail inhale sharply, but he ignored it. "Does he talk to you?"

"Occasionally, he shouts at the camera," Ray said. "He used to ask us questions when we delivered his food, but he stopped that after a while. I guess he realized the futility of it."

"Tell him about the shit," one of the other guards said.

That elicited a chuckle. "Yeah, late one night he went a little berserk and he smeared his own shit all over the lens that covers the camera."

"Jesus," Gail said. It sounded like a moan.

"Yeah, this is a real special job I've got," Ray said. "Let me know when you're ready to go down."

"A couple of ground rules," Jonathan said. "I want cameras and microphones turned off. There can be no record of the meeting."

"Not a problem. Apparently, no one wants a record of this. There's not even a capability for it. Now, I've got a ground rule, too."

Jonathan waited for it.

"If this turns out to be a hit—I mean if you're here to kill the guy—we're not going to let you pin it on us."

Jonathan recoiled. "I assure you that is not our mission. Nor are we here to take him away. We're only here to chat with him. Point us in the right direction, and we'll take it on our own."

From the outside, the secret prison in South Dakota looked a lot like dozens of surrounding farmhouses. It stood a story and a half, white clapboard with a wraparound covered porch. The remnants of a garden drooped in the surrounding flowerbeds. Ray led the way up the two steps from the ground to the porch and pushed open the front door.

"Not a lot of security," Boxers observed.

"As much as we need," Ray said. "I'm guessing the owners of this little slice of hell want passing aircraft to have no idea who we are or what we do." He entered the foyer and waited for the others to file in behind him.

The layout reminded Jonathan of a thousand ramblers he'd been in that looked just like it. The living area lay to the right of the door. A redbrick fireplace dominated the far right-hand wall, and in between sat five metal government-issued green desks that had been arranged in no apparent order. Laptops sat on each, as did an assortment of paperwork and food trash.

"This is our main area," Ray explained. "The dungeon is downstairs in the basement."

"The dungeon," Gail said, tasting the word and clearly not liking the flavor.

"That's what we call it. You'll know why when you see it." Ray pivoted to indicate a hallway that branched off to the left. "Restrooms and our personal equipment lockers are down there."

“How well are you guys armed?” Jonathan asked.

“We’re fine,” Ray said. “Hard stop. I don’t care who you are, you’re not cleared to know that.”

That was fair, Jonathan thought. Out here in the boonies, these guys would be on their own for a long time if they had to repel some kind of a breakout attempt. It made perfect sense that they wouldn’t want anyone to know just how much bad-assery they could bring to the party.

“Anything else we need to know before we head downstairs?” Jonathan asked.

“Nothing I can think of,” Ray said. “Other than to take a good lungful of air up here so you’ll remember what it smells like.”

Chapter Six

The route to the dungeon took them through the kitchen and out onto a covered back porch that Jonathan suspected had been built for the specific purpose of camouflaging the double doors that angled up from the floor. No doubt inspired by Tornado Alley storm cellars, these doors were constructed of heavy steel and were each six feet long by three feet wide.

As they approached, Ray explained, “There’s no way to open these doors from the inside. When you’re done with what you need to do, there’s an intercom at the bottom of the stairs. Push the button, identify yourself, and we’ll open the doors from up here. All good?”

Boxers made a growling sound so low that Jonathan wondered if he knew he was making it. Big Guy was a borderline claustrophobe. “You want to wait up here?” Jonathan offered.

The glare he got in return made him smile.

“Okay, here we go,” Ray said. Using his body to shield what he was doing, he opened what might have been a police call box on the wall and punched in a code. A pneumatic solenoid valve hissed, and the massive doors lifted to reveal a stairway that descended into a dimly lit space that looked a lot like a bunker. The pitch of the stairs was nowhere near as steep as Jonathan had expected, leading him to suspect that the footprint of the underground prison was substantially larger than that of the farmhouse.

"Last cell on the right," Ray said. "Shouldn't have any trouble finding him." He smiled at his deployment of the obvious.

"Remember," Jonathan said as he stepped toward the doors. "Cameras and microphones off."

Ray held up three fingers of his right hand. "Scout's honor."

Boxers took a menacing step closer to the mercenary so that he towered over the much smaller man. "You do not want to jam us up," he said.

Ray tried to look unintimidated, but like so many others so much stronger than him, he couldn't pull it off. "I got no reason to," he said. Then he swallowed hard.

Jonathan held the man with a glare of his own and then led the way down into the dungeon.

Everything about this underground space was the opposite of what Jonathan expected from the exterior of the farmhouse. Ordinarily, a descent into a root cellar or a storm cellar would show rough stone or concrete shoring materials, but the walls here were smooth, clearly made of poured concrete. Where he expected dim yellow light from exposed bulbs or maybe fluorescent tubes, the illumination was, in fact, a bright white, almost as if to simulate the light of the sun. But the temperature was the biggest surprise. The thermometer was supposed to plunge as you went deeper, but as he approached the bottom of the stairs, he found the air uncomfortably warm, hovering north of eighty degrees, he guessed. He waited for the others to join him at the bottom and then watched as the heavy doors closed again, sealing them in. When the lock seated, the loudest sound in the dungeon was the hum of the air handler.

At a glance, it became obvious to Jonathan how ambitious the secret prison program had been at its heyday. A long, straight hallway stretched thirty feet ahead of him. The walls on either side were constructed of steel bars set in concrete. He counted five doors on a side, for a total of ten cells, each separated from their next-door neighbor by a foot-thick slab of concrete that ran from the floor to the ceiling.

"Which one of you assholes is it this time?" a voice called from the far end of the hall.

Jonathan put a finger over his lips to tell Boxers and Gail to remain silent.

"What, you don't like me anymore?" the voice said. "Did I hurt your feelings last time?"

Jonathan beckoned his team to bend closer. He whispered, "You two stay out of his sight and listen. See what I can get done one-on-one. When we've exhausted that, I'll bring you in to ask whatever I missed."

Boxers bristled. He didn't like to let Jonathan engage without him closely in tow.

"There's a wall of steel," Jonathan said with a smile. "I think I'll be okay."

They approached as a group, then Gail and Boxers

stopped at the middle of the fourth cell, one short of their target.

"Wearing different shoes today," the voice said before he was visible. "A little early for dinner, isn't it?"

Jonathan remained silent as he crossed into view, then forced a straight face as he took in the horror.

Logan Masterson sat naked on a thin green plastic mattress that provided precious little padding against the concrete shelf that served as his cot. He'd angled his back into the corner, and he sat with his legs splayed, one knee cocked up. His beard looked splotchy and fresh, giving Jonathan the impression that it had not been grown intentionally. His hands and his feet were black with filth, and his hair dangled heavy with grease. The stench of body filth hung like an invisible fog. But that wasn't the most disturbing smell.

The dressings on Logan Masterson's bullet wound hadn't been changed in far too long. The trauma pads had soaked all the way through the bandages that held them in place, and even from his side of the bars, Jonathan could see the telltale yellow traces of a growing infection.

"Am I a pretty sight or what?" Masterson asked.

"When was the last time you saw a doctor?" Jonathan asked.

"Who the hell are you?"

Jonathan pointed to his badge. "FBI," he said. "Names don't matter. I asked you a question."

Masterson's gaze narrowed as he studied his new visitor. "Why don't you already know that?" he asked. "Aren't you the assholes who put me here?"

"Outrage from the guy who shot up a high school football game."

Masterson stared back. Finally, he said, "Get with the program, Agent Nobody. I'm here to die. That doesn't jibe with seeing doctors."

As Jonathan listened, he watched the prisoner's eyes. There was a lot of physical pain there, and he was doing a yeoman's job masking it. People in that line of work didn't fear death. They insulated themselves from the emotional and spiritual pain that plagued normal people. What they feared was indignity. Masterson's background in Special Forces meant, nearly by definition, that he'd foreseen a noble death for himself at one point—certainly at the beginning. Youngsters saw themselves as immortal, anyway. When they considered the possibility of their demise, how could it not be amid flags and explosions?

"You're not dying on my watch, Logan," Jonathan said. "I'll be back." He turned and walked past Gail and Boxers, beelining toward the doors.

"Where are you going?" Gail asked.

"I'm going to have a chat with our friend Ray."

Boxers jumped to life. "Coming with you," he said.

"I'm staying," Gail said.

That brought the guys to a halt. Jonathan turned, cocked his head.

"There's a wall of steel," Gail parroted. "I think I'll be okay."

Jonathan hid his displeasure. His efforts to protect her from harm while respecting her as an equal part of the team had always been a difficult balance for him. "Okay," he said. "See you in a while."

Boxers followed as he walked to the base of the stairs and looked into the lens of the security camera. Jonathan made a rolling motion with his fingers to indicate they needed to open up. He made no indication that he was angry.

"Are we going to go violent on their asses?" Boxers asked through an innocent smile.

"If we have to."

"Promise me I can bear your child," Big Guy said.

Jonathan laughed in spite of his anger. The solenoid hissed again, and the doors rose. "If they even think about going to guns," he said, "take 'em out."

"Roger that."

No one was waiting at the top of the stairs. As Jonathan cleared the hole, he looked at the camera on the porch and indicated the doors. "Leave them open," he said. He'd learned a long time ago that when you project authority, authority is often granted. The fact that the doors didn't close proved his point.

Boxers followed as Jonathan retraced his steps back into the house and on into the living room, where Ray and a minion were busy on their laptops.

"That was fast," Ray said without looking up.

Jonathan walked to the man's desk and swept his computer and half of the shit on his desk onto the floor with a giant move of his arm. "What the hell are you doing here?" Jonathan said. He didn't raise his voice, but he was confident that Ray heard the fury in his words.

Ray jumped back at the move, clearly startled. "Me? What the hell? Jesus."

The minion at the other desk started to rise.

"Sit," Boxers said.

The guy sat.

"And stay," Boxers said. He sold it with a smile.

"Hey, asshole," Ray said, regaining his composure. "FBI or not, you can't come in here and—"

"When was the last time Logan Masterson saw a doctor?"

"I don't know. Before my time."

"Why so long?"

"What do you mean, why?"

"He's a human being, dickhead. You can't treat him like an insect."

Ray stood up.

"You sit, too," Boxers instructed.

"Screw you," Ray said, and he stayed on his feet. He glared at Jonathan. "First of all, he's *not* a human being. He's a goddamn child killer, and he deserves to die."

Jonathan felt himself puff up bigger. "That's not—"

"Shut up and let me finish," Ray snapped. "He's all those things, but it is not my call to determine when he sees a doctor. That's on you guys."

Jonathan recoiled. Not at all what he'd been expecting. "Who's *us guys*?"

"Fibbies, you sanctimonious prick. You were guarding him when I got here, and the orders were to let him bandage himself and die. My job was to keep him fed and watered. That was it. And it's been a pretty goddamn soul-stealing experience."

"Who told you that? What was his name?"

"Names don't matter, remember?" Ray seemed genuinely pissed, and as a result, his stock rose on Jonathan's exchange. "He said he was FBI, and he showed me a badge. He gave me a quick tour of the place, and then he and his crew di di mau'd the hell out of here."

Jonathan recognized the verbal remnant from the Vietnam years that were way before his time. *Di di mau* more or less translated to *run like a bunny rabbit*. "How long had Masterson been here when you took over?"

"Hard to give definitive timelines to things that happened before I was in the loop."

Good point.

"How did you guys get hired?" Boxers asked. He'd dialed back on the bad-assery. "I mean do you all work for the same contractor, or are you a group of freelancers?"

Ray cocked his head and planted his fists on his hips. "My bullshit bell is shaking the rafters," he said. "This is stuff you should already know."

Jonathan considered his reply for a few seconds before saying, "Ray, I think it's plainly obvious to everyone on this property that nothing about what's going on here is anywhere close to normal." He looked to Boxers. "I think it's best that we all stop asking questions before we dig holes we can't get out of."

That seemed to make Ray happy, make him feel relieved.

"Now, about the doctor," Jonathan said. "Do you have one to call, or do I need to summon one of mine?"

* * *

Gail Bonneville pulled a folding metal chair from the corner and set it up in front of the wall of bars that separated her from Logan Masterson. She'd seen more than her share of naked men over the years, and more than a few of them in more startling conditions than this prisoner. He watched in silence as she positioned herself, and for five minutes or more, they just stared at each other.

His tough veneer began to fray. She saw it first in his eyes, and then around his mouth. They twitched, and it clearly bothered him that she could see it.

It takes a lot of energy to project toughness that you know you don't possess, and sooner or later, a person can't do it anymore. She'd seen versions of the same process work dozens of times in police interview rooms as tough-as-shit-just-ask-me thugs whittled themselves down to little boys who wanted their mommies. She didn't think it was a function of fear as much as it was a realization of helplessness. Of hopelessness.

"Want to talk?" Gail asked, finally.

"What, are you the good cop to the other guy's bad cop?"

She fell silent again. It made no sense to engage in the dick-knocking banter. She'd spoken too soon. In time, he'd come to realize that speaking with someone was better than being alone with his demons. The fact that she was a woman—and not a bad-looking one at that—could only help her cause.

Minutes passed before Masterson said, "What do you people want from me?"

"Information," Gail said. She tried to make it sound like the most obvious answer in the world.

"I'm not a snitch," Masterson declared.

"Good for you. That's admirable."

"And now you patronize."

Gail laughed. "Oh, come on, Logan. What am I supposed to do with *I'm not a snitch*?"

He allowed himself a smile that transformed into a wince. Point taken. "What are you looking for?"

"Let's start with *why*," Gail said. "What could possibly drive you to open fire on a stadium full of innocent civilians?"

"The same thing that drives you to a shithole like this to grill me with questions."

"Excuse me?"

"Ah, nice going on the shocked expression," Masterson mocked. "Want to show me your badge again, *Special Agent*?"

Gail didn't try to perpetuate the ruse anymore.

Masterson continued, "I recognize your guy, you know. I worked with him in the Army. Can't remember his name, but I know he was a D-Boy." Something dawned behind his eyes. "Oh, now I get it. Because we crawled through some of the same trenches, maybe he can get me to turn snitch."

There was that word again. Clearly, there was no worse crime in Masterson's world. "You were talking about your reason," Gail prompted.

"Money!" Masterson shouted the word and made her jump. "Come on, be honest. Isn't that why all of us go back and double dip in the killing business? Money. Gobs and gobs of it."

Gail bristled. That wasn't at all why she did what she did. He was trying to get a rise out of her. "Somebody paid you to shoot up a high school football game?"

A smile crept into his pain. "They don't call it Black Friday because I shot up a football game," he said. "They call it that because a bunch of people shot up a bunch of high school football games."

"But *why*?"

"I didn't ask. They handed me a pile of cash and gave me an assignment. I did my job."

"Who would pay for such a thing?"

"People who want to sow terror." Masterson stated that last part without emotion, as if he were stating the obvious.

Gail leaned forward in her chair. "That's a big step, Logan, from Army Special Forces to terrorist."

Masterson winced against something, a stab of pain, she imagined. "You think I'm a terrorist?"

"You opened fire on a stadium."

"But I'm not the terrorist," he said. "I'm just the tool. The terrorists are the guys who pay me."

Gail was engaged now and saw no reason to back away. At least he was talking. "That's a hell of a rationalization," she said. "How do you sleep at night?"

"I don't," he said. "Sure as shit not in here. "But I've been killing people for money for my whole adult life."

"For the military," Gail said. "That's different."

"Now who's rationalizing?" Another stab, but he seemed proud of himself for making his point. "When I was in the Sandbox blowing away Hajis for Uncle

Sam, how do you think the people downrange from me thought about the asshole who was shooting at them?"

"You were doing your duty."

"I was doing my duty on Black Friday. People who are getting shot never think heroic thoughts about their shooter. They think they're being singled out unjustly, because they've talked themselves into believing that the shit they're doing—the shit I'm killing them for—is at least as noble as the shit I've talked myself into believing. That's what rationalization is all about. Ask your fellow mercenary out there. It's about the adrenaline and the money. I gave up on causes a long time ago. And I'm sure it's no surprise to you that pulling triggers in the private sector pays a shit ton more than it does on Uncle's dime."

Gail was dumbstruck. Literally, as in struck dumb by what she was hearing. How does anyone go that far off the rails?

"You look like I smacked you," Masterson said.

"I kind of feel like you did," Gail confessed. He'd knocked her off message—if she'd ever had one—but keeping him talking was better than having him lock up. "How many like you are there?"

"What, burned-out SF shooters? I'm gonna guess as many SF shooters as there are, minus maybe a hundred."

That wasn't possible, and Gail knew it. He was trying to scare her, and frankly, it was working. If he was trying to engage her in an argument, she was going to disappoint him. "I meant how many of *you* are there? How many on your team?"

"Three thousand four hundred and seventy-eight," he said.

Gail felt her jaw drop.

Masterson laughed. "Shit, I don't know. It could be that many, I guess, but I have no idea. It's not like we have a clubhouse where we sign in. I'm what you call a lone wolf."

Gail's bullshit bell rang. "Then who were you afraid of snitching on?" Her gut tensed as she heard her words. That was the last thing she wanted him to be thinking about.

And he shut down.

Gail changed gears. "So, as far as you know, you're part of a pack of lone wolves."

"We're done here," Masterson said. "Let me die in peace."

"My partners have gone to get you a doctor," Gail said. "You're being treated horribly here. We're going to change that."

"I'm going to die here anyway," Masterson said.

Gail sat back in her chair and nodded. "Yeah, you are," she said. "And it's going to be pretty awful. The question you need to ask yourself is how awful do you want it to be?"

"I want a lawyer."

Gail's laugh was genuine, and it made her feel terrible. "That's not happening. This is not that kind of prison. This is a place designed to suck information out of you and then leave you bleeding to death. Did you know that no one even knows you're here? Hell, they don't even know that you were taken from the shooting scene. The world is still looking for you."

Something changed behind his eyes. She may have scored a hit.

"So, here's the choice you have to make," she continued. "You already know how the current landlord wants to treat you. This is not nearly as bad as it can get. Or, you can cooperate a little and you get morphine and antibiotics to take the edge off the awfulness. Either way, you're going to die here. Do you want to pass in your sleep, or do you want to go out screaming for your mother?"

Chapter Seven

"The chopper will be here in forty minutes with a medical team," Jonathan said as he clicked off and slid his phone into his pocket.

Ray looked both impressed and confused. "You have air ambulances on speed dial?"

"Doesn't everyone?" Fact was, in Jonathan's line of work, bad things sometimes happened to good guys—injuries that couldn't be reported or treated through normal channels—and systems were in place to handle such things off-the-books, in total secrecy. The original purpose of these secret medical facilities was to cater to the needs of counterespionage agents back in the days of the Cold War. If a KGB informant fell ill or got himself shot, it was not acceptable to have him transported to a community hospital. The FBI would shut down the scene until their own medical teams could swoop in and take control. The same thing often happened with people in the Witness Security Program.

The doctors and the technology were some of the best in the world, at least in part because money flowed like rivers in the world of covert operators. Money kept tongues stilled. And once silence was bought, because the stakes were so high, the penalty for revealing them was extraordinary.

"Only forty minutes?" Ray pressed. "Where are they located?"

Jonathan pretended he didn't hear the question. "Tell me about the crew that you and your team relieved here." He sat on a desk, legs dangling.

"Nothing to tell, beyond what I've said. We got here, they gave us a tour, and then they bugged out."

"Do you think they really were feds?"

"I don't think *you're* really feds." That came from the other member of Ray's team, who sat in a chair in the corner.

"I didn't catch your name," Boxers said. The subtext from his tone was, *sit quietly and shut the hell up.*

The man stood. "I didn't offer one," he said. "But since you asked so nicely, you can call me Walter."

"I don't believe you're really feds, either," Ray said.

"Not the question I asked," Jonathan said.

"They had badges," Ray said. His frustration was building. "They flashed and they talked their talk, but they didn't have the swagger that Feebs have." He paused for effect. "Neither do you."

"You're going to hurt my feelings," Boxers said.

Ray ignored him. "They told us essentially to let Masterson die."

"Why didn't they just kill him?" Jonathan asked.

Ray answered with an extended shrug.

An electric bell erupted and made Jonathan jump a foot. It was the same sound as class change, back when he was in high school. "What the hell!"

Ray looked concerned as he shot to his feet and spun around to look at his computer terminal. "Visitors," he said. "Heading toward the front gate."

"Is that a problem?" Boxers asked. He moved to the window.

Jonathan caught the glances exchanged between Ray and Walter. They knew something.

"Talk to me, guys," Jonathan said.

"No visitors in weeks," Ray said. "Now, two sets in the same day. Wouldn't that seem odd to you if you were in my shoes?"

Hairs rose on the back of Jonathan's neck. "Yeah," he said. "That would seem very odd."

"What's really going on, Agent Bonner?" Ray asked.

Across the room, Walter's hand inched toward the pistol on his hip.

"Don't be stupid," Boxers said. "We're the good guys here."

"Spoken like a calm bad guy," Ray said.

Jonathan extended both hands, as if stopping two-way traffic. "Everybody, just cool it," he said. "Let's see what happens."

Jonathan raced through his options. Whoever was on the way, they were not going to be happy with the plan to bring medical assistance to the man they wanted to be dead. Jonathan had no intention of leaving without some humanity injected into the place.

"Tell you what," Jonathan said. "Tell your man at the gate not to let them pass."

Walter recoiled from that suggestion. "What will that do?"

"I don't know. Buy us some time, maybe."

"Your chopper gets here in forty minutes?" Ray said. "There's no way you can buy that much time."

"Why not?" Jonathan asked. "What are they going to do, shoot their way in?"

Ray heaved an enormous sigh. "You know, you're going to throw this big wrench into the gears, and then you're going to drive off, and me and my team are going to be left with the mess."

"You didn't really like this gig all that much, anyway, did you?" Jonathan asked with a smile.

Ray's shoulders sagged. "Goddammit, I hate every bit of this." He picked up the phone and punched in four numbers. "Hey, Grant. We've got visitors coming. Don't let them in." He listened. "Don't you worry about that. That's my job. You just keep them at bay. Tell them that you have to get permission from me and that you can't find me."

Ray didn't wait for an answer, but rather hung up abruptly. "Okay, Agent Bonner, what's our next move?"

"You have cameras on that entrance, right?"

"Shit, we've got cameras everywhere."

"Let's watch how they react," Jonathan said. "You got audio, too?"

"What, are you kidding?" Walter joked. "This place was built with tax dollars. The government may not spend smart, but at least they spend big."

Jonathan shot a look to Ray. That was a lot of talking out of a guy who hadn't said much of anything.

"The electronics are Walter's specialty," Ray said.

"I do like to play with my toys," Walter confirmed. Short and stocky, he moved with a certain elegance as he pivoted back around to the desk he'd been occupying. "It's better if you come around here," he said, and he pivoted his screen a little to make it more visible. He hit a key, and the speakers came to life.

The screen showed four angles on the same spot, the images arranged in a grid on the twenty-four-inch monitor. The upper left of the screen showed an elevated view, straight on into the windshield, and the upper right showed a similar view, but from behind. The lower left and right panels showed those respective sides, also from an elevated view.

They'd just gathered around the screen when a vehicle appeared. And then another. Two SUVs with darkened windows.

"They sure look like Fibbie vehicles," Boxers said.

The gate guard stepped forward and motioned for the driver to roll down his window. As the glass descended into the door panel, the guard leaned in a little. "Afternoon, folks. I'm afraid . . . oh, shit!"

The guard jumped backward as he moved his M4 up to a shooting position, but he never made it. An unseen gun from inside the vehicle barked three times, and the guard dropped in his own shadow. A second guard, positioned on the passenger side, seemed to be stunned into stillness for a second or two, and by the time he got his shit together, it was too late. Four more bullets brought him down.

"Holy shit!" Ray yelled.

"Long guns are all in the Suburban, Boss," Boxers said.

Jonathan drew his Colt. "Are these doors locked down?"

"They've got locks," Ray confirmed, "but they're not what I'd call secure."

"Then move," Jonathan said. "We don't want to let ourselves be killed with a single grenade." He pointed a finger at Walter. "Secure the prison doors."

"What about your friend?"

Jonathan glanced at a different monitor, saw Gail scrambling up the stairs. "She must have heard the shots. When she's clear, you lock those doors down."

He watched as Walter typed in a code and the heavy steel doors closed. "What's that code?"

"Not your business."

"We don't know who's going to live and who's not," Jonathan explained.

"Sounds like we need to keep me safe, then, doesn't it?" Walter said with a fake smile.

The gate camera showed a man in tactical gear taking bolt cutters to the fence.

"Is that enough leverage to get through the lock?" Jonathan asked.

"No way," Walter said.

"Good. That will buy us some time." Jonathan turned to Ray, but the other man was beelining toward an internal door. "Hey, Ray, you said there's a weapons locker?"

"Way ahead of you," Ray said over his shoulder. "Follow me. Walter, I'll bring you a rifle. Keep an eye on the cameras."

Ray led the way into what might have been a den if the building were really a house and over to a steel gun cabinet that had to be five feet wide and stretched from the floor to the ceiling. Jonathan stayed out of his way as the man spun the combination dial, turned the lock, and then pulled the door open.

"Looks like they've got C4!" Walter yelled from the other room. "They're going to blow the lock."

Gail stood in the doorway. "What the hell is going on? What's all the shooting?"

"We're under assault," Jonathan said. It was as much explanation as they had time for and pretty much said everything anyone needed to know.

Ray pulled a ballistic vest out of the cabinet and handed it to Jonathan, who tossed it to Gail. "This one's for you."

A second one came out, and Jonathan did the math in his head. There was no way they'd have a vest big enough for Boxers. So, if he was going unprotected, Jonathan was going along. "Just a chest rig with ammo for me and Big Guy," he said.

"Put it on, Boss," Boxers said. "I was born bulletproof."

An explosion shook the building, and then a second one knocked out the electricity. An emergency generator kicked on somewhere outside.

"They're inside the wire!" Walter yelled, and he appeared in the doorway.

Jonathan tossed him an M4 as soon as Ray had placed it in his hand, and the second one went to Gail.

Ray handed one to Boxers, a final one to Jonathan, and kept the last for himself.

"Ammo," Boxers said.

Chest rigs were a kind of vest, designed to hold ten or more thirty-round magazines. They could be worn by themselves, or they could be slid over ballistic armor.

Jonathan handed a rig to Boxers and lifted another one over his own head, extended his arms, and let the ammo carrier slide into place.

"Watch the doors and windows," Jonathan said. "Don't let anyone inside."

"This is a bad place to be, Boss," Boxers said. "We can't maneuver. They can wait and smoke us out."

"Then we need to smoke them first," Jonathan said. He worked the bolt on the M4 to chamber a round and thumbed the fire selector from SAFE to SINGLE-FIRE. "Reinforced doors?"

Ray shook his head. "Never thought—"

From the front room, the air shook with the staccato boom of an M4 on full-auto. "They're at the door!" Walter yelled, and then he slid into the weapons room. "Looks like five guys." He fired a burst around the corner.

Jonathan imagined himself as the attackers and visualized what he would do. Given the layout of the building, there was really only one play in the playbook. "Walter, get in here," he commanded. "Be ready for the flashbang."

As if on cue, the whole structure seemed to bounce with the detonation of a nonlethal grenade called a flashbang. Over the course of a couple of milliseconds, the grenade produced a million-candle-power flash and a 140-decibel boom. Used by SWAT teams around the world, it's a device designed to disorient hostage takers and give the invaders an edge.

Except when you know it's coming.

When the invaders got to the threshold, Walter tried to defend himself, but he was rattled, and they took him out with a double-tap to the head.

Jonathan, Gail, and Boxers all fired on the shooter simultaneously and dropped him. Ditto the second guy in their stack.

The combined pounding of the flashbang and the rifle fire left Jonathan's head feeling as if it had been stuffed with cotton. Even for an experienced professional, the overwhelming violence and noise could be disorienting, but the fight was not yet over.

Jonathan spun on his own axis to confront the attack that he knew had to be coming from the black side—the rear of the structure.

This time, the attacker made a critical error. As he pulled the pin on his flashbang and prepared to throw it through the door of the back porch, he exposed his head and shoulders above the wainscoting of the low porch wall. Boxers blasted him through the forehead, and he fumbled the grenade, dropping it at his own knees. When it blew, the second guy in their stack jumped back and up, creating a target for Jonathan.

Three shots. Two to the vest and one to the chin.

Silence.

Jonathan scanned the room. Walter lay dead on the floor, his blood trail combining with that of the dickheads who shot him. Ray and Gail both held aim at the door to the computer room, while Jonathan and Boxers held the rear.

"We'll clear first," Gail said. "What's your name again?" she asked the man with the gun next to her.

He looked rattled. "Um, Ray."

"We need to check to see if we killed them all. Are you up for it?"

He nodded.

"Say it."

"I'm up for it."

Jonathan couldn't help but smile. She spoke the same words he would have. He turned away and refocused on his sector of the fight. He listened as she advanced on the door, and in his mind, he watched her pie the corner, her rifle up and ready.

"Clear!" Gail called from the other room. No imminent hazard to worry about.

"Let's move," Jonathan said to Big Guy. They advanced in unison, in a carefully orchestrated and frequently practiced sequence of movements designed to spot and neutralize any hazards they encountered. Rifles up and ready at their shoulders, safeties off, fingers outside the trigger guard, they approached the door to the porch.

A thirty-second search proved the porch to be clear.

After a search of the exterior perimeter, Jonathan proclaimed the scene to be secure. Ray's two companions at the gate lay where they fell. Two attackers lay dead in their own juices sprawled across the floor of the front room. Both of the attackers in the back were still dead. Body five of five lay in the front yard. Apparently, Walter's unaimed defensive fire hadn't been for naught.

As Jonathan and the others re-formed on the back porch, Ray said, "Someone want to tell me what the *hell* just happened?"

"The good guys won," Boxers said.

"We just killed a bunch of FBI agents!" Ray exclaimed.

"Maybe," Jonathan said. "But I bet not. Even so, I don't think there's anything in the U.S. Code that says we have to stand still and be murdered. Remember, they fired on your friends first."

"They weren't my friends," Ray said.

The sharpness of his tone startled Jonathan. "What aren't you telling me?"

"Nothing. Just that they weren't my friends. We occupied the same space, but we were all individual recruits. I didn't wish them harm, but none of them were buddies. I knew them about as well as I know you."

"We can't stay here," Jonathan said. "Big Guy, you and Slinger go down and package Masterson for transport out of here. I need to pull the medevac to a new location away from here." Actually, he'd make a call back to Virginia and have Venice make the call.

"What am I supposed to do?" Ray asked.

"Choose a side," Jonathan said.

"The hell does that mean?"

Jonathan explained, "It means you can walk away and go home if you want. Or, you can stick with us and become part of the solution."

Boxers cleared his throat. "Uh, Agent Bonner? Can I talk to you for a sec?"

"He knows what he knows," Jonathan snapped. He drilled his glare into Ray's skull. "But as you choose, understand there's no going back. And if you choose to cross me—to cross any one of us—we'll destroy you and everything you love." As he heard his words, he thought they were a little over-the-top, but they accurately reflected his intent.

"So, I'm just supposed to trust you? I don't know who the hell you are, either."

"There you go," Jonathan said. "Glad to know you're a quick study."

"If I leave, where am I supposed to go?"

"We don't care," Gail said. "Home? Tahiti? Anyplace but here."

Ray scowled as he thought through his options.

"There's not a lot of time," Jonathan pressed.

Ray shook his head and rolled his eyes. "You guys are a spooky group, you know that?"

"Thank you," Boxers said. "We try our best. While you're thinking, how about you press the right buttons to get us back into the prison wing?"

Ray moved to the phone box on the wall outside and typed in the proper code. Jonathan and Gail both watched as he did it. The heavy doors lifted out of the way.

It was Boxers' turn to glare. "I don't want to see those doors come back down while I'm in there."

"I won't go anywhere near them," Ray said, backing away and holding his hands up, as if surrendering. "I promise."

"You can help me get fingerprints off of these assholes," Jonathan said.

Gail added, "And Big Guy, you and I will go down and get Masterson."

"Why me?" Boxers asked. "He's disgusting."

"I can't carry him on my own," Gail said. She started down the stairs.

"Hey," Ray said.

Gail turned.

"The keys are in a box on the wall at the base of the stairs."

"Is the box locked?"

"No need."

Gail looked like she wanted to ask another question,

but headed back down the stairs instead. Big Guy followed.

When Jonathan and Ray were alone, Digger led the way back inside. "I need your answer," he said. "And I need some paper."

"I got printer paper up front," Ray said.

"Index cards would work better," Jonathan said. "You get better prints."

"I've got some of those, too."

Jonathan let Ray pass, and followed as they made their way back into the front room, sidestepping the bodies and the gore. "You know, I used to be a gunman for Uncle Sam," Ray said. "I was what you might call *special*. As in, Special Forces. I punched out after nine years, thinking I'd make my fortune in the civilian sector."

He worked as he talked, so Jonathan didn't complain about the long trip to a short answer. Sometimes, people needed to talk their way through a decision, so he'd force himself to be patient. Until he couldn't.

"Turns out that the civilian sector sucks," Ray went on. He arrived at the desk he'd been sitting at earlier and pulled open a drawer. He closed it and opened another. "There they are." He produced a packet of three-by-five index cards. "Now what?"

"Try to print at least three fingers from each of the corpses," Jonathan said, reaching out and taking a short stack of cards for himself. "Use the blood for ink. I'll print the ones in the back." He watched as Ray stooped down to the body closest to the door. "You still haven't told me your plans."

Ray stayed concentrated at his task of manipulating

the dead man's hand to get his prints. "I'm not sure when the world turned into the shit-sucking place that it's become," he said, "but I'm ready for something brand new."

"Do me the favor of putting that in the form of an answer."

Ray pivoted his head to look at Jonathan. "If you'll have me, I'll come along with you guys. Maybe there'll come a point when you can tell me who you really are."

Jonathan winked at him. "I wouldn't hold my breath for that one," he said. He turned to walk into the back room.

"One more thing," Ray said.

Jonathan stopped.

"What do we do with these guys after we get their prints?"

"Nothing," Jonathan said. "I'm going to make a few phone calls, and the people on the other side will drive those next steps." He pivoted back to get to work. "Tick tock. We don't have a lot of time."

His own words echoed in his head as he walked back to the porch. He needed to get Mother Hen involved sooner than later. He pulled his phone from his pocket and pressed the speed dial.

Venice answered after one ring. "You're early," she said. "Is there a problem?"

"Can't discuss it now," Jonathan said. "I need three things from you. One, contact our incoming chopper and redirect him to a different, nearby LZ." He knew she would recognize the abbreviation for landing zone.

"Where do you have in mind?"

"Not a clue. You've got better maps and more time than I do. Just keep it within a few miles. Upload the coordinates to my GPS when you decide."

He could hear her making notes in the background. "Okay, what's next?"

"I'm going to be sending some high-def pictures of fingerprints in a few minutes," Jonathan said.

"Oh, that can't be good."

"It's been an interesting day," Jonathan said. "And finally, have our special friend reach out to his special friend and let her know that she and I need to yell at each other very soon."

"Didn't go well?"

"Couldn't have gone worse. She needs to know that the people she thought were assets were exactly the opposite. She needs to watch her back."

"Are you in danger?"

"Not anymore. Let me know when we've got a usable LZ." He clicked off.

Chapter Eight

"What in God's name is going on up there?" Masterson had drawn himself into a tighter ball on the concrete slab that was his bed. "And who the hell are you?" That was directed at Boxers.

"I'm the guy who's going to carry your sorry ass up the stairs and out of here."

"The hell you are."

Gail scowled at him. "You're not really in a position to stop us," she said.

"What's with all the shooting?"

"That was us fighting off the troops who were sent here to kill you," Boxers said. He held out his hand for the key and Gail gave it to him.

"We're taking you to the hospital now," Gail said. "We're going to get you some real treatment."

"Unless you piss me off," Boxers said. "I'll spike you like a football if you push me. Are we clear on this?"

Boxers pulled the door open all the way and entered the cell first. "Here are the rules," he said. "Get your pissing and shitting out of the way now, because if you do it on me, I'll make you eat it. Judging from those dressings, it's gonna hurt like hell when I lift you. Yell if you have to, but try to keep it under control."

"Where is this hospital?" Masterson asked.

"I can't imagine a less relevant question," Boxers said.

"It's a safe place," Gail added. "It's a real hospital. We'll get you real care there. Real doctors."

"Why?"

"Because we're idiots," Boxers said. "And my boss is a hell of a lot nicer than I am. Now, about that pissing and shitting."

"I'm good," Masterson said.

Boxers looked to Gail and softened his tone. "Do me a favor and see if there are any clean blankets down here. Even a murderous asswipe like him deserves better than this."

Gail left the cell and toured the rest of the block. The other cells were as devoid of supplies as they were of prisoners. She was about to head back upstairs when she noticed the black metal cabinet tucked into the corner at the base of the stairway. It looked like a supply cabinet from any office, vertical doors with shiny chrome handles. She opened it, and there she found not just blankets, but all manner of first aid supplies as well as a stack of orange jumpsuits.

She brought the first aid supplies first. "Look what I found," she said.

Masterson's eyes grew huge as he seemed to be hit with panic. "Oh, no," he said. "I'll wait for the doctor."

Boxers eyed the supplies and nodded to a spot on the floor. "Put 'em down there," he said.

Gail had brought sterile saline solution, some fresh

trauma dressings, and Kling bandages to hold it all in place, and she laid it all on the concrete floor.

"It's your choice," Boxers said, his tone softer still. He sounded nearly clinical. "But I'll tell you this. There was no better combat medic than me when I was in the Army."

"Was that your MOS?" Military occupational specialty.

"Coulda been," Boxers said.

"We've got a jumpsuit for him, too," Gail said, hoping to raise the ante.

"Call the ball, Masterson," Boxers said. "I'm willing to help, but your clock is ticking. We need to get out of here."

Masterson's gaze shifted to Gail.

"I'll wait outside," she said. Really? After flashing her nonstop, this was where he decided to be shy?

"Won't take but a few minutes," Boxers said. "*Can't* take more than a few minutes."

Gail stepped back into the hall and busied herself with a more detailed tour of the prison. What a depressing damn place. As a former sheriff, she'd seen her share of human warehouses, but this sterile, windowless hellhole was particularly soul-stealing. And maybe that was the point. The people who were renditioned to places like this were at the end of their useful cycle in society. They were here to be milked for information—through God only knew what forms of enhanced interrogation techniques—and then they were left to rot. Or, maybe they were sent to the CIA's sister prisons in the Middle East or Indonesia, where these miseries in South Dakota would look less like a prison and more like a tourist hotel.

Gail could *feel* the suffering that went on in this place. In her quiet moments, she wondered how she had wandered so far from her roots as a sworn officer of the law and an officer of the court. Not so long ago, her conscience was tortured by the extralegal, sometimes lethal actions that defined the missions of Security Solutions' covert side. But now, after only a couple of years, she'd surrendered herself to the expediency of justice over the complexity of the law. Sometimes, the world's bad players so egregiously fractured the social contract that they surrendered their right to fairness in general, let alone a fair trial. They needed to be milked for information, and then incinerated in the human trash heap.

The bitter irony of it all was the inherent hypocrisy of the American people. As intense as their need for action when they were frightened was their self-righteous anger once a sense of peace was restored.

This was why governments so often failed at their mission to keep people safe from terror. Law enforcement agencies were ultimately managed by elected politicians whose fealty to the will of the people made it ultimately impossible for the law enforcers to do their jobs. Justice and principle took a backseat to re-election and pandering. Politicians forgot what they ordered the street cops and soldiers to do, and in the end, they turned on them and vilified them for doing what they were told.

When she had been a part of that career morass, Gail hadn't realized that she was a perpetuator of the problem. As a part of the FBI's Hostage Rescue Team, she had merely followed orders. It had not been within her pay grade to determine right from wrong—that was the purview of judges and juries. But now, looking at reality from the outside, she realized that judges and juries saw only what the bosses—and by extension, the politicians—wanted them to see. Not so long ago, when an FBI agent took the stand, the government's case was half won. Everybody watched television. Everybody knew that the FBI was infallible.

Gail had nothing but respect for Irene Rivers. As director, she was the exception to the rule, but there were limits to the scope of her effectiveness. The people below her—her assistants and deputies and field office agents in charge—all had their own career ambitions and would turn on her in a heartbeat.

So the dirty work of true justice—the wet work—fell to contractors like Jonathan and Boxers and Gail. And God knew how many others. These contractors were invested with nearly limitless power and were managed at arm's length. It fell to the moral compasses of the soldiers of fortune who answered only to themselves to determine how far was too far, how brutal was too brutal. The world was steadily evolving into a society she did not recognize.

"Okay, we're ready," Boxers said from the cell down the hall.

Gail turned and started that way. "Do you need help?"

"Actually, yes," Boxers said.

As soon as Gail eyeballed them, she understood why. The height differential between the two men was so great that Masterson had a hard time being guided by Big Guy. Or, maybe it was the other way around. "I thought you were going to carry him," she said.

"I begged him not to," Masterson said. He wore an

oversized orange jumpsuit but remained barefoot. The overall effect was far less disturbing that what she'd been watching before. "I saw this fireman's carry in my mind," he continued, "and that sounded like a lot of pain that I'd rather not have."

Gail took the prisoner's arm and let him set the pace. She noted that he was trembling but said nothing about it. Masterson smelled like disease, a rotten, musty stench that was equal parts filth, blood, and infection. She supported his left forearm with her right and noted, again silently, that his steps were short and halting.

"It's been a while since I've done this," he said.

"Take your time," Gail said.

It took all of two minutes to move the distance to the base of the stairs. Masterson stopped and craned his neck to look at the climb. "I don't think I can do that," he said.

"Then I'll take it from here," Boxers said. He moved to Masterson's right side and stooped to maneuver the prisoner's arm around his neck.

"Be gentle," Gail said.

"At least as gentle as he was to all those dead people in the stadium," Boxers said.

For all the bluster, he was gentle, anyway. Masterson winced in anticipation of pain, but didn't yell as Big Guy cradled the prisoner's knees across his forearm and lifted him as if he weighed no more than a child. Size notwithstanding, it was hard sometimes to comprehend just how enormously strong Boxers was. He led the way up the stairs, across the porch, and then back into the house. Gail brought up the rear.

"Hey, Boss!" Big Guy shouted as he stepped over

one of the corpses that littered his path from the gun room to the front room.

"Holy shit," Masterson said, taking in the carnage. "You guys had a war."

"More like a skirmish," Boxers said. "If you haven't figured it out already, screwing with us is always a mistake. Boss!"

Jonathan's voice called from outside. "Here!"

Gail and Boxers, with Masterson in his arms, crossed to the front door and on out into the yard, stepping over yet another body on the way. Jonathan stood next to the Suburban. Ray stood next to him. Both wore their rifles slung muzzles-down across their chests.

"Where are we going?" Masterson asked.

"Where we take you," Boxers said.

"To a doctor," Gail said.

Boxers stooped low and stepped high to fit himself and his charge through the door. He maneuvered past the captain's chairs in the second row and back to the bench seat that ran along the back. He laid Masterson onto the black cushions with a gentleness that surprised Gail.

As Big Guy backed out of the vehicle, he hooked a thumb at Ray. "What about him?"

"He's going with us," Jonathan said.

Boxers stepped closer to Ray, towering over him. "Did you already get the speech about what happens if you get sideways with us? The penalty for betrayal?"

Ray took a concomitant step back and tossed a glance back to the carnage. "Got the speech and saw the demonstration," he said. "You'll have no issue with me."

Chapter Nine

Fred Kellner pulled the buzzing phone from his pocket and checked his watch. 16:04 hours. He connected the line and brought the old-fashioned flip-style burner to his ear. "Yep." Only one person knew this number, and Iceman was not one to care about pleasantries.

"We're a go," Iceman said. "Any questions?"

As far as Kellner knew, they'd never met, but he felt that he would recognize Iceman on the street. In his mind, he saw the ubiquitous Special Forces physique, thick battle beard, and carefully mussed hair. Perhaps he saw himself. "H-Hour sixteen forty-five." It was a question, but he framed it as a statement.

"Affirm. Stay alive."

"How many this time?" Kellner heard the click before he got the last word out. The question was inappropriate at its face. Kellner knew that his was only one of several targets to be hit this afternoon, and while his curiosity was real, the details were none of his business. His assigned target was all he needed to worry about.

Well, that and getting away.

He started the engine of his plain vanilla white cargo van, pulled the shift lever into gear, and eased out onto the street. A squatty little motel sign at the driveway's apron read THANK YOU FOR STAYING WITH US!

Kellner smiled. "You're welcome." He made sure he had a wide clearance and took care to obey all traffic laws. He used his turn signals, and he kept his speed at twenty-seven miles per hour, two over the limit. Nothing piqued a cop's interest quite as readily as a vehicle that nailed the speed limit straight on. That was a sure sign that the driver had something to hide.

And brother, did Kellner have cargo worth hiding. His was a plan that could never work in New York City or Washington, DC, but it was perfect for the little town of Bluebird, Indiana, where the crime rate was miniscule, and if a homicide occurred, it was because somebody's neighbor got too big a snootful of whisky and settled a bar bet with a bullet. Terror didn't come to towns like Bluebird, so it made no sense to build bollards or security barricades at soft targets. Not even the County Office Building. Who'd want to hurt the mayor or police chief or a member of the Board of Supervisors here? If somebody had a beef with one of them, they could just as easily attack in the school parking lot on the way to a PTA meeting.

Sometimes it disturbed him how soft America's soft targets were. Two weeks ago, when Kellner opened up on those kids and parents and coaches at the football game in East Texas, he was stunned by the level and depth of confusion that defined the emergency response plan. After thirty kills with thirty shots, Kellner had been able to disappear without even a real effort. The evasive procedures he'd planned and geared up for never came into play. No roadblocks. Not so much as an increased police presence, as far as he could tell. These burgs were ripe for whatever the Bad Man brought.

On the night of that attack—Black Friday—Iceman had coordinated identical hits on six different sites. At the time, Kellner believed he was truly a lone wolf. The only reason he knew about the others now was because of the media coverage. Wall-to-wall and nonstop, with the usual talking heads beating the same predictable themes about gun control and mental health.

It was the Russians! No, it was the Islamists! White supremacists. The NRA.

Truth be told, Kellner neither knew nor especially cared why he'd been hired to do these things. But he cared about his bank account, thank you very much, and when this was all done, it would be a long time before he ever needed to work a day again.

But it was more than money. Kellner liked the juice, the adrenaline. What did he care who he was killing for or why? He didn't give a shit when he was in the Sandbox, and he didn't give a shit now. This was a hell of a lot better way to use his skills than on some two-hundred-thousand-a-year security contract guarding businessmen who wanted to feel important.

Kellner had tried that bodyguard bullshit before, and it didn't suit him at all. He was an *offensive* operator, addicted to bringing violence to his assigned targets and living on to fight another day. That's why he'd joined the Navy to begin with, and that's why he persevered all the way through BUD/S training to become a SEAL. And then the Navy lost its nerve. According to his discharge papers, he was *too* willing and anxious to deploy the skills they'd taught him. They stopped short of a dishonorable discharge but being removed from the teams was the same as far as he was concerned.

Politics were not his thing.

Morality was not his thing, either, but he had to confess that this job—this extended series of hits that had only just begun—had thrummed his conscience. Not much, but it was there. For the whole of his career, the deaths of innocents were a sure thing, part of the package that delivered justice to the bad guys and liberation to their victims who survived. It had always been part of the job—baked into the cake, as a former CO used to say. And that's what this killing gig had always been to him—a job. A noble job, in fact, in which he prided himself with damn few bad hits and never a single negligent discharge. He'd never cared what his targets had done to earn his bullets, and while their transgressions were always a part of the mission briefings, he'd never embraced their importance.

The one given was that a man—and it was always a man, in the Sandbox—was going to die. Kellner didn't want to know him or anything about him. Hell, everybody's got a mother and a father, most have siblings, and most have children and women to make them with. Everybody had someone to mourn them, and Kellner deeply didn't give a shit about any of that. He had targets to spot, wind and weather to compensate for, and triggers to caress. If he did those things well, he'd consider it a job well done and his bosses would be happy. Truthfully, he didn't give much of a shit about the bosses, either, but keeping them pleased made his life a hell of a lot easier than dealing with them when they were pissed.

As if there were ever a two-hour period when some boss somewhere wasn't pissed about something.

So, at its face, the current mission shouldn't move him too deeply, and in fact it didn't. But it was hard to feel good about this kind of killing, to feel proud. There still was the rush of a mission accomplished and the challenge to get away unseen, but in the wake of such emotional media coverage, he found it progressively harder to stay focused and shut out the noise.

But focus he would. Whining and mourning were counterproductive, even when done silently. Emotions made no difference because Kellner had already seen his payment money tucked away in its offshore account. Once paid, a professional always did his best, always kept his promises—a commitment that also allowed him to stay alive.

He'd been driving only ten minutes when he saw Memorial Circle looming ahead. A miniature version of the massive obelisk that marked the center of Indianapolis, Memorial Circle celebrated the Union victory in America's Civil War. Here, the circle marked the leading edge of the business district. Kellner had been here in town for six days, letting his truck be seen parked along Main Street. Everybody noticed strangers in a small town, until the stranger said hi, and maybe bought a cup of coffee and some breakfast in the Drip 'N' Donut Diner.

The locals knew him as Bain—short for Bainbridge, originally from Cincinnati—who'd just opened a franchise delivery service in town. He was staying at the Bluebird Manor Motel until he could settle down and find a place to live. When he did that, he'd bring his wife and two kids out to join him. These rubes loved family. The more you talked about them, the more the locals warmed up. Didn't matter that they'd never met the family—or, let's be honest, that the family didn't really exist. They saw a clean-cut white guy who wanted to move in and they were all over it.

All of that—his bullshit and his smiles—were a kind of social artillery, the sole purpose of which was to prepare for the moment when he could park his delivery truck in front of the County Office Building and run inside for a few minutes, no doubt on a delivery. If someone peeked inside the van—and no one would do such a thing in Bluebird, where everyone had manners—they would see stacks of cardboard boxes, each one addressed to a business in town. The real shock would come if one of the boxes was opened. That's when they'd find blocks of C4 and Semtex. Four thousand pounds, in all. When this baby went off, it wasn't just going to level the building.

It was going to leave a crater that was deeper than the three-story building was tall.

H-hour at 4:45 guaranteed that the sidewalks would be full and that offices inside the building would be closing down. The police, who also resided in the County Office Building, would be in the midst of shift change, at the moment of maximum confusion and carnage and minimum involvement in their surroundings.

Achieving maximum casualties wasn't difficult if you took the time to study your opponent.

Kellner took the second turn off the circle. The clock on the dash read 4:17. Right on time. Locals referred to morning and evening traffic as "rush hour," but clearly they'd never seen the real thing. Or, perhaps they were being ironic and Kellner missed it. The final half mile of the approach to the "Commercial District" was lined with one- and two-story homes, all about two-thousand square feet, and all with huge yards. More brick than siding. Autumn was fairly advanced here, with the leaves bright and brilliant. With the sun hanging low, it occurred to Kellner that this place looked like a postcard—no, a love letter—from Norman Rockwell's Middle America.

The County Office Building had been built in 1858, according to the numbers engraved in the worn white cornerstone. The redbrick edifice appeared to Kellner to be original construction. A part of him marveled at the history the building had witnessed. It was from here that the boys of Bluebird would have formed up by company to march off to the trains that would take them to the fighting of the Civil War. It was from here that soldiers returning from two World Wars would have been cheered as heroes after setting the world free.

In twenty-eight minutes—no, make that twenty-seven now—it would all be gone, and this spot would forever be known as the place where everything changed forever. They would know the futility of trying to hide from violence.

The closest spot to the building's front doors was arranged for parallel parking and the pavement was stenciled DELIVERIES ONLY. 30-MINUTE MAXIMUM. Kellner smiled at the irony that at least he would not commit a parking violation.

He pulled into the spot, threw the shift lever out of gear, killed the engine, and set the parking brake. He lifted the lid of the center console, and without looking, he flipped a toggle switch that activated the countdown timer. Actually, he supposed it was a count-*up* timer—a digital alarm clock, essentially, because the timing of the detonation was as important to Iceman as the devastation it wrought. The alarm clock had no hands or digital numbers. If a Bruce Willis wannabe stumbled upon his creation, there'd be no clue that a timer existed or what the intended time of detonation was. And just to frustrate the television tropes even more, all of his wires were black. Never made any sense to him why a bomber would use red and blue, other than to provide that moment of tension when the movie hero was trying to decide which to cut.

Anyone in Kellner's line of work understood that life was, in fact, driven by Murphy's Law. Anything that could go wrong would go wrong and at the worst possible time. Thus, if 16:45:00 passed without incident, he needed only to make a phone call to detonate secondary or tertiary double-redundant initiators.

Kellner lifted a heavy envelope that would give him probable deniability off the passenger seat, opened his door, and slid to the ground. He closed the door, locked it, and headed for the front doors of the County Office Building.

As many times as he'd done this over the years—no matter how convinced he was in his own competency—it was difficult not to hurry as he crossed the lobby to the security desk. He scrawled an illegible signature and listed "PD" as his destination in the logbook. The uniformed guard checked his watch as he waved Kellner past, clearly marking time till the end of his shift.

Kellner passed the elevators and instead headed down the adjacent corridor toward the restrooms and the emergency exit. The sign on the exit door announced that an alarm would sound if it were opened, but employees had disabled it. From the look of the cuts in the wires, it was done quite a while ago, probably about the time when smoking was banned in the workplace.

Three twenty-somethings were out there on the little porch, pulling on their last cigarettes of the day, and they smiled at him when he passed. If they wondered why a deliveryman would continue down the short stairway toward the Dumpsters, none of them said anything. Beyond the trash collection area lay a parking lot that was largely occupied by private vehicles, but this also was clearly where the cops and building inspectors left their vehicles while they were in the office.

Entrance to the parking lot was controlled by a guy at a guard gate on the far side of the lot, one hundred yards from the building. He checked passes and identification, but he paid no mind to Kellner as he *left* the lot.

"Have a good night," Kellner said as he sidestepped the wooden lift gate.

"You, too," the guard said with a smile and half-assed salute. "See you tomorrow."

Kellner took a couple of steps, then paused and turned. "Excuse me," he said. "What's your name?"

The attendant looked puzzled, but he answered, "Grant Duncan." The *What's it to you?* was silent.

"You need to leave this place."

Duncan smiled. "Love to. But my shift don't end till six, and bills got to be paid."

"You're not hearing me," Kellner pressed. "You

need to leave this place. Be somewhere else. *Anywhere* else. Because in a few minutes . . . Look I'm trying to save your life here."

Duncan's smile turned to a laugh, but then the sound froze in his throat. Something he saw in Kellner's eyes, perhaps. "You're serious, aren't you?"

Kellner held the man's gaze for another couple of seconds, then started walking again.

"Where am I supposed to go?"

Kellner turned and kept walking backward. "Literally anywhere but where you are. But not that way." He pointed toward the County Office Building. "And don't follow me."

Kellner turned around again and continued walking, picking up his pace to make up for the time lost to conversation. Grant Duncan was a nobody, Kellner told himself. Why should he die for a minimum wage job? He'd either take the advice and save his life or he wouldn't. Kellner had done his good deed.

At 16:26, after a walk of two blocks, Kellner unlocked the door of the quaint little 1950s bungalow for which he'd paid six months' rent up-front in cash. He'd never slept there, he'd never used the restroom, and he'd never so much as washed his hands in the sink. The house existed as a place to hang one shirt, which dangled in the hall closet, still freshly wrapped in its plastic dry cleaning bag.

Moving quickly now, as time was short, he stripped off his deliveryman's shirt and pulled the powder blue oxford cloth shirt off its hanger. He was still shrugging into it when he took the other shirt to the fireplace at the far wall of the living room. A red plastic five-gallon gas can sat on the hearth. Kellner pushed the deliveryman's shirt into the firebox, placed the gas can on top of it, and then used his pocket knife to cut a slit along the bottom.

The stench of gasoline filled his sinuses as the fuel spilled everywhere. Taking care to keep himself dry, Kellner stood and headed for the kitchen and the garage beyond. He paused in the kitchen archway to lift a dish towel from the counter, which he wrapped around the top handle of an open-coiled portable electric space heater. He cranked the setting up as far as it would go, and then set the heater itself on the carpet of the living room, out to the extent of its power cord.

Sooner than later, the gasoline vapors would find the coils, and when they did, there'd be a hell of a fire. And the cute little bungalow would burn to the ground because the fire department would be way too busy to fight it.

At 16:43, Kellner lifted the garage door by hand, bypassing the automatic opener. He climbed behind the wheel of his late model Ford Taurus and pulled down the driveway. As he reached the end of the apron, he was startled to see Grant Duncan standing in the street, off to the side of the dented aluminum mailbox. He projected no threat, but exuded fear and confusion. There might have been tears in his eyes.

Kellner opened his window.

Duncan spoke quickly. "I know you told me not to follow, but—"

Kellner cut him off. "I don't care about that," he said. "Keep going. You're still too close. Good luck." He left the window down as he cranked the wheel and headed down the street. He'd barely made it to the end of the block before a fireball blew out the front windows of the bungalow. A glance back showed Grant Duncan little progressed from before, but squatted over, with his arms shielding his head. Kellner had no idea why he cared about a stranger's safety, or even if he really did. He drove on.

Four blocks later, a giant flash and burst of smoke erupted in his rearview mirror. Three seconds after that, the Taurus's steering wheel jerked in his hand as the shock wave rippled beneath him.

Chapter Ten

Site J was one of many unpretentious estates that were nestled in the Black Hills of South Dakota. Jonathan knew the place as Juliet—the verbalization of its designation in the international phonetic alphabet. He'd been here only once before, and he had no idea what the origins of the place were, or even how it was organized. He'd always assumed that its funding came through a CIA cost center, but for all he knew, the place could be part of the South Dakota National Guard.

But probably not.

The medevac turned out to be an old-school Bell Jet Ranger that had been spiffed up with modern aeronautics and night vision capabilities. Jonathan didn't ask questions, but he figured that the owners didn't want to fly anything fancy when they landed in a wheat field to pick up passengers. You know how neighbors talked.

The secondary LZ was only a fifteen-minute drive from the carnage house, and from the LZ, the flight to Juliet was another forty-five minutes. Because of the small size of the aircraft the team had split up. Jonathan and Gail joined Masterson in the chopper, and

Boxers took Ray in the truck. They'd drive to Juliet, where they'd all reunite.

From the exterior, Juliet looked like a rich man's estate. It covered what Jonathan estimated to be at least a hundred acres, maybe two hundred, and the visible part of the structure looked like a Frank Lloyd Wright–inspired mansion. Built with a low profile and constructed of mostly natural materials like stone and timber, the structure had so many windows that it appeared to be constructed of equal parts glass and wood. But Jonathan knew from previous experience that the cosmetics of the estate were largely an effort to disguise itself from airborne snoopers.

Upon closer examination, the windows revealed themselves to be glass panels that had been installed in front of reinforced concrete walls. Lights came on as the sun set, and then went off again around midnight to simulate occupancy, but the panels were tinted darkly enough that any effort to spy through the windows would be thwarted.

The Jet Ranger flew past the private landing strip and flared a landing on the trimmed grass helipad near the pool in the backyard. As the rotors powered down, staffers dressed in casual civilian clothes swarmed the aircraft and took charge of Masterson. A not-unattractive woman in her forties led the phalanx of attendants, and Jonathan noted that she wore a stethoscope slung haphazardly around the back of her neck. As far as Jonathan was concerned, that made her a physician.

After they transferred Masterson from the chopper stretcher to a gurney, Jonathan approached the woman and extended his hand. "Hi, Doc, I'm Neil Bonner. I was—"

She didn't even make eye contact. "I'll find you and let you know when you can squeeze him for information." And she was gone.

"Friendly sort," Gail quipped.

"Sites like these are always packed with twitchy people," Jonathan said. "Nobody is here because it was their first choice." He started strolling across the grass, away from the building. He didn't have a place in mind to go, but walking was always easier on his back than standing still.

Gail fell into step with him. "I thought you said you didn't even know who ran things here," she said.

"Doesn't mean I can't guess," Jonathan said. "This is a spooky place run by spooky people. Pretty short list of choices."

"What is a place like this all about?" Gail asked. A tableau of rolling hills and clusters of trees played out in front of them. It was gorgeous.

"A little bit of everything," Jonathan said. "Not everything can be trained in Quantico, you know? Ditto Camp Peary. Defectors need places to stay while they're being squeezed and before they move into their permanent digs. Covert operators or witnesses sometimes turn up injured or wounded, and they have to be treated somewhere. Community hospitals are simply out of play for people like that."

"So, they bring them here."

"Or, a place much like it."

"It's really all a hospital, then?" Gail asked.

"Part of it is," Jonathan. "But nothing Uncle does is all anything. Yes, there's medical here, but there are also training facilities. I bet if we look hard enough we could find a shooting range."

"And a golf course?" Gail asked with a smile.

Jonathan laughed. "Maybe, but not necessarily. It's not an Air Force base."

"You've been here before?"

"Once," Jonathan said. "And you should remember the occasion."

His comment drew the confused look he'd been going for.

"We'd just met," he said. "Up in Pennsylvania, when I got shot."

Recognition came instantly. "They took you all the way out *here*?"

"Not initially," Jonathan clarified. "At least, I don't think so. Some of the details are a little fuzzy."

"You were kind of bleeding out," Gail reminded.

"Yeah, there's that. As I recall, my first stop was someplace local. The pain was pretty intense by then, so they gave me a shot, and yada yada, I woke up here with a bowel that was about two feet shorter than it was when I arrived."

"How am I just now hearing about this?"

Jonathan shrugged. "Never asked?"

"And how come when *I* got hurt I got sent to that nasty place in Texas to recover?"

"You were at Foxtrot, and I don't know for sure why they sent you there," Jonathan confessed. "I imagine it had something to do with the fact your issues were largely neurological and mine was gut-related. And the place wasn't *that* nasty."

"It wasn't anywhere near as posh as this."

Gail's secret hospital was a quarter of the size of Juliet, and it sat about five miles outside of Port Arthur. There really was no way to spin that into a nice place.

"You're right," he said. "Next time you get wounded, take it in the belly."

Even as he joked, he wished he could take his words back. Jonathan wasn't superstitious about many things, but he believed that success often hinged on a refusal to recognize the possibility of failure. It was bad juju to speak of sustaining wounds, even in the abstract.

They wandered together in silence for a minute or two, then Gail asked, "Have you got any theories on what just went down at the black site?"

"You mean along the lines of who and why?" Jonathan walked with his hands stuffed in his pockets. The suit-and-tie FBI disguise felt strange. He missed all the pockets and the roomier leg space of his usual 5.11 pants.

"That would be a great start," Gail said. "I'll prime the pump with a question. Do you think the shooters who showed up were actually FBI?"

Jonathan took his time answering. That very question had been gnawing at him since before the smoke had cleared. "We'll know after Mother Hen processes the fingerprints, but I don't think so," he said. "Maybe in the sense that we are FBI agents—part of the lend-lease agent program—but I'd be surprised if they were sworn agents. In fact, I'd be horrified if they were sworn agents."

"Because we killed them?"

"Yeah, that, too," Jonathan said. "More because the thought of federal agents committing cold-blooded murder is damned disturbing. What do you think?"

"I think I'm with you," Gail said. "I know for a fact that their assault tactics were not by any book I'm aware of. If they really thought we were a threat and they were making a SWAT-type assault, there'd have been backup. Even more than that, there'd have been patience. Whoever they were and whatever they were doing, it was all about making sure that people went home dead."

Jonathan stopped walking and turned back to face the mansion. They'd wandered a good half mile. He pointed to the building with his forehead and started strolling back. "The question for us, then, is why."

"Does it matter?"

Jonathan stopped abruptly. "Are you serious?"

She explained, "I don't see how knowing the reasons behind their assault is going to change much of what we have to do."

Jonathan was shocked that they were having this conversation. "It affects everything we have to do," he said. "If those assholes back at the prison were, in fact, sworn FBI agents, that means Wolverine has a shit storm on her hands. She's got rogue operations going on among the people we're supposed to interact with. It means we can't trust anyone."

Gail chuckled. "You don't trust anyone, anyway."

Jonathan chuckled, too. "Fair point," he said. "But it's a whole different world of mistrust if you suspect that your coworkers are trying to kill you."

Her chuckle became a laugh. "With the exception of the coworkers in Fisherman's Cove, name one person that you don't suspect might try to kill you. It's part of your charm, Dig. You don't like *anybody*."

Again, a fair point. He was not the right guy to surprise with a hug.

His cell phone buzzed in his pocket. "Maybe this is Wolfie now," he said as he fished for it. He was surprised to see a number that rarely reached out to him. He connected the call and said, “Scorpion.”

Dom D’Angelo’s voice said, “You know who this is, right?”

“I do,” Jonathan replied. “We really need to get you a radio handle. What’s up?”

“More tragedy, I’m afraid. Are you near the news?”

“Don’t tease me,” Jonathan said. “Tell me what you’ve got to tell me.”

“They hit again,” Dom said. “Bombs this time. All in Midwestern small towns, and all huge.”

“Ah, shit,” Jonathan said.

Gail dialed in on his tone. “What’s wrong?”

He held up a finger. “What’s the death toll?” He saw Gail tense at the question.

“Too early to tell yet, but probably hundreds. Appears that the attacks were simultaneous. Whoever you’re chasing, the guys are sick bastards.”

At one level, God help him, Jonathan admired the terrorists’ methods. They knew how to maximize the psychological damage wrought by their attacks. “Okay,” he said. “Anything else I need to know?”

“I think you have work to do,” Dom said. “I’ll let you get to it.”

As Jonathan disconnected, he looked to Gail. “I think it’s safe to say that Wolfie’s not going to be much help in the near future.”

Once inside Juliet’s front doors, the faux mansion looked like any other government building constructed by the lowest bidder. A twelve-by-fifteen-foot security vestibule blocked entry into the rest of the facility.

Molded plastic chairs in alternating orange and yellow lined the beige concrete block walls, giving the area a 1970s throwback vibe. The overhead fluorescents were a tad too bright, and the wire-reinforced glass that covered them was spotless. In fact, the entire area was uncharacteristically clean for a remote government facility. The security station lay to the right, at the far end of the vestibule, manned by a high-and-tight soldierly young man dressed in a white shirt, blue sport coat, and a red, white, and blue Republican tie. But for the heavy bulletproof glass and two gun ports, it could have been a receptionist station at a dentist's office. The guard greeted Jonathan and Gail with a look that was neither friendly nor un-.

Jonathan badged the guy from five feet away as he approached. "Special Agent Bonner," he said. "I'm here to speak with Logan Masterson. He was brought in about an hour ago."

The guard was either disinterested or expecting them, because he didn't say a word before reaching under his desk and causing the heavy door on Jonathan's right to buzz. Jonathan pulled it open to reveal a corridor of closed steel doors that stretched fifty feet in both directions. A massive sign on the wall opposite the door announced that the hospital wing was on the right and downstairs.

"Kinda creepy," Gail observed.

The stairway lay next to the elevator, about halfway down the hallway on the right. Jonathan avoided elevators in spooky places run by the government. An elevator car could be turned into anything the designers wanted it to be, from a jail cell to a gas chamber. Stairwells could be scary, too, but the extra space allowed for maneuverability, and maneuverability gave you options.

As he opened the stairwell door, Jonathan paused a moment to take in the surroundings. Surveillance cameras along the ceiling provided full coverage of the concrete chute to the basement.

"Why are we waiting?" Gail asked.

"Not waiting," Jonathan said. "Observing. I don't like how easy it was for us to get this far."

"You expect some kind of trap?"

"Why not?"

"And if that's what this is, what's your plan?"

Jonathan smiled. She'd got him. They were already in the monster's maw, if that's what this was. "In for a dime, right?" he said, and he led the way down the stairs.

This was no ordinary basement, he realized, after they'd gotten to the bottom of the fourth flight of stairs with another four flights yet to descend.

"Is this what bomb-proofing looks like?" Gail asked.

"Either that, or they have very high ceilings in the basement," Jonathan said.

When they finally bottomed out, they were met with massive steel double doors. To Jonathan's eye, they looked like blast doors, nowhere near as large or effective as the famous blast doors at Cheyenne Mountain, but on the same spectrum. Bigger than any bank vault doors that he'd ever seen.

"Are we supposed to knock?" Gail asked. The smile in her voice made it hard to tell if she was kidding.

And he had no idea. "Manual methods first," he

said. He wrapped his fist around the massive steel handle and pulled. The door opened with almost no effort. "Wow. This thing's really well balanced."

On the other side of the threshold, the world transformed into a hospital. About the dimensions of a medium-sized city emergency department, the medical wing was built as a square surrounding a central nurses' station.

"Bring back memories?" Gail asked.

"Too many." In the initial days after his surgery, he must have logged fifty miles around this nurses' station, rolling an IV stand in his wake. "I hate these places."

It was time to go to work. As they approached the nurses, the pinchy-faced doctor from the helipad exited one of the operatories and walked toward them. Her features had not softened. "I told you I'd call when he's ready to talk."

"I don't have that luxury," Jonathan said. "His friends just blew up half of the Midwest, and I need information now."

The cranky little doctor didn't move. She stood with her feet planted and her arms folded across her chest. Jonathan admired the feisty pose, but it was wasted.

"Look," Gail said. "What's your name?"

"Doctor Jones."

Gail rolled her eyes. "Of course it is. Doctor, we have authorization from the highest authority to interview Mr. Masterson."

"I am the highest authority in this facility," Jones said.

Jonathan leaned in closer and lowered his voice nearly to a whisper. "You can't win this."

Jones looked at once angry and defeated. It clearly pained her when she said, "All right, you can speak to him. He's over there." She pointed to the operatory from which she'd just exited.

As Jonathan and Gail headed that way, Doctor Jones followed. Jonathan stopped short. "Alone," he said.

"Absolutely not. He's my—"

Jonathan hardened his expression. She'd just stomped on his last nerve. He leaned in closer than last time and bored his gaze into her eyes. "Alone," he said.

That time it seemed to do the trick.

Without another word, they entered Logan Masterson's cubicle and closed the curtain behind them.

Chapter Eleven

Masterson looked a hell of a lot better than the last time Jonathan had seen him. Improved lighting helped, he supposed, and he was easier to look at while wearing a hospital gown. But the kid's features had improved, too.

He was sleeping—or pretending to—when they entered. Jonathan cleared his throat, and the patient's eyes snapped open. He adjusted his position and in the process revealed the shackle that bound his wrist to his bed.

"Feeling better?" Gail asked.

"That's not a high bar," Masterson said. "Any chance you can tell me what the hell just happened back there?"

"We saved your life," Jonathan said.

Masterson shifted his head so he was looking at the ceiling. He seemed to relish the comfort of a pillow. "Why?"

"Because it was the right thing to do," Jonathan said.

Masterson laughed, and he was rewarded with a jolt of pain. "I know what you do for a living," he said.

"Or, I know what you used to do. The *right thing* was irrelevant."

Jonathan let a flash of anger pass. He wasn't going to go toe-to-toe with a burned-out, shot-up shooter. He decided to tease him along. "Someone has to do Uncle Sam's dirty work," he said. "As long as you follow orders—"

"You can shoot up all Hajis you want," Masterson interrupted. "Women, children, insurgent, or innocent. Didn't matter."

"How many deployments?" Jonathan asked.

"Too many. Nine, I think. Four in the Sandbox and five in Afghanistan."

That matched what Jonathan already knew. "Okay, I get it," he said. "You're bitter. How does collateral damage on combatant soil lead to shooting up a school?"

Masterson shifted in his pillow. "What would you guess?"

Jonathan approached the bed and rested his arm on the folding rail. "I don't have time to guess. I'd like you to tell me."

Masterson winked at Gail. "Life's full of disappointments."

"Your mission mates left you to die," Gail said. "They sent men to kill you rather than talk with us."

Masterson looked back to the ceiling.

Jonathan walked to the other side of the bed, where he found a rolling stool. He pulled it up close and sat down. "I'm not going to bullshit you, Sergeant Masterson. This is unlikely to end well for you. But you're not a victim. You launched this shit show. The question for you is, How do you want to spend your years in confinement?"

"A prison is a prison, as far as I'm concerned."

Jonathan shook his head. "Not so. Have you seen a Pakistani prison? An Uzbek prison? Man, those places are brutal."

That drew Masterson's attention.

"Here's the thing, Logan," Jonathan went on. He wanted his tone to sound calm and businesslike. "You don't exist. As far as the world is concerned, you were never caught, you were never arrested, and you were never shot. You're not even here, because *no one* who's here is here. Are you following me?"

Masterson's face folded into a mask of deep confusion. "No, I'm not."

"You weren't arrested," Gail explained. "You were renditioned. There are no limits on the harm that can come to you."

"Or the kindnesses," Jonathan added. "The choice is up to you. I'm not going to be here in two hours. I didn't know and didn't care what your treatment was like before I saw it, and I won't know or care after I'm gone."

"And there's another detail that might help you choose a course," Gail said. "Your colleagues just set off bombs at soft targets throughout the Midwest. Hundreds more are dead, and authorities are still no closer to having a suspect."

Jonathan picked up on her thread. "If you think this through—just on the dignity issue—there's not a lot of that to be found when some Paki interrogator takes a blowtorch to your balls. Are you catching my drift here, Logan?"

Finally, the fear arrived in his eyes.

"From where I sit," Jonathan continued, "the only chance you have for keeping your fingernails and kneecaps whole and healthy is to start cooperating. That is your single bargaining chip. One of one."

"So, I squeal, and they kill me, anyway."

"Maybe," Jonathan said. "Or, maybe not. I guess it depends on the value and timeliness of what you have to offer. You'll have to take me at my word when I tell you that I have quite a bit of clout at the levels where clout will serve you best. A kind nod from me can work wonders."

Masterson again focused on the ceiling. Jonathan could almost hear the gears turning in his head.

"And an unkind nod from me can have you buried alive," Jonathan finished. He fell silent for the better part of thirty seconds to let the starkness of Masterson's choices sink in.

"Let's start at the beginning," Gail said. Sometimes a softer voice tipped the balance. "How were you recruited for this? Or, were you the recruiter for others?"

Masterson took a huge breath and brought his free hand to his face to cover his eyes. "Oh, how far the mighty have fallen," he said, apparently to himself. Then he dropped his hand to the mattress, found the right button on the controller and raised himself to a more upright sitting position. "No, I was not the recruiter. I heard about this through another team guy. He found it on some Dark Web chat room for people like us. You know, team guys."

Jonathan stiffened at the first-person plural—there was no *us* between this animal and himself—but then he realized that he was referring to the buddy who reached out to him. "What, was it like a want ad? Killers-R-Us?"

"What is your friend's name?" Gail asked.

"That's a step too far," Masterson said. "At least for today. And yes, it was very much like a want ad. At least that's how my buddy explained it to me. I never saw the initial piece. He just gave me a link to an address. I'm not a computer guy, so I don't know the ins and outs."

"What was on the other end of the link?" Jonathan asked.

"At first, a lot of grief. Lots of running around. I had to get a burner phone and a new laptop for the communications. There was security on top of security on everything electronic. Iceman is friggin' paranoid about getting spied on."

"Who's Iceman?"

"The guy on the other end. And before you ask, I don't have more of a name for him. When we finally got in touch with each other, he told me that he had a client that needed some work done. He wouldn't tell me what the nature of the work was until I committed to do it."

"Why would you do that?" Gail asked.

"Five hundred thousand dollars," Masterson replied. "Cash deposited wherever I wanted it."

"Where did you put it?" Jonathan asked, and instantly regretted wasting a question. What the hell did he care where the guy kept his money? That was for the FBI and IRS to figure out.

"Also, a question too far," Masterson said.

"You had to have some indication what he was looking for," Jonathan said.

"I suppose I did. Most well-paying gigs for former operators involve carrying guns."

Very few require terrorism, Jonathan didn't say. "So,

once you were in and you got your mission brief, what was it?"

"It was long on strategy but short on objectives," Masterson said. "I got a date and a time and instructions to inflict as many casualties as possible at a Podunk high school event of my choice. Only guns. Iceman was very specific about that. No explosives, only guns, and it had to happen straight up at zero one hundred Zulu."

"Is Zulu his word or yours?"

"His. And I'm assuming here that Iceman is a he. In reality, I don't know one way or the other. But he did use Zulu, which made me think that he was trying to coordinate something across time zones."

"As he did," Jonathan said.

"Yes," Masterson agreed.

"Why?" Gail asked. "What's the reason behind the carnage?"

"I don't know, and I didn't ask. Once you take the money, it's just following orders."

"You could have gone to the police," Gail said.

"When you get that much money, ma'am, you want to stick around long enough to spend it, you know? And there was a wicked threat to my family. I don't have kids, but I've got siblings and nieces and nephews. Iceman had pictures of all of them. And I mean recent, real-time pictures. There was no backing out. I didn't know there would be other attacks."

"Except Zulu," Jonathan reminded.

"Yeah, I had my suspicions, but those aren't facts. If I didn't go through with what I'd agreed to, then I'd just end up dead, along with a lot of people I care about. That was a nonstarter for me."

"And you never thought to ask why?" Jonathan pressed.

"No, I didn't. Because the why was unimportant. Dead is dead. Mission success is mission success. What difference does the rationale make?"

"What was your exfil plan?" Jonathan asked.

Masterson allowed himself a bitter laugh. "That part didn't go so well, did it? I was going to leave the rifle where it was—it was untraceable—and then blend in. I had a car stashed behind the water tower, and then another one stashed in a shopping mall parking lot about a mile away. Nobody would know what they were looking for to begin with, and I'd have nothing to hide. Simple stuff."

"Until you got shot," Gail reminded.

"The bystander is always the big variable, isn't it?" Masterson said. "I didn't anticipate one guy having the balls to climb all the way up there to pop me."

"What were you to do after the high school event was over?" Jonathan asked.

"Sit and wait," Masterson said.

"For what?"

"For whatever. For nothing."

Jonathan scowled. "I don't understand. What were your instructions for after the mission was completed?"

"Iceman said there'd be more, but he never said what or where."

"How were you supposed to report in?" Gail asked.

"I wasn't. What would be the point? The results would speak for themselves. Either a school got shot up or it didn't. More contact means more opportunity to get caught. That's bad business."

Jonathan felt a twinge of hope, a feeling that these

guys might have just made their first major blunder. "Did you have reason to expect today's assaults? This current batch of explosions?"

Masterson considered his answer for a few seconds before delivering it. "Not specifically, but I wasn't surprised when you told me about them."

"How much lead time would be necessary to pick a target for a bombing attack?" Gail asked.

"I don't understand the question. Lead time?"

Jonathan explained, "Do you expect that you would have been supplied the explosives and assigned a target, or would that have been on you?"

"The school was all on me," Masterson said. "I didn't know anything about the bombing stuff, so I don't know how to answer that."

"Could you get your hands on large quantities of explosives if you had to?" Gail asked.

Masterson looked amused. "Of course." He looked to Jonathan. "Couldn't you?"

Jonathan moved on. Gail had, in fact, asked a silly question. While commercial or military-grade explosives were a challenge to acquire, any middle schooler with a chemistry set could make explosive compounds in his bedroom.

"I'll tell you what," Masterson said. "I'll throw you a bone. Iceman indicated to me that he had a plan to bring terror to a new level. He wanted the American people scared of their own shadows. Those were his words."

"What did he mean?"

"I don't know for sure, but from what you told me today, putting it into the context of my previous dealings with Iceman, I'd say that he plans to make the attacks bigger and bigger. Isn't that how you make people shadow-scared?"

Jonathan looked to Gail, who answered with a shrug. He supposed it made sense to escalate the attacks to keep people off-balance, and the small Midwestern strategy was a good one, too. The more unsheltered people felt, the greater the mass anxiety.

"I think he wanted things to get to the point of anarchy," Masterson explained. "He talked to me once about what a beautiful thing it is to see neighbors turn on each other. He wants to see paranoia and racism and other-isms spinning completely out of control."

"Holy shit," Jonathan breathed.

"Once society boils down to that point, there really *is* no society anymore. Laws won't matter because no one will trust the government to stop the threat."

Jesus. Masterson painted the picture just as Jonathan imagined it would evolve. The next stage would come when government forces would have no choice but to turn on the crowds who began to take justice and safety into their own hands. He envisioned the Posse Comitatus Act suspended and federal troops pulled in to control the chaos. Those troops would have to come from outside the town or the region of the civilly disobedient, because to use locals would require homeboys to choose a side.

Even under the umbrella of the U.S. Constitution, with clearly defined branches of government and separation of powers and courts of blind justice, the rule of law was as fragile as the public's belief in The System. Courts were presumed to be just because citizens *chose* to believe that. Money had value because citizens agreed that it does—without that agreement, the par value of cash was identical to the scrap value of the paper it was printed on.

The world had seen this devolution of society countless times over the centuries. In fact, in the modern era, it had happened in almost every other civilized country *except* the United States. Ancient Rome and Greece and Egypt. More recently, all of Europe before and after two World Wars, and since then, the Soviet Union, Philippines, much of Central America, and the list rolled on. The United States persevered because its citizens and the citizens of the world saw Uncle Sam as a secular savior.

Except those opinions were changing. Protestors in countless capital cities around the world gathered by the hundreds and thousands to burn American flags. Jihadists would spare no effort to bring death and destruction to any American, whether vacationer or politician.

At home, in certain quarters, things were little better. In the American bastion of law and order, large swaths of the citizenry had declared open warfare on law enforcement officers, and shocking numbers of politicians flocked to the defense of the killers. In neighborhood parties and in office places and in social media, millions of Americans demonized fellow neighbors and coworkers who held dissonant political beliefs, choosing to end friendships and disown family members over philosophical differences. Jonathan knew more than a few pessimists who believed with all their heart that total societal collapse was merely a matter of time. Most had already assembled their bugout bags and stockpiled food and ammunition.

Jonathan was the very opposite of an alarmist, but he could see how easily coordinated terror attacks could provide the tipping point for the loss of everything for everyone.

"There's another reason why I think this thing is going to be big and bad," Masterson said.

He had Jonathan's attention.

"Iceman gave the op an name," he explained. "He's calling it Retribution."

Chapter Twelve

"Retribution for what?" Boxers asked after Jonathan finished filling him in. What had been a forty-five-minute chopper ride had translated to nearly four hours in the rental Suburban, and Big Guy had arrived cranky. The fact that they had to turn right around and drive back to the airport did not improve his disposition.

"It's the name a madman gave to a terrorist operation," Gail said. "I don't know that it needs to mean anything."

Jonathan explained, "The real takeaway is that this thing is blossoming way out of control. There's real danger to the country here."

"You should get the *real* FBI involved," Ray said from his seat next to Gail, behind Boxers.

"Careful of the pronoun," Boxers grumbled. "It's *we* now. Not *you*. We."

"And they're already involved," Jonathan added. "But unless and until we find out that that strike force back at the prison wasn't also the *real* FBI, I'm resistant to pulling the Bureau any deeper into this thing."

Jonathan twisted in his seat to look at Ray. "Tell us about you."

"I've already shared everything with Big Guy during the drive."

"Humor me," Jonathan said. What he didn't say was that Ray's were among the fingerprints he'd sent to Venice. Thanks to her, Jonathan already knew who Ray really was and what he was all about. None of it was scary in and of itself, but Jonathan wanted to know whether the guy was a liar. "You can start with your real name."

"Who said it's not?"

"You did," Jonathan reminded. "When you first pointed a rifle at me."

"Ah, that wasn't personal," Ray said.

"We knew that," Boxers said. "That's why you're still alive."

"Fair enough. The name is Stephen Spencer. Call me Spence. Eight years in the infantry. Ground pounder. Turned into a merc once I got home and found out that 'rifleman' is not an element in most résumé review programs. Tried it straight for almost two years. Long enough to run my wife off and take the kid with her."

That matched perfectly with what Jonathan had been told. "What company do you work for?"

"Why do I get the sense that you're testing me rather than seeking information?"

Jonathan chuckled. "Because I'm testing you rather than seeking information," he said. "Didn't know I was being that obvious. I can't abide dishonesty. Who do you work for?"

"I'm an independent contractor. You know, we've already discussed this, right? You and me, I mean."

"Again, humor me. I want to make sure the story stays straight."

And it did. He spun it out over ten minutes, and Jonathan noted no notable change.

"Okay," Spence said when he got to the end. "Now it's your turn."

"Not gonna happen," Jonathan said. He pointed through the windshield to a gas station that might have grown out of the cornfield. Still functioning and with a snack shop attached to one end, the place looked like it had been there since the days of the Model T.

Boxers took the prompt for what it was and pulled into the parking lot, such as it was. More of a cleared area, really. Big Guy threw the transmission into PARK and stepped out and around to Spence's door.

"Time for us to part company," Jonathan said.

Spence looked shocked. And angry. And a little afraid. "I don't understand."

"It's not complicated," Boxers growled. "You stay here, we move on."

"What am I supposed to do from here? We're in the middle of nowhere."

"Ah, come on, Spence," Jonathan said. "Uncle Sam invested millions of dollars in you to make you resilient and resourceful. Don't let him down."

"So, that's it? I'm not a part of this anymore?" Spence looked to Gail, presumably to get a vote for his side.

"Sorry," she said. "We fly too close to the sun as it is. You're a variable we don't need."

Spence looked hurt.

"If I were you," Jonathan said, "I'd find a ride to the local Walmart and buy some clothes that looked a little less soldierly. It's been a pleasure." He was careful to leave no room for argument or negotiation.

"This is a done deal, Spence," Boxers said. "There's been enough violence for one day."

"People are going to come looking for me after all that shooting."

"That's why you shouldn't waste any time," Jonathan said. "You've got your phone, right?"

"Yeah, but—"

Boxers laid a hand on his shoulder. "The time for talking just expired, buddy," he said. "Best of luck to you."

"Bite me," Spence said as he slid out of the seat and stepped out.

"There's the spirit," Boxers said.

Fifteen seconds later, they were back on the road.

"Think he'll be okay?" Gail asked.

"Don't give a shit," Jonathan said. "He tortured a guy. Let him taste some of his own medicine." He pulled his phone from his pocket and pressed a speed dial button. "Besides, the last thing we need is a mercenary we don't know peeking behind the scenes of what we do."

"Who are you calling?" Boxers asked.

At that instant, Mother Hen answered her phone.

Venice listened and took notes. With every additional word, the task before her grew progressively more difficult. In order to get ahead of the conspiracy that now had a name—Retribution—Jonathan thought it was essential to learn the identities of the conspirators, and the job of accomplishing that mission fell to Venice.

Jonathan often depended on her skills as a renowned computer wiz and hacker extraordinaire to achieve the impossible under crushing time constraints. Eight times out of ten, she was able to rise to the task and make it all happen by herself. That other 20 percent of the time, she was forced to reach out to others within the hacking community for reinforcements.

Almost no one else in the world knew that Venice had an alter identity that triggered fear in the hearts of people like her who understood the awesome power of cyberspace to both create and destroy great things. When the hacking community heard of FreakFace666, they undoubtedly envisioned a geeky, brilliant young man with no social skills, living in his childhood bedroom. Or, because FreakFace666 was the leader of Gloomity, the hacker army that single-handedly brought down a pedophile political candidate and stirred other mayhem, perhaps they envisioned him in a position of power, a *Game of Thrones* great room where he meted out praise and punishment at his whim. Certainly, no one saw FreakFace666 as a young African American woman working out of a spectacular office in the little burg of Fisherman's Cove, Virginia.

Or, alternatively, out of her recently-opened satellite office on the third floor of the Resurrection House administration building, which also served as her home. After too many overnighters at the Security Solutions firehouse headquarters, she'd finally opened the satellite to exactly zero objection from Jonathan. In fact, he asked her why she hadn't done that years ago. Some of the more advanced data stuff still demanded her presence down the hill, but for the boys' overnight missions when her greatest task was to keep in touch, it was nice to be at home in the mansion.

Venice reviewed the details of what lay ahead. She opened a page on her computer and typed the heading, *What we don't know.* Then she skipped a line and started a list.

She wrote, *Who are they?* According to Jonathan, Logan Masterson didn't know who his fellow terrorists were—or even how many were in play. The only safe assumption was that the others likewise toiled in the dark. That spoke of a well-organized structure that emphasized operational secrecy. Actually, that wasn't true. One person had to know it all.

She typed, *Iceman.* If Jonathan could find Iceman, he'd have real leverage to rip open the whole network. If.

What's next? She wrote the words because they were appropriate to write and because knowing that—getting ahead of the terrorists' plan—was the key to everything. But she skipped to the next line.

Why? What could possibly motivate a plot such as this? The motivation for the worker bees who were responsible for the death and destruction was money, pure and simple, hard stop. If there was one thing that Venice had learned through Jonathan's years of bringing justice to animals dressed in human skin, it was that morality was easily bought for nothing more than wads of cash. At one level, that made these jerks no different fundamentally than common street thugs.

The next thought that hit her took her breath away. She typed, *Soldiers?*

Masterson had told Jonathan that he was recruited via a soldiers' site of some sort. Could it be that every member of every assault team was former military? If so, that changed everything. It separated them from everyday street thugs. That would explain the competence and precision of what they'd been able to pull off. And the secrecy.

Masterson had also told Jonathan that he'd been paid half a million dollars for his efforts in Nebraska. If each of the conspirators received similar payment, that was a lot of money, no matter how many of them there were. Add to that the money that was necessary to fund the planning and execution—the expenses—and the list of people wealthy enough to fund it all grew short.

She ran some numbers through her head. The night of the Nebraska incident, a total of six high school games were attacked. That was three million dollars just in pay if everyone got the same half-mill as Masterson. Yesterday, there were five explosive attacks, so if—

Venice bolted upright. Yesterday, there were only five attacks. With Masterson in custody, there were only five attackers in play, so that meant the original team numbered six, right? Six minus one is five. It was a number to work with.

What was it that Jonathan had told her? All of the communication between Iceman and his pawns was done electronically, through encrypted email or messaging.

Her heart rate picked up. There was a kernel of an idea in her head, and she needed to develop it. The idea teased her, taunted her. It was *right there*.

Iceman couldn't know that Masterson was in custody. So, when the time came to communicate with his teams to plan their next strike, he would have reached out to everybody, not knowing that one of his team members was out of service.

This was a hacker's dream. If she could nail down one variable, then she'd have a place to start searching for all the others. In a perfect world, she could have Masterson's phone or computer, but the world was never perfect. If those things existed in anyone's custody, it would be with the FBI, and she didn't expect them to be in the mood to share.

Venice opened a new window on her computer and went to the list of evidence that was seized from Logan Masterson at the time of his arrest. Sure enough, a phone was on the list, and the evidence clerk had been thorough enough to include the make and the serial number. It no doubt was a burner, but that didn't necessarily matter.

How many burner phones could there have been in Indian Spear, Nebraska, in the days surrounding the shooting? Every time electronic devices talked to each other—or attempted to—they left a trail. If you could discern the trail, then you could identify both sides of the communication—or in this case, *all* sides of the communication.

She saw a glimmer of hope. If she could identify the communications from Indian Spear that involved the brand of burner phone that was found on Logan Masterson, she'd be on her way. She could trace it back to its origin. Then, if she could find a second effort to contact the same phone around the time of the bombings, then she'd know for sure that she'd found the source of Iceman. Using Iceman's identity, she could then scour around and find out the electronic identities of the other conspirators.

Unless, of course, they were super computer savvy themselves. There were ways to route data needles through electronic haystacks, but for this first stage, she couldn't focus on the negative. There had to be a way.

But it was an enormous task that would require lots of time and resources, all while the clock was ticking.

What she needed was a thousand times the computer power to handle the de-encryption and the analysis, along with a coconspirator of her own help nail down data.

And she knew just the guy who had just the resources. And a really hot body.

Venice stood from her desk and walked across her office to her wall safe, where she kept her Gloomity computer, the one dedicated exclusively to her moonlight hacking. The machine booted up, and she took a few minutes to make her home base appear to be in Vietnam before she reached out to TickTock2.

Because of security restrictions at the Puzzle Palace, it could take Derek as long as a few hours to get back to her.

Art Evers—Arthur to his mother, Artie to his friends, Iceman to his team—entered the National Air and Space Museum through the main entrance on Independence Avenue. He waited in line as a dozen tourists in front of him filed through the magnetometer and subjected their purses and backpacks to rudimentary security checks, if that's what you can call the process by which bored, nearly comatose automatons poked sticks into bags and ignored whatever they hit.

People like Evers—people who *understood* security and the meaning of hard targets versus soft ones—recognized the show for what it was: empty posturing. He didn't know how the security guards could take it. He hoped they were at least paid well, because the monotony of it all had to be soul stealing.

When it was his turn, Evers prepared himself for the inevitable. He stepped through the portal, and the magnetometer squealed.

"Empty your pockets," said the three-hundred-pound somnolent woman with three chins and a badge.

"I have a prosthetic leg," Evers said.

"Empty your pockets."

She handed him what might have been a gray plastic dog bowl into which he put his wallet—the entirety of his pocket contents.

"Is that all of it?" the guard asked.

"Yes."

"Go through the detector again."

He took three steps back to get around the structure of the metal detector and then walked through a second time. Because the laws of physics had not changed in the last thirty seconds, it squealed a second time.

"Okay, step over here and hold your arms out to your side." The guard powered up a handheld wand.

"Ma'am, did you hear me?" Evers said. "I have a prosthetic leg."

"That might be an excuse," Lady Genius said. She scanned his armpits and crotch, got a return from his leather-banded wristwatch, and then got an even bigger return from the scan of his left leg, the pegged one.

"Would you mind pulling up your pant leg to show me?" she asked.

He did, and she seemed satisfied. "Thank you," she said. "And have a nice day. Don't forget your belongings."

Clear of the checkpoint, he walked straight to Friendship 7, the Mercury capsule that had propelled astronaut John Glenn three times around the Earth back in 1962. There, he found Porter Brooks standing right where he was supposed to be. The other man checked his watch. "You're late," he said.

"Got stopped at Checkpoint Charlene," Evers said. "I guess your badge makes you exempt from all that."

Brooks's expression remained stern. Tall and fit, he was a poster boy for the FBI agent that he was. His shoes were shined to mirrors, and his suit was tailored to emphasize his physique. Every time they got together, Evers felt a pang of remorse for what he might have been if he hadn't donated his leg to the Iraqi desert.

"Let's walk while we talk," Brooks said. Of all the museums in Washington, DC, the Air and Space was one of the most popular, especially among families. Dinosaur bones, dioramas of taxidermized animals, famous paintings and sculptures, and wax reproductions of people appealed to certain targeted groups, but who didn't like airplanes? And they were everywhere—on the floor, hanging from the ceiling, and featured in film in the IMAX theater.

"What's this about?" Evers asked.

"Are you shitting me?" Brooks said. "Are you *shitting* me?"

Evers sensed the other man's anger—it wasn't as if he were trying to disguise it, after all—but he was anything but intimidated. Brooks had the advantage of size, but Evers had killed people who were far larger. "How about you stop the posturing and get to the point?" he suggested.

"The South Dakota shoot-out, for God's sake," Brooks said. "What were you thinking?"

Evers was confused. "What did you think I would do when you told me where Masterson was?"

"It was a slaughter," Brooks said. "Why did you send such incompetents?"

The question knocked Evers off-balance. "Incompetents?"

Brooks pulled them both to a halt. "Are you telling me that you didn't know?"

Evers felt something melt in his gut. "Know what?"

"Masterson got away. He's still in custody. Your guys were the ones who were slaughtered."

Evers closed his eyes and leaned against the metal stairs that led to the SkyLab exhibit. He didn't know all the guys on the assault team, but the ones he did know were good. "All dead?" he asked.

"Every one of them. A couple of our contractors, too."

Now Evers was pissed. Not at Brooks, but at himself. Trying to hit Masterson was a mistake. A temper tantrum. It was unprofessional, and now he'd incurred the ire of the FBI for the attack on their contractors.

"So, where is Masterson now?" Evers asked.

"I don't know," Brooks replied. "I'm not even sure my boss knows."

Evers wasn't buying. "She's the director of the whole Bureau," he said. "She has to know."

"I think maybe she doesn't want to," Brooks explained. "For years, Director Rivers has talked about plausible deniability."

"Where I come from, that's called cowardice," Evers said.

"In Washington, it's called survival. It's called *politics*. What you need to worry about now is the same thing that I need to worry about: she's gonna want to know the source of the information leak."

"That sounds much more like a problem for you, Mr. Security Detail."

"Do you really think she's not going to turn the world inside out trying to find out who those attackers worked for?"

"Of course she will," Evers said. Brooks was playing directly into his hand, and he had to suppress a smile. "But I'm confident that as the guy who's most likely to lose his pension, you'll find a way to knock her off the trail."

Something changed behind Brooks's eyes. He'd been hit with an idea, and it triggered an emotion that looked a lot like fear. He pinched his lower lip and walked a couple of paces away.

"What's going on?" Evers asked.

"There's another thing I should tell you, and now I think it makes some sense to me."

Evers stood quietly as Brooks sorted his thoughts.

"In South Dakota," Brooks began, "during the shoot-out, there were more people present than just the rent-a-soldiers that were supposed to be there. That comes from just an initial analysis of shell casings. Lots of five-five-six. Of the rentals who were on duty, only one of them survived, and we don't know where he is. It appears that the others were killed early on, in the first seconds of the assault."

"I'm not sure I follow what you're telling me," Evers said.

"The people who shot your guys were not our guys," Brooks said.

Evers connected a couple of dots. "Plausible deniability?"

"I think so."

"I'm still not seeing what you're trying to show me," Evers confessed.

Brooks explained, "Your guys didn't have credentials, right? That's why they had to shoot their way into the compound. But the unknown shooters *had* to have creds or they wouldn't have been let in."

"So, they're FBI agents?" Evers asked.

Brooks shook his head. "No. Well, maybe, but I don't see how. That's the sort of thing that I'd probably know about. I think it's a covert team, and I think it might be working for the director."

"You mean personally?"

Brooks thought a little more. "Let's talk outside," he said, and he led the way across to the Jefferson Drive exit. A security guard started to object, but Brooks badged him. "This gentleman is with me."

There weren't a lot of tourists in town this time of year, and the street on this side of the building was fairly free of traffic, both vehicular and pedestrian.

"So, here's the thing," Brooks explained. "Every now and then, Director Rivers meets with this mysterious guy from someplace I don't know. He's got a tough guy look to him, and he's got lots of attitude. Very full of himself. He goes by the name Richard Horgan, but I question whether that's his real name."

Evers was no less confused. "Surely, the FBI director meets with a lot of people every day."

"Not this way," Brooks said. "It's almost always over at St. Matthew's Cathedral in Northwest, and when it's there, it's always in the same little chapel."

"What do they talk about?"

"I don't know," Brooks said. "You can't hear anything, and she's never shared any of the details with me."

"So, why is this an issue?" Evers asked. "I still don't understand."

"Think about it. A guy who looks like he could be a Navy SEAL has a clandestine meeting with my boss, and then within a day or two, there's a shoot-out at a clandestine jail, and they're able to transfer the prisoner no one is supposed to know about to another clandestine location. That's a lot of coincidence all in one place."

Evers weighed the words he'd just heard. It was no surprise that the feds were throwing everything they had at stopping Retribution, but it was troubling to know that they were using such strange methods.

"You still don't get the significance, do you?" Brooks pressed.

"No, I guess I don't."

"This means that there'll be no due process in taking care of you and your teams," Brooks explained. "No warrants, no arrests, no trial. They can just take you out."

Chapter Thirteen

For many years, Jonathan had been able to trade the services of his team for access to his wealthy clients' corporate jets. Such arrangements had sunset clauses, unfortunately, but time and again another client with a jet would pop up more or less exactly at the time when the previous arrangement was expiring. Alas, good luck doesn't always prevail, and when the last deal expired, there was no other to take its place.

For his part, Boxers was thrilled. Their last aircraft had been a small Lear that Big Guy liked to call a sardine can. There wasn't a lot of moving-around room, and it was damned comical to watch Big Guy get in and out of the flight deck.

So, with Jonathan's blessing, Big Guy went shopping for a new airplane. From the beginning, Jonathan's greatest concern about owning the aircraft that delivered them to their missions was the traceability of the tail numbers. These days, by opening an app on your phone, you could trace any corporate jet in the world simply by entering its tail number—its *N*-number. The app would disclose the plane's location along with the details of its ownership.

It was clear, then, that Security Solutions could not own the aircraft, and neither could Jonathan Grave. Instead, ownership would fall to Bekin's Environmental, a fourth-tier cutout corporation whose website said that it specialized in compliance with the EPA's Resource Conservation and Recovery Act and hazardous waste site reclamation. Jonathan knew what all those words meant individually, but when they were all stitched together, they translated as tree-hugging cleanup shit.

In reality, the sole purpose of Bekin's Environmental was to own airplanes and employ mechanics to fix them.

Them, as in plural. By the time Boxers was finished with his shopping spree, Bekin's owned not one, but *two* executive jets, both previously owned but with all of their certs current. For longer trips, he dropped eighteen million dollars for a Global 6000, but for shorter hops like this one to the Midwest, he paid nine million for the Hawker 800 that Boxers was aiming at the runway at Manassas Regional Airport in Virginia. It was a haul to drive here from Fisherman's Cove, but it was the closest FBO—fixed base operation—with runways long enough to handle either jet, even when loaded with maximum fuel and cargo. Jonathan also thought the separation from Fisherman's Cove aided with operational secrecy.

When Jonathan and Boxers worked as a twosome, Jonathan more often than not sat in the right seat next to Big Guy during the flight to keep him company. With Gail on board, though, he sat in one of the gray leather captain's chairs in the passenger cabin. Gail leaned back in an identical chair across from him, facing him, her eyes closed.

"You're staring at me," Gail said.

"Your eyelids are leaking if you can see that," Jonathan replied. "Like the new digs?"

She opened her eyes and stretched. "What, this old plane?" she teased, looking around. "It can't even go the speed of sound."

"Eight-tenths of it," Jonathan said. "Or, so I'm told by the driver."

"You'll have to explain to me one day how this expense makes sense."

"I'm a billionaire," Jonathan said. "Good place to start. And TSA would spaz up and die if they got a glimpse of our usual cargo."

Gail smiled but closed her eyes again as she said, "Do you have any idea how hard it is for us fiscal mere mortals to wrap our heads around those kinds of numbers?"

The speaker in the ceiling popped to life and Boxers' voice said, "Good afternoon, lady and dickhead, this is your captain speaking. I see a runway ahead of me—or maybe it's just a long road—but I intend to plant this machine onto the pavement. If I were you, I'd bring my seat up and put my seatbelt on. Only one set of ass cheeks per seat."

Jonathan and Gail both laughed. "You know, he does seem to be in better moods now that he gets to fly the new toy," Gail said.

Six minutes later, they were on the ground, and five minutes after that, they were rolling to a stop outside the hangar that Jonathan had rented on a twenty-five-year lease, along the perimeter road.

"We've got a wrinkle," Boxers said over the loudspeaker. "Quinn Parker wants to come on board and talk to us before we park."

That brought Gail's eyes open again. "Quinn Parker?"

"She's one of the mechanics I had to hire to take care my new air force," Jonathan explained. For years, Quinn had been a mechanic for the Air Force's 160th Special Operations Air Regiment (SOAR), headquartered out of Fort Campbell, Kentucky. He found her and her fellow mechanic, Matt Wacklowski, also a veteran of the 160th, through yet another Army buddy who had hung out his shingle as a headhunter specializing in spooky civilian jobs.

Jonathan elaborated, "She's part of the same ground crew who tows us in and out of the hangar and takes care of the whole shebang between flights."

"Why would they want to come in and chat? Why not just wait till we're on the ground?"

The fuselage shook a bit, and the air stairs started to deploy.

"Ask me in a few minutes," Jonathan said with a smile. "As for being surprised, you see those nondescript white planes over there?" He pointed through the tiny window to a small fleet of corporate jets a couple of hangars over.

Gail craned her neck to see.

Jonathan said, "Agency."

Gail's jaw dropped. "As in CIA?"

"As in CIA."

Boxers stepped into the cabin from the flight deck. "I hope this doesn't become a regular thing," he said. As the stairs fully deployed, he stood with his fists on his hips, filling the opening.

Jonathan rose from his seat and wedged past Big Guy to stand in front and beckoned the mechanic to come aboard. As she cleared the door, he asked, "What's up?"

"I'm sorry for the intrusion, sir," she said. "But there's a visitor inside the hangar that I think you should know about."

Jonathan had long ago given up on trying to break both of his new mechanics from calling him *sir*. He didn't rate it when he was in the Army, and he sure as hell didn't require it now, but some habits were impossible to break. He waited for the rest.

"He says his name is Derek Halstrom, and—"

"Oh, shit." Jonathan, Boxers, and Gail all said it in unison.

Quinn looked startled.

Jonathan laughed at the look in her face. "Did he say what he wanted?"

"Only that he needed to speak to you."

"As in, *me*?" Jonathan asked. "Or, as in *all of us*?"

"Just you, sir," she said. "He specifically said that he didn't want Mr. Van de Muelebroecke there."

"Boxers," Big Guy said. "And that's your only warning."

Quinn gave a shy smile and blushed a little.

"How did he get in?" Jonathan asked. "I mean, onto the airfield?"

Quinn's shoulder twitched in what might have been a shrug. "It's not that hard," she said. "I believe Ms. Alexander gave him the code for the keypad."

Under his breath, Boxers said, "Venice and Derek, sittin' in a tree. K-I-S-S-I-N-G . . ."

Gail slugged him in the arm while Jonathan tried to suppress a laugh. In the years he'd known Venice

Alexander—which was her entire life—he'd seen her smitten by Cupid only a few times. One ended in a terrible marriage followed by a baby and a divorce, and the others kind of fizzled and died. This thing she had for Derek seemed very real, and for once, the man she'd fallen for was a decent guy.

"I think I know what this is about," Jonathan said.

"Anyway, I thought you should know, in case . . . Well, I thought you should know. I didn't know if it would be a good surprise or a bad surprise."

Jonathan offered his hand. "You did a good job, Quinn," he said. "Thank you."

"You're welcome. Matt and I will tow the aircraft into the hangar after you're off." She turned and headed back down the stairs.

"You should be nicer to her," Gail said. "She's trying so hard to be noticed. You treat her like an annoyance."

Jonathan looked to Boxers. "I vote you just leave the gear on the plane until we figure out what lies ahead in this mess."

"Works for me," Big Guy said. "What's the computer geek here for?"

"I'll let you know. Just don't leave without me." Jonathan descended the stairs and headed for the hangar. The crew had already brought up the Batmobile, Security Solutions' armored and highly customized Hummer, and parked it at the base of the stairs. Beyond that, just outside the hangar door, a black Jeep Cherokee sat just this side of the hangar door.

Jonathan was halfway to the ground when the Cherokee's door opened and revealed a thin young African American man who sported a closely-cropped beard and wore a suit that looked like it was too small for his skinny body. It was, Jonathan had been told, the in look these days for the cool kids. Derek Halstrom.

The young man stayed in place next to his opened door as Jonathan approached. "Mr. Grave!" he shouted as the distance closed to a few yards. "Thanks for agreeing to meet with me."

"I don't remember doing that," Jonathan said. "But since you're here . . ."

"I'm wondering if we can talk in the car," Derek said.

"What's wrong with talking here?" Jonathan heard his own words and realized he was being a dick.

Derek seemed startled. "I just thought that maybe . . ."

"Don't worry about it," Jonathan said, and he moved to the passenger side. As he was about to climb in, he glanced back to the plane's door and saw the curious look on Boxers face. He yelled, "We're not going anywhere!"

The Jeep smelled new and was outfitted with a leather interior. Nothing over-the-top, but this was likely not a vehicle whose four-wheel drive would ever be engaged. Jonathan kept his door open until Derek was fully committed behind the wheel and closed his own door.

Derek turned awkwardly in his seat, till his back was propped against his door. "Has Venice been in touch with you?"

"All the time," Jonathan said.

"About this meeting, I mean."

For an instant, Jonathan got this brief flash that he was going to ask for Venice's hand in marriage. Surely not. "No, not about this meeting."

"She's brought me in on your search to find the conspirators who pulled off Black Friday and are now behind yesterday's explosions."

Jonathan held his expression blank, but no, Venice had not mentioned that to him. He knew that Derek had been of considerable help in the past, but he felt anger beginning to boil that she had pulled an outsider in without consulting him first.

If Derek had been waiting for a response, he didn't show it. He just plowed on. "We've got to crunch some huge numbers to find the source of all the planning that went into the hits, and that's what she needs me to do."

Jonathan settled himself with a deep breath. "If Ven thinks it's important, then it's important. I thank you for your willingness to assist. So, why are we sitting in your Jeep at a little airport?"

Derek grew uncomfortable. He shifted his gaze, and his posture squirmed. He was a man who should never play poker. And if he did, Jonathan prayed that he could be on the other side of the table. "Well, the thing is, there's a lot of risk in doing things like this. I mean, if I get caught, I could lose my job."

"As I understand it, Derek, if you get caught, you *would* go to jail."

"Exactly. That's what I mean about high risk."

Jonathan made it a point to keep his body language locked down. "Are you feeling coerced into doing this?" he asked. "If so, then don't do it."

"No, no, that's not it at all," Derek said. "I'd do anything for Venice. It's just I was thinking that risk should bring with it some reward."

"You mean, she didn't offer to pay you? In dollars, I

mean." That last part slipped out unintentionally. Yeah, okay, he had some fraternal protective instincts when it came to Mother Hen.

"Oh, yes, she's paying me. In dollars." The significance of nonmonetary compensation seemed to hit him at that moment, and he blushed.

"But it's not enough?"

"The money is fine, I guess," Derek said. "It's the exposure that I'm not being compensated for."

Jonathan waited for it.

"I want to join your team." There, he said it.

And it was exactly what Jonathan had been expecting. "You're already on the team," he said. "That's why you're getting paid."

"No, I want to be a permanent part of the team. I want to work for Security Solutions."

"As a private investigator?" Jonathan was being deliberately obtuse, but for a reason. This kid had to see for himself what a ridiculous thing it was that he was asking to do.

"What? No, as part of the covert side."

"I don't know what covert side you're talking about," Jonathan said. "Security Solutions is a private investigating firm."

Derek cocked his head. Jonathan thought of it as a confused puppy look. "You know that I know, right?"

"Did Venice tell you something I wouldn't like?"

"Of course not! I figured it out on my own. And then I deleted what I'd found."

"That was to impress Venice, was it not?"

"Well, yeah. But what difference does that make? I made your covers stronger."

"And I appreciate that," Jonathan said. "Let me make this whole conversation easier. We don't have any positions available."

"But I'm very good at what I do," Derek pressed.

"Which is why Venice keeps coming back to you for help," Jonathan said. He knew what he paid this kid, and it was not an amount to apologize for.

"Think of what you could do with my mad skills on your payroll. Your *permanent* payroll."

"I've already got someone with mad skills on my permanent payroll," Jonathan said. "And she's got great judgment. That's why when she says she needs help, I'm happy to sign the check."

"But I'm tired of committing felonies every time I lend you guys a hand."

Jonathan gave him an annoyed look that said, *Really*?

"Okay, okay," Derek said. "I guess that's kind of part of the job. But at NSA, they come hunting for people who do what I do for you."

"Which is why you need to be careful." Jonathan shifted in his own seat so that he could face Derek more or less head on. "Way back when, Ven told me that you'd given her a speech about how important it was to you to see justice brought to bad guys. You told her that this line of work inspired you. Was that just a line of bullshit, or do you really think that?"

"It wasn't bullshit," Derek said.

"I'm glad to hear it, because bullshitters and I don't get along at all. I respect you for your *mad skills*, as you put it, and I like you because Venice likes you. If she stops, I stop. I pay you what I pay you because you bring additional value to what we already do very well—and have been doing very well for quite a few years."

Derek's head cock grew more severe, as if he were totally confused.

"Here it is, between the eyes," Jonathan said. "That extra value you bring is one hundred percent tied to your job at the NSA. You give us access to things that we would otherwise not have access to. If you want to quit, quit. I can't stop you from doing that. I'd prefer that you continue to help because you meant what you said about justice."

Derek looked hurt. "Maybe sometime in the future?"

"Ask me sometime in the future," Jonathan said. "Is that the sole reason you came out here to meet us? To ask me for a job?"

"Ven thought you'd say no."

"She knows me pretty well."

"And there's one other thing," Derek said. "I've got a strong lead on how to find Iceman."

Jonathan gave him a hard look. The guy seemed ambitious and honest, and maybe even a little naïve, especially considering his line of work. "Tell you what," he said. "You know where the office is, right?"

"Yes, sir, of course."

"Meet us there in ninety minutes, and you can brief us all at once."

Derek looked stunned. "I can come into the office?"

Jonathan winked and opened his door.

Chapter Fourteen

It made no sense to close Derek out of the War Room. While the guy had no place on the permanent team, he did have useful skills and being close to the seat of power seemed to be important to him. Fewer than ten people in the world had ever visited the War Room of Security Solutions' headquarters because fewer than ten people had earned that level of trust.

Derek wasn't trustworthy so much as leverageable. Jonathan had enough dirt on the guy that it would be foolish for him to turn into an enemy and do something stupid, so why not bring him into the warmth from the cold? Boxers, on the other hand, hated the idea and had not been shy in letting his thoughts be known.

"I got it," Jonathan had said in the Batmobile. "And your point is duly noted."

"But you're going to bring him in, anyway?"

"Yep."

"You know, if he goes rogue and tries to take us down, we *all* go down. It's not just you."

Jonathan had laughed at that. "If that happens, Big

Guy, I promise I won't stand in your way when you teach him the lessons of how he was wrong."

Boxers shot him a look, then smiled. "It's not much," he'd said. "But it's something."

Presently, they sat around the big teak table—Venice in her command chair, plus Boxers and Jonathan along the left edge, Gail on the right edge, and Derek in the pressure seat at the far end, under the 106-inch projector screen that was currently dark. Derek looked to be equal parts jazzed and nervous.

So did Venice, Jonathan noticed. She clearly wanted her boyfriend's first all-hands impression to be a good one.

"The floor's yours," Jonathan said after they'd all settled in. "Who is Iceman?"

Derek's shoulders sagged at the question. "Um, I, uh, didn't mean to imply that I know who he is—at least not yet. What I have for you is a way to find him. Well, Venice and I figured it out together."

Venice smiled, but didn't say anything. If that wasn't an expression of infatuation, nothing was.

Gail caught Jonathan's attention with a little smile that said, *This is so cute.* On his left, Boxers made a quiet retching noise.

Derek rose from his seat, nodded to Venice, and the big screen came alive, displaying "Who Is Iceman?" in bold red letters.

Jonathan steeled himself for a long one.

"Acting on an idea presented to me by Venice, I redirected some assets at the Palace and scoured the metadata from the six sites that were hit on Black Friday and crossmatched them with the five sites that were hit next." Numbers appeared on the screen. Lots of them. And while they no doubt represented important revelations to the two megageeks in the room, they meant nothing to Jonathan.

Big Guy's retch transformed into a barely audible growl. He hated big-reveal drama when it came from Venice, but he'd learned to accept it in deference to the source. Jonathan worried about how he would endure it from a stranger he didn't think belonged here in the first place.

Derek continued, "I'll be honest and tell you there were a lot more hits on burner phones than I thought there'd be. That was true across all the locations."

"But we only care about one or two per location, right?" Gail asked.

"Exactly. So, I worked backwards from Masterson's phone. He told us that he got a call from Iceman just a few minutes before he had to commit to his attack in Indian Spear. That call went back to a SIM card in Sediment, Oklahoma. So, leveraging that one known point, we found the phones in the six other towns, all pinging back to the phone in Sediment."

"So, we've got them?" Jonathan asked.

"No," Derek said.

"Of course not," Boxers grumbled. "What would be the fun in getting to the point?"

Big Guy's words seemed to knock Derek off his game, and he looked to Venice.

"He's always like that," she said. "Even with me."

"*Especially* with you," Boxers corrected.

"Just go on," Jonathan said.

Derek nodded to Venice, and the slide changed to show the silhouette of a faceless man. Very dramatic.

"We'll assume that the Sediment phone belonged to Iceman because that number is the common denominator. Problem is, after that night, the signal disappeared and never returned."

"He killed the phone," Jonathan said.

"Exactly," Derek confirmed. "But he gave us a pattern to look for. Phone calls to the killers' numbers within an hour of the time of the attacks." The screen changed again, this time to show a map of the United States with the cities where the bombings took place expanded out of the map in starburst explosive graphics. "And the second hits, the pattern repeated itself. Same numbers out in the field, contacted by a different number, this time from—where do you guess?"

"Mars," Boxers said.

"Wrong," Derek replied, unfazed by the irony. "Lincoln, Nebraska."

"Oh, for Christ's sake," Boxers groaned.

"It means that Iceman is moving around," Derek explained. "And he's careful about turning off his phone till he needs it, which means he's not traceable. At least not yet."

"I don't get it," Jonathan said, feeling some of Boxers' frustration. "I thought you said we had a lead."

"We do," Derek said. He was beginning to look and sound flustered. "Please bear with me. In the weeks between attacks, all the operators involved turned on their phones for one hour beginning at nine a.m. Eastern on Mondays, Wednesdays, and Fridays. For most of them, those signals come from all over the map. Iceman, on the other hand, stays dark."

"That means the operators are waiting for a message from Iceman," Venice said. "At least that's what we think." It was her way of bringing Derek back on point.

"All of them clearly are mobile," Derek continued. "Except for one."

Jonathan sat a little taller.

Derek explained, "The best I can figure is that one of them must have roots to a place called Winterset, Iowa." The screen changed to show a picture of a beautiful Midwestern town that could have been lifted from a Disney movie. "At that hour on those mornings, his phone comes alive from the same coffee shop."

Silence fell as the enormity of this settled on them. Jonathan said, "Are you telling me that we know where one of the terrorists is?"

Derek smiled as he nodded. "It would seem so, yes. At least we know where he is every Monday, Wednesday, and Friday morning."

"Today's Tuesday, Boss." Boxers said.

Jonathan addressed Derek. "How long have you known this?"

Derek looked to Venice for confirmation. "A few hours?"

She nodded.

"You knew this at the airport."

"Yes."

"Why didn't you say anything?"

"I did. I told you we had a lead."

"You didn't tell me you had a location!" Jonathan felt his temper meter tipping into the red.

"I wanted to do this as a presentation," Derek said. He seemed deflated. "You know, to make a good first impression."

Jonathan shot a glare to Venice.

She smiled. "He's used to doing things Uncle Sam's way," she said. "He'll learn."

"Especially if you're my teacher," Derek said.

"Oh, my God," Boxers declared, and he shot to his feet. "I'll gas up the Batmobile so we can drive all the way back to the airport we just came from." He left the War Room after damn near tearing the door off the hinge while opening it.

"Is he mad?" Derek asked.

Jonathan laughed. "Yes, he's mad. But I'll stipulate that sometimes it's hard to tell the difference." To Venice, he added, "You'll get the address and send it to my GPS?"

She nodded.

"Teach him well, okay?" Jonathan said as he let Gail lead the way to the door.

Back out in the Cave, the larger area that housed the offices on the covert side, Gail said, "Isn't he supposed to be a badass cyber warrior in his other life?"

"That's what I hear."

"Venice could kick his ass."

Jonathan smiled. "That's fine by me," he said.

Six hours later, it was well after dark when Boxers painted the Hawker onto the runway for a perfect landing at Ottumwa Regional Airport. Triple the distance to Winterest than Des Moines International Airport, Ottumwa Regional allowed the kind of high-end executive service that Jonathan's team required. Thanks to Venice's efforts, a black rental Suburban was waiting for them when they parked the plane, along with a red Ford sedan. After another forty-five minutes to tie things down and transfer the gear and equipment, they set out for the hundred-mile drive to Winterset.

"You okay to drive, Box?" Jonathan asked.

"I'm fine," Big Guy said. "But I like the way you pretended that there was a choice."

Their plan—if you could call it that—needed to account for multiple chases. Jonathan and Gail took the sedan.

Venice had also rented them a furnished house at the edge of Winterset's business district for a week. It was longer than they'd need, but the shortest rental duration the owner would accept. Jonathan had learned the hard way over the years that hotel rooms didn't work well for what they did. Too many curious eyes. Neighbors got curious, too, but this town was headquartered in Madison County—famous for its bridges—and was the birthplace of John Wayne, so tourists were accepted as routine.

As promised, the keys to the rental house were under the mat. Yes, it was that kind of community. To err on the side of safety, the three of them checked the house for burglars or bums before moving their equipment from the Suburban into the bedrooms. One of the benefits—and banes—of having their own airplane was the freedom to travel heavy. The nondescript duffel bags contained a wide variety of rifles and pistols, and God only knew how many rounds of ammunition for all of them. Explosives filled one bag, while initiators filled another, much smaller one. And then there was the comms gear, night vision, body armor, and other assorted kit.

An inviolable fact of Jonathan's business was that it

was better to have something and not need it than need it and not have it.

"All right, kids," Boxers said as he planted the last duffel on the floor of the bedroom he'd declared to be his own. "I'm done. See you in the morning. If romance strikes, try to keep quiet." He closed the door without waiting for an answer.

Gail led the way to the other bedroom, with Jonathan close behind. "Do with me what you wish," she said, "but try not to wake me up."

Jonathan and Gail entered Carol's Coffee Café shortly before 7:45 the next morning. Located on Jefferson Street, across from a town square that housed a domed courthouse, Carol's was a throwback to a time Jonathan had only seen in movies. Aqua-clad swivel stools stood sentry down the long aqua-and-orange service bar on the left, while four-top Naugahyde booths lined the wall on the right. Narrow and deep, this was clearly the place to be for breakfast in Winterset.

A bell slapped against the glass door to announce their arrival. No one seemed to notice, except for an ample woman who looked up from a customer in a cheap suit who was eating at the bar. She held a bulbous coffeepot in her fist, and she lit up with a smile.

"Good morning, folks," she said. "Sit wherever you like. I'll be with you in a minute."

"This entire town is a movie set," Gail whispered as they walked to a booth about halfway down the line. Her tone sounded more complimentary than critical. There was no denying the charm of this little burg.

Jonathan took a seat facing the front of the café while Gail faced the back. Their plan was as loose as it was simple. They were here to observe. If Derek and Venice were correct, their terrorist was here in this building, or would be, beginning at eight o'clock—nine Eastern. Back East, they were monitoring the terrorist's burner phone, waiting for an alert call to come in. Of course, there was no guarantee that today would be the day, but if it didn't happen, Venice would call the number at 8:50 local time. Whether it rang or buzzed, someone would answer something, and when that happened, they'd be over the first hurdle.

In part because it was impossible for Boxers to remain unnoticed, he waited outside to follow the bad guy as he left.

The proximity of the courthouse explained a lot about the diversity of the clientele. If suits and ties meant lawyers, then lawyers preferred eating at the bar. Jonathan decided that the men wearing ties with no suit jackets were either witnesses or litigants. Then there were the people dressed like regular folks, who he decided were assorted townies or tourists like he and Gail.

As if in homage to Norman Rockwell, a boy of about thirteen sat by himself at the bar, flanked by lawyers who towered head and shoulders higher than he.

"What do you think the kid's story is?" Jonathan asked, leaning in close so he wouldn't be heard.

Gail glanced over. "Owner's son, maybe? Hanging out on his way to school? I wish I had an idea of who we're looking for."

"Give it an hour," Jonathan said.

The woman from behind the counter appeared with

the ever-present coffeepot in one fist and two white ceramic mugs in the other. “Welcome to Winterset,” she said as she approached. “Y’all look like you need some coffee.”

“Is it that obvious?” Gail asked.

“I’m Carol,” the waitress said. “That’s my name on the door. I own the place, but I’m also the accountant and custodian.”

Jonathan laughed because that felt like the right thing to do. This clearly was not her first time delivering the line.

“When did you get into town?” Carol asked as she filled the mugs.

Jonathan and Gail exchanged looks. They hadn’t prepared any small talk.

“Don’t look so surprised that I know you’re not from around here,” Carol said with a big smile. “Sooner or later, every tourist drops by. That’s why I keep it looking like a movie set.”

Another shared look. *Did she hear us?*

“We’re from back East,” Jonathan said. “Newbern, North Carolina.” It was the first Carolina city to pop into his head.

“You military?” she asked. “You’ve both got the shoulders for it.”

Jonathan forced a smile. Honest to God, the CIA was missing its mark by not hiring bartenders and short order cooks as interrogators. No one was more adept at pulling information out of people.

“I used to be,” Jonathan said. “Navy. Got out awhile ago.” He almost choked on the *N*-word, but the fewer intersections this conversation had with the truth, the better off they’d all be.

"You too?" Carol asked.

Gail nodded. "Yes, ma'am."

"Well, God bless you both. Any idea what you want to eat?"

They *had* discussed this. In keeping with remaining as invisible as possible, they each went for eggs, bacon, and toast. When it arrived ten minutes later, Jonathan said to Carol, "Looks like you have a lot of regulars."

"And a lot of new folks like you, too," she said. "I've been open here for over fourteen years now, and the lesson I've learned is that good food is always welcome. You should stop by here for dinner one night while you're in town. You'll never have a better meatloaf, and that's a money-back guarantee."

As she spoke, Jonathan pulled his wallet from his back pocket. "How much do I owe?"

She waved him off. "Oh, there's no hurry, sweetie. That can wait till you're done. Need anything else?"

He really wanted to pay, to be unencumbered if the time came for them to leave in a hurry. But there was no easy way to press the point.

And then Carol was gone.

The food was, indeed, great, but in all fairness, the ingredients were hard to screw up. By the time they were done, there'd been a 30-percent turnover in diners. Most of the lawyers were gone now, but roughly half the litigants remained engaged in conversation.

Jonathan checked his watch. "Mother Hen makes her call in six minutes." He continued looking at Gail as he moved his hand to the control knob on the two-way radio he wore on his belt, under his denim jacket on the left side—the side not occupied by his Colt. He switched the radio on, then flipped the toggle to

VOX—voice-activated transmission—which would broadcast their conversation live without him having to push a transmit button.

The tiny transceiver bud in his ear popped as it came to life. "Howya doin,' Big Guy?"

"Cutting it a little close there, aren't you, Boss?"

"Nothing's happened here so far," Jonathan said. He used his eyebrows to ask if Gail was also on the channel.

She gave a subtle thumbs-up.

The plan was to make the terrorist panic. When he answered his phone—and for good or ill, Jonathan was convinced that the bad guy was, in fact, a *guy*—he'd hear a message that was sure to flush him out.

Boxers said, "You know, if this thing goes down, it's gonna be really hard for this guy *not* to know he's being followed. There's like zero traffic out here."

"One thing at a time," Jonathan said. "Two minutes till something happens."

Chapter Fifteen

Seth Provost did his best not to look at the clock on the wall. Instead, he passed the time on his phone, texting with his buddy, Benny Branch, a.k.a. AXL7433. They'd reached a deal yesterday to rescue Seth's algebra grade, but the plan had gone off track when Seth's plans for the morning changed unexpectedly.

The morning bell had already rung at school, and Benny's homework still resided in Seth's backpack. Benny was on the edge of panic. One of the problems with having a four-oh grade point average was that even a single zero on a single assignment stood out like a zit on a school photo.

Benny was, like, melting the hell down.

AXL7433: Dude where are you?? I need my homework back!!!

MSTR_CHIEF1485: I'll be there. Got this 1 thing

AXL7433: How long????? Math is in a hour. Ur gon b late and if you go 2 the office, FML

MSTR_CHIEF1485: Gotta hang til 9. Then I'm done.

AXL7433: WTF you doing?

MSTR_CHIEF1485: Makin $$$$$$

AXL7433: Screw your $$$. Get back here.

MSTR_CHIEF1485: I'll be there.

This shit could go on and on without stop if he let it. A hundred bucks was a hundred bucks, and if that meant Benny wouldn't be his friend anymore, there were worse things in the world. He only had to hang out here till nine, and after that—

The other phone buzzed in his pocket.

"Oh, shit." He said it aloud, but he didn't think anyone heard him. He fished the old style flip phone out of his jeans and opened it. "H-hello?"

When he heard the voice on the other end of the call, it felt as if his spine had dissolved. It was a horrible, growly sound, like something from a horror movie. "Your cover is blown," it said. "The FBI is coming for you. Take evasive action now. You have no time."

Then the line went dead.

Seth snapped the phone closed much too loudly, and he felt tears pressing behind his eyes. His heart rate jumped to a million beats a minute, and suddenly, he felt like he might throw up all the breakfast he'd just scarfed down.

Holy shit. The FBI! What the hell?

He hadn't signed up for this. He was supposed to answer the phone—if it rang, which it probably wouldn't—memorize the code that he was told, and then meet Tony behind the tobacco store on Court Avenue. That was it. Period.

Nobody said anything about the FBI!

Holy shit, holy shit, holy shit.

Everybody was looking at him now. Everybody knew. Maybe they were all FBI agents, and they were there to arrest him.

Without moving any other part of his body, Seth rotated his head to the left and to the right, and no, they really *weren't* looking at him. Well, maybe that one guy at the end of the bar, but as soon as they made eye contact, he looked away.

Carol was over at the order window, doing what Carol always did—talking and laughing.

Directly across, the fisheye mirror near the ceiling showed everybody doing normal things. They hadn't seen him slam the phone shut, and maybe they really couldn't hear the hammering of his heart. How was that possible?

This was bad. Really, really bad . . .

Wait. Seth hadn't done anything wrong. Not unless skipping morning bell was a crime. Did they still have truant officers? He'd heard about them on an old TV movie he'd watched. The FBI weren't coming for him. They were coming for Tony!

What the hell should he do now? He could just leave the phone on the counter and walk away, but then Carol would call him back because he'd forgotten it. Then everyone really *would* be looking at him.

What was he doing still sitting there? The guy on the phone said they were coming right now. Sure, it was easy for Seth to say he'd done nothing wrong because he really hadn't, but were the FBI going to understand that? They were famous for stacking false evidence against people they didn't like. He'd been hearing about it in the news. Hell, he'd been hearing about it *everywhere*.

He had to get out of here. He glanced at his neighbors again, and they were still lost in their own worlds. When he looked in the mirror, though, he locked eyes with a guy in a denim jacket who seemed to be looking at him and talking to the lady he was with.

Did he know? Was he the FBI?

Seth had to move carefully here, needed to think things through all the way to the end. He didn't want to go off *half-cocked*, as his mom always said.

No, if they were the FBI, they'd have made their move, right? That's what the guy on the phone said. He didn't say that the FBI was *there*. Said that they were *on the way*. Those are different things.

Seth decided that he had time, but that he needed to move. He needed to get the phone back to Tony, and while he was at it, he'd give back the hundred dollars, too. He didn't want anything to do with anything the FBI was doing.

In five minutes, he'd be free of all this shit. In fifteen, he'd be back in school with one hell of a story to tell Benny.

Should he say good-bye, or should he just walk away? Call attention and act normal, or simply disappear?

He decided that invisibility was the way to go. He'd already paid for his food. Before spinning around on his stool and dropping his feet to the floor, he looked in the mirror one more time.

The guy in the denim jacket had gone back to eating his breakfast.

* * *

"What do you mean, it's a kid?" Gail whispered.

"Remember that boy at the bar when we first came in?" Jonathan asked.

"Yeah."

"It's him. He just took the call."

"He's not even a teenager yet. Hardly terrorist material."

"Maybe he's a mule," Jonathan said. "Doing the dirty work for the real bad guy."

"Quit the chit chat," Boxers said. "I've got eyes on the front door. Do I copy that I'm looking for a kid?"

"Affirmative, Big Guy."

"Got a description?"

Jonathan shifted his eyes to the kid at the counter. "He's white, brown hair. Green windbreaker, looks like black tennis shoes. As far as I can tell, he's the only kid in the restaurant."

As Jonathan was relaying his description, he met the kid's eyes in the fisheye mirror over the service counter. The boy looked frightened.

Jonathan cut his eyes to Gail. "Shit," he said. "I think I've been made."

"Is he moving yet?" Boxers asked.

"Looks like he's about to," Jonathan said. "I'll need to give him a thirty-second head start or more when he leaves. Otherwise, if he sees us, I think he'll panic."

"Don't hurt him, Big Guy," Gail said.

Boxers replied, "I'll pretend you didn't say that."

Jonathan understood. As wicked as Big Guy's violent streak was, he'd moved heaven and earth in the past to *avoid* hurting children.

Through his peripheral vision, while feigning conversation with Gail, Jonathan watched as the boy eyeballed him again, spun on the stool, hit the floor, and started for the exit.

"He's moving," Jonathan said.

As soon as the kid was clear of the door, Jonathan fished his wallet out of his pocket.

"We don't have a check," Gail said.

Jonathan dropped two twenties on the table. "Forty bucks is sure to cover it."

"I've got him," Boxers said. "He's scared shitless."

Gail stood.

"Where are you going?" Jonathan asked.

Gail explained, "You need to wait. I don't. He didn't see *me* staring at him. Big Guy can't do it all from the truck."

"Good idea," Boxers said.

As Jonathan watched Gail exit, he realized that he might not be capable of waiting to follow. But he had to. Venice's call had knocked the kid off-balance—who in the world thought there'd be a child involved?—and that in turn had knocked their plan off its trajectory. If Jonathan moved too quickly, he'd amp things up to panic mode.

He decided to put the time to use. He slid out of his booth and walked to the eating counter. "Excuse me, Carol?" he said.

She looked up from whatever she was doing and greeted him with a big smile. "Oh, no, honey," she said. "I can come to the table for the money. I haven't even brought—"

Jonathan put the twenties on the counter. "Keep the

extra as a tip," he said. "Who was that boy who was just sitting here?"

The frumpy lawyer on his left looked up at the question. "Whoa there, Mr. I-Don't-Know-Who-You-Are. The hell kind of question is that? What business—"

Jonathan produced his FBI badge. "I'm not talking to you," he said. "Carol, I have to know."

Carol brought a hand to her chest. "Oh, my God, did Seth do something wrong?"

"Seth what?" Jonathan pressed. "I need a last name."

"What did he do?"

"I just need to talk with him."

"Then how come you don't know his name?" the frumpy guy pressed.

"I don't have time," Jonathan said. "Seth does not have time. Now, tell me."

"Don't say anything," the frump said. "Carol, that boy—"

"Provost," Carol said. "Seth Provost. But he's a good boy."

"Seth Provost," Jonathan repeated, mostly for the benefit of his team. "Thank you, Carol. Breakfast was terrific."

As Jonathan headed for the door, the frumpy lawyer moved to follow.

Jonathan froze him with a forefinger thrust to his nose. "If you want to be on a liquid-only diet, go ahead and follow me."

The lawyer went cross-eyed as he focused on the finger. His altruistic indignation seemed to have taken a backseat to reality. That was a good thing. For both of them.

* * *

As Seth stepped out into the chilly sunshine, his spine felt as if it were crawling with ants and spiders, chills racing up and down from his butt to the back of his head. Was the FBI already there? Was he being watched? And what was Tony involved with that could get Seth arrested and sent to jail?

Did they send thirteen-year-olds to jail? He'd read books and seen movies about juvenile detention centers. This had been a stupid, *stupid* idea. This shit was worth more than a hundred bucks—more than a *thousand* bucks. This shit was *crazy*.

"Keep it together," Seth mumbled to himself. He tried to look calm and uninterested as he glanced back to see if the guy in the denim jacket was following. Nope. Then he looked ahead at the courthouse and down the streets and sidewalks. FBI agents wore those nylon windbreakers, right?

Just a few more minutes and this whole thing would be over.

Tony would be in a white pickup truck. A big one with dual rear axles, the kind that's designed to haul heavy stuff. He'd be sitting behind the tobacco store.

What was Tony going to do when he found out about the FBI? Tony looked like he got pissed a lot. And he looked a lot like a guy to be afraid of when that happened.

All for a hundred dollars. "Seth, you're a moron," he mumbled.

His mom would shit a cow if she knew what he was doing.

Maybe he didn't owe Tony anything. Maybe Seth

could keep the phone and the money and just disappear.

Except, how hard would it be for Tony to find him when he lived in a town this small?

No, this was important. He needed to make the handoff, and then he needed to fly away.

It took way longer for Seth to cross the courthouse lawn than he thought it would. You didn't pay attention to how long it took to get to a place you knew unless there was a reason to be in a hurry. And man oh man, was he in a hurry.

He crossed Court Avenue directly in front of the tobacco store, but because all of the buildings touched each other—essentially forming one big building—he had to turn left at the sidewalk and then right onto John Wayne Drive toward Washington Street. That took him to the rear of the businesses into an alley marked by red brick and back doors on the right, and a line of telephone poles on the left. In the middle was a lot of nothing, some Dumpsters and a few parked cars.

There weren't many corners of Winterset that Seth hadn't explored at one time or another, but the last time he'd been down here, he and Benny had seen a huge rat chewing on something that had fur on it, and it had kind of freaked him out.

Yet here he was again, *totally* freaking out.

He saw the truck. It was parked in a part of the alley that wouldn't be visible to passing vehicles on John Wayne Drive or Washington Street. In fact, it wasn't visible at all. Tony was sitting behind the wheel, smoking a cigarette and studying his phone, seemingly unaware that Seth was even there. Seth was half a second from turning around and quitting this whole thing.

Then, as if drawn to Seth's eyes, Tony looked up from his phone and waved at him.

Seth hesitated, then waved back. He was going to do this thing. He hadn't yet cut the distance by half before Tony opened the driver's door and stepped out to stand next to his vehicle.

"How'd it go?" Tony asked. Then his expression hardened. "What's wrong?"

Chapter Sixteen

"I've lost him," Boxers said. "He disappeared behind the trees."

"I'm still on him," Gail said. "It looks like he's heading straight across the courthouse lawn. He's certainly walking with purpose."

Jonathan listened to the radio traffic and tried to imagine their plan. Was Seth Provost merely a mule, or was he part sociopath? Jonathan remembered when the DC area was shut down for weeks by a sniper who turned out to be a child. Either way, the kid could not be working alone on this. There had to be others involved. His father, maybe? Older brother?

"I'm moving my vehicle," Boxers announced. "If he's moving to the other side of the square, I want to be in position." He was not asking permission.

Jonathan decided to walk a parallel route to both Gail and Boxers, using the sidewalk along John Wayne Drive, which defined the eastern edge of the square. He was twenty yards to Gail's left and probably a hundred yards behind. On the far side of the square, Boxers cruised the Suburban slowly along, finally choosing a parking spot at the southwestern corner of the square.

"The boy is approaching the street," Gail said.

"I see him now," Boxers said.

"Be careful, Gunslinger," Jonathan said. "Don't get too close."

As the boy crossed the street and then turned left, Boxers said, "Looks like he's not done walking yet. Another block or two, maybe?"

At the corner with Court Avenue, Seth turned onto John Wayne Drive. "I've lost him again," Boxers said.

"He's headed toward Washington Street," Jonathan said. Ahead and to the right, Gail crossed Court Avenue and followed the path Seth had just walked.

Still a hundred yards back, Jonathan had a perfect view of it all. "Slinger, feel free to turn the corner normally. He's not checking his six at all."

When Seth turned right at the rear corner of the closest building, Jonathan's gut tightened. "He turned into the alley," he said. "I can't see him anymore. Big Guy, turn left on Washington. That will give you the best opportunity to eyeball him."

When Gail reached the end of the building, the point at which Seth had turned, she stopped. "I don't see him."

"Dammit." Jonathan picked up his pace. "Big Guy?"

"I'm just turning onto Washington, but I can tell you now that I'm going to have a limited view past the buildings on this street to see into the alley. Want me to go back and cruise the alley itself?"

"You can't drive through a narrow alley and stay out of sight," Jonathan said.

"He's a little boy, Scorpion," Gail said in her most scolding tone.

"He's just one kid," Boxers countered. "We're working to save a lot more than that."

"I'm going down the alley," Gail declared. "I'll just be a curious tourist. If he sees me, he sees me, but then I'll know if he's okay."

"Suppose he's inside one of the businesses?" Jonathan asked.

"Then we'll know that, too, won't we? I'll keep you both in the loop."

Jonathan picked up his pace to a jog.

"I need an order, Boss," Boxers said.

"Sit tight for now," Jonathan said. "Wait for intel from Gunslinger."

Fifteen seconds later, Gail said, "I've got him. He's talking with a guy—maybe thirty, looks like he could be an operator. They're standing next to a big white dually pickup. The driver is getting out to meet him."

Jonathan hated being the blind guy on the team. "Are you seeing it, too, Big Guy?"

"Affirmative. Well, sort of. I don't see the kid, but I can see a fender of the truck. Big sucker."

"That's the one," Gail confirmed.

As he listened to the chatter, Jonathan reached the entry to the alley, where he could see Gail downrange, pressed up against a Dumpster, doing her best to observe while staying out of sight. Jonathan walked past the alley, closer to Washington Street, then turned right and cut across a gas station parking lot, keeping the alley trash receptacles between him and the target. Up ahead and to the left, he saw Boxers' rented Suburban idling against the curb.

Finally, Jonathan had a usable angle, with both Seth and the driver in full view. The driver had a tough, athletic look about him. He wore a bushy beard and the kind of clothes worn by tactical operators of all stripes—and by countless classes of hangers on. Khaki shirt, forest green 5.11 Tactical pants, some kind of light boot or heavy tennis shoe. Jonathan had a couple dozen outfits that looked just like it. This did not look like a happy meeting.

"Gunslinger, can you hear anything?"

Her replay came in a whisper. "No."

Jonathan made a decision. "If he moves to hurt the kid, we move in to intervene."

Seth chatted with the driver for a solid minute, and as the meeting droned on, the boy's anxiety seemed to grow while the driver went through a spectrum of body language. At first suspicion, then followed by a posture of intimidation that made Jonathan nervous.

Jonathan repositioned himself to get a little closer. He didn't want to be so close that he'd be noticed, but close enough to intervene if the driver started whaling on the boy.

Seth reached into his pocket and handed the phone to the driver. Gail relayed that on the air.

"Definitely looks like Seth was a mule," Jonathan said. "Carrying the phone for the real bad guy."

Once the driver had his phone, he gave Seth another stern look, and then rumpled his hair and gave his shoulder a friendly smack.

"Looks like it's over," Gail said.

"Not yet," Jonathan countered. "Big Guy, whatever happens next, you stay on the truck. If the kid gets in, we'll hop in with you. If he doesn't, Slinger and I will follow the kid on foot, then catch up with you."

"Gonna be tough not to be noticed in a one-vehicle pursuit," Boxers said.

"I have every confidence," Jonathan replied. Big Guy didn't like it when the action got split. He liked to be a part of everything that went down everywhere.

As the driver climbed back into the truck's cab, Seth started walking back toward Gail.

Jonathan watched the pickup as it pulled out, and he said, "Big Guy, our target is turning left onto First Avenue. He's going to cross behind you."

"I'm on him," Boxers said.

Jonathan turned his attention back toward Seth. He walked quickly, but with his hands stuffed into the pockets of his windbreaker and his head held low. When he walked past Gail, he didn't even look up. Clearly, that was one distracted kid.

Seth walked to the spot where the alley met John Wayne Drive, and he stopped. He stood there on the sidewalk for a few seconds, then sat heavily on the curb and put his face in his hands.

"Hey Slinger, I think you should approach him first. He probably doesn't need any more trauma in his morning."

Seth had seen from the look in Tony's eyes that he knew something was wrong, and because Tony was Tony, Seth knew he was going to follow through with the awful things he had promised to do. All for a hundred goddamn bucks. As he pressed his hands into his face, he willed himself not to cry. Crying wouldn't accomplish anything.

He heard footsteps approaching from behind, but he didn't think anything of them until they stopped. He lifted his face from his hands and looked up to see a lady with a ponytail smiling down at him.

"Hi, Seth," she said as she squatted to take a seat next to him on the curb. "Are you okay?"

Seth didn't like her. He didn't know why, but something about her didn't seem right. It was time for him to go. He stood without answering, and as he did, he saw the guy from the mirror walking toward him, too.

"Please don't run," the lady said. Seth turned back to her and saw that she was holding up a gold badge. "FBI," she said.

Seth whirled again, and now the mirror guy was holding a badge.

The lady said, "Please take a seat. I promise that you're not in trouble. Yet."

Mirror guy was only a few yards away now. "This is my colleague, Agent Bonner," the lady explained. "I'm Agent Culp. We need to talk to you."

Seth's ears grew hot, and he imagined his eyes were turning red. As Agent Bonner drew near, he put a hand on Seth's shoulder and gently pressed down, trying to get him to sit again.

Seth spun away and jammed his hand wrist-deep into his pants pocket to grab the fistful of bills, and he thrust it toward the FBI guy. "Here," he said. "I don't want it anymore."

Agent Bonner smiled. "We don't want your money," he said. "We just want to talk. Please have a seat."

Seth had never been so scared—not even when he was approaching Tony's truck. His heart hammered in his ears, and his breakfast was again threatening to come back.

"Please," said Agent Culp, tapping the spot next to her on the curb. "We've got a few questions, is all. Ten minutes, tops. Then you can go."

"Am I under arrest?" Seth asked.

"No."

"Can I leave?"

"If you do, we'll have to arrest you," Agent Bonner said.

Seth knew he'd been beaten. He had no choice. Not anymore. He lowered himself to the curb, and Bonner sat down next to him. Seth was trapped now, with the others so close that if he tried to run they'd just grab him and pull him back.

"Let's start with what just happened," Agent Culp said.

"How did you know my name?" Seth asked.

Agent Culp gave a kind smile. "We're the FBI. Knowing things is what we do."

Seth knew that she was trying to be nice, but he wasn't having any of it. "It was just a phone," Seth said. He heard his voice crack with emotion, and that pissed him off. "What's wrong with answering the phone?"

"How did you get the phone?" Agent Bonner asked.

"He gave it to me."

"Who?"

"Tony."

"Who's Tony?"

"That guy in the truck."

Culp asked, "How did you come to know Tony?"

"He paid me a hundred dollars to sit in Carol's and answer the phone if it rang."

"Didn't that seem odd to you?" Agent Bonner asked.

"It was a hundred dollars!" Seth exclaimed. "Of course, it seemed odd. But the money was real, and who can't use a hundred bucks?"

"How did he find you?" Bonner asked. "Or, maybe how did you find each other?"

Seth explained, "I was on my way to school this morning, and he just drove up to me. Gave me the phone and a hundred bucks and told me to wait in the diner for a call. I'm not the only one he's asked. There've been rumors in school about the guy, but I never believed them."

Culp asked, "What were you supposed to do when you answered the phone?"

"Just listen and remember what I was told."

The agents looked at each other. They seemed to think he'd just said something important, but he had no idea what that might have been.

"How would that work?" Bonner asked. "I mean, if it rang and they told you XYZ, how would you get that information back to Tony?"

"I'd just walk it to him in his truck."

"And then what?"

Seth answered with a shrug.

"So, what did you tell him today?"

Seth felt his heart skip even faster. "Nothing," he said. Then he had another thought. "Is Tony the guy you're really looking for?"

"Yes," Culp said.

"What did he do?"

Bonner took this one. "That's none of your concern," he said.

Another piece fell into place for Seth. "Wait. Why haven't you asked me what they said to me on the phone?"

Another look between the two agents.

"That was you, wasn't it?" Seth guessed.

Agent Bonner took a big, deep breath. "It wasn't *us*, exactly, but it was part of our team. We knew that someone in there would have that phone, but we didn't know who it would be. We for sure didn't expect it to be you. A kid."

"Why do you need the phone?"

"Why didn't you tell Tony about the message you received?" Culp asked.

Seth looked down at the curb, at the space between his knees. "I guess I was scared," he said. "If he's doing something that would bring the FBI down on him, I didn't want him to know that I knew. I just wanted to be done with everything."

"So, you told him what?" Bonner pressed. "I mean, we saw you talking to him. What was that about?"

"I told him that the phone never rang. I'm not sure he believed me." Seth was surprised by how good it felt to come clean with all of this. "He promised to hurt me and my family if I ever told anybody about what I did."

Agent Culp tapped his knee. "Don't worry about that," she said. "You did the right thing," she said. "Now, go on to school." She stood, and so did Agent Bonner.

"One more thing," Bonner said. "If you had told Tony the truth, he probably would have killed you. From his perspective, he'd have no choice."

The words and the tone in which they were delivered were terrifying. Seth took a step back. "Seriously?"

"Seriously," Bonner said. "Keep that in mind next time somebody gives you a stupid amount of money to do something that doesn't seem right."

Jonathan wondered sometimes how children in general, but boys in particular, could be so stupid in adolescence yet still live long enough to become adults. Seth walked back down John Wayne toward the courthouse, but after maybe a dozen steps, he turned to address them.

"I have a question," he said.

"Go ahead," Jonathan replied.

"Does my mother have to know anything about this?"

Jonathan suppressed a smirk. "As long as you don't tell her, she doesn't have to know a thing."

That seemed to make him happy. He turned again and continued on his way.

"What do you make of all that?" Gail asked.

"Two things," Jonathan said. "One, that there are still active plans in the works, and two, that we need to get the car and join Boxers' car chase."

Chapter Seventeen

Earlham Road, like most roads in this part of the world, might have been laid out with a straight edge. Iowa was the land of the right-angle turn. Boxers had followed Tony—as if that were his real name—out to a modest farm about a mile and a half up Earlham Road from 210th Street, just a few miles from Winterset. Tilled and harvested land stretched endlessly in every direction, but gently rolling hills and thick, meandering lines of trees and undergrowth marked the pathway of streams and rivers.

Per Boxers' instructions, Jonathan drove the rental Ford Taurus about a quarter of a mile past the target house to a spot along the road that was fairly shielded by trees. When he and Gail arrived, they found Boxers at the rear of his vehicle, under the lift gate, studying the screen of his laptop.

"So, what do we know?" Jonathan asked as he approached. As he got closer, he saw that Boxers was watching an aerial view of a farmhouse.

"I launched Roxie while you were on your way,"

Boxers said, referring to the UAV—unmanned aerial vehicle, or drone—that had recently become an important part of their kit. Small and quiet, Roxie captured high-definition live photos and videos and, with Boxers at the controls, was capable of going just about anywhere they wanted to take her. The man literally could fly anything.

Boxers rotated his big frame out of the way to make room for the others. "Take a look."

The house in the video was an unremarkable two-story frame structure with porches in the front and the back. The white dually pickup sat in the driveway next to a blue Toyota Prius.

"Two vehicles," Gail observed.

"That means two people are home," Jonathan said.

Boxers pointed to the lower right corner of the screen. "There's more than that," he said. "A bicycle and a tricycle."

Jonathan checked his watch. "The kids should be at school," he said.

"Unless the one with the trike is too young," Boxers said.

Jonathan forced a wry chuckle. "That would be consistent with our luck so far. Have you dialed Mother Hen into this?"

"Yeah," Big Guy replied. "About ten minutes ago. She's researching the property and its owners."

"Did you actually see the driver pull in?" Gail asked.

"I saw him make the turn into the driveway. It's a long driveway, too. I was a couple hundred yards back, so when I crossed the apron, he was out of sight. That's one of the reasons why I wanted to get Roxie up in the air. Since I've been watching, no one has come in or out."

"Can you bring us in closer?" Jonathan asked.

Boxers worked the controls on his remote, and the image zoomed in to the twenty-foot range. From here, they could see details of window coverings and the dust that had accumulated on the sills.

"Give me a three-sixty tour," Jonathan said.

Boxers worked his magic, and the image moved in a large circle, revealing the locations of all the doors and windows and the fact that the building was an old one, from the 1940s at the latest. And not much had been done in the way of improvements.

"Doesn't look like entry will be difficult," Boxers said.

"The place looks like it would burn easily," Gail said.

Jonathan agreed. "And hot."

Jonathan's ear bud popped. "Scorpion, Mother Hen. Are you on the channel?"

He reached behind his left hip to press the transmit button on the radio on his belt. "Right here, Mother Hen. What have you got for us?"

"Are you still monitoring Big Guy's computer?" she asked.

"Affirm."

"Have him open up his encrypted chat window."

"I'm right here," Boxers said. He worked the keyboard and opened a second window. "Got it," he said.

The screen showed a happy family of four, mom, dad and two girls, smiling at the camera. "Any of these faces look familiar to you?" Venice asked.

The mom might have been American Indian, and she'd passed her dark hair and high cheekbones on to the girls. Dad could have been Swedish, blond on white with a thick neck and wary eyes. "The guy in the picture is the one who gave the kid the phone."

"Well, meet the Talley family," Venice said. "Angela and Eric, with daughters Maria and Angelina. He's former Army, a Green Beret, and she is a nurse at Madison County General Hospital. Specializes in pediatric emergencies. Their credit is terrible—low five hundreds—and they've got at least two mortgages on their farm. Neither of them has an arrest record, not even a traffic ticket."

"Not exactly the profile of a killer, is it?" Jonathan wondered aloud.

"Did we just stumble onto the motivation?" Gail asked. "He needs the money?"

"Half a million would do it," Boxers said.

Over the radio, Venice said, "Are you still there?"

Jonathan keyed his mic. "Sorry, Mother Hen, he said. "We were just thinking aloud. Mostly about motivation. But this is definitely the guy we saw."

Venice said, "I don't know what this means in the larger picture, but the record says he was dishonorably discharged. I have TickTock2 looking into the details. His record is sealed."

Boxers scowled at Jonathan. "Who?"

"The horny kid from the NSA," Jonathan reminded.

Gail slugged his arm. "Be nice."

"Are you making fun of our new team member?" Venice asked.

Jonathan keyed the mic. "Who, us? Hey, thanks for the intel, Mother. We'll let you know the plan when we have one." He looked to the others. "I think we have to go in."

"You mean break things and shoot stuff?" Boxers said with a grin. "I'm good with that."

Jonathan turned to Gail, on whom he depended for less lethal, more rational approaches.

"I think you're right," she said. "There's some kind of organized plan in the works, and this guy knows more about it than anyone else we're aware of. We need to take him out of the equation and learn what he can tell us."

"How do you want to do it?" Boxers asked.

"Fast and loud," Jonathan said. "We know he's got firearms and explosives, and we know he's not shy about using them. If we can get him before he has a chance to draw down, that's our best chance for not having to shoot him."

"Yeah, I'd hate to kill a terrorist," Boxers said.

"We need to know what he knows," Gail said.

"What makes you think he'll be willing to share anything?" Boxers asked.

"So far, we're one for one," Jonathan said.

"Well, if he points a gun at me, he's going to die," Boxers said.

"I worry about the wife and the kids," Gail said. "Background is really important on this one. That's old construction, and we don't know what's behind any of the walls."

Jonathan shifted gears to a more tactical view. "When we hit them, I want everybody in full armor, plates in their carriers. We'll combine into the Suburban. Box, you come in the back, Gail and I will come in through the front. No flashbangs. We don't know where he's storing his explosives, and we don't need a secondary detonation."

"We think that the wife is there," Gail said. "At *least* the wife. What do we do with her?"

"We don't know if she's part of the conspiracy or not," Jonathan said. "We handle her just like we handle him. If she poses a threat, respond to the threat."

"And if there's no threat from her?" Gail pressed.

"We zip-cuff her and leave her be," Jonathan answered. "When we're done, we'll contact Wolverine, and she can contact the locals to come in and clean up the mess."

"Shouldn't we be talking to Wolverine now?" Gail asked. "I mean, we know that he's one of the bad guys. We're going to screw up the evidence chain. There'll be practically no chance to get a conviction when they prosecute."

Boxers coughed out a bitter laugh. "There won't be any prosecutions for these assholes. They get nabbed, squeezed for information, and then given a dirt nap."

Jonathan thought Boxers was overstating the fate of Eric Talley, but not by much. Uncle Sam wanted this terror plot to go away as soon as possible.

Why the hell aren't the FBI here?

That thought coursed through Jonathan's mind as he was changing from his FBI haberdashery disguise into the tactical kit that he preferred. The thought startled him. Was it possible that the FBI was silently working against them while pretending to push them forward?

That would explain the attack on the prison house. And it would explain why the federal government, with all the resources that were available to them, didn't think of performing the same phone trick in the diner that Security Solutions had devised on its own.

Jonathan pulled one of the duffels closer, unzipped it, and lifted out the gun belt that would soon hold his Colt 1911 .45 on his right thigh and his H&K MP7 on his left. He'd done this so many times that his hands worked on their own. He racked a round into his M27 carbine, and set the safety.

As he was reaching for his ballistic vest, he shared his question with the others. "Am I missing something?"

"It's about warrants," Gail said without dropping a beat. "Everything we've done these last few days is against the law. If a fed tried it, he'd be fired and maybe prosecuted."

"So, we *are* being used," Boxers said as he pulled his vest over his head.

Jonathan bounced his shoulders a few times to get his own vest to seat comfortably. "Of course, we're being used," he said. "That's what we do when we're working for Uncle. Doing the shit that they can't do on their own."

"Everybody go to VOX," Jonathan said, flipping the switch on his radio. "Mother Hen, we're ready to roll."

"I copy," Venice replied.

Boxers said, "Mother Hen, I'm sending you the video feed from Roxie. Are you getting it?"

"Stand by." After a few seconds, Venice came back

with, "I'm very proud of you, Big Guy. Maybe someday you can teach your boss how to use a computer."

"That's why I have staff," Jonathan said.

Boxers explained, "I've set her to hover over the farmhouse. If she runs out of juice, she'll return to the controller."

The availability to use UAV technology had revolutionized much of Jonathan's business. Not that long ago, they needed to tap into satellite feeds to get a bird's-eye view of a target—and sometimes that was still necessary—but with Roxie, they could go pretty much everywhere and see everything before exposing flesh and blood to danger.

"Final safety check," Jonathan said. Boxers had his 7.62-millimeter H&K 417 slung across his chest and an H&K 45 tactical pistol on his thigh. Gail's preferred loadout was an M27 like Jonathan's but with a nine-millimeter Glock 19 as her sidearm. All wore Kevlar ballistic helmets and vests, the latter with "FBI" emblazoned on the front and back.

"We're good to go," Jonathan said. "Big Guy, try to drive quietly into the driveway. Let's not spark a panic if we don't have to."

Boxers parked the Suburban directly behind the Talleys' vehicles to slow down any exfil plans they might have. As he threw the transmission into PARK, he said, "Give me thirty seconds to get in position at the back door, and say the word."

Jonathan and Gail glided as silently as possible up the porch steps. He carried a battering ram, and she carried a Halligan bar in case the entry got complicated. Jonathan positioned himself on the knob side of the front door on the right while Gail took the hinge side. In the back, if Boxers was true to form, his entry tool for a house of this era would be the sole of his boot.

"I'm set," Boxers said over the air.

Jonathan said, "On my count. Three . . . two . . . one . . ." On the silent *zero*, Jonathan heaved the ram into the spot where the lock's hasp met the jamb. The wood splintered and disappeared under the impact. The reverberation shook the whole structure to its foundation. He released his grip and let the ram's momentum carry it airborne into the living space. Gail dropped her Halligan onto the porch deck at her feet and brought her rifle to her shoulder.

With his rifle at high ready, Jonathan crossed the threshold and swept his muzzle left. He ignored the back door as it exploded open and Big Guy stepped in.

"FBI!" Jonathan yelled. "Federal agents! Down, down, down!" Boxers and Gail shouted the same words, with the effect sounding damned intimidating.

He'd taken only three steps into the room when he saw through the dining room that Angela Talley was standing frozen in the kitchen. She looked terrified.

"One in the kitchen," Jonathan reported to the others on the channel. "Angela Talley, put your hands up and drop to your knees!"

She complied, but she wasn't the one he wanted.

"Where is Eric?" Jonathan shouted.

"I'm right here," a voice said from somewhere ahead and to the left.

"Show yourself with empty hands," Jonathan commanded.

Angela said from her awkward position on the floor, "What's going on?"

Jonathan ignored her. "We've got this in here, Big Guy," he said. "Cover the green side in case he tries to rabbit out a window."

"Eric, show yourself now. Don't make this any worse than it needs to be." As he spoke, Jonathan sidestepped oh so slowly to his right—cutting the pie, as they liked to say in his business—to gain a visual on his target.

"I've got eyes on him through the window," Boxers said. "He's standing against a wall of cabinets, inside and to your left. I can't see his hands."

"Don't be stupid, Eric," Jonathan coaxed. "This doesn't have to end in tragedy."

Finally, Eric Talley stepped into Jonathan's field of view. He held a knife in his right hand. It looked like a six-inch carver, the kind that you'd expect to pull from a kitchen knife block.

"He's got a knife," Jonathan announced. "Put that down, Eric. Don't bring a knife to a gunfight."

"I can't do what you want me to do," Eric said. His tone was matter-of-fact, yet amped with emotion.

Angela stood again.

"Get down!" Jonathan ordered.

"Shoot me," she said. To her husband: "Eric? What the hell?"

The man's eyes showed no fear, and that bothered Jonathan. What bothered him more was that they showed commitment. Something bad was about to happen.

"What's going on, Eric?" Jonathan asked. "Don't make me shoot you in your own house. In front of your wife. Just put the knife down."

"I've got a reticle on his ear, Boss," Boxers said.

"Don't shoot yet," Jonathan instructed. "He's still too far away to pose a real threat."

"I'm tellin' you just in case," Boxers said.

Jonathan didn't respond. He kept his sights locked on Eric as Gail crossed behind him to open up yet another shooting lane.

"Come on, Eric. It's over."

"*What's* over?" Angela snapped. The frustration had converted her voice to a squeak.

"I'm sorry, Angie," Eric said. He looked straight at Jonathan as he brought the point of the knife up to the side of his own throat, and then used the palm of his left hand to punch the blade all the way through the other side of his neck. His knees buckled, but on his way down, he pulled the knife free with a slicing motion that launched a fountain of gore.

"Holy shit!" Jonathan yelled.

Angela screamed, "Oh, my God! Oh, my God! Eric!" She turned on Jonathan like an angry dog and launched herself at him. "What did you do!"

He felled her with a single punch, and she hit the floor hard, clearly unconscious.

"Tie her hands behind her," Jonathan instructed.

Gail objected. "Oh, come on, Scorpion."

"Please do what I say. This is some of the weirdest shit I've ever been involved with, and as far as I'm concerned, she's part of the problem. Mother Hen, our target just cut his own throat."

As Boxers reentered the kitchen, he drew to a stop. "Oh, holy Christ."

If a stopped heart truly defines death, then it took Eric Talley at least thirty seconds to die, with each ventricular contraction launching a crimson streamer into the air. The first six pumps or so hit the ceiling, but then it dwindled to a flow and finally stopped. When it was over, the kitchen had a macabre Jackson Pollack vibe to it. Jonathan stomach churned when he realized that the air itself tasted like copper.

"Okay, kids," Jonathan said. "We take ten minutes to scour this place for whatever we can find, and then we get the hell out of here."

"What about her?" Gail asked as she rose from the task of cuffing Angela.

"We'll call Wolverine when we're on the road, and she can figure out what to do from there."

Eight minutes into their burglary, Angela Talley regained consciousness. The screaming was awful.

Chapter Eighteen

As Jonathan swung his BMW M6 from Ox Road into the main entrance of Burke Lake Park, he reminded himself of the least likely advice he'd received from the least likely source. On his way to his car, Boxers had warned him not to lead with his anger. So saith the monster of a man who woke up angry and got steadily crankier during the day.

The ticket taker had abandoned his station, so Jonathan forewent the ten-dollar admission fee for out-of-county residents and piloted his M6 down the lake road and into the woods. A thousand years ago, as a little boy, he'd attended a fire service event here at the park, courtesy of the guys at the Fisherman's Cove Fire Department, who'd allowed him to be their firehouse mascot after his mother died. He didn't remember much about the place beyond a miniature train that he thought was fantastic and an old-fashioned merry-go-round with a brass ring dispenser that he couldn't quite reach.

This would be a new venue for meeting Wolverine.

Jonathan was too pissed to drive all the way into DC, and according to Dom, Irene was too pissed to put the meeting off. She was the one who proposed meeting here, a spot near her house. A later phone call established the specific picnic pavilion number where they'd meet.

The leaves were at the height of their autumn splendor, the thermometer on his dash said it was sixty-two degrees outside, and if this had been a different day, he'd probably have thought it was beautiful. For now, it was hard to see any color but red.

The pavilion sat by itself, about twenty yards off the road, surrounded by trees. Jonathan was the first to arrive, but he was ten minutes early. He parked the BMW, climbed out, and walked to the picnic tables. There were at least a dozen of them spread a comfortable distance apart, about half of them under the protection of a wooden pole barn roof with no walls. He could imagine this as a great venue for a family reunion, provided you could see past the spiderwebs and bird shit.

The woods provided lots of shade, and if you squinted just right and cocked your head a little, you could see the glitter of the sun off the surface of the lake itself.

The sound of crunching gravel drew his attention to an official Washington black Suburban with the requisite black Suburban follow car pulling down the access road. The Tweedle brothers stepped out of the front doors, while two other security pukes flanked the follow car. With that phalanx in place, Tweedle Dee (or was it Dum?) opened the rear door, and Irene Rivers climbed out. She was dressed for a work day in a gray business suit. Her hair was tied back in a ponytail, and her eyes showed murder.

She strode toward Jonathan with the intensity of a torpedo homing in on a destroyer. When she'd closed to within ten feet, she said, "Have you lost your mind? What were you thinking?"

"Don't lead with your anger," Jonathan said. "A friend of mine told me that once."

"Don't you even," Irene growled. "Do you have any idea the position you've put me in? The position you've put the *Bureau* in?"

"You're talking about the Winterset thing?" Sometimes, Jonathan enjoyed the simple thrill of pulling her strings.

"You're goddamn right, I'm talking about the Winterset thing. Was there anyone in the town you didn't tell that you were FBI?"

"Really?" Jonathan said. He felt his own anger control system beginning to fail. "With all the shit that's gone down in the last couple of days, you're most worried about a public relations problem?"

"You harassed a thirteen-year-old boy, Digger! And you knocked a woman unconscious after attending the horrific death of her husband. Let's not forget the cherry on top of the poo sundae: you tied her up while she was unconscious."

Jonathan cast a nervous glance toward Irene's guard dogs. "Let's use our inside voices, okay, Wolfie? First of all, that kid was a witness and a potential victim. Second, I had nothing to do with Eric Talley's death, and third, zipping up the wife was standard procedure.

I did nothing that you would not have done in the field."

Irene smacked the picnic table with an open hand. "But I'm *actually* an FBI agent!"

"I didn't steal my creds, Wolfie. You gave them to me with instructions to make this Retribution thing go away."

Some of the wind left the director's sails. "Retribution?"

"Yeah. This terrorist op has a name. They're calling it Retribution."

"Retribution for what?"

"I have no idea," Jonathan said. "Maybe there wasn't enough foam in his latte one morning. And by the way, the reason we know that tidbit is because we were able to rescue Logan Masterson from the guys you sent to kill us. Let's talk about that for a moment, shall we?"

Irene's sails faltered a bit further. "Our people were *victims* of that attack."

"Boo-hoo," Jonathan said. "I mean no disrespect, but . . . No, I take that back. They were running a torture chamber, so I do mean disrespect. We left some extra bodies for you to examine. What has that shown?"

Irene motioned with her head for Jonathan to follow her toward the woods. "They're all former military," she said. "Special Forces types."

"How are they linked?"

"We don't know that yet."

"Let me give you something to look at," Jonathan said. "I guarantee that all of their credit scores are in the crapper. I think we're looking at a mercenary army that's doing what it's doing for the paycheck. Masterson told us he got half a million for the high school hit. Talley's farm was in trouble. And how the hell did that assault team in South Dakota know to hit the prison?"

That last question startled Irene, made her jump. Her face was uncharacteristically blank. Jonathan couldn't tell if she was trying to construct a bluff or if she'd been genuinely taken off guard.

"Come on, Wolfie," Jonathan said. "This can't be the first time you've thought about this. You've got a major leak somewhere in your system. I don't know if it's your Bureau or the Agency, but somewhere people are talking, and the talking is posing a threat to me and my team."

Irene seemed to deflate. "This isn't our first rodeo together, Dig. You know I've always been plagued with leaks. When I plug one, another springs open. I try to limit the sphere of knowledge to as small a crew as possible, but I can't do my job if I keep *everybody* out of the loop." She grew uncomfortable as she cleared her throat and asked, "How certain are you that the leak isn't from your shop?"

"One hundred percent," Jonathan said. "And I know this because most of my team were the ones getting shot at."

"And Mother Hen has a crush on you," Irene added. "It must be nice to be surrounded by loyal team members."

The image of Derek Halstrom in his ridiculous too-tight suit appeared in Jonathan's mind. He pushed it aside to stay on point.

"You know, Wolfie, a question came up among my team that I didn't have an answer for, and I confess that it troubles me."

Irene arched an eyebrow and waited for it.

"How come my loyal little team is smarter than the entire intelligence and law enforcement apparatus of the United States government?"

"I have no idea what you're talking about," Irene said, and her expression doubled down on her confusion.

"We tracked down Eric by tracing his cell phone. Why didn't you guys think to do that?"

She smiled. "Honestly? Because I was hoping you'd think to do it. Your methods are so much faster and easier."

"What if we'd failed?"

"Then the Bureau would have had to do it the old-fashioned way. You know, following all that Fourth and Fifth Amendment stuff. The framers never foresaw what we're living through. I think there's a civil war coming, and anger levels across the country are so high that I don't know that we can stop it. If my team and I go all Wild West on these assholes and deliver old-fashioned justice, we dead-end at the courthouse and go to jail."

"The same place I will go if I get caught," Jonathan observed.

Irene gave him a playful slap on his shoulder. "That's why you get the big bucks," she said as she reached into her jacket pocket. "I have something for you here." She handed him a thumb drive.

"Oh, Wolfie, you shouldn't have. And I didn't get you anything."

"Take it to Mother Hen and let her loose on it."

"What is it?"

"It's a direction for you to go."

"How about more of a hint that that?" Jonathan said. "It's been a long few days. Coyness is less appreciated than usual."

Irene winked at him. "I'm giving you a face. Not much of one, but it's a face."

"Of a terrorist?"

"Yup."

"Why aren't you guys pursuing him?"

"We are," she said.

"Then why do you need me?"

"Because, for reasons previously discussed, I'd rather you find him first."

Jonathan didn't like the implication of her words. "I'm not an assassin, Irene. I've told you that before."

"I'm not saying you are. But I'm fairly certain that when you come eye to eye with him, he'll give you reason to shoot."

Two hours later, as the sun was nearly done with its daily journey, Jonathan and the team sat in the War Room, watching the screen as Venice waded through the files on Irene's thumb drive. So far, it remained blank.

"You know we're waiting, right?" Boxers grumbled.

"You know that being snarky doesn't make me go any faster, right?" Venice grumbled back.

"The information is more important than the reveal, Ven," Jonathan said. "If we've got a face and a name—"

"Do you think I'm stalling you?" Venice snapped. "Do you think I am unaware of the time crunch here? I know as well as you that lives are at stake, and I'd like to believe that you had enough faith in me to understand that."

Jonathan caught Gail's glance, and she twitched her head. This was not the time to push.

So, they waited.

Finally after thirty minutes that felt like ninety, Venice gave her keyboard a final, triumphant poke, and the big screen at the end of the conference table jumped to life. The first image was fuzzy at best. Clearly lifted from some kind of enhanced security camera footage, it showed what appeared to be a man in nondescript clothing stepping away from a plain white van.

"This is from Bluebird, Indiana," Venice explained. "One of the bombing sites. The FBI believes that this is the van that held the explosives."

"And that the blur is the guy who set them?" Boxers asked.

"Exactly. Now, take a look at this." The screen changed to reveal what appeared to be a parking lot. An attendant's booth occupied the foreground, and behind it they could see a swath of dormant emergency vehicles.

"This is the parking lot for the city administrative building in Bluebird," Venice explained.

"Why are the pictures so blurry?" Gail asked. "Even by security camera standards, these are awful."

Jonathan said, "I'm going to guess that all the close-in cameras were destroyed by the explosion."

"Exactly," Venice confirmed. "That's in the case notes. According to the time stamp, this picture was shot about thirty minutes before the blast. Can you see our bomber there in the lot?"

It took some imagination, but someone was clearly walking through the lot. Jonathan was willing to stipulate that it was the person the Feebs declared him to be.

The screen images changed about once per second for the next few frames, showing the blurry man approaching the guard booth in a kind of jerky animation.

"Here's where it gets strange," Venice said. "This bomber has set God only knows how many pounds of explosives to kill dozens of people and destroy a sleepy little town, but watch this."

The blurry man, who was more in focus than he'd been, stopped at the attendant booth.

"There," Venice said, pointing. "He's talking to . . ." She referred to her notes. "Grant Duncan. That's the parking lot attendant. Now, look at this."

The picture changed to the same angle, but showing devastation. The attendant booth was shredded and scattered over a wide swath of parking lot. "This is that same spot just a few minutes later."

"Duncan was killed?" Gail asked.

"You'd think so, wouldn't you?" Venice said with a knowing smile.

The picture went back to the suspect and Grant Duncan.

"I've jumped back to the timeline," Venice explained. "Mr. Duncan lived to speak to the police about this," Venice explained. "That's how we know that this man—the one he's talking with in the picture—told him that it was unsafe to stand where he was while standing in the booth. He told him to seek safety somewhere."

"He *warned* the guy?" Jonathan asked.

"Yes," Venice confirmed. "How does that make sense?"

"Maybe they knew each other," Gail suggested. "Maybe they were coconspirators."

"The FBI is wondering that, too," Venice said. "But so far, as of the date of these files, they haven't been able to find a link. There's more."

The picture on the screen switched to show parallel rows of neat little houses lining a residential street. Again, the magnification on the images made them fuzzy.

"Keep watching the right side," Venice said as she clicked through the images. "There," she said, pointing. "That guy on the sidewalk is the same one who parked the truck and talked with Mr. Duncan."

"Where's he going?" Boxers asked.

"Wait for it," Venice replied. The man turned right—his left—and walked to the front door of one of the cookie-cutter houses.

"Oh, my God," Gail breathed. "He's a local?"

"Renter," Venice said. "Rented the place for three months, starting two weeks ago."

"Please tell me he paid by credit card," Jonathan said.

"No such luck. Keep watching." On the right, in the top half of the screen, another figure was visible approaching the house. "Look familiar?"

"That's the parking lot guy," Gail said. "Danby."

"Duncan," Venice corrected. "He told the FBI that when our bomber— Remember, he didn't know yet that it was going to be a bomb—"

"Pretty good bet, given what he was told," Jonathan said.

"Fair enough," Venice conceded, "but he maintains he didn't know yet. What he figured was, if the area itself was unsafe, by following the guy who told him, he'd end up in a place that was. Sort of by definition."

"Does he go inside?" Boxers asked.

"Keep watching."

"Oh, for Christ's sake, Ven, this isn't a goddamn movie. You're allowed to give away the ending."

Venice didn't flinch. It was as if Big Guy had never spoken.

"A few minutes pass here in the timeline," Venice explains. "Duncan just stands there. Except there. Looks like he thought about getting closer, maybe to look into a window, but then he changes his mind."

Between two of the stills, the garage door on the target house switched from closed to open, but Duncan remained on the sidewalk. "Here you'll see a car backing out of the driveway," Venice said, and that's exactly what happened.

"According to his testimony to police, Duncan didn't know what to do when he made eye contact with the bomber because the bomber specifically told him not to follow. Now watch."

The sedan cleared the apron of the driveway and started driving toward the camera.

"Grant got left behind," Boxers said.

"More than that," Venice said. "Keep watching."

Four frames later, the house from which the sedan had just pulled away erupted in a ball of fire that obscured their view of Grant Duncan.

"Holy shit," Boxers said.

Venice kept advancing the slides. The sedan had exited the bottom of the frame, and as the fireball lifted, Grant Duncan was revealed on his hands and knees.

"Doesn't look like he was hurt," Gail observed.

Venice said nothing as she continued to advance the slides. Four or five images later, the distant background lit up. After that, they watched an eruption of debris. "That was the main bomb," Venice said.

"So, who's our guy?"

"I passed this on to Derek," Venice said. "He ran the images through really advanced state-of-the-art facial recognition software."

"Dammit, Ven," Jonathan said, "I wish you wouldn't do that without talking to me first."

"Because you're the technology expert?"

"Because I'm president of the company." Jonathan cringed at his own words.

"I didn't realize we were quite so structured," Gail said.

Jonathan pointed to the screen. "Keep going, please."

"Thank you. And for what it's worth, I think you'll be interested in the results. In fact, Derek just sent me this."

The screen switched to the discernable face and shoulders of a white man in his thirties with dark hair and a goatee. Thick of neck and shoulders, he had that same operator look that they had seen with the others.

"Is that our man?" Jonathan asked.

"According to Derek, it is. Thanks to facial recognition technology that only certain people in certain jobs can obtain."

"That's Ven being subtle," Boxers said with a grin. "In case you didn't get that."

She shot Big Guy a look that was not entirely disapproving and continued. "Given that there are seven billion people on the planet and the enhancement process sometimes emphasizes clarity over accuracy—"

"God*damm*it!" Boxers boomed.

"I'm *reading* what Derek just sent me!" Venice boomed back. "You can sit in silence while I break it down, digest it, and reprocess the information like I usually do, or you can sit in silence and listen to me read. Which do you want?"

Jonathan had rarely seen her so spun up, and it kind of scared him. Boxers was on his own in this fight.

Big Guy grew uncomfortable, and he cleared his throat. "I was out of line," he said. "I'm sorry."

Jesus, hell's frozen over and pigs are flying, Jonathan thought. Boxers just apologized.

"Then quit being such an asshole," Venice said.

Jonathan shot a look to Gail, who seemed as startled as he. Mother Hen *never* cussed.

She went back to reading her screen. "Duh, duh, duh, 'sometimes emphasizes clarity over accuracy, a total of twelve people in the NSA database meet the ninetieth percentile probability that this picture is them. But given circumstances and known information, the most likely identity of the man in the picture is former SF operator Fred Kellner, originally of Hattiesburg, Mississippi.' "

When Venice fell silent this time, no one said a word. If only for his own safety, Jonathan was willing to wait for as long as it would take for her to resume. During the silence, he watched her retreat into what he'd come to call Veniceland, where all that mattered to her was the research thread she was chasing.

After ten minutes of typing and scowling, she once again offered her keyboard a triumphant poke with her finger, and the screen filled with a picture of a younger version of the man in the enhanced photograph. This man was a little skinnier, but still heavily muscled, and he was dressed in a Class A Army uniform with a green beret cocked oh-so-precisely on his head. His lapel insignia showed him to be a staff sergeant, and his beret flash showed him to be a part of a Special Forces Group.

"Meet Frederick Kellner," Venice said. "In the interest of time, I'll skip over the early life details and the ins and outs of his military service. Cutting to the chase, he and Uncle Sam parted ways in other-than-honorable ways, and now he has a credit score in the low-five hundreds." She looked up. "Sounds like a match to me."

Jonathan liked it. Not a sure thing by any means, but in his line of work few things ever were. "Okay," he said. "Frederick Kellner it is. How do we find him?"

Venice beamed. "As of a few minutes ago, every security camera at every ATM, library, gas station, light pole, and every other place whose feed is run or monitored through cyberspace is actively looking for the man who meets that description."

Jonathan's jaw dropped. "We can do that?"

"No," Venice said. "*We* can't do anything like that. But we know people who can."

"But the NSA can't surveil people in the United States," Gail said.

"Obviously, they can," Jonathan replied.

Venice explained, "What they *can't* do is use the results of that surveillance to prosecute the surveilled."

"This is all fruit from the poisonous tree," Gail said. "None of the evidence that follows finding Kellner through these methods can be used against him in court."

"I'll tell Wolfie about this and let her decide what to do about it," Jonathan said. "But she made it pretty clear to me that there's literally zero expectation that this prosecution will ever make it to the courthouse steps."

Boxers rumbled out a laugh. "God, I love this job."

Chapter Nineteen

Arthur Evers watched out the window of his U Street apartment in Northwest Washington as he rubbed moisturizer into the stump of his leg, and he mulled just how much his life would soon change. And how he'd gotten to this terrible, wonderful spot.

He'd never owned much of what most Americans considered to be important in their lives. He grew up in Belle Vernon, Pennsylvania, the son of a union welder who was blinded by an explosion at work when little Artie was only seven. The injury rendered the old man pretty much useless to the rest of the family, so Mom picked up the slack working two jobs at a time. Dad's drinking didn't help. Looking back, it was hard for Evers to remember a day when his father didn't wake up drunk and go to bed drunker.

The Army was supposed to be Evers's big break—his chance for a reset, and for a while the world felt right. In fact, it felt right for nearly eighteen years.

Evers was all-in. There wasn't a shithole in the world that he hadn't visited and spilled blood in—both his own and that of his enemies—and he made it his quest to be as close to the point of the spear as he could be. As he closed in on sergeant major's stripes, his soldiers liked him, his senior officers respected him, and his junior officers feared him, just as they should.

And then he shot himself.

It was a stupid mistake holstering his Beretta M9 pistol without decocking it. He wasn't even done with the weapon yet. He just needed to free his hands to look at a map, and the trigger snagged on the waist adjustment cord for the hoodie he was wearing, and in that microsecond, everything got derailed.

Normally, a leg wound from a nine-millimeter pistol wasn't a big deal. They hurt like hell, and you could bleed out if a major blood vessel were hit, but in the grand scheme of war wounds, they were usually minor league. Not so for Evers's wound. The bullet he fired entered at the back of his thigh and tumbled through the length of his right leg to exit three millimeters above his ankle. On the way, it shredded his posterior tibial artery, the distal end of his sciatic nerve, and pretty much the entirety of his tibial nerve. It was a one-in-a-million shot.

His team called a medevac, and he was on an operating table within ninety minutes of being wounded, but there wasn't enough useful structure to save. Thus, the stump and the damnable prosthetic peg leg.

Looking back, he supposed he could have stayed in the Army, but what would be the point? If there was one immutable commandment never to be broken in the U.S. Armed Forces, it was "Thou shalt never shoot thyself nor thy fellow troops." A close corollary applied to senior noncommissioned officers: "Thou shalt never make an idiotic, high-profile mistake in front of thy troops." Even as he fell to the sandy ground, he knew that he'd ended his career. And rightfully so.

Hard to believe that five years had passed since then. After he separated from the service, he was able to milk his injury to qualify for 8A status for some deskbound security contracting work, but that never floated his balloon.

His consuming passion in that time evolved into navigating the nightmare that was the Veterans Affairs benefits office. Weeks would pass between requests and responses, and all too often the eventual answer would be no. No, he couldn't have more pain meds. No, he couldn't qualify for an upgraded prosthesis. No, they didn't give a shit about how much of his life he'd devoted to the cause of promoting America's freedom.

Evers saw a lot of his old man in himself as he drank progressively more, and the irony was not lost on him. They say it's a bad idea to drink and type, but Evers was never much of a rule follower. He spent hours every night—tens of hours every week—posting on various internet sites that promoted vets' venting of grievances about the shoddy way that Uncle Sam treated his soldiers after they were no longer useful trigger-pullers.

Some of the posts were wildly off-the-wall, and Evers understood that many of his own posts walked too close to the line that separated truth from lie, but those communities grew to be his family. Those were his new troops—his new cadre of guys who got it.

Explorations of the Dark Web were the natural next steps in his explorations of anger, and soon he found himself in places where he knew he didn't belong. Jihadist sites, but in English. His distaste for American bureaucracy had never approached hatred for the country itself. He thought himself immune to such beliefs, and it was his confidence in the American Way that emboldened him to read what the Jihadis had to say. Hell, he'd killed enough of them over the years. Maybe the least he owed them was a ready ear (ready eye?) for their point of view.

What he found were people in pain, people who'd lost family members to drones and air strikes that they'd never seen coming. Many of the angry posters were Americans here on U.S. soil whose extended families remained in the Sandbox, unable to escape in time to save their own lives.

Intellectually, Evers understood that much of what appeared on the screen was entirely fabricated, specifically designed to foment anger, but at a more intimate level, he saw where they were coming from. He saw that he, as a soldier in the United States Army, was the cause for their suffering, or at least a part of it.

When a child lost a parent or a parent lost a child, the geopolitical justifications were all bullshit. The loss was personal, and the desire for revenge—no, the *need* for revenge—trumped every other element of the equation. While he was in the shit, Evers had never allowed himself to think of the humanity associated with the missions he accomplished for his commanders. They were merely orders to be obeyed.

Then there were the friends we tossed aside in theater. The moment a source had been exploited to its maximum capacity, we turned our backs and walked away, all too often leaving them and their families to the rabid wolves that were ISIS and the Taliban. It was a despicable thing to do. No wonder their world hated our world so much.

Another irony not lost on Evers was the fact that he himself had been so readily abandoned by his beloved military. They might not have liked how he received his injury, but as far as he was concerned, there was no denying that it was sustained in service to God and country. But his chain of command saw only the embarrassment of it all.

What, exactly, was a combat arms noncom supposed to do with his life after being tossed aside without prep work for his résumé? How was he supposed to make a living? Yeah, there were consulting gigs, but let's not kid each other. The revenue from those jobs just kept the lights on, they didn't provide a lifestyle. Even combined with his disability pay—much of which went to private doctors because he couldn't stand the wait to be seen by VA docs—he barely stayed afloat.

Evers was willing to admit that he wasn't solely a victim in his current state. Beyond the self-inflicted nature of his injury, there were a couple of bad business decisions—the least wise of which was a calamitous gambling trip to Atlantic City—but desperate people did desperate things, right? And he was on painkillers when he lost it all.

He understood this stuff about anger. And abandonment. And betrayal.

So, he came clean. In one long stream-of-consciousness rant on a Jihadi message board, he let the frustration flow. He mentioned no names, but he wrote about some of the missions he'd run and some of the people he'd killed. He made it clear that he respected the commitment of the warriors he'd killed and that he understood the anger that propelled the discourse on the site.

The response surprised him. He expected to be cursed and trolled out of the community—and there were some attempts at that—but by and large the community embraced him for his honesty and expressed admiration for his own commitment to duty. To be sure, some of those posters were FBI agents posing as Jihadis, so much of the praise needed to be taken in context.

He needed to disappear off the grid for a while after that, just in case. He didn't know of any law he might have broken, but these days, with that useless Tony Darmond sitting in the White House, anyone could snoop on everyone. Evers wondered sometimes if this was how things started in 1938 Berlin. Don't like the opposing party? Send the IRS after them. Don't like a news report? Name the reporter as a coconspirator in a felony.

About six months ago, he learned that no one is ever truly off the grid.

He was at a friend's fishing cabin on the edge of Shenandoah National Park when he saw a guy in a blue parka approaching him through the woods. This guy wasn't a wanderer. He walked with purpose, as if he were a magnet and Evers were a hunk of iron.

As he thought back on it, Evers remembered how his warning radar had pinged in his head. The man who had targeted him was wearing too much coat for the temperature of the day, and Evers had ventured all the way out to the edge of the water without a weapon. He supposed a few fishhooks and a fileting knife could save his life in the pinch, but only if the new guy didn't know what he was doing.

The man in the blue jacket was still fifty yards away when he waved his arms and yelled, "Hello, friend! Do not worry about me. I am not here to hurt."

Evers had heard the same Pakistani accent—if not the same voice—thousands of times over the years. "Do I know you?"

Blue Man had stopped his approach. "No, Mister Arthur Evers, but we will soon be friends."

"I've got enough friends." Evers didn't like the guy's approach, didn't trust him.

"Suppose I can make you a very rich man?"

Evers launched a laugh. "You a Nigerian prince with nineteen million dollars you've got to get rid of?"

Blue Man looked confused. "No, I am not Nigerian."

Interesting way he put that. "But you've got the nineteen million?"

Blue Man's face didn't change much. "Can we please sit and talk? My business is not the kind that should be shouted."

Evers reeled in his line, put his rod down on a deadfall, and turned uphill to head back to the cabin. Without looking back, he beckoned for Blue Man to follow.

The cabin had a dead bolt on the door, but if there was a key, Evers had never seen it. Presumably one was not needed out here, at least until such time as bears figured out how to turn knobs and pull doors open. Inside, the place was . . . *rustic*. No running water, but he had plenty of kerosene and firewood. A tiny gas-powered generator provided enough electricity for a dorm fridge and a toaster oven. Other cooking was done on the woodstove that doubled as his central heating system. He enjoyed the isolation.

Which was why he was not keen on having a stranger stop by.

Blue Man was still outside when Evers snagged his little SIG Sauer P365 off the drainboard and slipped it into the pocket of his jeans. Next, he pulled two Bud Lites out of the fridge, stripped the cap off one, and had the other at the ready for Blue Man when he crossed the threshold.

The visitor stopped just beyond the doorjamb and held up his hands as if to surrender. "I think you know that my religion does not allow alcohol," he said. His tone sounded light. If he took offense, he didn't show it.

"Well, you know we Americans aren't allowed to make assumptions about such things anymore. Trigger warnings and all that."

Blue Man looked confused again.

"Never mind," Evers said. "Say your piece."

"May we sit down?"

"Nope. For all I know, you're some Jihadi assassin here to kill me. I want some maneuvering room if it comes to that."

"Of course. My name is Amal Al-Faisel. I come from Pakistan to make you a very rich man."

Evers's gut tumbled. "Oh, God," he said. "The proverbial nineteen million."

"Only eight, I am afraid," Amal said. His face showed only earnestness. "May we sit now?"

And so it began. Amal and some unnamed associates had drilled down on Evers from his board posts.

The opportunity he offered could not have been simpler: terrorism by proxy, to be codenamed Retribution. For the sum of eight million dollars, Evers would manage all aspects of launching exactly three multifocal simultaneous mass killings. All the killers would have to be American, and all attacks needed to carried out in Middle America, where complacency ruled. The body counts needed to be high, but the absolute value of hearts stopped mattered less than the elegance and thoroughness of the execution.

Amal's presentation took fewer than ten minutes to deliver, and when the man was done, Evers stared back at him. He literally did not know what to say.

"I need you to agree," Amal said.

"I don't know that I'm ready to do that," Evers said.

Amal groaned. "That's troubling," he said. "Having laid this out, I don't know how I could walk away without a deal."

"You want to kill me?" Evers said. He stood. "Give it your best shot. We'll see whose body gets fed to the coyotes."

Amal threw back his head and laughed. It was a hearty, phlegmy thing. "I love you Americans and your swagger. You all learned to speak by watching Bruce Willis movies."

"That's a lot of talk in the middle of a fight, Mister Amal."

"Sit, sit, sit," Amal said. "I am not here to fight you. Nor will I engage in a fight if it starts." He leaned in. "If I'm being honest, I am not very good at fighting with my hands." Then, as an afterthought, he added, "Or with guns."

Evers waited for the rest.

"Sit back down, Arthur. I promise you that there will be no violence here today."

"I can't make that same promise," Evers said.

Amal continued pointing at Evers's chair with an open palm. "Please hear me out."

Evers didn't like it. To make his position clear, he removed the SIG from his pocket as he sat and rested the pistol on his knee. Muzzle pointed to a neutral spot, his finger off the trigger.

"Here's how this works, and why you will say yes to getting rich. I'm going to reach into my pocket now, so don't shoot." Amal moved very slowly as he unzipped his parka and withdrew a manila mailing envelope. It had no markings that Evers could see. Amal dangled the envelope with two fingers from its corner as he handed it over.

"What is this?" Evers asked. It felt like paper.

"Good old-fashioned photographs, I'm afraid." He waited until Evers was pulling out the contents to expound, "I'll bet you can guess what you're about to see. Your brother and your sister, their respective spouses, and their collective eight beautiful children."

Evers felt his bowels rumble. "Why are you showing me these?"

Amal gave him a coy smile and wagged his finger at him playfully. "You're not a stupid man, First Sergeant Arthur Evers. You know why I show these to you, but I suppose it's fair that you want to assume nothing. Very well. If you do not perform your mission as directed, these are the people who will die at the hands of my compatriots, and they will die with all the imagination that the West has come to expect from my part of the world. Surely, you have seen the videos."

Oh, God, yes, he'd seen them. Heads sawed off with dull knives. People burned alive. People drowned in cages.

Evers said nothing as he slid the pictures back into the envelope and handed them back.

"No," Amal said. "I think you should keep them. Look at them whenever you need encouragement to continue."

"I . . . I don't understand why you want me to do this. Why don't you do the killing yourselves with all the flair you want?"

Amal stood. "Because I want you to do it," he said. "I'm paying for a service. You do not need to know why." He took a huge breath. "I need you to decide. Two beautiful families await your answer, even if they do not know that yet."

And the decision was made.

In the ensuing weeks and months, as he carefully recruited his team from among disgruntled former soldiers, he came to understand without asking why Amal had chosen him for the attacks. It didn't matter that Arthur Evers, per se, lead the effort. Rather it mattered that the attacks be led by America's fallen heroes. Even if the public never discovered their identities, the team members themselves would know.

There was a symbolic satisfaction to knowing that they had successfully turned America on itself.

If he were a more introspective man—or a less wounded one, physically and psychologically—he supposed he would feel traitorous in his execution of Retribution, but given the inevitability of his participation, he'd come to think of it as just another mission. And like every other mission he'd led in his lifetime, he committed himself heart and soul to exacting maximum carnage. At the end of the day, killing was killing, and he was an expert at it.

His team members were all expert at it, and they were proving their worth.

This next thing—the biggest hits of all—would be the end for him. With three million dollars nestled in a bank offshore, when the smoke cleared—the other five million would be distributed among his ad hoc army—he would be on his way to the Caymans. He had no choice but to count on Amal to keep his word about leaving his family alone after the missions were completed, but just to be on the safe side, Evers had every intention of disappearing again, but this time he'd disappear deeper.

If Amal Al-Faisel could not find him, then he would have no reason to leverage his family again. Evers would be rich, free, and able to afford whatever healthcare he wanted, without having to jump through all the goddamn hoops.

The chirping of an incoming message broke him from his ruminations. He turned from the window and settled in behind his computer. He had a new email on his personal account, and his heart jumped when he saw the source. "How did Porter Brooks get this address?" he wondered aloud.

Evers hesitated before opening the email, wondering if this was some kind of virus sent by Brooks as retribution for the way he had spoken to him during their last encounter. Then he figured, what the hell?

There was a reason why he paid a commercial service to backup all that data. He opened the email.

The text read, "This is your guy. I think your operation is deeply compromised. No record on the guy through facial recognition software, but got a fair match with the face in the attached article. Have fun with this."

He'd attached a photo of a man and woman talking. It looked like they might be in a park. He recognized the woman to be Irene Rivers, director of the FBI, but she was not the focus of the photo. The picture presented remarkably good detail of a fit, good-looking guy, probably in his forties.

When he clicked the link below the picture, he opened an article from the *Washington Tribune* that showed a gaggle of men and women in formal wear chatting in the blazing red environment that could only be the Kennedy Center for the Performing Arts in Washington. When he zoomed in, he got a better image of a familiar-looking man rocking a tuxedo, chatting with a stunning lady in a clingy red dress and stiletto sandals. The caption identified the man only as Jonathan Grave, president of Security Solutions, located in Fisherman's Cove, Virginia.

This is your guy, Brooks had said. This is the guy who's been shoving sticks into the spokes of his operations.

The attached article confirmed that the locale was the Kennedy Center and the stuck-up event was a fundraiser for the Resurrection House Foundation, also located in Fisherman's Cove.

"Fisherman's Cove," he said, tasting the words.

He'd heard of the place, but he'd never been there. A few taps of the keys, and there it was along the Northern Neck of the Potomac River. What was that, an hour, hour-and-a-half drive from DC?

"I think it's time for a nice autumn drive," he said to the room. But first, he had a few administrative details to take care of.

Chapter Twenty

Fred Kellner hadn't expected the next operation to start so soon. The others had been separated by weeks, but now only three days had passed before his dedicated burner buzzed in his pocket. A text message read merely, "*p23 t91.*" Of the two numbers, the second was by far the most disturbing. *T91*—tango nine-one in Kellner's mind—meant that something was wrong and it was time to burn the burner phone. Without hesitating, he powered the phone down, tore open the plastic body and ripped out the SIM card, the brain of the phone. He dropped them all onto the concrete floor of the garage in his rental house in Herndon, Virginia, and crushed them one at a time with a hammer.

The first number in the message—papa two-three—represented one of four Dark Web sites whose numeric URLs he had memorized long ago. The sites were dormant—that is, nonexistent—until Iceman brought them up, and then they lived for only a short period of time. Kellner didn't know how long that period was, but he'd never pushed it past eight hours.

Kellner made his way to the Herndon Public Library and planted himself behind one of the public access computers. For reasons he couldn't begin to understand, the county let just anyone work at a computer station, even without benefit of a library card. They thought they were making life easier on county residents, but apparently never considered how easy they made things for people like him.

He was in and out in under ten minutes. The website featured a series of geometric angles, dots, and boxes that would mean nothing to anyone unfamiliar with the cryptic cipher of the Freemasons. For those who *were* familiar with the cipher, the figures would still be nonsensical because the message they presented was likewise encrypted. Kellner snapped a picture of the screen with his phone, then closed the site and double-checked to make sure that his search was not retained in the computer's cache.

His town house in Herndon would have been a nice starter home for a newly married couple. Located on Elden Street, arguably the main drag through the once-charming town, the narrow brick attached homes soared three stories over street level, and they provided garage parking for any vehicle smaller than a clown car. At least Kellner's Ford Expedition was partially sheltered by the second-floor deck. The twelve-hundred-square-foot floor plan was divided into three floors of four hundred square feet. Kellner couldn't stand the place.

But small rooms meant thin walls, which in turn meant a virtual shopping mall for wireless internet servers. The strongest signals came from routers that were "secure," but he got into the Beachum House network by typing in the word *password* as the WEP key, and he was in. He linked with a computer in Dubai, which then linked to a server in Croatia.

When his signal was scrambled, Kellner ran the Freemason cipher through the decryption site that Iceman had established. He'd never had to jump through this many security hurdles just to get to a message—not even when his jobs in the Sandbox dealt with the kinds of secrets that could topple nations.

When the decryption was finished, he had a series of letters and numbers:

38D 28 21.70Nx77D 59 74.00W 0744 1028

That was all of it. No description. Something about the pattern looked familiar, but the rest made no sense. As he leaned back in his desk chair, he opened a bottom drawer, withdrew a bottle of George Dickel, stripped off the cap, and took a pull. Iceman was not one to send gibberish—certainly not with this much effort—so the meaning was there. All he had to do was figure—

He saw it. The first bit of the message was GPS grid coordinates: 38 degrees, 28 minutes, 21.70 seconds of north latitude, by 77 degrees, 59 minutes, 74.00 seconds of west longitude. It looked strange because the Freemasons did not allow for degree markings. Deal with this stuff long enough and you get a feel for where longitude and latitude locations are, and this one was pretty close, he thought.

He entered the numbers into a commercial mapping program, and he came up with the northwest corner of Main and Culpeper Streets in Culpeper, Virginia.

The rest was just a guess, but he imagined 0744 to

be a time of day, albeit unusually specific. Since today was October 27, he was going to roll the dice that 1028 meant tomorrow. That was a damned early time to be at a place that was easily an hour away, but he'd be going against traffic.

As a final step before leaving the Beachum family alone, he checked his offshore bank account. Sure enough, additional money was there. Soon, it would be time to go hot again.

Kellner left Herndon at 06:00 to make the one-hour drive to Culpeper. At its face, that seemed like a lot of lead time, but in the Washington Metro area, traffic was always a crapshoot. All it took to lock things up for hours was for one asshole to check his text messages at the wrong moment. Kellner wasn't sure what would happen if he blew a deadline set by Iceman, but his gut told him that it would be unpleasant. In his experience, people who had those kinds of financial resources also had formidable human resources at their disposal.

Resources like the rest of Team Retribution.

As it worked out, Kellner arrived in Culpeper with nearly an hour to spare. As modern small towns went, this one still seemed to have a lot of life in it. There were the obligatory coffee and trinket shops, but he also saw shingles for insurance companies, law offices, and more than a few antique stores. The retail establishments hadn't opened yet for the day, but the Culpeper Diner seemed to be doing impressive business.

The business district was a few blocks square, beyond which he saw older-style homes that ultimately gave way to what he figured was farmland.

The corner of Main and Culpeper Streets was remarkable for its lack of remarkableness. The northwest quadrant, the specific geospatial point he'd been given, didn't even have a building on it. Rather, it was a parking lot, itself largely unoccupied, surrounded on three sides by a low brick wall.

He drove slowly past the assigned point in space, looking for some clue of what might lie ahead. And he saw it. Good thing he was Old School in his tradecraft. Someone had placed a ten-inch-long white chalk stripe at about thigh height along one of the redbrick walls. In Kellner's corner of the Special Forces community, that meant there'd be an old-fashioned brush pass at an hour to be otherwise determined. A yellow stripe would have meant to check a dead drop at a predetermined location.

Of course, it could also mean that kids had been playing with chalk, but under the circumstances, that seemed unlikely.

He drove to one of the two-hour parallel slots on Main Street, opposite Antigone's Antiques and parked. Now came the tricky part. There was no surer way to draw attention to yourself than to sit alone in a car on an otherwise unoccupied street. People would wonder if you were sick or if you were up to no good. Either way, that knock on the window by a cop wouldn't be important in real time, but it would give the cop something to remember in the future.

With a half hour left till his commitment, he decided to peek into the diner and grab a cup of coffee and a muffin, both of which were outstanding. No wonder the place was so crowded. When it was time to go, he paid his bill, added a generous tip, and headed down the street.

Kellner hadn't practiced basic tradecraft in a long time, but there wasn't a lot that could go wrong with a basic brush pass. Even if he fumbled the pass or dropped it, this wasn't exactly East Berlin in the 1970s.

Seven forty-four is actually a minute long, and sixty seconds is a long time to kill when you're trying to look natural in a strange place. Kellner paced himself to arrive at the corner precisely at 07:43:60, and was pleased to see that he was not the only punctual one.

A pretty young thing in her early twenties approached from the opposite end of Main Street and made too much of a show about not making eye contact as they closed in on each other. If this had been a couple of years ago in Kabul, Kellner would have had his left hand on his pistol as he passed on the right, and as the distance closed to within feet, his heart jumped a beat. Had he made a mistake? He didn't know this contact from—

As they passed, he opened the fingers of his right hand, and the young lady pressed what felt like a plastic ball into his palm. She never broke stride. With a little tweak to her body language, she would have made a good operative.

One key to this line of work was to never review the received message in public. He didn't even look into his palm until he was back into his car. The girl had handed him what could have been a miniature container of Silly Putty, a black plastic ball that split in two. It had been wrapped in tamper-proof tape and clearly had not been opened.

His curiosity piqued, Kellner started his Expedition and drove to the parking lot of the Walmart he'd seen on the way into town. If ever there was a place to hide in plain sight in America, it was in the parking lot of a Walmart, where the corporate policy invited weary travelers to spend the night parked outside their store.

Using the folding knife from his pocket, Kellner cut the tape and peeled the tiny egg open to reveal the contents as a flash drive. He lifted his laptop from the slot where he kept it between the driver's seat and the center console, opened it up, and inserted the drive. It was encrypted, of course, so it took nearly a minute to run it through the program that would make it legible.

As the computer worked its magic, Kellner checked his mirrors and craned his neck to make sure that this wasn't some kind of a trap. Finally, the plain language message appeared on his screen.

Change your appearance asap. Facial recognition software is looking for you. Visit Claude at 134 Simpson there in C-pep. Pass=I'll be just fine. Your choice on Claude's tomorrow.

Next event must be huge, then we go dormant for a while. Check out Capital Harbor. Halloween, 21:23. Shoot for 100.

Text new burner when able.

Eliminate your street contact. Details attached.

Iceman.

"Well, shit," Kellner said aloud to his truck. Somehow, he'd been made, and he still had lots of work to do.

* * *

In his line of work, Kellner had come to expect every illicit contractor to be old, twitchy, and male. They were the kinds of people who grooved on the notion of the killing business but never wanted any actual blood on their hands. Sort of like gamers, he supposed—men who give themselves lethal-sounding names and arm up with enough virtual guns and ammo to blow up the virtual world and feel powerful while doing it, while in fact having never once been punched in the face.

He was surprised then—no, call it shocked—when the resident of 134 Simpson Drive turned out not to be Claude, but rather Claudette, and she was anything but old or twitchy. In fact, she was pretty hot in a plus-size Ellie May Clampett kind of way. Big country-girl blond hair, western shirt that emphasized her God-given gifts (as Kellner's mother used to refer to boobs), and blue jeans, but without the rope belt from the television show.

His surprise must have been evident because she laughed when she opened the door to her 1940s-era farmhouse and saw him standing there. "Can I help you?" she said.

"I, uh . . ." He found himself stammering.

"Can I help you." This time she said it as a statement rather than a question. She was prompting him.

"I'll be just fine," Kellner said. The pass phrase.

She held out her hand for him. "Call me Claude," she said. "I know you ain't got no name, but I got to call you something, so how's Wilbur?" She didn't wait for an answer but rather stepped aside and motioned for Kellner to come in.

"I hope you got cash," she said, "because checks and credit cards ain't welcome here." She laughed when she said it, but the humor escaped Kellner.

"Is it the boobs?" she asked as she led him deeper into the tiny house. All the rooms were small, and there had to be five of them on the first floor, separated from one another by archways.

"Excuse me?"

"The look on your face. Was it the boobs? Not what you were expecting?"

"I, uh, I guess not," Kellner said.

"So, how much you need?" Claude asked. She was still walking, leading him to a doorway under the stairs. Sensing his hesitation, she added, "My workshop isn't the kind of thing that should be visible through the windows, don't you agree?"

"I suppose," Kellner said.

Claudette opened the door and flipped the switch for the single exposed lightbulb that barely illuminated anything. "You didn't answer my question," she said. "How much do you need?"

"I didn't answer it because I didn't understand it," Kellner said.

"You're after a disguise, right?

"Right."

"So, who are you trying to hide from? If it's just cameras, that's a whole different animal than if you're trying to hide from family or the laws. With them, you gotta change everything from face to posture to walk to voice. Ain't impossible, but ain't easy, neither."

Okay, so maybe Claudette *was* a little bit twitchy.

"I guess I'm mainly just going for face," he said.

They were in the cellar now, and it looked like

something from a horror movie. Claudette flipped on another switch, and brilliant light erupted to reveal droopy latex faces, stands draped with wigs, and little plastic containers filled with teeth, eyeballs, and fingernails.

"Business must be good," Kellner thought aloud.

"I do a lot of theater work in addition to . . . well, in addition to this kind of work." She walked to a full-length makeup mirror on the far wall, lined with bare lightbulbs all around the top half of the frame. "Come over here and let me take a look."

Kellner did as he was told. Claudette swung in behind him and for a few seconds they stared at him together.

"Okay, Wilbur," she said, smacking Kellner on his ass. "Take off everything but your underpants."

"What? Why?"

"If you want, you can take those off, too," Claudette said. "You ain't got nothin' that I ain't seen a *lot* of over the years." To emphasize her point, she winked and bounced her boobs.

"No, I'll be fine, thanks," he said. Except he really wasn't. As a wearer of old-fashioned boxer shorts, once the restraining compression of his jeans was removed, his arousal was plainly evident.

Mostly naked now, he returned to the mirror, and they stared together again. "Well," Claudette said with another playful spank, "at least I know you like me. But don't even *think* of unsheathing that thing at me."

Unsheathing?

"Folks like you are a challenge," Claudette said. "You're fit, you got a six-pack, angled features, and one great big eyebrow. And we gotta change all of that.

Go have a seat in the chair and give me a bit to work my magic."

"How much is this going to cost?" Kellner asked.

"Does it matter?"

The starkness of her question startled him. "No, I suppose it doesn't."

"Then go sit down and quit askin' stupid questions. I'll have my back turned in case you want to jerk that thing off. I promise I won't look."

Kellner gaped at her. As did Little Fred.

Claudette leaned back and launched a hearty laugh. "I'm just kiddin' you," she said. "You go spunkin' in here and we're done. I just like getting' young men like you thinkin' about not havin' a hard-on 'cause that just makes 'em harder and every one of you blush like schoolgirls when it happens."

Okay, twitchy and *crazy.*

Over the course of an hour, Claudette cycled Kellner four times from the chair to the mirror. She took studied dimensions with a tape measure, and then she'd pinch bits of skin and have him strike various poses. He suspected that half of the pinches and poses were more for her entertainment than for professional reasons, but the weirdness of it all had come to feel less weird, and that eliminated a lot of the stress.

"All right," she announced. "We're finally about done. Now, unless you want me traveling with you doing whatever it is you're going to be doing—for all I know, you could be one of them terrorists that's been shootin' people and blowin' them up, right?—you're gonna need to know how to put all this stuff on."

It started with shaving off the middle of his unibrow, and then resculpting the remaining brows to look different. He learned how to make wrinkles appear in his face and how prosthetic teeth, combined with latex chins and cheeks, changed all the outlines. And perhaps most important of all, he learned how to feather the makeup from the appliances onto his skin in a way that would look normal even under close scrutiny.

Throughout the entire lesson, though, Kellner had difficulty concentrating. He needed the knowledge—it was about his own survival, after all—but it troubled him that once he was certain that he'd milked Claudette for all the skinny he could get, he would have to kill her. That was the problem with talkative people. They never knew when to shut up. As soon as she made her little joke—was it really a joke?—about the possibility of him being one of the Retribution killers, she'd sealed her fate.

Iceman must have had his doubts about her, else why would he have written, "*Your choice on Claude's tomorrow*"?

In his heart, Kellner didn't believe that she had any kind of inside knowledge of him or of Retribution, but the penalty assessed if his intuition proved wrong was simply too high. He could take no chances on this one. For all he knew, his poker face wasn't the wonder that he believed it to be, and at the mention of the shootings and the bombings maybe something had registered in his eyes.

Even if it didn't strike her now, maybe it would strike her in the future. And she was the only other person on the planet who had any idea what he looked like!

Such a shame. The death penalty for talking too much.

Claudette's body language told him that they were about done, so as she turned back to her worktable to arrange her things for the last time, Kellner rose from his seat. He'd try to make it quick, maybe take her out before she could—

It was the quick hitch of her shoulders that gave her away.

Kellner knew that she'd grabbed a weapon before he saw it just from the way her stance changed, and that half-second bought him a chance. When Claudette spun around, she led with a pistol, a little purple Kimber 1911-style pocket gun, and from the way she held it, he knew that she knew how to use it.

She brought it around at face height from Kellner's left, but he got his hand out in time to catch the gun in his fist, between the hammer and the front sight. As the pistol fired, the flame of the muzzle flash hurt like shit, making him wonder if maybe she'd got him in the hand. What he knew for sure was that he'd kept the slide from cycling completely and that the shell casing was stove-piped in the breech, effectively transforming the weapon into a paperweight.

In the same motion, two seconds into the fight, Kellner pulled Claudette in closer, then slammed his right elbow into the bridge of her nose. As blood erupted and she backpedaled into her worktable, she left her little Kimber in Kellner's hand.

He cycled the action, cleared the spent casing, and leveled the muzzle at Claudette's forehead.

She cowered, bringing her hands up in front of her

face. "Please don't," she said. Only, her voice was different. Lower. Manly. "I only tried to shoot because I thought you were going to kill me. I saw it in your face."

"You're a guy," Kellner said.

"I'm a makeup specialist," he said. "I was trying a new persona. Please don't shoot."

Kellner shot the makeup specialist through his left eye. "Yeah, well, I'm a killer, so . . ."

As Kellner gathered his new toys and gadgets and started back up the stairs, he wondered how long it would take before someone found Claude(tte)'s body.

Chapter Twenty-one

Jonathan hated waiting. Yes, it was part and parcel of his military years, but back then he'd be waiting for orders from others. This kind of waiting—hanging around for another shoe to drop—was torture to him. It had been twelve hours since they'd nailed down Fred Kellner's face, and no one had yet to see the son of a bitch.

During his dinner meeting with Wolfie the night before, after he'd dropped the bomb about their facial recognition discovery, Director Rivers at first showed anger. "You should have told me before now," she said.

"I *am* telling you," he countered.

"How do you know that the face belongs to Kellner?"

Jonathan relayed the logic without throwing Derek Halstrom under the bus. He was grateful but not surprised that she didn't press for details. In all their many years of working together, Wolverine had adapted to the fact that Jonathan and his team had access to means and methods that they had no right to.

Jonathan said, "If you can re-create an evidence trail, you can probably still use it."

She cocked her head and gave him *that look*. "I have always admired your deep knowledge of the law and prosecutorial standards."

He winked and took a sip of his martini. The site of their dinner—Café Renaissance in Vienna, Virginia—was a new one for them, and he liked it. The old-school charm and outstanding food were a surprise, given its location in an out-of-the-way strip mall on Glyndon Street, but it was quiet, and the owner was kind enough to give them an even-quieter table in the back where they would not be overheard.

The Tweedle brothers occupied the only other table in this section of the restaurant. When Jonathan caught the eye of the taller one—Brooks, he thought—he blew him an air kiss.

"Why are you such an ass with my security team?" Irene asked, exasperation obvious.

"Because they're so friggin' self-righteous," Jonathan said. "And because they have a shitty job that they want everyone to think is a cool job."

"It's not cool to protect me?" Irene asked the question with a smile. No offense had been taken.

"Merely being in your presence is an honor, Madam Director." They clinked glasses. Hers held a vodka tonic. "Now, back to the issue of stopping crazies, can you at least send agents to Kellner's known former residences and see if they can track him down?"

"Sure, I can," Irene said. "I'm not sure what that end game would be."

"We have to make certain assumptions," Jonathan said. "One is that Kellner is the right guy, and two, that he's still involved in this Retribution thing. If we can find him, then we have a good idea of where the next event is going to be. Or, you can follow him to see where he's going."

"No, I can't." The annoyance was back. "I can't justify a surveillance team without a warrant—or at least a reasonable likelihood of getting one. You're talking a dozen or more agents just for one target."

"You've got a more important case than this one, do you?"

"Jesus, Digger, it keeps coming back down to your own words: fruit from the poisonous tree. Without probable cause, I've got nothing. And you're right, this is the most important task before us right now, and I'm not going to redirect resources away from operations that I know will pay off."

"Do you have other suspects on the radar?"

"Yes, we do."

"Did you know about Kellner before I told you about him?"

Irene grew uncomfortable and cleared her throat. "We certainly knew about the security footage."

"I know that," Jonathan said. "You sent it to us."

"But we didn't have a name, and we couldn't make the facial recognition work. Which is another reason why I can't divert resources for your guy."

Jonathan scowled. "I don't get it."

"I'm not sure I believe your results," she explained. "Mother Hen is very good at what she does, but am I really to believe that she has access to better technology than the FB friggin' I?"

Jonathan recognized the question as an opportunity to expound, but he didn't take the bait. He made a show of opening his menu. "I understand that this Café Renaissance makes the best Irish coffee on the planet," he said. "Be sure to save room."

The rest of the night with Irene was largely non-case-related small talk because neither one of them had information that the other was cleared to hear. Just as well—

"We've got a hit!" Venice yelled with a war whoop. "He's in Culpeper, Virginia!"

Jonathan shot to his feet. "Kellner?" He hurried out of his office to join Venice in hers.

"The one and only," she said. "Yesterday morning." She leaned in closer to her screen. "Time stamp says seven-fourteen. This image is from an ATM across the street."

"Across the street from where?"

"From where Kellner is."

Jonathan pointed to the far wall. "Bring it up on the big screen." While she tapped the keys, Jonathan picked up the landline that sat at his station at the conference table. He punched four digits and listened to the ring.

A familiar gruff voice answered, "Fortress of Solitude, Kent speaking."

"Come back to the War Room," Jonathan said to Boxers. "We've got something." Big Guy had been down in the basement armory, truly his happy place. Jonathan made a second call, and Gail picked up on the first ring. He delivered the same message to her.

While they waited, Jonathan asked Venice, "Need I ask where this video feed came from?"

"Only if you're in denial," she said. "I reiterate that we should hire him."

"I know that's what you want," Jonathan said. "But you know, if he worked here, he wouldn't have access to this same stuff."

She offered a dismissive snort of a laugh. "Have you talked to him about that?"

"Yes, I have. At the airport."

"No, you talked *at* him, not with him. You made a speech and essentially shut him down."

"The way it is, is working."

"The way it is, is unfair," she countered. "You know he risks arrest every day he helps us out."

"We all risk arrest every day," Jonathan said.

"It's not the same, and you know it."

She had him. He did know it. The NSA teemed with armed guards who could swoop in and yank Derek out of his chair and send him to jail in a place that his coworkers likely didn't even know existed.

"He doesn't have to help us," Jonathan said. "It's his choice to do so."

Venice's head whipped around, and now she was angry. "You know he's trying to impress you. He hates his job."

Jonathan inhaled deeply and didn't reply.

Venice's expression changed. "What?" she said.

"What, what?"

"You're not telling me something," she pressed.

"Oh, come on, Ven. You're not the mind reader you think you are."

"I've known you for as long as I've known my own mother," she said, stating fact. "Jonathan *Gravenow* wasn't as shut down as Jonathan Grave is. You still have the same mannerisms now that you had then. So, let me have it."

Jonathan deeply did not want to chase the rabbit down this hole. "We'll talk about it after this meeting," he said. "I promise."

As if summoned as cavalry, Gail arrived at the door to the War Room. "What've we got?"

Boxers arrived a minute later. When they were all caught up, Big Guy said, "Culpeper. I've been to that town. There's nothing worth attacking. Hell, even the hardware store closed down."

"Maybe we should watch what he's doing there," Venice said. "TickTock was able to put a number of sources and images together in a timeline."

"If that guy is going to be around here, we need to get him a different name," Boxers said. "TickTock is a name for an elf, not an operator."

"He's not an operator," Jonathan said.

"The screen, people," Venice snapped. "Watch the screen."

Kellner seemed to be looking around the town, not engaged with anything or anybody.

"He likes that parking lot," Gail said. "Seems to be something there that intrigues him."

And then he was walking again.

"Wait a second, Ven," Jonathan said. "Go back to the lot Gail was talking about."

The pictures changed.

"How long was he there, watching?"

She clicked through the various time-stamped photos, clearly stitched together from different angles. "Looks like about two minutes," she announced.

"That's a long time compared to everything else he's doing," Gail observed.

"Okay, go on," Jonathan said. Three images later, he

was gone, and then he was back again. Watching stop action like this gave the impression that he disappeared and then reappeared, a la Harry Potter. "That was weird," he said.

"Again, look at the time stamp," Venice said. "Twenty minutes passed. He must have gone into that diner."

"And they don't have a camera?" Boxers asked.

"I can only presume not," Venice said, "or I'm confident that we'd have footage."

They watched as Kellner walked back toward the parking lot. He didn't seem to be concerned, and he no longer seemed to be scouting the place out. He was walking with purpose.

The angle changed again, and now there was a second person in the frame.

"Hel-lo," Boxers said, with a God-awful attempt at a British accent. "Who have we here?"

"She looks young," Gail said.

"Goes with the pattern, doesn't it?" Jonathan said. "Even down to the diner."

"No, it doesn't," Gail said. "The Provost kid was the one eating in the diner."

The way the images were timed, they couldn't see the actual moment when Kellner and the girl passed.

"I say she's just another pedestrian," Boxers said. "Other people are allowed to be out on the sidewalk."

The angle shifted again, and now they saw Kellner continuing on his way.

"Wait!" Jonathan said. He'd nearly shouted it. "Go back one."

The image changed.

"What?" Gail said.

"He's just walking," Boxers agreed.

"You're looking at the wrong person," Venice said.

Jonathan smiled. They really did often think alike. "It's the girl," he said. "Look at the top of your screen. She's turned around and looking back at Kellner."

"Think he said something crass?" Boxers guessed.

"We don't know," Jonathan said.

"Maybe it was a brush pass," Gail said. "Or, maybe he smelled bad. We can guess at this all day."

"But it was *something*," Jonathan said. "And in the absence of pretty much everything, I'm happy to take a something. Ven, how can we find out who that girl is?"

Venice stared back at him. "I have no idea," she said after a few seconds. "I suppose we could run her face through the local high school yearbook and try to get a match."

"I don't think she's *that* young, do you?" Jonathan asked.

"Probably not, but chances are that she's too young to be in any other database. Her drivers' license, maybe. Let me check."

Venice spun her chair back to her keyboard and started typing.

"You're not suggesting that we go to Culpeper, are you?" Boxers asked.

"I don't know what I'm suggesting," Jonathan said. "At this point—"

"Oh, no," Venice moaned, genuine sadness in her tone. "I think I have a name for our girl. Cindy McVeigh, age twenty."

"Holy crap, that was fast," Jonathan said. "Why do you think it's her?"

"Because twenty-year-old Cindy McVeigh was

killed yesterday afternoon while she was alone in the shop where she works."

Jonathan felt his stomach flip. It had to be connected to Kellner. How could it not be?

"The news is just hitting the internet," Venice explained. "And the police have posted a picture of their unnamed person of interest." She clicked, and the screen filled with yet another fuzzy security camera image, this one of an overweight man with a bald head.

"Not our guy," Boxers said.

"I'm not so sure," Jonathan said. "Can you get that image to TickTock and see if he can work some magic?"

"I don't understand what you're doing, Dig," Gail said.

Jonathan looked back at the screen. "I hope I'm wrong, but right now, the smart money says that Kellner spent the day getting a new identity."

Evers piloted his stolen Kia Serrano to the end of Church Street, where it teed with Water Street, and was surprised to find a firehouse there. According to his research, this was the location for Security Solutions. Could he have gone to the wrong spot?

He parked and checked the mirror to make sure that his nose and chin prostheses looked natural. The fake teeth made his real teeth ache, but he hoped that the subtle squint of pain would add character to his now-blue eyes. Satisfied, he climbed out of the vehicle and rolled a quarter into the meter, granting him two hours in the space. "How could anyone possibly spend two hours here?"

He supposed the place was charming enough in that old Virginia small-town way, and being on the water was always nice, but Jesus, living here would drive him nuts.

Just up the hill, a majestic stone church rose from a massive churchyard. The brown sign with gold letters along the street identified the structure as St. Katherine's Catholic Church. In smaller letters were the words FR. DOMINIC D'ANGELO, OSFS, PASTOR.

"Huh," Evers said. His research into Resurrection House had highlighted Father D'Angelo as a prominent player in Resurrection House's administration. And the school itself was affiliated with St. Katherine's. Not only was this a small town, but it was the center of a small world.

As he walked up the hill, past the church, he considered going inside to find out more from this D'Angelo guy, but decided to put that off. Instead, he kept going. He wanted to check out the ginormous mansion that he'd passed on the way in. Honest to God, the place was a palace, occupying what had to be six or seven acres of land. The architect had clearly been inspired by Tara of *Gone with the Wind* fame, but this was Tara on steroids.

He was surprised that the house itself sat so close to the road, less than a hundred yards, but then, judging from the age of the place, he imagined it had something to do with the run of underground utilities.

As he got closer, he saw that there were other buildings behind the mansion, far more modern in their construction, with a more utilitarian look. The complex bore no signage, but he figured that this place had to be Resurrection House. An iron fence ran the length of the property in the front along the road, but the gate was open, and beyond the gate, about halfway between the street and the house, a stout African American woman appeared to be attending to a bird feeder.

Evers climbed the few steps to the front walk, passed through the gate, and approached the woman. He walked easily, a smile on his face.

The woman seemed startled at first, but then she smiled, too.

"Good morning," he said. Then he checked his watch. "Oops, I guess it's afternoon now. My name's Joe Vitale." He extended his hand.

The woman shook with him, but she clearly didn't like it. "Mama," she said. "And if you're sellin' or tryin' to get me to vote for one guy over the other, you are in the wrong place."

Evers laughed. "None of those things, I promise. This is a beautiful building. Did you say your name was Mama?"

"I did, and yes, it is."

"Just Mama?"

"That's all you need. Mention Mama to anyone in town and half the county, and they'll know who I am. Been here a long time. Now, how can I help you?"

"Is this Resurrection House?"

Mama recoiled. She didn't like the question. "Who are you?"

Evers took a step back. Literally. "I seem to have offended you. I'm sorry. I'm just here on business, and I'm a fan of Southern architecture. I've heard of Resurrection House and the great work you do, and when I saw you I just wanted to say hi."

"Well, hi, then," Mama said. "What's your business here?" Behind her, a uniformed guard with a short-barreled rifle slung across his chest stepped out from inside the front door onto the mansion's porch. He didn't say anything, but his posture communicated for him. *State your business and get out.*

"My business isn't actually here," Evers said. "I'm looking for a place called Security Solutions. I went to the address, but there's a firehouse there."

Mama's face bloomed with amusement, and she laughed. "No, you got the right place," she said. "That's where they're located. On the third floor. Use the door on the left."

Evers made a point of smiling. "Thank you very much, Mama." He didn't bother to shake hands again. Instead, he turned and headed back down the walk.

He'd taken maybe ten steps when Mama called to him. "You got an appointment? You won't get very far in there without an appointment. My Jonny's a stickler on appointments."

Evers smiled. "Who's Jonny?"

Something passed in Mama's eyes, as if maybe she she'd said something she shouldn't have. "He's the man who runs the place," she said.

"Jonathan Grave," Evers said. "Yeah, he's the man I need to talk to. "It's a private investigating company, right?"

"That's right," Mama said. "It's all in the name. They take the *security* part of it pretty seriously."

"I'll keep that in mind. Thanks, Mama. Have a great day."

By the time he got to the bottom of the hill and turned the corner of Water Street, it was clear that the folks in Resurrection House had called ahead. A uniformed security guard, a clone of the other one, right down to the MP7 machine pistol, had positioned himself outside the entrance door.

"You Mr. Vitale?" the guard asked. He bore no name tag and no visible rank insignia, but he clearly had a military background.

"I am," Evers said. "You guys expecting a war?"

"How can I help you."

"I'm here to see Jonathan Grave."

"We don't have you on the visitor's list."

"I don't have an appointment."

"Then I'm afraid you've wasted your time."

"Can you at least tell him I'm here?" Evers asked.

"He's busy."

"Please tell him it's important. A matter of life and death."

The guard seemed amused by the cliché. "Whose?" he asked.

"Mr. Grave's, for one. And everyone else he cares for." Evers hardened his features.

The guard settled his hand on the pistol grip of his MP7. "You need to be careful about making threats, sir. And I mean *really* careful."

Evers took a menacing step forward. "I know it doesn't show," he said. "But I'm trembling all over. Could you deliver the message, please? I'll wait here."

The guard's eyes never left Evers as he pulled his cell phone from his pocket and punched a speed dial button. After a few seconds, he said, "Yes, sir, this is Unit One. We have a visitor at the door who says it's important to speak with you. His name is Vitale. Joe Vitale. He presented a direct threat to your life. How do you want to handle it?"

A pause as he listened.

"Yes, sir. I'll tell him, sir." As the guard clicked off and slid his phone back into his pocket, he said, "Mr. Grave will be down in a few minutes."

While they waited, two more security guards materialized, one from up the street and another from inside the building. "You've got quite a fortress in this town," Evers said.

The guards remained silent.

"I guess billionaires deserve a little extra security," Evers said.

"Yes, they do." These words came from behind Evers, from a stubby, mean-looking cop with a gold badge that read CHIEF. His name tag read KRAMER.

"Did someone call you?" Evers asked. "I haven't done anything wrong."

"Am I arresting you?" Kramer asked. "I'm just here to see what the crowd is about."

Five minutes after Unit One made his phone call, the firehouse door opened, and Jonathan Grave emerged into the chilly sunshine. He was accompanied by one of the largest men Evers had ever seen. He had the body of a linebacker, the height of a point guard, and he exuded menace. For the first time, it occurred to Evers that this might not have been a good plan, after all.

Grave approached to within five feet and positioned himself so that the cocked and locked 1911 pistol was clearly visible in its holster. The monster was armed, too, but Evers couldn't make out the model.

"This is a lot of firepower for a chat," Evers said.

"This is your meeting, Mr. Vitale," Grave said.

Evers made a point of scanning the stern faces. "This is kind of a sensitive matter," he said. "Can we speak in private?"

The big man said, “Nope.” He had the kind of voice that made the concrete rumble.

“Say your piece and move on,” Grave said. “I trust every one of these men with my life.”

Evers was in too deep to stop now. “All right then. I happen to know that you’re involved in something that you shouldn’t be. I came to warn you to leave it alone.”

“I don’t know what you’re talking about,” Grave said.

“I think you do,” Evers said. He had to walk a fine line here, especially with the cop standing there. “I have a job to do, and if you get in the way, I will be very angry.”

“Isn’t that cute?” the monster said. “The little man needs a hug.”

“Up yours,” Evers said. “Deny what you want, but I have a job to do, and I happen to know that everything that’s important to you is here in this little town, and all of it is vulnerable. Breakable.”

Chief Kramer stepped in closer. “Are you making a threat to Mr. Grave?”

Evers smiled. “No threat. Just an observation.”

Grave said, “It sounds like he’s talking about some form of *retribution*.”

Vitale tried his best to keep expressionless, but Jonathan saw the flash in his eyes when he leaned on the word *retribution*. He’d catch hell from Boxers later for showing their hand, but this Vitale guy—clearly a cover name—somehow already knew that they were involved. The denial game would accomplish nothing.

"Again," Vitale said. "I'm merely making an observation."

"And a promise, perhaps?" Jonathan asked.

Vitale's features twisted into a pained smirk. "Perhaps. Let's call it an implied promise."

Jonathan took a step closer to the man. Vitale didn't step back until Boxers advanced, too. "Let's match promise for promise," Jonathan said. "You stop doing what you're doing, and we never have to cross paths again."

Vitale eyed Jonathan for a long time before he said, "I suppose that's a fair deal." Then he turned away. "Excuse me, Chief," he said, and he started to cross the street.

"Hey," Jonathan called after him.

Vitale turned.

"You're right that everything important to me is in this town. You cannot imagine the lengths I would go to protect it."

Vitale smiled. "I admire that," he said. "I always admire a man willing to fall on his own sword. Have a nice day."

Jonathan and the assembled posse of gunfighters watched in silence as Vitale walked to his Kia, pulled a U-turn out of his parking spot, and headed back up Church Street.

"You want to tell me just what the *hell* that was about?" Kramer asked.

"I'd love to," Jonathan said, "but I can't. But I know this, gentlemen. Sometime in the next week or two, that asshole is going to bring violence to Fisherman's Cove, and we need to be ready for it."

"Come on, Dig, you've got to give me more than that," Kramer said.

"Boxers will beat me up for having told you too much as it is." Jonathan had known Doug Kramer since they were kids, and while the chief didn't know the specifics of Security Solutions' covert side, he had to be aware that it existed, if only through osmosis.

Something changed in Kramer's face as a thought dawned. "Does this have anything to do with that string of shootings and bombings all over the country?"

Jonathan took his time as he considered the wisdom of answering. The only way to truly keep a secret was to keep the damn secret. He threw a look to Big Guy, who offered a little nod. "You're in this deep, Boss," he said. "A little deeper can't hurt but so much."

"Okay, here it is," Jonathan said. "Officially, I have no idea if Mr. Vitale, or whatever his real name is, has anything to do with . . . the terrorist incidents." He thought it unwise to reveal the name Retribution, though he could not articulate why. "Unofficially—and all of you need to keep this close to your vests—I suspect he's involved."

"How?" Kramer asked. "How is he involved, and how do you know?"

"I said I *suspect*, Doug, not that I know, and I'm not being difficult."

"Yet you know he's bringing violence to town."

"That's a suspicion, too," Jonathan said.

"That's not what you said."

"Call it a *strong* suspicion."

"Dammit, Digger," Kramer said, not a shout, but

close to it. “It’s my job to protect this town. If you’ve got information—”

“I just told you everything I can tell you,” Jonathan said. “Damn near everything I know.”

“Look, Dig, I can’t get the county or state boys here to reinforce us without some kind of details.”

“You won’t get them,” Jonathan said. “I’m not being obtuse, here, Doug. If the violence comes, we’ll be on our own for the first shots. After that, you can call the cavalry. I just can’t give you any more than that. When I can, I swear to you that I will.”

“You know I’ll be there, sir.” This from the first guard at the door, Rick Hare.

“I do know that, Rick, and I appreciate it.”

The second guard to arrive from inside, Charlie Keeling, said, “Me, too.”

The third guard, Oscar Thompkins, threw his hat in the ring, as well. He was a supervisor of the security team up the hill at RezHouse. “What do I tell the rest of the team?” he asked through a Tennessee accent as think as honey.

“Tell your security teams the truth, just as I told you,” Jonathan said. “I’ll ask Father Dom to explain it all to the faculty and staff. We’ll sell it as heightened security precautions.”

“What’s our time frame?” Keeling asked.

Jonathan shook his head. “When I know, I’ll tell you.”

“Okay,” Kramer said. His face had reddened, and he’d pressed his lips into a thin line. It was his mad face, and Jonathan knew from experience that a mad Kramer could become a bad Kramer. “You and I need to talk,” he said. He glared at the rest of the crowd, then added, "Privately." He turned and started walking toward the marina across the street.

As Jonathan moved to follow, Boxers stepped out, too, but Jonathan waved him off. Doug Kramer was one of those guys who needed to vent when he was angry, the sooner the better. Jonathan knew he was going to get a stern talking-to, and if Big Guy was there, he'd get offended by proxy, and everything would turn ugly.

Kramer walked all the way down to the end of what locals called Millionaires' Row, the long dock with extra clearance to allow for the kind of yachts that common folk rarely see, let alone sail in. As Jonathan followed, he was reminded yet again how much he wished that he didn't hate boating.

Kramer never looked back to see if Jonathan was following as he led the way past the few vessels that were moored and on to the very end of the dock.

"You're not gonna try to drown me, are you, Doug?" Jonathan quipped.

Kramer whirled. He looked ready to fight. "Who the *hell* do you think you are?"

Jonathan kept his distance. "I need more than that."

Kramer planted his hands on his Sam Browne belt, and for half a second, Jonathan wondered if they were going to have a gunfight. "Look, Dig, I know that you do crazy shit through your business, and I know that most of it involves violence. You're the only guy I know who returns from every *business trip* with bruises and a new limp. I don't ask questions because I respect your privacy, and frankly, I don't think I want to know the answers."

"But you think I owe you this one," Jonathan said.

The comment seemed to knock Kramer off-balance,

as if he had a speech prepared and wanted to deliver his own punch line. "Yeah," he said. "Yeah, I think you do. And if you think you can't trust me with a secret that can save this little burg from harm, then you're not the friend I thought you were."

The words hit hard. Jonathan wanted to push back, but when he put himself in Doug's shoes, he knew he'd be furious. Like Jonathan, Doug had grown up in Fisherman's Cove, and the better part of three generations of his family still lived here. They were the ones who would be placed in danger if Retribution came.

Jonathan heaved a deep breath and walked closer so he could speak as quietly as possible. "Doug, you are about to be the fifth person in the world to know what I'm about to tell you, and right up front I warn you that I cannot and will not tell you how I obtained my information."

"Let me guess. And after you tell me, you'll have to shoot me."

Jonathan wasn't in the mood. "We think we've found a way to track one member of this terrorist group. Not the guy who was just here, but another one."

"Where is he now?" Doug asked.

"Not here," Jonathan said. "Beyond that, you have nothing to worry about."

"You said you *think* you found a way," Doug parroted. "That means maybe you haven't."

"Maybe we haven't. But I'm confident that we have."

"Why haven't you told the police? Are they following him, too?"

"Let's say that the authorities are aware and leave it

at that, okay?" To open up the can of worms about warrantless searches and illegal interdiction would be a step too far.

"So, what about the guy who was just here? Vitale? Should I arrest him?"

"If you can think of a charge, knock yourself out," Jonathan said.

"How about fomenting terrorism?" Doug said.

"Is that even a thing?" Jonathan asked. "And when I play back the conversation in my head, I don't remember hearing him say the *T*-word."

"Then what the hell was he doing here?"

"Trying to intimidate me, is my guess." Jonathan took a deep, noisy breath and rubbed the back of his head. "Let me ask you this, Doug. On Black Friday, how many terror attacks were there, do you remember?"

Kramer scowled as he thought about it. "Six, right? All simultaneously."

"Right," Jonathan said. "And for the second attack there were only five. My team and I had something to do with that reduction in number. And when one happens in the future, there will be only four. We had a lot to do with that, too."

Realization bloomed in the chief's face. "You've been hunting them down? Killing them?"

Jonathan rocked his head noncommittally. "Not exactly, but that's close. My concern is that only two people outside my immediate team could possibly know that, and at least one of them is beyond reproach. I have no idea who Vitale really is, but he wanted me to know that he knows what I'm doing. If I let him do his thing in peace, he'll leave Fisherman's Cove alone."

Kramer looked at his feet and then out at the river. "You're not going to do that, are you?"

"I can't Doug. I can't stop all of them, but I'll do what I can. If they come here, they come here. And we'll fight them off."

Kramer's head snapped up as another thought occurred to him. "Holy shit," he said. "You're using this town as bait. You're *trying* to draw them here."

"That wasn't even on my mind a half hour ago," Jonathan said. "But now that you mention it . . ."

Kramer's shoulders sagged, and he closed his eyes as he looked at the sky. "Oh, goddammit, Digger. Maybe I should arrest *you*."

Jonathan chuckled. "Do you really want Boxers to blow the walls of the jail?"

Kramer fell silent for the better part of thirty seconds as he stared out over the water. "Okay, then" he said. "Sounds like this thing is inevitable. So, what do we do?"

Jonathan hiked his shoulders to his ears and arched his eyebrows. "We develop a plan," he said. Most obvious thing in the world.

Chapter Twenty-two

Fred Kellner pondered his latest instructions as he strolled among the tourists and passersby that packed the park at the end of America Avenue. Ten, maybe fifteen years ago, this strip of land on the Potomac River was a little-known nothing of a largely unoccupied swamp called Oxon Hill, Maryland. Now, it was called Capital Harbor, and the swamp had been transformed into a pretentious little city. Grass and trees had been transformed into concrete and steel, and rental rates were astronomical—for reasons that made no sense because the place was impossible to get to during rush hour, and in their infinite wisdom, the developers had decided to block the most impressive views of the river with views of other buildings.

Even the buildings with the best view really had no view at all. The second favorite tourist draw in Capital Harbor was a God-awful monstrosity called the Potomac Eye, a two-hundred-foot-tall Ferris wheel that provided none of the thrill of the amusement park original yet cost fifteen dollars for a once-around.

When Iceman's text specifically mentioned Capital Harbor as the site for the next launch, Kellner was at first concerned by the proximity to his own backyard, only one state away. But the more he thought about it, the more he realized that it was the perfect venue for maximum impact. Tomorrow, on Halloween night, the area would be packed with revelers of every age. When the shooting started and the panic spread, they'd crush themselves. The bullets would be only a small part of the damage inflicted.

At one level, Kellner hated himself for admiring the images such carnage brought to focus in his mind, but it was a thing he could live with. His spot in hell had been reserved a long time ago, so moral trepidation was not in play. Killing one person was fundamentally no different than killing dozens. And after having left over a hundred corpses in a steaming crater in Bluebird, Indiana, now was not the time to turn soft. He had a job to do, and it paid really, *really* well.

Kellner shifted his stance as he read the information on the plaque at the base of the Eye. He was getting used to his new look. No fat suit this time, nothing like the costume he wore to kill the girl in Culpeper. This look would have to get him through a couple of days, while at the same time be easily changed out of when the op was completed. Disguises were never his expertise—in fact, Claude had expanded his lifetime knowledge manyfold—but he thought he'd hit the highlights. The bridge of his nose was thicker, his jaw pointier. Rather than wearing a wig, he opted to bleach his hair blond and cut it down to an old-school crew cut, complete with the flattop. The wig would come later during exfil. The sunglasses were old-school technology, but he couldn't do without them. Even if they did no good in the long run, they made him *feel* hidden.

He was to meet someone here in just under an hour. According to the message he'd received, his *asset*—no mention of man or woman—would be wearing a green jacket and a red Washington Nationals hat. He would ask a specific question and receive a specific answer, and from there, they would work together to plan the Halloween operation.

Kellner wasn't sure how he felt about stepping beyond the lone wolf paradigm, but he was never asked. At this stage, his choices were literally to do or die. Or, on a really bad day, both. Historically, he wasn't known for working and playing well with others.

While he waited for the meetup, he thought he'd take a ride in his future target. He paid his money at the ticket gate and walked right up to the waiting gondola. With no crowd to speak of, he wondered how they could afford to run the attraction all day. A pretty young girl named Molly, according to her name tag, met him on the loading platform, which was little more than a diamond-plate strip of decking that linked two sets of metal stairs, one on each end.

"Good afternoon, sir," she said. "Please watch your step."

Kellner smiled. "Thank you," he said. The gondola had a lot in common with its cousins at ski resorts around the world. It was a perpetual motion machine, never stopping its oh-so-slow progress. As it moved through the loading zone, the double doors on the opposite side of the platform slid open of their own accord, presumably to let passengers step off, and a few seconds later, the doors on his side opened.

"Please watch your step," Molly repeated.

"I'll do my best," Kellner said. He wondered how many times she spoke those words in a day and whether she could turn them off in her sleep.

Kellner helped himself to the padded bench seat on the left-hand side of the gondola. An identical bench seat lined the opposite wall. The rules he'd read outside on the sign mandated a maximum occupancy of twelve people. "It's a long damn ride for the eight people who can't sit," Kellner mumbled.

He'd been seated for a few seconds before the doors slid shut, and then he was off.

He'd positioned himself to rotate backward, watching the harbor development fall away rather than facing the river and maybe revealing the DC skyline from above the trees. As he rose, he noted that the gondola had been built for maximum visibility. But for a strip of steel that ran around the belly of the enclosure and a substantial steel cap overhead that kept the roof attached, the entire enclosure was made of plexiglass—or some more modern version of it.

When he rapped on the plexiglass with his knuckle, he was pleased with what he found. It was thick enough to be weatherproof, but nowhere near thick enough to be bulletproof. This made the task ahead many times easier.

Shooting through glass was always something of a crapshoot. The crystalline structure of glass often rendered trajectory and penetration difficult to predict. Throw in the fact that the glass was installed at an angle—as car windshields are—and a carefully aimed shot could zing away ten or twenty degrees from the intended impact point.

Plexiglass, on the other hand—or any other polycarbonate product—was composed of solid, poured, and molded sheets, and the molecules were happy to give way to the physics of a rifle bullet. This would be too easy.

With his marksmanship guaranteed, now he needed a sniper's nest. And a single glance at the Maryland skyline told him exactly the spot. Three blocks back from the water's edge, one building was three stories taller than the buildings in front of it.

With his phone, Kellner zoomed in on the building and snapped a couple of pictures. With the magnification, he saw everything else he needed to know.

Doug Kramer, Boxers, Gail, and Jonathan leaned heavily on the mahogany conference table that lined the wall opposite Jonathan's desk, studying a map of Fisherman's Cove. It wasn't especially detailed—more the kind you'd get from an auto club—but they didn't need to see details of the town they knew so well.

"Let's look at this from a tactical point of view," Jonathan said. "These are hit-and-run teams. They want to come in, wreak as much havoc as they can in as short a time as possible, then get out in one piece. They're not suicide bombers, and I don't think they're interested in being occupiers."

"How much of what you said is what you know and how much is wild-ass guess?" Kramer asked.

"More knowledge than guesswork," Jonathan said. "We've been following these assholes for a while. There's a pattern. One guy outright told us about the family threat, and the other guy cut his own throat rather than be caught. That suggests a lot of leverage."

He turned back to the map. "There are three basic routes of attack," he explained. "Land, air, or sea. If they come in by sea, their exfil options will be limited to virtually nothing, so I think that's unlikely."

"They could boost cars for exfil," Boxers pointed out.

"That's a lot of extra time," Gail said. "A lot of exposure."

"But it's possible," Jonathan conceded.

"Do you really think an attack by air is feasible?" Kramer asked.

"Drones," Boxers said. "You can turn them into little bombers."

"But what's the range?" Jonathan asked.

Big Guy rocked his hand noncommittally. "Half mile for a civilian model, maybe a little more."

"So, that makes it a land attack." Jonathan said

"If and when they come, we assume they come in by the road," Boxers said. "There's only two of them into town. We can set up roadblocks."

Kramer recoiled from the thought. "What are we going to tell the residents? We don't want to spark a panic."

Jonathan unbent from the table and stood tall to stretch his back. "Can we increase awareness without sparking a panic?" he asked.

"You mean tell people that we're going to be attacked, but not to get too concerned about it?" Kramer formed the question as an absurdity.

"Not everybody," Jonathan said. "But the right people. People who won't run from a fight. You know who they are. Start with the vets who still salute during the Fourth of July parades."

"The people who've lived in Fisherman's Cove their whole lives," Gail said.

"Can you still deputize people?" Boxers asked. "Or, is that just in Westerns?"

Kramer's expression had changed from mocking disbelief to interest. "We don't have to be specific," he said. "We can form a kind of hometown militia and call it a way to send a message to the terrorists that our town is not as soft a target as it looks."

"Wait a second," Gail said. "We've got to tell them something of the imminent threat. They need to know that this is more than a symbolic gesture. They need to know that real bullets may very well start flying."

"Gail's right," Jonathan said. "That's where the fine line comes between awareness and panic. We need to use a soft touch." He looked to the chief. "Can you recruit one person at a time? I don't think this is a town hall kind of announcement."

Kramer nodded as he thought it through. "Yeah, I think I can. But I'll need to give them something to do. What am I asking for, other than a hypothetical yes?"

"First of all, encourage them to arm themselves," Jonathan said.

Kramer laughed. "This is Virginia. Half the population is packing heat anyway."

Jonathan smiled at the point. "Think like a terrorist," he said. "What are our most attractive targets?"

"That Vitale asshole already told us that the targets are what's important to you," Boxers said. "That puts RezHouse at the top of the list."

"I agree," Kramer said. "I think I can sell people on

the notion that until these Black Friday attacks are over with, we should increase the security presence outside the school. Especially since it's already been hit once."

"Talk about attracting attention," Gail said. "The press will have a field day with pictures of civilians standing guard with battle-slung ARs in front of a school."

"These are scary times," Boxers said. "Who gives a shit about public relations?"

"I do," Kramer said. "And the mayor does. What do I tell him?"

"Billy Babcock's a town lifer," Jonathan said, referring to the mayor to Fisherman's Cove. "I'd make him your first recruit and then take him along for the others."

Two quick raps drew Jonathan's attention to the open office door. It was Venice, and she seemed agitated. "I have news," she said. She cut her eyes to Doug Kramer and then back to Jonathan.

He got the hint. He turned to the chief. "Do you feel like you have a plan?"

Kramer laughed. "Absolutely not. But I have things to do. I believe I'll be on my way."

As he headed toward the door, Venice stepped back to let him pass.

"Thanks, Doug," Jonathan called after him. "Let me know if I can help."

Venice waited till the chief had exited the Cave before she said, "You and I need to talk." This was directed straight at Jonathan.

"That's your news?" Jonathan asked.

"No," she said. "My news is that we've got a new

hit on Mr. Kellner. But you don't get it until we finish our conversation."

"Oh, for God's sake, Ven," Jonathan scoffed.

Her features hardened. This thing had to happen.

Jonathan turned to the rest of his team. "I need you to leave us, please. But don't wander far."

He got nothing but confusion from the others, but they left, closing the door behind them.

Alone together, Jonathan gestured to the collection of leather chairs and sofa that framed the stone fireplace. Soon, it would be time to stoke that hearth up. "Let's have a seat," he said. "Give my back a rest."

Venice took the sofa. Jonathan's reserved seat was a wooden rocking chair emblazoned along the back with the Seal of the College of William and Mary in Virginia. More than a memento of his alma mater, the chair was the only seat in the office—apart from his Aeron desk chair—that gave his lumbar spine the support he craved. Ah, the price of a misspent youth.

"You go first," Jonathan said once they were in place.

"Not me," Venice said. "You're the one who has a problem with Derek. You're not my big brother, you know."

Jonathan recoiled in his seat. "No, I'm not your brother, but I *am* your boss. Do you really think this is personal?"

Venice said nothing. She pressed her lips to a thin line and tears rimmed her lids. "This is important to me," she said. "*Derek* is important to me. If you know something about him—if you *think* you know something about him—you need to share it with me. After all these years, you *owe* me that much."

Jonathan leaned back in the rocker and closed his eyes, pressing his head into the Great Seal. How was he going to say this?

When he opened his eyes, she hadn't moved.

"Okay," Jonathan said. "I'll just put it out there. I think your buddy might be a spy."

Venice's face fell. And her lips pressed tighter. She was beyond pissed. "He's not my *buddy*," she seethed. "His name is Derek."

"Fine. Derek then. I think your *colleague* Derek might be a spy. And before you go ballistic and quit, look at things from where I sit. Derek finds a secret prison on our behalf, and the prison is invaded. We've *never* been identified before, yet after he joins the team, some psycho sails into town and threatens me directly. The *only* variable is Derek. What other conclusion could I possibly draw?"

Venice's expression hardened even more. "You could draw any conclusion that did not insult me."

"I'm not insulting you."

"When you think that I'm stupid enough to invite that level of danger into our lives, you insult me. Do you believe for a moment that I haven't vetted him? Do you think I don't know every corner of his life?"

Jonathan started to object. "But—"

She slammed her hand on the arm of the sofa. "You didn't even have the courtesy to ask me before you passed judgment on him. Derek has been a joke to you and Boxers since the first day his name came up, and Gail isn't much better."

Jonathan started to say something but withered under her glare. "I have never been this angry with you, Digger. Don't forget that I remember when you were Jonny.

I remember when you and I first talked about starting Security Solutions, and yes, I remember when you intervened to keep me out of jail. Do you have any idea how many times I have intervened to get you out of trouble or keep you out of it? I can't count that high."

The tears on her eyelids finally spilled onto her cheeks, and she angrily wiped them away. "In all these years, Dig, this is the first time you've shown me utter disrespect. Now, you have a decision to make. Am I a part of this team or am I not?"

"Of course, you are." Jonathan heard the meekness of his tone.

"Don't just say it if you don't mean it," she snapped. "Skills don't come much more marketable than mine, you know. Just ask Wolverine."

Something clicked in Jonathan's head. "Wait a minute," he said with a snap of his fingers.

"I'm not done yet," Venice said. "In fact, I'm just barely—"

"What? Oh, fine. Sorry about the Derek thing. You were right, I should have talked to you first. That wasn't right of me." He'd already moved on to a more pressing bit of news. "Derek isn't the only moving part. There's Wolverine, too. Your mentioning her brought that into focus."

Venice gaped. For a few seconds, she said nothing, clearly knocked off balance by Jonathan's effortless capitulation. "So, now you think Irene Rivers is spying on us? How could she possibly benefit from that?"

Jonathan was too far inside his head to hear anything she was saying. "At the park," he thought aloud. "When I met with Wolfie, one of her security guys gave me a weird look." He rose from his rocker and walked to the window on the opposite wall, through which he could watch the masts in the marina sway gently in the calm river. "Normally, it's a ballbusting interaction with those guys, but this time Tweedle Dum didn't rise to my bait."

"Because he didn't insult you back you assume that he's a spy?" Venice said. "That's a big leap."

"It's the other variable," Jonathan said. "It's sure as shit not Wolfie herself, and with you vouching for Derek, there aren't a lot of feasible options."

"Except all the unknowns we don't know," she said.

"Yeah, those. Can we call in the others now?" Jonathan said. "Are we done here?"

"Can Derek join the team?"

Jonathan turned away from the window to face her again. "If we can figure out something for him to do, yes," he said.

"And you'll keep Boxers at bay?"

Jonathan's shoulders sagged. He couldn't believe he was having a high school conversation like this. "No," he said. "And that's a job for Derek. You know the rules here. Respect is earned, and you can take the heat or you can't. I'm not going to tell Box what he can and can't say. Jesus, that would just spin him up more. We play by big boy rules. To be continued. We have countless lives to save. Can we back-burner the personnel shit till later?"

Venice's anger was fading. Jonathan could tell she wanted to be more pissed than she was, but she wasn't exactly new to the dynamics of the place.

"I don't believe you just said *personnel shit*," she said. "Suppose the network news heard you? I'd have to file suit."

"And then I'd have to shoot the reporters." He sold it with a smile, then yelled, "Okay, team, let's get back together!"

A few seconds later, the door opened, and Boxers and Gail entered.

"Have a seat around the fireplace," Jonathan said. As he walked back to his rocker, he added, "I think we've been unfair and dismissive of Derek Halstrom. There's a good chance he's going to join our team in some capacity, and we all need to wrap our heads around that."

Boxers made a growling sound. "He's got to change his friggin' name, then."

Jonathan laughed. "I'll come up with something." He sat in his seat and opened his palms to Venice. "Ms. Alexander, you have the floor."

She looked uncomfortable. "Um, not here," she said. "We need to go back to the War Room."

Boxers made a show of hauling his huge frame out of the leather chair he'd just collapsed into. "Oh, this is fun," he said. "Not only do we have to cool our heels for the information, we get to march around the office, too."

Gail smacked him on the arm. "You know you're a baby sometimes, right?"

"I like the diaper," Boxers said. "Especially when it gets all squishy."

"And now it's time to puke," Jonathan said.

Thirty seconds later, they were gathered in their seats around the big teak table. The projector was already fired up.

Venice clicked, and the screen filled with pictures of Frederick Kellner in his natural state posted next to the fat man from Culpeper. "I can't take credit for this," she said. "It comes from information sent by Derek."

Jonathan could not possibly express how tired he was of hearing that name. And she always said it with that singsong quality that spoke of new love.

As they watched, the fuzzy picture of the fat guy who killed Cindy McVeigh superimposed itself over Kellner's face. The combined image magically magnified and rotated until they had a mildly fuzzy picture of a fat Kellner.

"There's a ninety-eight point three percent chance that Kellner murdered Cindy McVeigh, the young girl who did the brush pass," Venice said.

Jonathan noticed that she was reading from her screen.

Venice continued, "It turns out appearance and identity are two different things. You can change the look of your nose, for example, but you can't change its location on your face. At least not in a meaningful way. You can't change the position of your eyes or your ears, and two of the biggest tells of all are posture and gait. People can disguise as many of those factors as they like, but on a minute-by-minute basis, it's too many moving parts to keep track of, and all but the most experienced operators drop the ball on something."

"So, what we see up there," Jonathan said. "Where the fuzzy profile turns and morphs into a full face. Is that the new technology from your guy?" He couldn't make himself say the name. Baby steps.

"It's *evolving* technology," Venice said. "I don't know what parts fall into the supersecret category, but the totality of what we're watching is what the FBI doesn't yet have. Make sense?"

Jonathan nodded.

Venice continued, "The more factors that remain undisguised, the easier it is to find the person you're looking for."

Boxers grumbled, "Is there a 'so, therefore, we've got the bastard' at the end of this?" He recrossed his legs from left-over-right to right-over-left.

Venice said, "So, therefore, we've got the bastard."

Jonathan leaned into the table. This was not what he'd been expecting.

She smiled. "At least we think we do. Eighty-four-point-seven percent chance."

"How good is that in the world of facial recognition?" Gail asked. "It's not nearly enough for a sniper to take a shot, for example."

"Is it enough to take a trip to Alexandria?" Venice asked with a smile. She tapped her keys and another image of a man appeared on the screen. This one was the opposite of the fat guy. This one was athletic, tall, and young, and he sported an old-school crew cut. Not quite full-face, it was still a distant image.

"This comes from an ATM security camera," Venice explained. She tapped some more, and the image shifted and magnified and bloomed over the fat suit disguise. When she was done, all three images—Kellner in his natural state, in his fat suit, and in his new look—were ghost-like images, all stacked on top of each other. "Note how the features line up," she said.

It was remarkable. The eyes, noses, and ears all lined up perfectly.

"I don't understand why this is only an eighty-five percent match," Jonathan said. "I mean, everything looks spot-on."

"It's the digital manipulation," Venice explained. "Every time you zoom and magnify, you shave a couple of points off the probability."

"Definitely worth a trip to Alexandria," Jonathan said. "Can you track him somehow once we're there?"

"Not in real time," Venice said. "Once we program the camera management software to keep an eye out for the latest disguise, we can tell you where he's been, but the information will always be old."

"How old?" Boxers asked.

"As much as an hour."

"Crap."

Gail turned her head to look at Jonathan. "When are you going to tell Wolverine?"

Jonathan leaned back in the rocker and cast his eyes toward the ceiling. "I don't think I am," he said.

Gail gasped. "Digger! You have to. Too many lives are at stake."

He met Gail's gaze. "I think she's got a mole in her shop," he said. He shared the concerns he'd discussed with Venice.

"Then she needs to know *that*."

"Why?" Boxers said. "She's got thousands of agents working for her. If they can't find a mole in their own ranks, that's their problem, not ours."

Jonathan agreed. "Look, I don't know for sure about the mole. Here's where eighty-five percent means nothing. It's high enough for me to shut off the information spigot, but not enough to create ill will with Director Rivers."

"But if there's a terrorist plot in Alexandria, somebody needs to tell them," Gail persisted.

"We *don't* know that there's a terror plot in the works," Jonathan said. "We think we've got a guy who's the guy we suspect might have caused a terror incident elsewhere. That's a suspicion on top of an observation on top of a guess. That's not much. If you want to clear your conscience, feel free to call their tip line—preferably from a pay phone and without giving your name."

It was a rude kiss-off, and Gail clearly did not appreciate it. "It's not the same, Dig, and you know it." Color was rising in her cheeks. "Coming from you, the alert will carry more weight."

"It will also expose Derek," Venice said. "We've always protected means and methods. This is not the time to start breaking our own rules."

Her words sucked the air out of the room. Gail's shoulders settled, and she leaned back into the sofa.

Case closed.

"Let's go to Alexandria," Jonathan said.

Chapter Twenty-three

Kellner had never considered how long a time forty minutes was when you're riding in a big circle and you're tired of looking at the view.

Finally, the Potomac Eye finished its revolution, and Kellner was waiting at the door to pop out as soon as it opened.

"Have a nice day!" Molly called to him. While he was on the ride, she'd shifted to the arrival side of the machine.

"I'll do my very best," Kellner said. He prayed that he'd just issued his last forced smile of the day.

Now to find his contact. This would be a one-way effort, because Iceman had no idea what Kellner looked like now. There weren't but a few people within his field of view, so how could he not see anyone in a green coat and red hat?

As he left through the exit turnstile, he buttonhooked to the left and started walking back toward the buildings along the shore. He saw a man and a boy standing together pointing to something in the distance. A young lady sat on a bench reading her electronic tablet, while a man of the same age read his phone. From their physical closeness, Kellner assumed they were a couple. Maybe they were texting their love to each other.

When Iceman told him to meet his asset at 13:00 hours at the Potomac Eye, Kellner had acknowledged without having yet seen the place. For all its boring design, the wheel took up a lot of real estate. Beyond the physical footprint of the ride itself, you had the complex of ticket booths, chained off areas where lines formed, and two picnic areas on either side. Where, specifically, were he and his contact supposed to meet?

Maybe they were supposed to share a gondola on the wheel itself. If that were the case, then Kellner was going in the wrong direction.

He turned and looked back again toward the Eye itself. Of the three people waiting to get on, none were in the proper attire.

He checked his watch again, hoping that he was a few minutes early, but he was actually three minutes late. He shielded his eyes to see if he could make out the occupants of the various gondolas, but the glare made it impossible.

This standing and scanning had to stop. There was no better way to draw attention than to look lost. He turned again and started walking back toward shore.

It was possible, he supposed, that his contact couldn't make it for some reason, but if that were the case, he'd have expected to hear from Iceman.

Then, there he was. A guy who appeared to be in his sixties sat on the wooden bench closest to the shore, one hand resting on a silver-handled cane, the other holding a phone to his ear. As disguises went, this one was outstanding. The red Nationals hat couldn't have been more obvious, but the jacket he wore was more of a forest green than the brighter color Kellner had been expecting.

Kellner didn't walk directly to the guy, but rather took his time, moving at a slow stroll. The guy never looked at him, just kept talking on the phone. Great tradecraft.

When Kellner finally made it to the bench and sat down, he seated himself only a foot or two away to facilitate quiet conversation.

The man shifted to his left, away from Kellner, and shot him a look that rang a warning bell. Maybe this wasn't—

Somebody sneezed. It was a loud thing that pulled Kellner's head around. Twenty-five feet up the dock, closer to shore, a younger man in a green jacket and a red Nats hat was approaching. When they made eye contact, the guy gave a subtle shake of his head and kept walking toward the Eye.

Kellner let him pass and was going to give him a ten- or fifteen-second lead before he followed, when the old man on his left said, "Can I help you?" It was not a friendly offer. From the way he held his phone, the line was still open.

"Probably not," Kellner said.

"Then how about you give me some space?"

Kellner moved over a bit and then stood.

"This guy," the old man said into his phone. "Plops down like we're lovers and just sits there . . ."

Yeah, that was awkward.

Green Jacket was waiting for him all the way at the end of the dock, staring out over the water, or at least pretending to.

"Hi, Steve," Kellner said, following his script.

The contact turned. "Hey, Chuck."

"Redskins or Bills this year?" Kellner said.

"I say Falcons," the man said. "Maybe Chargers."

That was it. The sign and countersign were disposed of. Now all Kellner had to worry about was that this guy hadn't tortured his real contact to learn the script. Of course, Steve had to worry about the same thing, and that was what provided the needed balance for this association.

"I'll be straight up front with you," Steve said. "I don't like this arrangement. We shouldn't be together." If he'd altered his appearance, he'd either done it subtly or he was really damn good with disguises. He presented as early forties and athletic, but not in the way that most operators were athletic. He looked more like a fit cop than a fit snake eater.

"Not going to argue with you on that," Kellner said. "But I was never asked for my vote."

"Did you even get instructions?" Steve asked.

The on-the-nose nature of the question put Kellner on edge. "Tell me about yourself first," he said.

"What is this, a fraternity meeting?"

Kellner took a step back. "How about you dial it down a little? Look, dude, I don't know you from Adam. Try this, then. Back there when you forced the sneeze. How did you know it was me?"

"I didn't." Steve said. "I knew that the other guy

wasn't me but could have been. Throw in the fact that I'm running late, and I had a hunch. Now, what the hell are we doing here?"

"Didn't Iceman give you a target?"

"And a date," Steve said. "Clearly, we're to wreak havoc here, but what's the plan?"

Kellner jerked his head toward the shore. "Let's walk and talk. This is exactly the wrong spot to discuss what I want to talk about."

Chapter Twenty-four

The Golden Buoy Hotel on America Avenue sat three blocks back from the waterfront. At ten stories, it defined the first row of tall structures. Its marketing brochures touted the best views of the river, perfect for Independence Day fireworks. Who wouldn't pay extra for an unobstructed view of the Potomac Eye against a backdrop of beautiful pyrotechnics?

The lobby staff greeted Kellner and Steve with warm smiles and hearty good-afternoons, to which they responded in kind. The lobby itself was a utilitarian space, designed for weekday businessmen and weekend families, where the seats needed to be functional yet not necessarily comfortable. The color palette melded blues and yellows in ways that Kellner thought induced more stress than comfort, but who was he to judge? He was a beige kind of guy.

At the elevators, they waited for a middle-aged couple to clear the car before they stepped in. The top two floors required a special card to access, so Kellner pressed the button for the eighth floor. From there, they walked down the green-and-yellow carpeted hallway—honest to God, who paid people to design these spaces?—toward the exit door at the end of the hallway. The exit stairway was blessedly bland and concrete, and he was happy to see the sign that read FD ROOF ACCESS. This was where firefighters would go if they needed to get to the top to take care of fires or utility issues on the roof.

As the stairway door clicked behind him, he rattled the knob. It was locked. That meant a long walk down when they were done here. They climbed the four half-flights past floors nine and ten in silence, and another flight later, they were confronted with the locked access door to the roof.

The lock was barely a lock at all. Kellner pulled his pick set from his pocket—the same one, in fact, that a Secret Service neighbor had given him as a gift way back when Kellner was a teenager. The neighbor's name was Al, and he was always anxious to impress the kid next door. Kellner inserted the tension bar, raked the top pin tumblers and then the bottom ones, and the cylinder turned.

"Well, that was easy," Steve said.

Kellner replied with a grunt. Steve's newly found aggressive friendliness put him on edge. The guy seemed nothing like a killer.

As they stepped out onto the gravel-covered roof, Kellner thrust his arms out, as if making a presentation. *Ta-da!* Seeing the vista made the mission plainly obvious. The entirety of the Potomac Eye lay before them.

"There it is," Kellner said. "I was just on that puppy. Moves at a snail's pace. The range to the front of the gondolas is four hundred yards, give or take. The glass isn't glass, and the shots aren't hard. We can plink at those sons of bitches all night long, and they'd have no place to hide."

Steve smiled and put his hands on his hips. "You are one sick man," he said. He clearly meant it as a compliment.

"Well, I try," Kellner said. "I'm thinking a suppressed AR in seven-six-two. A little bit of overkill, but it will make some damn big holes."

"Even suppressed, it's going to draw a lot of attention," Steve observed.

"That's kind of the point, isn't it?" Kellner said. "People will hear shots, but there'll be no muzzle flash. Among these buildings, I figure the noise will bounce around so much that they won't be able to figure out where it's coming from. At least not for a few minutes. And that's all we'll need to get a couple hundred rounds downrange and get the hell out."

Steve pinched his lip as he listened to the plan. "So, how do you see my role?"

"I see you as the opening act," Kellner said. "There's going to be a lot of security down there because of the holiday. I'll act as your spotter at first to take them out. Use whatever weapon platform makes you more comfortable. Once we identify the uniforms and wipe them out, that will buy the time I need to go to work on the Eye."

"I can be a second shooter on that," Steve offered.

"I think that's a bad idea," Kellner said. "The cops are going to go apeshit when this goes down and their own people drop first. I need you to keep an eye out for them and neutralize those threats as they arise. Then, when my mags are empty, we're done. Thoughts?"

Steve chuckled. "I've already said it, dude. I think you are a sick man. I love the plan." His expression changed to one of curiosity. "Do you know if we're the only show for Halloween? Are there other ops going on simultaneously?"

"I don't know the answer to that," Kellner said. "I do sense that this is our last op for Iceman and that he wants it to be huge. So, I wouldn't be surprised to see more. But I just don't know."

"I don't get why he's doubling us up like this. We could make a lot bigger mark if we worked separately."

"Hey, the check cleared," Kellner said. "Everything other than that is above my pay grade." He started walking across the rooftop, examining the details. It was difficult to walk more than a few feet without bumping into a vent pipe or an air handler, big gray boxes that hummed more quietly than Kellner would have expected.

"What are you thinking for cover?" Steve asked, articulating Kellner's thoughts.

"Everything up here is one shade of gray or another," Kellner said. "At night, it would be pretty monochrome."

"We could build a couple of shelters," Steve said.

"Exactly," Kellner agreed. "Hell, we could drape ourselves under a gray blanket and be invisible from the air."

"Put gravel on top of the blanket," Steve said.

"Yes, exactly," Kellner said. "Exactly. The cover only has to last for a few minutes, and then we're out." It was time to test his new companion. "What do you have in mind for an exfil plan?"

Steve pinched his lower lip as he pivoted slowly on his own axis, taking in the details. "First of all, I'm leaving my weapon right here. They can track it all they want, but they'll just end up at a National Guard armory somewhere in Texas, where the gun was stolen five years ago. I've never been to the place, and my prints cannot be on it."

"Agreed," Kellner said. "But you'll need to be careful in the hotel room, too."

"What hotel room?"

"I booked two rooms for the next two nights. Your name is Steven Boyer, by the way, in case you lose your key or something."

"Isn't that a little risky?" Steve asked. "Anything that prolongs our exposure seems like a bad idea to me."

"If you don't want to stay, then don't," Kellner said. "Just have a good excuse as to why you're going up to the occupied room levels when you don't have a reservation. Don't get confused by the lackadaisical security effort you saw downstairs today. I expect security to be tight as hell at this place on tomorrow night. We've created quite the panic over these past few weeks. I'll have my rifle in a guitar case."

Steve acknowledged the logic with a quick twitch of his head. "Why two nights?"

"Less suspicious than checking out on the night of the op."

"Fine. So, on to exfil." He pivoted again, then he walked to the edge of the roof and looked down. "That's a long-ass rappel," he said. "You've been brooding over this for longer than I have. What are your thoughts?"

Kellner cleared his throat and bounced his eyebrows. He liked being recognized as the expert here.

"The only reasonable way down from here is through the stairwells. So, I figured we need to flood the stairs with occupants we can blend into."

Recognition bloomed in Steve's eyes. "You're going to set the building on fire. That's a little short-sighted what with us being up here and everything."

"Incendiary bombs," Kellner said. "One in your room, one in mine. Put a flashbang in with the incendiary to get everyone's attention. Once the fire alarm goes off, we're set. We just go with the flow."

Steve thought about that for a while. "You know, given the mayhem out on the street, the cops aren't going to let everyone just flow past."

"You can't stop people from fleeing a burning building," Kellner said. "I plan to pull off my shirt and go down looking as if I'd just been rousted from bed. I think it's my best shot. In a perfect world, you'd go down a different staircase, and then we part ways and never see each other again."

Steve paced, clearly running the plan through his head. "Do you think we can kill the power to the hotel?" he said after the long pause. "That would really raise the stakes on the panic scale."

It was Kellner's turn to study the problem. "I imagine it's a lot harder to get into the electrical room than it is to get up here on the roof."

"One thermite grenade is all it would take," Steve said. "We shoot it remotely. The lights go out, and we get another fire and even more confusion."

Diversionary tactics had long been a staple in Kellner's life. The tactical equivalent of sleight of hand, where the magician draws you to look away from where the action is happening, a good diversion allows operators to do what they need to do and get out before the targets realize that they've been hit.

He liked the idea of killing the power, but blinding the enemy was only effective if you yourself had night vision. "How would we get NVGs out of here?" he thought aloud, referring to night vision goggles.

"Why would we need them?" Steve asked. "I figure we wouldn't kill the power until we were on our way out. The stairway will be lit by emergency lights."

Kellner liked the idea, but it had a flaw. "If we kill the power here, that's like firing a flare that says, *look at me*."

Steve waited for the rest.

"Why stop at the hotel?" Kellner said with a wink. "Why not black out the whole block?"

Steve smiled. "You know how to do that?"

"I guess we'll find out," Kellner said. "I've done it for Uncle Sam in shithole corners of the globe. Can it be a lot different to do it here?"

Boxers parked at the curb outside the People's Bank. "This is the place," he said. It was from this ATM that the camera had captured Kellner walking by.

Jonathan opened the door on the shotgun side and stepped out. He adjusted the Colt on his belt on his right hip and the radio on his left, all hidden by the suit jacket he was tired of wearing.

He didn't know what he was looking for, exactly, but he hoped that he'd recognize it when he saw it. He'd visited Alexandria many times over the years—the locals called it Old Town—and he'd always found it to be beautiful. On a chilly fall afternoon like this one, the view across the Potomac was stunning. Hard to believe that this wide expanse of water was the same narrow river that coursed through Fisherman's Cove.

The bank building was only a block up from the water. In the distance lay the Woodrow Wilson Bridge, the site of a mass shooting of which he was a victim—or a potential one—not so long ago.

From the angle of the security photo, it was clear that Kellner had been walking toward the water when the picture was snapped.

Jonathan took out his phone and took several photos of the buildings and businesses that surrounded him. Then he set them to Venice with a request for her to see if any of them had useful imagery.

Sometimes, when you walked in the steps of your enemy, you could learn to understand him better. That was his theory, anyway, when he started strolling toward the water. He was halfway there before he knew that Gail and Boxers had followed him.

The town fathers had torn down an ancient boat club at the end of the street to make room for a city park–slash-marina. They strolled to the end, where a guardrail constructed of three courses of horizontal iron pipes kept people from falling in. Given the median blood alcohol content of Old Town partiers on a Saturday night, Jonathan imagined that the rails were the first things built.

"Bridge give you flashbacks, Boss?" Boxers asked with a smile.

"Over the years, it's hard to find a view that *doesn't* trigger a flashback," Jonathan said. "So, what do you think Kellner wanted? Why did he walk down here?"

"Do we know that he walked here?" Boxers asked.

"Work with me," Jonathan said. "Pretend that he did. Why?"

"He likes the view," Boxers said. Clearly, he wasn't going to play the game.

"Recon," Gail said.

"That's what I was thinking," Jonathan said. Then, with a nod to Big Guy, he added, "Okay, that's what I was *hoping*. What was he looking for?"

"Targets," Gail suggested. "Or exfil routes, or, more in line with Big Guy's view of the world, a place to eat."

"No," Boxers said. "It was a target."

The words startled Jonathan. "That was a quick change of heart."

"Because I just saw the perfect target for the kind of work he does." He pointed toward the Woodrow Wilson Bridge.

At first, Jonathan thought he was pointing at the bridge itself, and he was inclined to disagree. Short of blowing the thing up during rush hour, it would be hard to get the kind of body count these guys had become addicted to.

But then he looked beyond the bridge, and it fell into place. Way in the distance, the loop of a giant Ferris wheel cut a half-circle over the bridge span.

"The Potomac Eye," he said. And there wasn't a doubt in his mind that they'd identified the next target.

Chapter Twenty-five

Thanks to the presence of the massive Greyson Hotel and Casino, Capital Harbor was at once everything Jonathan abhorred and everything Boxers loved. Jonathan looked at gambling as a form of regressive taxation, attracting people who couldn't afford the games to cast reason aside to joust at the Windmill of Luck, all the while surrounding themselves with a façade of opulence that was nowhere to be found in their own lives. He thought of gambling as a form of legalized addiction from which authorities looked the other way because the addiction lined their pockets.

There was a reason why history books mentioned gaming commissions and organized crime in the same paragraphs.

The three of them took a water taxi across the river from Alexandria, in part because Boxers wasn't sure that the Batmobile would fit into the parking garages at Capital Harbor. As they disembarked, Jonathan was immediately struck by the potential value of the place as a terror target. As darkness fell and offices closed, the place began to fill with all strata of people, from lawyerly types in their tailored suits and carefully loosened ties, to construction workers in their boots and denim, to homeless folks who knew when the gravy train had arrived.

"Talk about your target rich environment," Gail said as they walked past the fountain that was sculpted to look like a bowsprit, complete with a fully clothed mermaid. "Casino, restaurants, Ferris wheel. And that doesn't include the ones we haven't thought about."

"It's the wheel," Boxers said. "There might be others, I suppose, but it's the wheel."

They wandered that way. As Jonathan took in the crowds and the couples, it occurred to him that something was missing. "Where are the children?" he thought aloud.

Gail answered, "At home watching television and doing homework, I assume."

"I thought parents did their kids' homework these days," Boxers said.

"But our guy—this Iceman—he likes to include kids in his target packages," Jonathan said. "Makes sense if you're him. Nothing makes a bigger headline than kids killed by terrorists." As he said the words, he reflexively looked around to see if he might have been overheard. People were seeing something and saying something more readily now than they had a few weeks ago.

Gail stopped short. "Tomorrow's Halloween," she said. Then she pointed to a glass-enclosed advertisement kiosk ahead and to their left. "Look."

A three-by-four-foot poster announced in bright orange and dark black that the Capital Harbor Waterfront would be the perfect spot for trick-or-treating. Every shop would be open to provide special treats for every "witch, wizard, ghost, or goblin," and many would be offering "special brews" for their parents or guardians.

"Well, that will spike the number of targets," Boxers said. "And mostly in the kiddie demographic."

"It'll be a bloodbath," Jonathan said.

"We need to tell someone," Gail said, yet again.

"We still don't have anything to tell them," Jonathan insisted.

"How are you going to feel after the fact if this thing happens as we think it will, yet you didn't say anything?"

Jonathan regarded Gail with a quizzical look. Did she really think he wasn't worried about the next attack? Did she think for a moment that his heart wouldn't bleed if they somehow aided something as horrible as another Black Friday attack? He chose not to respond. The three of them walked the next three blocks in silence until they were at the base of the massive Potomac Eye.

"Look how slow it goes," Boxers said.

"Should we give it a ride?" Gail asked.

"Oh, hell no," Boxers snapped. "I mean, y'all are welcome to, but there's no friggin' way I would go into one of those airborne prison cells."

"Execution chambers," Jonathan corrected. "And I agree. I think we'll stay on the ground for tonight." He turned his back to the wheel and faced the development of bars and hotels and office buildings. "Okay, Gunslinger, say I promote you to chief terrorist. How would you do it if the Eye was your target?"

He wanted to get her out of pissed-off, hurt-feelings mode and into a more proactive, stop-the-bad-guys mode.

"Can I tell you that first of all the Eye would not be my target, not on Halloween."

Now, that was interesting. "No? What would it be?"

"I'd plant bombs where all the people would be."

"I don't know," Boxers said. "Don't get me wrong, it would be a hell of a plan if it went well, but don't you think under the circumstances that this place will be crawling with bomb dogs? Surely, the cops will do a sweep."

"I don't know if they will or they won't, but a good bad guy should really assume the worst," Jonathan said.

"Fine," Gail said. "If the Eye is the main target, you've got a few hundred stranded tourists who can't get away. If we can't talk about explosives, then you're pretty much left with snipers."

"Now your turn, Big Guy," Jonathan said. "Where are you going to snipe from?"

Boxers glared as if he thought Jonathan had lost his mind. "Are you going to ask me to snatch a pebble from your hand later?" A reference to the ancient student-sensei TV show *Kung Fu*.

"Humor me."

"I'm not your friggin' student."

"This once."

Big Guy laughed. "Yeah, *this once*. Humor me *this once*."

Jonathan waited.

"From someplace high," Boxers said. "If I was the shooter, it would be high and far away."

"Gail?"

"Agreed."

"Times three," Jonathan said. Then he pointed ahead. "What say we take a stroll up America Avenue?"

The long dock from the Potomac Eye ended at Freedom Plaza, a circular white concrete disc with a fountain in the center and surrounded by a decorative wall that doubled as seating space for tired revelers. There wasn't much of a police presence, but the cops he saw were tached out with long guns. There was nothing overly-aggressive about their presence, but clearly they were taking seriously the need for upgraded security.

America Avenue stretched off from Freedom Plaza Drive, the road that ran perpendicular to the river, and up a slight incline where the restaurants, hotels, and office buildings created a redbrick canyon. As the sun dipped, flickering gaslights atop lampposts spaced maybe thirty feet apart along both sides of the street gave the place a certain charm, and in Jonathan's view took some of the edge off of the nastiness of the area.

As they walked up the hill, Jonathan kept craning his neck to see where the first likely sniper's nest would be. When they arrived at the revolving doors to the Golden Buoy Hotel, he knew he had the right place. "Let's go take a look at the view," he said.

"What are we looking for?" Gail asked as they crossed the lobby.

"Just want to be sure this is really the best place for our guy to set up."

As he led his team to the elevator, he tried to remain inconspicuous, but with Boxers in tow that was always difficult in a crowd. He . . . stood out.

They took the elevator as far as it would go, then switched to the stairs. It was Big Guy's idea to stick a quarter in the doorjamb to keep the fire door from locking behind them.

A minute later, Jonathan was at the door to the rooftop cupola. "Don't they normally keep these doors locked?" he asked as he pushed the panel open.

"Maybe we're not the first to do recon work up here," Gail said.

"Interesting thought," Jonathan said. "Maybe he's still here and we can end it all early."

No such luck.

The moment he stepped out onto the rooftop, Jonathan knew that they'd found the right place. The view of the Potomac Eye was entirely unobstructed, and as he approached the edge, Freedom Plaza opened up as a killing field. "This is where he'll be," he announced.

"Look behind you, Boss," Boxers said, pointing. "The building behind us has an extra three stories over this one."

"The one next door is taller, too," Gail added. "Granted, it's only two floors, but still."

Jonathan shook his head. "Nope, it's this one. Sure, I could be wrong, but Box, the one back there adds another, what, hundred fifty yards to the shot, and I'm guessing that perch loses a lot of the plaza. Gail, see the parapet along the edge of the one next to us? Again, it makes the shots unnecessarily difficult. Plus, it's off-line to the Eye." He planted his fists on his hips and scanned the horizon, reassessing his conclusions. "Nope," he said. "It'll be here."

Boxer laughed and clapped him on the shoulder. "It's always good to be sure on a wild-ass guess."

"You know," Gail said, "if we sweet-talk the front desk staff, maybe we can scan their security footage for Kellner."

Jonathan grinned. "That's why you get the big bucks, Gunslinger. Let's do it."

Back on the ground floor, as they waited for the elevator doors to open, Jonathan said, "Let's be FBI down here. As he spoke the words, he pulled himself taller and soured his expression, going for the joke.

"That's not Bureau, Boss," Boxers said. "That's constipation."

They shared a laugh.

The doors opened and Jonathan led the three-person phalanx across the lobby. Jonathan strode to the front desk and presented his credentials to the teenager behind the counter. His name tag read ZEE. "Agent Bonner, FBI," Jonathan said. "I need to speak with the manager."

"Um, the manager is with a couple who are planning their wedding."

"We only need a few minutes of his time."

"Do you have a business card?" Zee asked. "I can have have the call returned."

Jonathan leaned his arms heavily on the counter. "Contact him, please. Now."

"She's a her," Zee said, suddenly offended. "And she doesn't like being disturbed in the middle of—"

"What's her name?" Jonathan asked.

"Ms. Filipi," Zee said. "And it's her policy that—"

Boxers leaned in past Jonathan and growled in his most menacing tone, "Get her on the goddamn phone, or I'm going to get pissed."

Zee melted. He snatched the phone from its cradle and fumbled it before he could get it to his ear.

Boxers stood to his full height and winked at Jonathan. "You're welcome," he said.

Zee turned his back as he spoke hurriedly into the phone, and as he came back, he stammered, "Sh-she's on her way."

"Thank you," Jonathan said. "Now, let me show you something." He retrieved his phone from his suit coat pocket and pulled up the ATM picture of Kellner. "Have you seen this man?"

Zee reached for the phone, and Jonathan pulled it back. "Look, don't touch," he said.

The kid put his hands behind his back this time as he leaned in closer. "No, I haven't seen him."

"You said that really fast," Jonathan said. "Take another look."

"Look, officer, I'm feeling aggressed here."

Jonathan recoiled. "You're feeling *aggressed*? What the hell does that mean?"

"I would like you to step away from me, please. I-I've already told you no."

"When did you come on today?" Jonathan asked.

"About an hour ago."

"Okay, Zee. Thanks for your time."

Two minutes later, a fireplug of a woman approached, maybe five-three, and she looked angry. She walked quickly with short little steps, her arms pumping inordinately hard. "I am Ms. Filipi," she said as she closed in to within a few feet. "What do you want?"

Jonathan produced his creds again. "Good evening, ma'am, I'm Agent Bonner with the FBI, and these are my—"

"Badges don't impress me," Filipi said. "I don't like people who beat up other people just because they can."

Jonathan cocked his head. "When did I beat somebody up?"

"You're a cop, aren't you? That's what you do."

Jonathan sent up a silent prayer that Boxers wouldn't weigh in on this.

"Ma'am, I'm not here to engage in political discourse. I'm looking for a person of interest in a criminal matter." He produced the photo again. "Have you seen this man?"

She glanced. "No."

Jesus. "Please try again," Jonathan said. "We have reason to believe he has been here within the last few hours."

"My shift didn't start until one hour ago," Ms. Filipi said. "What did he allegedly do?"

"I can't speak to that," Jonathan said. "Do you mind if we look through your security camera footage to see—"

"Have you got a warrant?"

"No, ma'am, but—"

"Then, no," Filipi snapped. "You people do enough illegal spying on Americans. I'll have nothing to do with it. You bring me a warrant, and we can talk. Short of that, then, no."

A crowd had started to form. Jonathan wanted to get out of this before the cell phones came out to take video footage. "Thank you, ma'am," he said. "I appreciate your time."

"Can I go back to work now?"

Jonathan leaned in close so only she could hear and said, "I don't care what you do, you nasty little bitch." He pivoted before she could react and led the way back toward the revolving doors.

"Where does all that attitude go when they *need* a

cop?" Boxers grumbled when they were back out on the sidewalk.

"Can't tell you how glad I am to be out of that game," Gail said. "What now?"

Jonathan made a phone call back to Fisherman's Cove and told Venice to tap into the Golden Buoy's security system and see if she could find their boy on the record there.

It was after six now, and night had fully fallen. The bars were beginning to get active, and the streets had begun to fill with the dinner and party crowds.

Jonathan and his team stood there on the sidewalk, as if a rock in the middle of a stream. "I think we need a plan, Boss," Boxers said. "Got anything in mind?"

"Sort of," Jonathan said. "Tavern Row starts one block south of here. If he's waiting till tomorrow to wreak his mayhem, maybe he's drinking some courage tonight. I say we split up and show his picture to as many people as we can."

"I don't like splitting up," Boxers said. "Let's do it as a group."

"The clock is ticking," Gail said. "I don't like spitting up, either, but it'll let us cover way more ground."

"If you get a hit, give a shout on the radio," Jonathan said. "Then we join up again and see what the next step is."

"I don't like it," Boxers said again.

Jonathan feigned a baby voice. "Is widdle Boxie afraid?"

Boxers' whole body seemed to swell. Ever played with a dog too long and you get that awful feeling that the dog's not playing anymore? That's what it was like with Boxers when you pushed him too far. Like an angry dog. The biggest most lethal angry dog on the planet.

"Oh, get over yourself," Gail said. "It was a joke."

That did the trick. Big Guy's anger passed.

"Well, that was fun," Jonathan said. "Tavern Row runs at least three blocks. Let's each take a block and see what we find."

"And if you get a hit, radio it in first thing," Boxers said.

They headed down the hill toward the water and turned left onto Freedom Plaza Drive. Gail peeled off first onto Constitution Street, where at least two dozen bars lined both sides of the street. Jonathan had been noting that Gail's limp was returning, a sure sign that she needed to take a break, so he figured that the less walking she had to do, the better off she'd be.

When they were alone, Jonathan asked Boxers, "Why are you so jumpy?"

"I don't know," Big Guy admitted. "I just have a bad feeling I guess. I don't like it when the team splits up. It's one thing when we're moving for advantage in a firefight because we're all still on the same targets. Going out individually is a bad idea. Sorry, Boss, but you asked me."

Jonathan smirked. "You don't think I know how to fight my own fights, do you?"

Boxers grinned. "You know I've *seen* you fight, right? Those little wounded-kitten punches." Big Guy made little mewing noises as he punched at the air with little T-Rex arms.

Jonathan laughed. "God, you're an asshole."

Boxers said, "I complete you."

When they got to the next corner, Independence Street, Jonathan stopped. "I'll take this one," he said. "I'll leave the long walk to you."

Boxers blew him an air kiss. Big Guy was in rare form tonight. But you know what? It wasn't uncommon for those bad feelings to turn into bad shit.

Jimmy Kraut and Allen Wade shared rolled eyes as they approached the boarding line for the Potomac Eye. "Oh, God, this is going to be so lame," Jimmy said.

"Oh, will you two please stop?" The request came from Lauren Stark, Jimmy's girlfriend and, he was pretty sure, his future wife. After they were both out of college, five years for him and six for her. "The view will be beautiful."

"It's nighttime," Allen said. "It's dark. What can you see in the dark?"

"The lights," said his girlfriend, Ashleigh. "And the night sky. If Jimmy wasn't here, you'd be fine with it. Just because you're 'Mister Tough Lacrosse Dude' doesn't mean that you can't enjoy pretty things."

Ashleigh was a bitch. Jimmy had known her since elementary school, and she'd always been a bitch. Even the spelling of her name was bitchy. *L-E-I-G-H, my ass,* he thought. She was going to suck the life out of Allen. Jimmy smiled at the irony. He happened to know that for now, it wasn't Allen's life that was being sucked dry, but something else. In confidence, Allen told him that Ashleigh had no gag reflex. And people wondered why they were still a couple!

"It's only forty-five minutes," Lauren said. "You can do anything for forty-five minutes." She pinched Jimmy's ass. "Think of it as doing a nice thing for me."

"Is that an offer to return the favor?" Jimmy asked with a wink and a grin.

"It all depends on how you behave," Lauren said.

"So, maybe a spanking if I'm a bad boy?"

"Oh, my God," Lauren groaned. "You just never grow up, do you?"

"I hope not." Jimmy put his arm around her and pulled her in close. God, he loved this lady.

Finally, it was their turn to climb aboard. During his half-hour wait, he'd watched enough other people manage the step off into the moving gondola, but it felt a little weirder than he'd anticipated. Once aboard, the couples split, with Lauren and Jimmy sitting on the left-hand bench, and Allen and Ashleigh on the right. But then three generations of an Asian family flooded their gondola, so Jimmy decided to move to the other side to be with their friends.

By the time the gondola door closed, the space was packed with twelve people. The family chattered in whatever language they were speaking, and whatever they were saying was apparently funny as hell because they all laughed raucously.

"Oh, yeah," Jimmy mumbled. "This is gonna be fun."

This time Lauren pinched his balls and made him jump. "Forty-five minutes," she whispered. "And if you're nice, I'll have a favor to return.

His pants grew very tight down there.

Now he appreciated the long ride. It would take him forty-five minutes of thinking about goat guts and calculus to be able to stand without getting cited for public display of perversion.

Chapter Twenty-six

Fred Kellner wondered if he'd made a mistake planting the C4 explosive on the power transformer so early. He liked the idea of blacking out the whole neighborhood when the balloon went up, and his rationale was to be done with it before the extra security arrived for the Halloween celebration tomorrow night. For sure, no one was going to find it by accident. It wasn't that big a block, and he'd concealed it well under the water guard of the sidewalk-mounted green box. He even camouflaged it with dirt and gravel.

But if the security teams brought dogs with them to sniff before the event and they hit on his bomb, they'd likely lock everything down and cancel the whole evening. Then he'd be in a spot, and it would be tough to explain to Iceman how he ended up botching his own operation.

He was thinking about removing the explosive charge, but doing so would be particularly tough now, given the number of people wandering about. If he was going to do it, he'd have to haul his ass out of bed at some ridiculous hour tonight (tomorrow?).

Where the hell was his *partner* Steve? After they'd split up earlier and went to their separate rooms in the Golden Buoy, they'd agreed to meet here at eight. It was 8:05 now, and Steve's chair was still empty.

He sat at an elevated two-top in a back corner of the Parker Brothers' Wild Dueling Pianos Bar at the top end of Constitution Street, and as he spun his Bud Lite bottle in its sweat ring, he wondered what his *partner* Steve's real game was. Or, better still, what Iceman's game was in pairing them up. If there was one lesson Kellner had learned over the years, it was that any break from expectation and routine was always a bad thing.

It was entirely possible that Steve was exactly what he purported to be, but in this job, retirement depended on trusting no one.

Kellner thought about giving Steve a call on his burner, but as soon as the notion formed in his head, the music started up. He wouldn't be able to hear a thing over the phone, and he wasn't yet ready to give up his seat.

Kellner decided to give him a half hour.

Lost in thought, he was startled when a guy pulled out the other stool at his table and helped himself to the empty seat. "Got a second?" the guy asked. He'd stepped out of Central Casting as a biker. Rocking a long red ponytail, he wore a denim vest over a plaid checkered flannel shirt, under which an ample belly challenged the jeans that appeared to Kellner to be at least two sizes too small. A red beard covered most of his chest, erupting from high on his cheeks.

Kellner fought the urge to draw down on this guy. "I'd prefer to be alone," he said.

The guy sat down, anyway. "Name's Smitty," he said, offering his hand. He leaned in close to be heard over the music without shouting.

Keller stared at the hand, probably for a second too long, then shook. "I'm Chuck," he said. "And I'd still rather be alone."

"Dude, I'm not here for a date. I thought you'd like to know that the FBI is looking for you."

Kellner felt something go liquid in his gut but worked to keep his face emotionless. "Huh," he said. "Why? What have I done?"

"I don't know, and it's none of my business," Smitty said. "All's I know is that there's this FBI lady cruising the bars with a picture of you, asking if people have seen you."

Kellner found it difficult to think rationally past his pounding heart. "How do you know she's with the FBI?"

"That's what she said," Smitty replied. "And I think she might have had a badge on her belt. I'm not so sure about that."

"And she didn't say why they were looking for me?"

Smitty shook his head. "And I didn't ask, either."

How could this have happened, he wondered. "Where were you when she approached you?"

Smitty tossed a nod toward the front door. "At Callahan's the first time. About three bars down the hill from here."

"There was more than one time?" Kellner asked.

"I don't think she's paying all that close attention to who she's asking, you know? It's like, if you've got a heartbeat, she's gonna show the picture."

Kellner reared back a little. "They've got a picture?"

"Yeah," Smitty said. "On her phone. I think it's lifted from some security camera somewhere, but it's a pretty good photo."

Shit, shit, shit, shit . . . There had to be a way to put this genie back in the bottle. He just had to figure out how.

"Why are you telling me this?" Kellner asked. "What's in it for you?"

"I did eight years in the penitentiary because of DNA analysis that they lied about," Smitty said. "I don't know if you remember the case a few years back, where the FBI's lab manager was caught with his thumb on the blind lady's scale. They held back details that would have shown me to be innocent and then misrepresented the rest in court. Wasn't just me, either. Affected a whole shit ton of people. They fired his ass and let my ass go free, but that's eight years out of my life, you know? *Eight years.*"

Kellner noted the tears in the guy's eyes. Jail would suck under any circumstances, but he couldn't imagine how he'd handle the anger of being sent there under false pretenses and deliberate lies.

"So," Smitty continued, "I take whatever opportunity I can to ruin whatever those assholes are doing." He extended his hand again. "Welcome to my bad deed of the day."

Kellner accepted the hand again, then paused. "What does this FBI lady look like?"

Smitty scowled as he thought. "I'm not sure I know how to describe her. Normal height for a woman, maybe five-seven. Blond-ish ponytail, gray business suit—

pants, not skirt. Oh, yeah, and she walks with a limp. Nothing huge, but noticeable if you know what you're looking for."

Kellner listened and realized that he'd just described a couple million people.

Smitty broke off the handshake and stood to go back to wherever he'd come from and leaned in again. "Look, none of this is any of my business, but if you're going to get out, now would be the time to do it. She's for sure gonna get to this place, because she was working every establishment on the block."

He searched Kellner's face for a reaction and seemed disappointed in what he saw. "That's all I've got, dude. Chuck. Good luck."

As he watched Smitty navigate his way through the crowd to return to his seat near the bar, Kellner ran through his options. First choice: Stay or go?

If the FBI lady was traveling door-to-door and was only three doors down however long ago she was there, then she'd soon be here. If he left through the front door, would he run into this lady? Surely, he would encounter someone else she'd approached, and what would happen then? He already knew from a previous trip to the men's room that the back door had an alarm on it, and he knew from previous experience that it undoubtedly worked. No matter the cost of maintenance, it was always cheaper in the long run to keep the exit alarm in working order than it was to lose the revenue from unpaid-for bar bills.

In an instant, it became clear to him what he had to do. He grabbed his phone from his pocket and called Steve's burner. It must have rung a dozen times before a sleep-addled voice said, "Um, yeah. Hello?"

"Steve?"

"Huh? Who? Oh, yeah, hi, Chuck. Oh, shit! I slept too long. Sorry man. Shit. I can be there in five minutes."

"Forget that," Kellner said. "Everything's gone to shit. Execute the plan now. I'll join you when I can."

"I, uh. . . . What happened?"

"No time to explain. Get to the roof and get started. I'll try to give you ten minutes before I turn out the lights. It'll probably be closer to five, so get your ass up there. Don't wait for me. Just open up." He clicked off.

This wasn't about Iceman and his grand plan anymore. This was about the biggest diversion of all time to get Kellner to safety.

Chapter Twenty-seven

The pavement pounding was beginning to get to Gail. She'd made great progress since her injury, and for the most part she was back in true fighting form, but activities like this, walking slowly and dodging people, sometimes lit up her neck and back. Somewhere at the end of tonight, a long bath and a very long nap lay in her future.

She'd shown Kellner's picture to at least two hundred people, she figured—management, labor, and partiers—at thirteen different restaurants and bars, and the results had been mixed. Most took the obligatory cursory glance, but she'd had a few hits, too. Some of the sightings were hours old, and some were within the last half hour, forty-five minutes. While her heart told her that some were lying—probably just for the hell of it—she tried to push those thoughts away. The idea here was always to follow evidence where it took you. If the destination turned out to be a dead end, then at least you will have been guided there honestly.

As she reached the top of the hill, she paused for a few seconds to look down on the Capital Harbor complex. It was much more beautiful at night, she thought. Jonathan spoke derisively about the Potomac Eye, but she thought it was a pretty cool idea, and now that it was lit up, she thought it was spectacular. Freedom Plaza teemed with people, some of them in costume a night early, probably for a private party somewhere.

One last place to visit, and then it was quitting time. She keyed the transmit button on the radio she wore on her belt. "I'm pretty much at the end of the line," she said. "I'm entering Parker Brothers' Wild Dueling Piano Bar."

"I copy that," Jonathan said.

Each of them informed the rest of the team when they were entering or leaving a new place. That way, if trouble came, the others would know where to go to provide backup.

As she pushed through the door, the overamplified sound hit her like a physical obstacle. For the life of her, she didn't understand why things needed to be so loud these days. Armed with the photo pulled up on her phone, she walked to the thick-chested black man in the black T-shirt that read SECURITY.

She badged him, then presented the picture. "Have you seen this man?"

The bouncer looked at it, then scowled. "What did he do?"

"That's a question, not an answer," Gail said. "Have you *seen* him?"

"I see a lot of people," the bouncer said. "He looks familiar, but sooner or later everybody looks familiar, know what I mean?"

Yeah, she thought, *it means you've got nothing.* Time to work the room.

Though the construction here couldn't be more than five years old, the cavernous room had the feel of an old converted warehouse, with twenty-foot ceilings and brick walls. It was a giant sound amplifier. People at the tables had to lean close and shout to be heard. It felt like standing on a flight line.

The dueling grand pianos sat on an elevated platform that put them above the bar, which itself ran the length of the right-hand wall. To the left, looking front-to-back, the hoard of revelers occupied a sea of high-top tables.

There was no easy way to do what she needed to do. One table at a time, one person at a time, you show the picture and wait for a reaction. As she took a step forward to wade into it all, motion on her right caught her eye. A biker with a red beard was waving to someone in the back of the bar. Probably saving a seat for a friend.

Gail followed the biker's sight line and—

"Holy shit," she said aloud. She keyed her mic. "I've got him," she said. "I've got him, I've got him. Dueling Piano Bar."

"Wait for us before you take action," Jonathan said.

Kellner finally saw the biker's ever-more-frantic wave.

"Don't think that's going to be possible," Gail said.

Now that the biker had Kellner's attention, he pointed straight at Gail.

Here we go, Gail thought. She casually drew her nine-millimeter Glock 19 from its holster on her hip and let it dangle at her thigh.

Kellner moved with startling speed. He leapt from

his stool, and by the time he was clear of it, he had a pistol in his hand.

"Oh, shit!" Gail yelled reflexively. "Gun! Down! Everybody get down!" Her words were lost in the cacophony of chatter and music. She brought her Glock to high ready, but there were just too many innocents in the way to dare a shot.

Kellner had no such compunction. He opened up on the crowd, sending at least ten rounds downrange in Gail's general direction, but hitting her wasn't the point. He wanted stacked bodies and panicked patrons. There'd be a stampede for the front door. Preparing for the coming rush, Gail lowered her shoulder like the football player she never was and pushed forward toward the back of the room.

As people fell and panic bloomed, screaming became contagious.

The pianos stopped playing as the pianists dove for the floor.

Gail yelled into her radio, "Shots fired! Shots fired! I'm engaging."

Gunfire erupted again. These weren't aimed shots, but rather a mag dump, a percussive *boom-boom-boom* that sent bullets tearing into flesh and furniture.

Within seconds, the stampede was in full bloom, with everybody pressing toward the front while Gail was pushing toward the rear. "FBI!" she shouted, holding her badge high and her pistol low. "Get out of the way. Get down!"

Less than twenty seconds into the attack, the floors were already becoming slick with blood. As the dead and wounded fell, they became tripping hazards, and the panic bloomed even brighter.

As Gail continued to press toward the back, against the crushing stream of terrified patrons, she noted that the firing had stopped. Either he was changing magazines, or he was making his escape. Two seconds later, she heard the characteristic squeal of a door alarm, and she had her answer.

For reasons that never made any sense to her, building codes allowed emergency exits to be fitted with timers that allowed twenty- to thirty-second delays before the locks would open. Clearly, they were designed to stop pilferage, but in cases like a wildman shooter, those twenty seconds could prove deadly as the accompanying alarm drew fire.

Tonight, though, the crazy timed lock gave her precious time to close the distance. She got glimpses of Kellner at the door, and she noted that the slide on his pistol was locked back. He was out of ammo. His only chance now was to run for it. If she could get a reliable shooting lane, she was going to kill him.

"Frederick Kellner!" Gail shouted. "FBI! Freeze."

If he heard, he showed no sign of it.

Jesus, the sea of panic was exhausting. She kept pushing. She only needed a couple of seconds for a clear shot.

Out of nowhere, a beefy arm reached out from her right and shoved Gail to the side, knocking her off-balance. She stumbled over a wounded man but caught herself on a barstool before she fell.

It was Big Red, the guy with the beard who'd been trying to get Kellner's attention. "Oops," he said.

"Go to hell," Gail said. She launched herself up and off the barstool and moved to push past Big Red, but he moved to block her way again.

Gail fired a brutal front kick to the asshole's kneecap, dislodging it to the outside of his leg. He howled in agony and collapsed. On his way down, she pounded his nose with a lightning-fast left jab, and he was done.

Gail sidestepped Red and finally had a clear path to the back door. It stood ajar, and no one was there.

She keyed her mic. "Kellner made it out the back door," she said. "I'm following."

"Goddammit, Gail," Jonathan said. "Wait for our backup."

"Told you we shouldn't have broken up," Boxers said over the air, clearly running.

"Shut up," Jonathan snapped.

Gail ignored both of them. She was going to get Kellner.

He couldn't have more than ten-second head start, could he? Surely, her fight with Big Red didn't last longer than that. She moved quickly to the steel door—none of the panicked guests had thought to come this way yet—and as she opened it, she moved carefully. If the roles were reversed, and she'd just run out of ammo, she'd—

Gail was halfway out the door when the heavy steel panel slammed into her left side and knocked her to the right. It helped that she'd been expecting it, so while it knocked her off-balance, she didn't fall. She slammed the door back the other way, but it didn't hit anything.

With her Glock up in a two-handed shooting grip, in close to her body, she angled out a step at a time, ready to take a shot the instant she had one. By the time she'd cleared the cover of the door, she saw Kellner again. He was hauling ass down the alleyway, making his way to the corner.

Gail got a sight picture just as he was making the turn, and she snapped off a shot. She thought she'd missed, but he stumbled, anyway—just a quick step off to his right—but then he gained his stride again. She fired again for good measure, but she knew before the round cleared the muzzle that she'd whiffed it.

She keyed her transmit button. "Kellner's in the wind. He turned left out the back door of the Dueling Pianos and then left again at the alley. I'm in pursuit." And she didn't care what Jonathan thought about that.

She'd only made it three or four steps around the corner before the distance erupted with the sharp pops of gunfire. Within seconds, a wave of screaming people swelled from the street down below.

She keyed her mic. "We were wrong," she said. "The attack is now. It's underway right now!"

She didn't care about Kellner anymore. He was gone. So, who had opened fire down below? Was it from the sniper's nest they'd identified? How could it be?

Unless Kellner wasn't working alone this time.

The gunfire was relentless, but it didn't sound like rifle fire she would have suspected from a sniper. It was softer and sharper, more like a pistol than the throaty boom of high-powered, large-caliber ordnance.

The she got it.

She keyed her mic. "Be advised, I think the shooter is using a suppressor." Translation: the near total lack of a muzzle flash would make him very hard to locate.

Halfway down the hill, she encountered the bloodied and terrified patrons of the Dueling Pianos bar as they spilled out onto the sidewalk and street.

"Someone call nine-one-one," a voice shouted. "Oh, my God, we need an ambulance!"

Gail swallowed the lump that formed in her throat from the realization that there'd be many more ambulances needed tonight. And with the piano bar victims being four blocks up from the *real* slaughter that was evolving, these people may be waiting a long time.

She fought the urge to stop and help. It didn't feel right to focus on these pistol wounds when there would be so many horrific rifle wounds to contend with down below.

She took off at a run. After a few steps, an explosion rattled everything, and all the lights went out.

Lauren rubbed Jimmy's balls some more. It was her game to keep him hard, so he'd be embarrassed when he stood. It was also a promise for later. "Okay, you were right," she said. "This is pretty lame."

"Gotta love the view," he said. "I think I'd recognize any one of those butts anywhere I saw them."

"Plus, I'm learning Japanese," Allen said.

"That's Korean," Ashleigh corrected.

"Whatever," Allen said. Jimmy sensed that he was pretty much done with her, oral prowess notwithstanding.

The invading family had never sat down and never shut up. The youngest of the group—maybe eight or nine years old—kept dashing back and forth in the gondola to see the different views. At one point, the older of the two kids planted his feet on the plastic bench where Jimmy and his friends were sitting and stood there looking outside.

Allen snarled at the kid and made an excellent imitation of a feral dog growling.

The kid hopped down and stayed away for the rest of the ride. The kid must have said something to his dad because one of the older family members gave Allen the stink eye. God forbid they actually, you know, raise their kids.

"Parent is a verb *and* a noun," Allen said to the father. "Keep a leash on them."

Ashleigh was aghast. "You can't say something like that to someone else's child," she said.

"I didn't say jack to the kid," Allen said at normal volume. Clearly, he wouldn't have minded if this escalated to something bigger. "I said it to his lazy father."

"How about you dial it down a little," Jimmy said, sotto voce. "This is way too small a space to rumble."

"It's also too small a space to run around like it's a playground."

Jimmy had known Allen since their first day of kindergarten, and knew that he was smart as hell, but the boy had no filters. He often joked that it was even money whether Allen Wade would get a Nobel Prize in literature or a life sentence for killing someone who crossed him.

"Not now, okay?" Jimmy said. "We can trash talk the hell out of them afterwards, but for now—"

His peripheral vision caught some odd movement down on the ground, and it pulled his attention. People were scrambling about, as if in a panic. "What the hell is that?"

He pointed, and everyone moved to his side of the gondola to get a better look.

"Oh, my God," Lauren gasped. "People are falling. Just collapsing."

"Jesus, is that blood on the pavement?" Allen said. "It is! It's spraying out of that lady's neck. See? Over by the fountain?"

The Asian family was seeing the same scene, and they started to yell and cry. The parents pulled their kids close to them.

"It must be an active shooter," Jimmy said, drawing from the lectures he'd received at school. "But I don't hear any shooting."

"The car is soundproofed," Ashleigh said. "Wow, a lot of them are going down."

Thock.

One of the Asian ladies dropped to the floor of the gondola. Instantly, blood was everywhere.

"Jesus!" Jimmy yelled.

Thock.

A bullet hole materialized in the window behind Allen.

Thock-thock-thock-thock-thock . . .

Splinters of plastic and seat foam erupted on the inside of their gondola as the shooter took out his wrath on them.

Jimmy wrapped his arms around Lauren and pushed her to the floor, trying to shove her under the bench, but Ashleigh had already taken up most of the space. "Make room!" Jimmy yelled.

Ashleigh stiffened and expanded her occupancy of the space.

"Aw, come on, Ash—"

A crushing impact hammered the center of his right shoulder blade and knocked him into the plastic seat. At the same instant, a hole erupted in the seat, and he knew he'd been shot. He tried to throw himself to the floor, but a second bullet blasted through his left thigh before he could drop all the way. He landed hard on the floor, knocking the back of his head on the wall. A rose of blood and tissue had erupted out of his jeans, and he found himself screaming, even though nothing really hurt yet. His head hurt more than the wounds.

For now, he felt only a searing heat in his leg and shoulder, but mostly, things were numb.

And the bullets kept coming. *What the hell? Why the hell?*

Feeling began to return. He could feel the heat of his blood. And he could smell it and taste it.

He dared a glance down at where he wanted his shoulder to still be, and except for a hole in his leather jacket, surrounded by a little poof of blood-tinged lining, everything looked normal. Maybe it wasn't as bad as he thought. He reached with his left hand under the leather, and his fingers found hamburger. *Jimmy-burger,* he thought, and he found a way to smile.

In the midst of the screaming, he called, "Lauren! I've been hit. Are you okay?"

He only heard the voices that he didn't care about.

Jimmy tried to lift his head, but that lit up something in his neck that reignited the searing pain in his shoulder. "Ow! Shit! Lauren!"

A voice arrived in his left ear. "Dude. Ah, Jesus, look at you." It was Allen.

"Is it that bad?" Jimmy asked.

"I don't know, man. But legs aren't supposed to bend that way. But I think the shooting's stopped."

"How's Lauren?"

The silence that followed wasn't really silent at all. The wailing and crying had a kind of physical force to it. It was overwhelming. It made the gondola reverberate with grief. But through it all, Allen fell quiet.

Jimmy tried to turn his head to eyeball his friend, but the pain wouldn't let him do it. "Tell me, Allen," Jimmy said. "Please tell me."

"Just relax, Jimmy," Allen said. "We're going to get you help."

"Tell me, goddammit! Where's Lauren?"

Allen rubbed Jimmy's hair. Kind, gentle strokes. "I'm sorry, Jim," he said.

Jimmy felt the emotion rising, and with it the pain blossomed to excruciating. He knew what was coming, but for some reason, he needed to hear it. He needed Allen to feel the pain of saying the words as punishment for still being okay.

"She's dead, man. Instantly, I'm sure of it."

"You can't be sure."

"Yeah, Jimmy, you can. Trust me. Ashleigh, too."

Jimmy didn't give a shit about Ashleigh. "What about me?" he asked. "How eff'd up am I?"

Allen never stopped stroking Jimmy's hair. It felt good. A gesture of kindness in this swirling tornado of evil and death.

"We'll be on the ground soon enough," Allen said. "Then we'll get you to a hospital, and you'll be fine. I won't let you die."

Jimmy felt tears running toward his ears as a crushing sense of hopelessness and helplessness enfolded him. He forced a smile and said, "You're not going to kiss me now, are you?"

Somewhere out there in the night, an explosion shook the air.

In that same instant, the lights went out.

Kellner was wrong to second-guess. Setting the C4 on the electrical transformer was the smartest thing he'd ever done. With the FBI bitch on his tail and Steve going to work on the crowd, instant darkness was everything he needed to get away. When he pressed the four-digit code on his cell phone, gratification came instantly. The blast wasn't as startling as it might have been if the shooting hadn't started first, but it was big enough to reverberate off the bricks even four blocks away.

As the electric lights went out, the alley to the side of the piano bar transformed from charming to menacing, reminding Kellner of what the streets of White Chapel must have looked like during Jack the Ripper's reign of terror.

The people up here were free from danger for now, but there was no way for them to know that. In the dark, he was able to mingle with the bloodied and the wounded and disappear into the mayhem.

Sirens split the night, but as the cadence of Steve's gunfire picked up, those emergency responders were going to be spread so thin that only the most grievously wounded would receive treatment. Actually, that wasn't true. The really bad cases that would have qualified for a medevac and quick trauma surgery—the kind of heroic efforts that fail more than they succeed but are worth doing anyway—would be left to die. That was the nature of triage. The patient with only a 20 percent chance of survival without intervention got priority over the one with a 50 percent chance. But the guy with only a 10 percent chance? With so many patients to tend to, he would be left to die.

A well-planned act of terror affected everything and everyone at more than one level. And this one was brilliant.

But good old Steve would have to finish it on his own. Kellner had had quite enough close calls for one night.

The time had come for him to retire.

The first step on that journey was to stay out of the line of fire.

Chapter Twenty-eight

Jonathan heard the gunfire and knew in an instant that they were too late. He hadn't considered that Kellner might have accomplices. He keyed his mic. "Gunslinger, where are you?"

"I'm on the main road. Freedom Plaza. It's really bad, Scorpion."

"Big Guy?"

"On my way," he said. "No one do anything until we're back together, right?"

"Just stay out of their sights," Jonathan said.

When he got to the bottom of his hill, he turned right and sprinted toward the place where everyone else was sprinting out. Everyone, that was, except for those who were on the ground because they were scared or because they were hit. In the darkness, people and landmarks were just dark objects against dark backgrounds. Thanks to the gaslights that were unaffected by the power outage, the pools and streams of blood had a luminescence about them.

This was huge. Jonathan hadn't counted the rounds fired, but after so many years in so many gunfights, he had a feel for these things. His gut calculated them to be in the hundreds. And the asshole kept firing, and people kept falling.

And no one was shooting back.

Well, that shit was about to change.

"Where are you, Gunslinger?" he asked over the air.

"At the base of America Avenue," she said. "A cop's been hit."

"If past is precedent, a lot of cops have been hit," Jonathan said aloud to himself. He picked up his pace.

And the gunfire continued. They were easily a minute and a half, two minutes into the attack, and the shooter seemed to have no intention of letting up. At the rate that people were dropping, it seemed that many of his shots were aimed and accurate. This was a bloodbath.

Other than managing somehow not to get shot, his first order of business was to get more firepower than the .45 that was strapped to his hip.

When he found Gail, she was on her knees, tending to a wounded police officer. He lay on his back, a human island in a sea of his own blood while she applied a tourniquet to a spurting wound in his leg. Another cop lay dead of a head wound, sprawled just two feet away.

"Thank God," Gail said when Jonathan joined her. "Give me a hand."

Jonathan didn't reply. Instead, he went to the dead officer and lifted him to a sitting position. He wrestled the man's slung rifle off his shoulder and ruined head and laid it on the ground. Then he stripped the Velcro of the cop's vest and wrestled that over the cop's head as well and put it on himself.

Jonathan didn't care about the protection provided by the vest—the guy hadn't inserted any plates, so he might as well have been shirtless against rifle fire. The pouches for the guy's extra magazines were integral to the vest itself, and since Jonathan was about to go and pick a gunfight, he wanted as much ammo as he could get.

After he'd donned the vest and slung the rifle over his own head, he realized that Gail had been talking to him. Whatever she was saying, it could wait.

"Get to cover, Gail," he said. "You've done what you can for him."

"Where are you going?"

"We started this," Jonathan said. "Now, I'm going to finish it."

He started his long sprint to the Golden Buoy Hotel.

Gail felt overwhelmed by it all. The screams. The moans. The thrashing of the wounded, the stillness of the dead. And the blood. Oh, good God, the blood.

The police officer she was attending—his name tag read HINTON—was the first wounded person she'd encountered after getting to the bottom of the hill, so she went to him. He'd been trying to press on his femoral geyser with one hand while fishing for the first aid pouch on his vest, but the blood continued to spew. She took control and grabbed his tourniquet.

Now that she was done, he lay so quietly that she didn't know if he was alive or dead. Jonathan had been correct. There literally was nothing more she could do for him. Not here. Not now.

"Gunslinger!" a voice boomed. She snapped her

head around, and there was Boxers, his chest heaving from the exertion of his run. "Where's Scorpion?"

"He said he was going to end this. He took a rifle and ran off toward the hotel."

Boxers kicked at the pavement. "God *dammit*! This is why we don't split up." He bent to Officer Hinton and dragged him to a sitting position by the collar of his vest and roughly relieved him of his AR15.

"Hey, be careful!" Gail said.

Boxers laid the cop back down. "He's dead," he said, and he stripped three mags from Hinton's vest.

"Are you going to help Digger?"

"Haven't decided yet," Big Guy said. "I might kill him, instead."

Alone again among the carnage, Gail found herself overwhelmed. She didn't have another long run in her. Not now. Not after everything else.

Digger was right. She should seek cover and take it.

But she wasn't going to. Not with this many wounded and not with the rest of her team in harm's way. Like all members of SWAT teams everywhere, Gail had received high-end combat medic training when she was with the Hostage Rescue Team. She didn't have any supplies, and she didn't have any help—not yet, anyway—but she had skills, rusty though they may be.

Gail stood, then bent and tore the first aid pouch off of Officer Hinton's vest. While bent, she also checked his pulse. Boxers was right. Hinton was dead. That meant he didn't need his tourniquet anymore. She released the windlass from its anchor loop and let it spin itself off. Then she unhooked the attachment and pulled the woven nylon free from his thigh.

She noted with grim sadness that there was no spray of blood anymore.

"I'm sorry, Officer Hinton," she said. "I tried."

And now she had work to do.

She could still hear the gunman firing away, but for now, he seemed to have shifted his focus to another direction. Of the people on the ground, the wounded outnumbered the dead, but the numbers were astounding. She didn't have time to count, but it had to be north of fifty.

In the darkness, everyone was a shadow. Gail had a penlight on her belt, next to her holster, but she didn't dare use it. Bright light in a sea of darkness would undoubtedly bring the shooter's sights back around to her.

"Who needs help?" she said softly, but loud enough to be heard within fifteen or twenty feet. "Listen up, people. Please be quiet."

She heard shushes among the wounded. "I'm with the FBI. You're not safe here. If you are wounded and can move, get inside a building. Right now, while the shooter is focusing the other way."

"Where are the police?" someone asked. "The fire department?"

"I can only assume that they're on the way. Now, please move." What she didn't say was that with the number of police officers who'd been killed or wounded, none of the civilians would be high on the first responders' priority list. She also didn't mention that if the local operating procedures were like those at every other place she'd worked, the firefighters and medics wouldn't be allowed near this scene until the shooter was secured.

A few people stood easily, but more stood uneasily, clearly in pain but ambulatory. As they did, Gail started to check those who couldn't stand yet clearly were alive.

The first patient she came to was a teenage boy who'd been shot in the belly.

"What's your name?" Gail asked.

"Oh, God, it hurts."

"I know. My name's Gail. What's yours?" To hell with the cover names. Right now, nothing seemed less important.

"Glen," the boy said. "Glen Joyce."

"Hi, Glen. You've been shot. Did you know that?"

He grunted against a wave of pain. "It occurred to me, yes."

"Okay, I need to help you, but it's going to feel uncomfortable."

"Anything," he said. "Just keep me from dying."

Gail didn't respond to the request. She pulled the bandage scissors out of the first aid kit and slit Glen's T-shirt from waist to neck, and then down both sleeves to bare his belly and chest.

"Do we really know each other that well?" Glen quipped.

Gail smiled. A sense of humor was always a good sign. It meant that he still had enough blood circulating to keep his brain sharp. But that could change quickly.

She pulled the shirt completely free from his body and held it in her hand. "Okay," she said. "Here comes the uncomfortable part."

"Can't hurt worse than I already do."

Then Gail started stuffing the fabric of the shirt into the bullet wound.

* * *

Jonathan sprinted in the dark down Freedom Plaza Drive on his way to the Golden Buoy Hotel. He keyed his mic. "Hey, Big Guy, where are you?"

"On my way to save your sorry ass," Boxers replied.

Jonathan looked back down the sidewalk but didn't see him.

He kept going. As he swung the turn onto America Avenue, he literally ran into a cop who looked and sounded dazed. "Hey, who are you?" The cop grabbed him by his vest.

Jonathan badged him. "Neil Bonner, FBI."

"What are you doing in Bob Driscoll's vest?" The cop fingered the trigger guard on his slung MP5.

The decorative gas lamps provided just that much illumination.

"He'd dead. I figured his rifle and mags could go to a better cause. Come with me."

The cop hesitated. The flickering light also highlighted his fear. "To do what?"

"To stop the slaughter," Jonathan said. "The shooter's on the rooftop of the Golden Buoy."

The cop looked up the hill, then cranked his neck to look to the top of the building.

Jonathan didn't have time for this. None of them had time for this. "Look, Officer . . . What's your name?"

"O'Brien."

"Officer O'Brien," Jonathan said, "I'm going up there, and I'm going to stop that killer. I'd love to have you along."

More hesitation.

Jonathan tried again. It would be his last attempt. "You wear a badge, and that means people count on you to do the dangerous thing. This is your defining moment. Are you coming or not?"

Jonathan pushed past O'Brien and started running again. It had been a long, long time since he'd encountered a shooter on his own.

Watching the reactions of bystanders as he passed them with his rifle at low ready he was thankful that he'd thought to bring the vest. The word POLICE at the shoulder and across the back meant a lot when people were scared. How quickly they forgot the recent attack on a Northern Virginia's Mason's Corner Shopping Center that was spearheaded by bad guys dressed as police.

That was one Jonathan could never forget.

He never broke stride as he ran across the hotel lobby to the emergency stairwell. "Make a hole!" he shouted to the confused crowd. "Out of the way!"

Many shouted questions to him, asking what was happening and what he was about to do, but he ignored them all.

"I hope you arrest that son of a bitch and put him in jail forever!" someone yelled.

Again, he didn't respond. The lady probably wouldn't want to know the truth of what he was about to do.

As he passed the elevator shaft, he could hear stranded people in the cars screaming for help. *Careful what you ask for,* Jonathan thought. This was probably one of the first emergencies in the history of emergencies where the elevator was the safest place to be.

The escape stairwell was well enough lit by the battery-powered emergency lights to see where he was going. "God help me," he said aloud as he hit the first step. He had a long way to go, and it was all straight up. Over the air he said, "I'm running up the stairs to the roof of the Golden Buoy."

"Copy," Boxers said. He sounded especially winded.

By the time Jonathan got to the seventh landing, his legs and lungs were burning.

He pushed on.

Tenth floor. Top floor. Only one short flight to the rooftop.

"Hey, Bonner," a winded voice said from below.

Jonathan turned. It wasn't Boxers. He looked down to see Officer O'Brien only two flights down.

"You slowed down a little after the fourth floor," O'Brien said. "I expected more from Feeb."

Jonathan smiled. "Thanks for coming to the party."

"You only die once," O'Brien said. "It might as well be in a blaze of glory."

Jonathan pivoted to the mission at hand. He'd arrived at the steel door to the roof. It was closed, but the knob turned. When he tried to push it open, though, it wouldn't move. Made sense that the shooter would barricade access to his sniper's nest.

"Hey, Big Guy, where are you?"

"Don't wait for me," Boxers said.

This wasn't right. Jonathan didn't get it, but he didn't have time to stew over it, either. He turned to O'Brien. "It's blocked."

"We've got choppers in the air on their way here," O'Brien said. "Maybe we should wait for reinforcements."

"Negative," Jonathan said. "You've heard his rate of fire. Every second of delay is another body."

"So, you just want to add two more on the roof?"

Jonathan felt a flash of anger, but he swallowed it.

"Talk like that gets people killed, O'Brien. If you don't think we can win, then stay behind."

Even in the dim glow of the emergency lights, Jonathan could see that he'd hit the shame button that he was aiming for.

"Okay," Jonathan said. "We're going to go in on this fast and hard. Getting past his barricade is likely to be noisy, and if it is, it will draw his attention. Speed is our friend, have you got that?"

"I'm not a coward," O'Brien said.

"Then prove it." That came out more harshly than he'd wanted. "And to be clear, when I see this puke, I'm going to kill him. We're not going to talk, I'm not going to put him under arrest. Are you good with that?"

"You were in immediate fear of your life," O'Brien said, the key phrase necessary to justify the use of lethal force.

"Appreciate it," Jonathan said. "Now, I'm going to open this door fast, move in, and pivot left. You go right. If you see him—"

"Shoot him in the friggin' face," O'Brien said.

Jonathan smiled. "You remind me of a friend of mine. Three . . . two . . . one . . ."

Jonathan slammed his shoulder into the door. It gave a little, but not much. But boy, oh boy, did it make some noise.

"Give me a hand," he said. He counted out another cadence, and together they hit the door. It moved a little more.

"It's like yelling, 'Hey, look at me!' " O'Brien said.

Jonathan counted another cadence, and this time, the door opened enough to allow a man to pass.

O'Brien started to lead the way, but Jonathan pulled him back by his vest. "No way," he said, and he squirted through the door. He cut left and brought his rifle up.

The sniper had stopped shooting. That was a good thing for the folks on the ground, but a really, really bad thing for Jonathan. He kept low and swung left, his rifle up and ready. Behind him, Officer O'Brien came through the same opening and headed right.

Jonathan refused to give in to the urge to make sure the cop wasn't doing something stupid. He wasn't part of Jonathan's team, and therefore, the only natural assumption was that he didn't understand this level of tactics. But this wasn't a training exercise. If anything, this was the worst kind of final exam.

He scanned his sector of roof with both eyes open, but his right focused on the reticle of his red dot sight.

I bet this guy has night vision.

Jonathan would if he were in that position.

Well, shit. That gave the bad guy all the advantage. But at least he wasn't targeting the people down—

He heard a *whiz* and a *clap*, and his left ear and cheek felt like they'd been set ablaze. Deafness enveloped his left side. He dove for the tar and gravel and rolled as a second shot slammed a hole through the cupola door where he'd just been crouching. He scrambled on hands and knees and threw himself behind a massive air handler. Depending on the sniper's chosen gun, this would or wouldn't be stout enough to stop a bullet.

"O'Brien! What's your situation?"

The silence pulled his head around to O'Brien's sector. The cop lay still, blood pouring from his head.

"Shit!"

A bullet blasted a hole through the air handler. One question answered. Maybe waiting for airborne reinforcements wasn't a bad idea, after all. He tested his cheek and ear to see how badly he'd been hit, and his hand came away wet and red. "I've had worse," he mumbled.

Another hole blew out of the air handler's steel case.

"God *dammit*!" This wasn't tenable anymore. Jonathan pressed his belly flat against the gravel and advanced an inch at a time toward the lower right-hand corner of the big steel box.

The bad thing about a two-way shooting range like this was the two-way sight lines. As soon as you could see the bad guy, he could see you. Add the fact that there were essentially only two points in space from which Jonathan could expose himself—the left side or the right side—

No, that wasn't right. He pulled himself back to cover and scanned the real estate of the rooftop. His was one of many air handlers, arranged in staggered patterns from here to the edge of the roof. If he moved fast enough and kept low enough, maybe he could use the current steel air handler as cover as he dashed to one of the ones that stretched out behind him.

There was no maybe about it. It would work or it wouldn't, but staying here was out of play.

Rising back to his haunches, Jonathan curled himself into a sprinter's stance, and keeping as low as he could, he dashed thirty feet to the next air handler and slid to a halt. Again pressing his belly to the rough rooftop, he dared to take a peek around to where he thought the shooter must be.

The view sucked. His sight picture was all about vents, air handlers, and utilities.

Where the hell was Boxers? Shit like this worked a hell of a lot better when you were part of a team.

Jonathan drew his feet under him, and with his rifle pressed to his shoulder, safety off, he frog-walked like an undertalented Cossack dancer, trying to get an eyeball on something that looked like his target without exposing himself.

Movement.

He caught it on his left periphery, but by the time he brought his muzzle around, it was gone. He froze in place and waited. In nighttime warfare, movement was what gave away most hidey-holes. One of the reasons humans are inherently afraid of the dark is because nighttime is so often owned by predators, whether they be rapists or hyenas. We're inordinately attuned to movement in low-light conditions.

And in this case, the shooter forgot that city darkness is never really dark at all.

Jonathan figured that his guy was moving for position on the spot where he thought he had Jonathan pinned down.

Then, there he was, night vision goggles and all. The shooter swung out from behind the cupola door for his final assault on the air handler. Jonathan settled his reticle on the attacker's ear, and as he moved his finger to the trigger, the shooter dropped to his knees, and half a second later, Jonathan heard the boom of an unsuppressed rifle. Then, as the shooter started to fall, his head blew apart the instant before the sound of a second shot was able to reach him.

Jonathan's radio broke squelch, and Boxers' voice said, "You're welcome. And you're clear."

Jonathan rose to his feet and jogged over to O'Brien to lend aid, but he was well beyond medical care. "Sorry, kid," he said softly.

The shooter's body was next. He was as dead as pretty much anybody Boxers decided to kill, and Jonathan didn't care. He rolled the corpse over onto what used to be his face and rummaged through his pockets. He got a wallet from the back pocket and a burner phone from the front.

Then he stood and caught a glimpse of Big Guy's enormous silhouette on the roof of the building next door. It was twenty feet taller than the Golden Buoy, the one with the decorative parapet that blocked the view to the street. Boxers waved, and Jonathan waved back.

"Is it Kellner?" Big Guy asked.

"Negative," Jonathan said. "You didn't leave a lot of face to look at, but what's left isn't his."

"Well, that sucks," Boxers said. "Hey, I see a chopper heading in here pretty hot. The next fifteen seconds or so would be a terrific time for you to get out of there."

He was right. Jonathan stepped inside through the cupola door. On the landing there, he unslung his rifle, dropped the magazine, and unchambered the round before he laid it on the floor. Then he pulled himself out of Officer Driscoll's vest and laid it next to the rifle.

He walked down to the ground floor and exited out

onto the sidewalk just as the SWAT team was swarming the front. One of them looked at Jonathan's face wound curiously, but a glance at the FBI badge seemed to satisfy him.

It was time to go home and shower. For many reasons.

Chapter Twenty-nine

Arthur Evers's phone buzzed with a news alert from a commercial site he monitored. More and more, the buzz pissed him off because the stories they were touting had more to do with a celebrity pregnancy than real news. Plus, he was entertaining a lady in his apartment. Or, maybe she was entertaining him. He thought her name was Rebecca.

"Oh, come on, Billy," she said, looking up from her work. Nothing *there* could be as good as what's happening here."

But he had to look.The thing about hookers was they they never really got a vote in anything.

He rolled Rebecca off of him and wandered the two steps over to the chair in the corner of his room. He fished through the left front pocket for the smartphone that was always there. He unlocked it with his fingerprint and read the incoming message. His stomach knotted. In that instant, he damn near reversed his dinner.

Shooter Kills or Wounds Scores in Capitol Harbor Sniper Attack

Rebecca either sensed or saw his horror. "Are you okay, Billy?"

Evers heard the question, but not really. It was as if his brain had frozen and could no longer process information. This was a disaster.

"Get out," he said, and he started to get dressed.

"What's wrong, sweetie?"

He found his wallet, fished out three fifties. "What's wrong is, you're still here. Pack up your shit and get out of here."

"What turned you into such an asshole?" she protested as she collected the money.

Evers didn't bother to answer. He cinched his pants and padded barefoot from the bedroom to his living room, where he stood at the window and stared out into the night.

What the hell had just happened? Why would Kellner and MacGregor go a day early and on their own? Without so much as a phone call to alert him.

This was a disaster. He didn't yet know the details of the hit, but the headline used the word *scores*, and that meant *twenties*. It was a huge hit.

And in its wake every community would ramp their security up to Defcon One. His other teams wouldn't have a chance. The other two hits scheduled for Halloween would have to be scuttled.

In the window glass, he watched as Rebecca stormed from the bedroom to the front door. "Eat shit, asshole," she said.

He smiled. "I might just have to," he said to his reflection.

How was he going to explain this to Al-Faisel? He'd

paid for massive simultaneous hits, not one-offs, and tomorrow night—Halloween night—was supposed to be the grand finale. Not only did the Capitol Harbor hit come a day early, it wasn't all that grand. In combination with the simultaneous hits of four bars in Lansing, Michigan, and the firebombing of the hospital in Westboro, Massachusetts, it would have been spectacular.

Now, the Capitol Harbor incident on its own would be written off as a couple of crazy guys with guns.

This time when a phone buzzed, it was a double-buzz, and it came from a spot behind *Huckleberry Finn* on his bookshelf. His burner phone, and the double-buzz meant a text message. This was madness. Exactly the wrong time to be firing electrons through cyberspace. Evers tilted the heavy Mark Twain volume forward and lifted the little folder phone. Sure enough, it was a message, in violation of his very specific standing order that they not connect to each other directly. His temper flared even darker when he saw the message was from ANON4, a.k.a. Frederick Kellner.

He opened the message because the fact of it being there had already done all the possible damage if the government was somehow monitoring them.

ANON4: Feds knew. Female agent challenged me directly. Had to move early for E+E diversion. Await instruction.

Evers stared at the message, trying to figure out the meaning. He interpreted *E+E* to mean "escape and evasion," but which feds? And how did Evers not know about it? If it was the FBI, Brooks should have told him. He sighed and closed his eyes. He knew what he was about to do was a bad idea, but he had no choice. He thumb-typed,

BOSS1: There are lots of feds. Which do u mean?
ANON4: FBI. Need instruction.

Evers's blood pressure spiked. He could feel it in his flushing face and in the pounding pulse in his temple. Kellner's instructions would have to wait.

Evers needed to talk to Porter Brooks right by-God now. The son of a bitch was not doing his job, and he needed to know why. Brooks's burner rang fifteen times without answer.

"I'm the wrong one to ignore," Evers said. He clicked off, and then called Brooks's home number.

This time, it rang six times before Brooks answered. "The hell are you doing, Artie? This is entirely inappropriate."

"I don't give a shit about propriety," Evers said. "Did you guys betray me? Tell the truth now, and I swear I won't hurt you or your family."

"Jesus, where does that come from?"

"Have you watched the news? That unfortunate event in Maryland?"

Brooks's tone darkened. "Yes, I have."

"Did you and the other feds know about it?"

"No, of course not."

"I happen to know that an FBI agent approached a friend of mine."

"Absolutely not," Brooks said. "Not unless it was some sort of renegade operation. If this is what I think you're talking about, I've already told you what I think. Who your enemy is."

Jonathan Grave.

Evers clicked off without saying good-bye.

"I promised you what would happen," Evers mumbled as he went back to his burner and began thumb-typing again. The first message went to ANON4.

BOSS1: 10-84 TBD.

Translation: *You and I are going to meet at a place to be determined.*

Then he thumbed a second message, this one address to ANONALL, which would go out to all of the Retribution team members.

BOSS1: X-ray. Zebra. NLT 11-3.

He clicked SEND, then sat heavily in his chair. All the plans for tomorrow were now aborted, and sometime on or before November 3, Operation Zebra would be in effect.

Scorched earth was on the way.

"What the hell does *X-ray. Zebra* mean?" Jonathan asked. He sat with the others in his living room on a wooden William and Mary rocker that was identical to the one in his office. He held a bag of frozen peas against the left side of his face. His wound was just a graze, but it had cut a stripe on the angle of his jaw and sheared off the last millimeter or so of his earlobe. Boxers had stitched it up, so a scar was pretty much guaranteed. When you had as many of those as Jonathan had, what was one more? The good news was that his hearing seemed to have returned.

"There's no way to tell for sure," said Derek Halstrom. He'd been yanked out of bed at zero dark early, did some research for a couple of hours, and then drove seventy minutes to get to Fisherman's Cove. Somehow his suit was perfectly pressed. He sat in the center of the wine-colored sofa with Venice on one side and JoeDog on the other, sprawled on her back, legs splayed, and snoring like an old drunk as Derek softly stroked her tummy.

Maybe Jonathan liked him a little more than he thought.

"My guess is it's their exfil plan," Boxers said from his spot in the oversized leather lounger that Jonathan had bought specifically to make Big Guy comfortable when he visited.

"Guesses don't count," Gail said from an identical lounger. She filled the extra space with her legs curled up under her. "Obviously, it's code for a plan, but how can we know what it is? An announcement to abort, maybe?"

Venice said, "The wallet you got from the shooter didn't produce anything of value, but grabbing the phone was helpful. BOSS1 made the same mistake twice."

"You're not going to like where the signals pinged," Derek said. "In addition to the one in your hand, we got another in Baltimore, then four in Lansing, Michigan, and two in Westboro, Massachusetts, of all places.

All of them are burners, no way to trace the identity of the owners."

"But we have signals we can trace?" Boxers asked.

"Not anymore," Derek explained. "They've all gone dark. That was probably part of the meaning of the code."

Jonathan rocked as he thought aloud. "Even without the details, we have usable intel," he said. "Vitale is breaking his pattern."

"Who's Vitale?" Derek asked.

"You know," Venice prodded. "The man who threatened to attack us all?"

"Ah." Yes, he remembered.

"According to Masterson, these attacks were all one-offs, lone wolf simulations. Now he's combining multiple assets in the same city."

"You look like you have a theory," Gail said.

"And theories are no better than guesses," Jonathan reminded. "But I think this concentration of resources reflects a plan to go bigger and better. I don't know what the prime targets are in those others cities. Ven, remind me to reach out to Wolfie so she can reach out to the police departments in those cities, even though I'm pretty sure the bad guys have aborted their efforts."

"Whoa," Gail said. "Aborted? Why do you say that?"

"Because I think our interference knocked them off their game. We forced their hand to go early with their attack."

Gail looked horrified. "Is that what you meant last night when you said that we caused the attack?"

"I didn't say we caused it," Jonathan corrected. "I said we started it. Once we pushed Kellner in a corner, he pulled the trigger early as a diversion."

"Hell of a deadly diversion," Boxers said.

"It worked, didn't it?"

"Do you ever listen to yourselves?" Venice said, clearly offended. "You know a lot of people died last night, and you speak of it as nothing."

"I do not," Jonathan said, but he heard the defensiveness in his voice. "At least that's not what I intend to do. But let's be honest. We've all been around this block a few times."

"That doesn't mean it should start feeling normal," Gail said. "I think that's Venice's point. So, what you're saying is that I caused all those people to die out there."

Jonathan groaned, "Oh, come on, Gail."

"I was the one who confronted Kellner, wasn't I? If that was the reason all those people were killed last night, isn't that the same as saying I'm responsible?"

Jonathan grunted his frustration. "How could I possibly think you're responsible? *You* didn't pull a trigger. *You* didn't blow out the lights. In fact, last time I saw you during the shooting was out in the middle of it all, rendering aid. So, hell no, you're not responsible."

He hesitated before going on but decided to throw caution to the wind. "But did you trigger the cascading events that ultimately made his cohort open fire? Yeah, you probably did. In fact, I'm *certain* you did."

Venice looked aghast. "Digger!"

"What? When have you known me not to be honest and direct? There's no shame to be found in this, Gail.

You did all the right things, and this time, the right thing had a bad effect. But even *that's* not a horrible thing. It's reasonable to extrapolate from past experience that whatever this larger hit mission was supposed to be, it was supposed to happen simultaneously in three different cities. Given the increase in manpower assigned to each, they were going to be huge. I think the fact that the Capitol Harbor incident was a one-off is definitive proof that they went off early."

"Jesus, you suck at pep talks," Boxers said, eliciting a wan smile from Gail.

Jonathan wasn't done. "So, here's the thing. If you want to throw yourself a pity party, have at it. Yes, you inadvertently started the ball rolling on last night's free-for-all. But if you're going to illegitimately take responsibility for all that, you also need to claim credit for all the lives you saved tonight, when I'm certain they had intended to attack."

"You can't know that they won't attack tonight," Gail said.

"Yeah, he can," Boxers chimed in. "In its own right, Capitol Harbor was *big*. Big enough to scare the bejesus out of every other community in the country. Assuming tonight—Halloween—was the intended night, security's going to be too tight everywhere for them to chance it. After Ven gets off the phone with Wolverine, the collective asses will be so tight you won't be able to drive a ten-penny nail."

Derek laughed.

"Oh, please don't encourage him," Venice said.

Boxers continued, "So, get over yourself and get a grip, Slinger. Not everything that goes wrong is your fault."

"Thanks for that," Gail said. "Condescension is exactly what I was trolling for."

"Stop," Jonathan said. "We're not doing this. Ven and Derek, work your magic. We need to figure out what their next move is and where they're going to hit."

"I thought we knew that," Boxers said. "Vitale pretty much promised that he was coming here."

Venice sat bolt upright. "Wait. What? What does *here* mean?"

Jonathan explained Vitale's threats in greater detail than he had before. *Thanks, Big Guy.*

When he was done, Venice looked wounded. "You knew all this, yet you interfered with their plans, anyway?"

"You'd rather I'd just let a few hundred people die?" Jonathan said. "And don't answer that question. I don't want to know the answer either way."

He stood and started pacing. "Here's what we need to know," he said. "If the team has disbanded and taken to the winds, they're not our problem anymore. They become Irene Rivers's problem."

"But you don't think that for a moment," Gail guessed.

"Not for a fraction of an instant," he confirmed. "Up until now, Kellner has been our vector into the group. Now we've got the guy who pretends to be Joe Vitale and seven unknown terrorists, one of whom we believe to be Frederick Kellner. Kellner's the key. He's got to be spooked, and unless he's got no other option, he'll be lying as low as he can. We need to find him. Gail, pull what strings you've got to find him. Reassign some of our own people to it.

"On the overt side?" Gail asked. "What do I tell them is the reason?"

"Tell them a client is paying to know where he is, and that that's all they need to know."

"That's not how we normally operate," Gail said. "They're going to want to access the file."

"Tell them that the fact it's different should be an indication of how important it is. Use those two new investigators you hired. What are their names?"

"Cody Johnson and Megan Bobbins," Gail said. "Aren't they a little green for something like this?"

Jonathan waved the thought away. "We were all green at one point. I figure they're hungry and they'll be anxious to please the guy who writes their paychecks."

"What about Masterson?" Boxers asked. "Think we could lean on him a little?"

"I think it's a perfect idea," Jonathan said.

"What makes you think he'll talk to you?" Gail asked. "What's in it for him? He wasn't all that cooperative the first time."

"I'll have to make it worth his while."

"You don't have the authority to do that," Gail said.

"But we all know who does. Ven, have Dom arrange that meeting with Wolverine ASAP."

St. Matthew's Cathedral was too far a drive at this hour. The morning rush up I-95 was always brutal, and Jonathan was in a hurry. He convinced Wolverine to drive south to meet him at the Maple Inn in Vienna, Virginia. Located just a few miles south of CIA headquarters, the Maple Inn didn't have much to offer in the way of aesthetics, but the food was good—the best chili dogs on the planet—and it was accepted by the intelligence community as a safe place to meet.

Jonathan thought that one of the reasons secrecy worked at the Maple Inn was that no one made a big deal about it. Local citizens composed most of the regulars, and they were too interested in their own conversations—or in their beer and food—to notice who else was sitting nearby.

Jonathan called ahead to make sure that the table in the far corner—the one under the ceiling-mounted television—would be vacant for him when he arrived. The young lady he spoke to—Tiffany—knew better than to ask why, thus cementing his appreciation for the venue.

Irene Rivers arrived wearing jeans and an unassuming shirt and a scuffed leather jacket that looked like it'd had seen a lot of use over the years. She entered alone, but by the time she'd reached Jonathan's table, the Tweedle brothers had also entered, one at a time. They wore their standard security dude suits, but without ties. They sat separately, but less than ten feet from their protectee, facing outward.

Jonathan stood to greet his guest, but she was not in the mood for pleasantries. She sat heavily in her seat, her face turned away from the rest of the diners. "It's your meeting," she said. "Go."

Despite her sharply angled features—or, perhaps because of them—Jonathan had always found Irene to be quite stunning, but man, oh man, did cameras not like her.

"Okay, here it is," he said. "We know that there are at least eight Black Friday terrorists still out there.

Maybe more.The business at Capital Harbor knocked them off their game. We're pretty sure that they've aborted their plan to attack tonight. I believe Father Dom told you about increasing security in Lansing, Michigan, and Westboro, Mass."

"I did, and I passed it along. Why am I here?"

"Because we're not allowed to talk on the phone, and I need help from you."

Irene leaned in closer. "What kind of help?"

"I need to give Logan Masterson a reason to give us information, and you're the only person I know who has the authority to do it."

"What do you have in mind?"

"Assuming he's forthright and helpful, let him go."

Her expression telegraphed her answer before she verbalized it. "You're out of your mind."

"Think about it, Wolfie," Jonathan said quietly. "No one knows you have him in the first place. He's not been charged and letting him starve to death in a black site or killing him outright just isn't you. It sure as hell is not me. Hell, you can fit him with a chip or make him report in every week somewhere."

"He killed dozens of people, Dig. We can't pretend he didn't."

Jonathan leaned in to whisper, "Who among us has not killed dozens of people, either directly or indirectly?"

As he leaned back, he watched her jaw set. "It's not the same thing."

"Look at it this way," Jonathan said. "If you stand fast against the killer of dozens, we'll be powerless to save the lives of hundreds more when these asshats go back to work."

"If he's got information, our people will get it out of him," Irene said.

"Jesus, Irene, you've had him for over two weeks, and hundreds have died in one and a half coordinated attacks. How's that interrogation model working for you? How many more have to die?"

Irene's cheeks reddened. Jonathan thought she wanted to say something, but the words wouldn't come.

"Don't get me wrong," Jonathan said. "I'm not trying to lay any of this nightmare at your feet, but this is a chance to learn something really useful. Masterson is a soldier, and he's looking at the end of everything. I'm telling you that I know his kind. For all I know, even freedom might not break him, make him turn on his buddies. Jesus, the guy in Iowa cut his own throat. But I think we have to try."

"Lie to him," Irene said. "Tell him that freedom's on the table if he cooperates. Tell him whatever you want. That we'll give him the Medal of Honor, whatever. Doesn't mean we have to do it."

Jonathan scowled and leaned away as he folded his arms. "I'll forget you said that," he said. "Just because times are tough doesn't mean ethical boundaries are no longer important. Not when the stakes are this high. That's just wrong."

"But letting a murderer walk isn't wrong?"

"It's a trade-off," Jonathan said. "The dead are already dead, and we can't do anything about that. But there are people walking around alive right now who will be dead if we don't intervene. If he sells us bullshit and the next hit happens, then you can still burn him. But if it works . . ." He let her finish the sentiment in her mind.

Something changed in Irene's eyes, and she sat taller, as if a piece of a puzzle had just fallen into place. "What *aren't* you telling me?" she asked.

"Excuse me?"

She leaned in again and smirked. "We've known each other a long time, Dig. You're never this passionate about your missions. You're holding something back, and I want to know what it is."

It bothered Jonathan that he was that transparent. He prided himself in his poker face. "I have reason to believe that the next target package includes Fisherman's Cove."

Now he'd piqued her interest. "Reason to know? What does that mean?"

Jonathan moaned a little. He really didn't want to disclose this next part. "I think I met one of the leaders of Retribution," he said. "And he warned me that if I didn't lay off on what they were doing, they would, and I quote, destroy everything I love."

Irene sat straighter still, deeply concerned. "How did they find you?"

"I have no idea," Jonathan said. "But it's concerning."

"Concerning my ass," Irene said. "The implications are huge. Where did a leak like that come from?"

"Not from my team," Jonathan said. "But that's tomorrow's problem. For now, we've got Masterson to think about."

Jonathan could almost hear the wheels turning in her head. She stewed for thirty seconds or more, then thumped the table. "Okay," she said. "We'll do it."

Jonathan smiled. It was a rare occurrence to change

Director Rivers's mind. "I'll need something in writing," he said.

"When are you leaving for South Dakota?"

"As soon as possible," Jonathan said. "Out of Manassas."

"You can't want to wait till I get back to my office," Irene said. "I can dictate the letter from the car and email it to you. Make him understand that this is contingent upon him being entirely forthright."

Jonathan's smile widened. "I'll scare the shit out of him. How's that? Actually, I'll let Big Guy handle the intimidation part."

Something about that image made Wolverine smile. "Go stop this thing," she said.

Boxers painted the Hawker 800 onto the runway at Juliet and taxied to the trailer-size hut that served as a terminal. As the engines spun down and he went through the shutdown procedures, three four-passenger golf carts approached, along with a fifth cart carrying six men in white shirts and blue sport coats, each of them armed with rifles.

"Dear Lord," Gail groaned as she saw the approaching motorcade. "Why do we have this effect on people?"

"Given their mode transportation," Jonathan said, "word must have leaked out about how bad my golf game is." He unclipped his seatbelt and walked to the back of the cabin, where he opened what on any other version of this aircraft would have been a coat closet and withdrew two M27s and an H&K 417.

As he walked back to the forward end of the cabin,

he handed Gail one of the M27s. "Hey, Big Guy," he shouted just loudly enough to be heard on the flight deck. "I presume you've seen our welcoming committee?"

"Yup."

"When you lower the doors, I want you to lower the forward port side door and the aft starboard side door simultaneously." He pivoted to Gail. "I want you to take a position back there. Don't know if this is going to go hot, but if it does, I want the greatest coverage we can get."

"Sounds like a plan," Gail said.

As she moved into position, Jonathan slung his M27 and handed Boxers his H&K 417 shoulder cannon.

"Where do you want me?" Boxers asked.

"Stay near the flight deck," Jonathan said. "If things *really* go to shit, getting out of here will be a priority."

"Roger that."

Jonathan took a breath and settled his shoulders. He glanced back to make sure Gunslinger was in place, and he said, "Lower the doors, and let's see what happens."

As the stairs lowered, the first thing Jonathan noticed was the blast of cold air. He stood in the doorway with his rifle at low-ready, safety off, fire selector on automatic. All six of the riflemen stood in an arc around the base of the stairs in similar postures.

"Kind of a harsh welcoming committee," Jonathan said from the top of the stairs.

None of them moved.

"Let me tell you what I'm thinking," Jonathan went on. "This is what people in my business like to call a target-rich opportunity. You look ready to shoot, and that puts you about half a second away from a firefight that not all of you will win." He gave the words a few seconds to sink in. "If I see a twitch or a change in stance, I'm going to kill you all."

He took another few seconds.

"So, let's do this," Jonathan said. "I'm not sure how we got to Defcon One here, but let's notch it back a bit. When I count to three, we all engage our safeties and take our hands off our rifles."

"You go first," said a guy that Jonathan recognized as the vestibule security guard he'd spoken to before.

"No, we go together," Jonathan said. "Don't screw this up, boys. I will not hesitate, and I will not miss. Reach down deep and ask yourselves if you can say the same."

He let another ten seconds pass.

"Okay, here we go," Jonathan said. "One . . . two . . . three." He made a show of twisting his fire selector switch to SAFE and lifted his hand a couple of inches off his rifle's pistol grip. "Together now." With his fingers splayed, he lifted his hand away from his weapon.

The others hesitated, but then did the same, more or less in unison.

"Excellent," Jonathan said. "I hate having a gunfight looming over my head." He descended the stairs until he was standing on the tarmac. "Who's in charge?"

The vestibule guard stepped forward. "I am. At least while we're here."

Jonathan walked down the stairs to the tarmac "Have you got a name?"

"Call me Mike."

"Right." Jonathan rolled his eyes. Apparently, everyone at Juliet had common Mid-American names. "Call me Neil."

"Right."

Jonathan shifted his posture to one foot and slid his rifle down until the muzzle was pointing at the ground. He felt confident that if someone tried to draw down, Boxers would take him out from somewhere inside the plane.

"So, why the posse?" Jonathan asked.

Mike reached into his pants pocket, then stepped forward. Jonathan braced for conflict, but Mike presented him with a business card. Jonathan accepted it and turned it in his hands so he could read it. The embossed blue logo made it clear at a glance that it belonged to an FBI agent. More specifically, *Arlon McCrimmon, Special Assistant to the Director*. "You know him?" Mike asked.

Jonathan shook his head. "Never heard of him." That was a statement of fact, but in the broader sense, he thought he was familiar with most of the names in Irene's immediate cloister, and he'd never heard the name. "Why are you showing me this?"

Mike's eyes narrowed to a squint. "You really expect me to believe that you've never heard of Agent McCrimmon? Special assistant sounds like a pretty important job."

"Yes, it does," Jonathan agreed. "But I don't have a clue who he is."

"Well, that's a shame," Mike said. "Because he's the reason why I have orders not to let you leave your aircraft."

Jonathan folded the card into his fist and planted his fists on his hips. "How about you stop talking in riddles and tell me what this is all about."

"First tell me why you're here."

"This isn't a secret," Jonathan said. "I understand that my people and your people have already worked this out. We're here to interview the guest we brought to you a few days ago."

"Logan Masterson," Mike said. "Just to be clear."

"I'm not entirely certain that we're allowed to speak his name, but yes, Logan Masterson."

"You're too late," Mike said.

"And why would that be?"

"Because that special assistant to Director Rivers killed him about forty minutes ago."

Jonathan said nothing. There had to be more coming.

"Officially," Mike clarified, "Logan Masterson killed himself. He just happened to do it at a time when he was alone with Agent McCrimmon. He hanged himself with a rope that wasn't in his possession when his room was swept a half hour before McCrimmon arrived. So, what's the real game here, *Neil*?"

Again, Jonathan said nothing. He was trying to make sense out of what he'd just heard.

"It's your turn to talk," Mike said.

"I don't know what to say." Jonathan was trying hard to control the anger that was swelling inside his gut. Just what the hell kind of game was Irene playing here? "What did this McCrimmon guy tell you he was here to do?"

"To talk to the prisoner."

Jonathan didn't know what to say or ask, so he was grasping at anything to keep the conversation alive. "What did he look like? McCrimmon?"

"Hell, I don't know. I'm *looking* at you and can't say what you look like. He was medium everything. White guy, dark hair, dark suit."

"Did he say anything when he left?"

"He didn't really say anything when he got here," Mike said. "He flashed a badge at the security officer, and she let him in. He left about a half hour later, and by the time we found out that Masterson was dead, McCrimmon was in the wind."

"How sure are you that he was really an FBI agent."

"About as sure as I am that you are."

In this business, the only safe call was to assume that everyone was lying all the time. "Can I see the body?" Jonathan asked.

"No." That answer came without equivocation. "I literally am under orders to shoot you if you don't get back in your plane and fly away. You Feebs are persona non grata until either we figure out what you're doing or until we get our shit together. Either way, have a nice day."

"I can't just take your word that Masterson is dead," Jonathan said. "I need to see the body."

"Then you're going to die a disappointed man," Mike said. "It's nothing personal, but you and your Bureau have made too many messes here over the years. Arguing is just going to make you leave later. Am I clear here?"

Jonathan tried to think of an alternative option, and nothing was there. "Clear as crystal," he said.

"Thanks for understanding," Mike said.

"I'm happy that I look like I understand," Jonathan said.

"Just what the hell *is* going on?" Mike asked. The swagger shield had thinned. He seemed genuinely concerned.

"I don't know," Jonathan said. "But I'll tell you

what I *do* know. This country is under attack, and in today's political climate, with a couple more successes, God only knows what might happen."

"I tell people it's time to start laying in food and ammo," Mike said with a smile.

"Not a bad idea," Jonathan said as he turned and headed up the stairs.

When they were buttoned up and airborne, Jonathan and Gail gathered near the door of the flight deck so they could all talk.

"I can't think of a more thorough waste of time than that trip," Boxers said. "Glad I'm not the one paying for the gas."

Jonathan handed the palmed business card to Gail. "Before we land, I want you to reach out to one of your folks and have them research that name."

She read the card. "Arlon McCrimmon? Sounds like one of the names that Wolverine gave to us. Kind of *out there*. You don't think . . ."

"That she double-crossed us?" Jonathan said. "I refuse to. But I think it's somebody in her immediate sphere."

"You gonna tell her?" Boxers asked.

"Not yet, I'm not. That's not a thing to speculate about with her."

"Any theories?"

"Yeah, I do," Jonathan said. "The list of people who could possibly have overheard us *and* who could point me out in a lineup is very, very short."

Gail brought a hand to her chest as a puzzle piece feel in place for her. "Her bodyguards?"

"That's who I come up with."

Boxers laughed. "Jesus, Dig. I'm gonna guess they've undergone some serious screening."

"So has every other government dickhead who's released classified information over the years." Jonathan turned pensive as he took the next step in his head. "I have to be careful here because I've never liked her security detail and I've never made a secret about it."

Gail feigned a gasp. "Oh, pray, say it's not true."

"Yeah, I know that's hard to believe."

"You've always been shy that way," Boxers added.

"Anywaaaay . . . A few days ago, when I met with Irene at Burke Lake, I caught the taller of the Tweedle brothers looking at me strangely."

"Maybe he thought you were hot," Boxers said.

"I *am* hot, so that's a real possibility," Jonathan said without dropping a beat. "But it wasn't that kind of look."

"What kind of look was it?" Gail asked.

Jonathan chuckled ahead of his answer. "You know that look JoeDog gets when she gets caught doing something bad?"

Both of the others laughed. "Yet they think that you show them less than full respect?" Gail asked.

Jonathan clapped his hands. "Okay, here's what we're going to do. Gail, get on the horn and start the wheels moving on finding out if Arlon McCrimmon is a real person. I'm going to reach out to Venice and get her to find out the names of Wolfie's security statues and then to dig into them. And Box, try not to fly the plane into a mountain."

Chapter Thirty

Three and a half hours later, it was late as they taxied to their hangar. The ground crew had every right to be cranky after they found out that what was supposed to be an overnighter turned out to be one very long day. Jonathan didn't know how Big Guy stayed awake and alert as long as he did. As always, he insisted on driving the Batmobile while Jonathan slept through most of the ride back home.

He was a little tense to find that his living room lights were on, but relieved when he opened to door to find Venice asleep on the couch. He was less pleased to see Derek crashed on one of the loungers, JoeDog at his feet. As the team entered, JoeDog perked up and jumped to her feet, startling Derek, who lunged out of slumber and startled Venice.

"Oh, you kids," Boxers teased.

"You know, you've got a whole mansion up the hill, right?" Jonathan said.

"This couldn't wait," Venice said, though her eyes weren't focused yet. "What time is it?"

"You don't want to know," Jonathan said. "Mind if I sit?"

"Of course not . . ." The words were out before Venice recognized that her boss was being ironic. Then she recovered. "But you won't want to do that for long."

The Maple Inn wasn't just a dive. It was a twenty-four-hour dive, and the only place it made sense to meet at this hour. When the ever-composed director of the Federal Bureau of Investigation entered, she looked somewhere between pissed and apoplectic. When she directed her security team to stay near the front door, Jonathan was reassured that Dom had delivered the entire message. Her hair was combed but not coiffed, and she wore the kind of jeans and T-shirt combination that one might expect of someone who'd just been evacuated from a house fire.

In short, she looked like just about everybody else who was drinking beer and eating chili dogs at zero dark early.

"Dammit, Digger," she said as she slid into the bench opposite him. "You know, I really do have other things to do."

"Sleeping is not a real thing to do," Jonathan said. "And since you like to make sure I get so little of it, I thought I'd share the wealth." He slid the business card he'd taken from Juliet and slid it across the table. "This guy a close friend of yours?"

Irene tromboned her arm to look at the writing.

"Arlon McCrimmon," she said, tasting the name. "Never heard of him. And I've never had a special assistant."

"Well, he just killed our only witness. Logan Masterson."

Wolverine's jaw dropped.

"Agent McCrimmon apparently heard of my plan to interview him, then leveraged your office's contact with Site Juliet to get there first. The security guard told me that I missed him by forty minutes."

Irene scowled deeply enough to make her eyebrows touch. "I assure you that I had nothing to do with that."

"Never thought you did," Jonathan assured.

"Juliet must have a leaker," Wolverine said.

"Oh, that it were so," Jonathan said. "It's your shop, Wolfie, and I can prove it."

"Absolutely not," she said.

He could see her defensive shields falling into place. Hell, he could almost *hear* them. "Give me a chance," he said. A waitress approached, then retreated from his quick shake of his head. "Remember our talk in the park?"

"I'm not doddering," she said.

He needed to get to the point. "We discussed then that there had to be a leak for that assault force to try to take out the prison. To kill Masterson. Now, earlier today, we determined to visit him in the prison, and assassins got there first. I don't know how many people you talked to about this, but my list is clean."

"That's why I think it had to come from someone at Site Juliet."

"Let me finish," Jonathan pressed. "It's no secret that I don't have a lot of respect in your security team, but they're the one constant in our meetings."

"Oh, for God's sake, Digger," Irene looked like she was ready to stand and walk away.

Jonathan made a pressing movement with his hands to keep her in place. "I know you don't want to hear this, Irene. At least hear me out, and then you can reject my theory if you want."

"You've got three minutes," she said.

"It'll take seven and a half," Jonathan said with half a smile.

It took a beat, but she smiled, too. And she relaxed.

"All right," Jonathan continued. "Here's where I broke a law or two."

Irene brought her hand to her chest to feign amazement.

"I had Mother Hen do some research on your security team." He didn't mention that she had a fair amount of help from the NSA.

"Digger!"

"Hey, if we didn't find anything, you'd never know. When she dug into Porter Brooks, she found some interesting stuff. Did you know he had a mistress in Crystal City?"

"How can that possibly be relevant?"

"It's not," Jonathan said. "I just thought it was interesting."

He got the eye roll he'd been expecting. "He's also way over his head in debt. And I think that *is* relevant. From what we can tell, it's a common denominator to all of these shooters. Now shooters *and* coconspirators. Two months ago, he managed to pay down a hundred fifty thousand dollars' worth of his debt over the course of two weeks. I don't suppose you gave him a big raise during that time?"

Irene scoffed. “That’s hardly proof that he’s involved in something like this.”

“I told you it’s a seven-minute presentation,” Jonathan said. “Hang in there. When Mother Hen went through his phone records—”

“Jesus.”

“—she found the smoking gun. On the night of the Capital Harbor shooting, he received a call on his home phone from one of the burners used to transmit what we think was the abort order. I’ll bet you dollars to donuts that if you execute a warrant on his residence—or maybe his person—you’ll find another burner on our list.”

Irene stared at Jonathan for the better part of a minute. He could see from her eyes that her mind wasn’t there, that she was trying to process it all. Finally, she said, “You’re sure about this.”

“One hundred percent.”

“If he had a burner phone, why wouldn’t the other conspirator call him on that instead of his home phone?”

“I don’t know,” Jonathan said. “In fact, it’s conjecture on my part that he even has the burner. What I’m positive of is that he took a call from a bad guy on a night that was bad for the bad guys.”

She thought it through some more. “I can’t use any of this,” she said. “It’s all inadmissible.”

Jonathan had anticipated those words. “He doesn’t know that,” he said. “Welcome to my world, Wolfie. Let’s play a little poker.”

“I don’t understand,” she said.

He explained.

* * *

Private investigator work wasn't anything like Cody Johnson expected it to be. He'd read the books by the old pulp masters, and he had images in his head of going door-to-door to ask thousands of questions that by themselves meant little, but after a while stitched together the solution to a mystery.

He had dreams of finding misplaced treasures and kidnapped children. He'd go nose-to-nose with flat-foots who didn't know what they were doing. He'd watched old reruns of *Mannix*, the private eye show from the sixties, where the P.I. drove a cool car and got all the hot women.

The reality of his job fell way short. Well, mostly. His degree in political science from Purdue gave him the skills that eased his way into the research, but so far, eight months into his job with Security Solutions, he'd yet to speak to a human being face-to-face during an investigation. He did mostly online peeping, exercising more of his ill-gotten skills as a lower tier hacker than he did the legitimate ones, but as long as he didn't cross certain lines—and, swear to God, he didn't fully understand where those lines were—no one questioned his results.

It bummed him out that the company billed his time at a considerable multiple of what he actually made, but it had been made very clear to him by Ms. Bonneville that it was industry standard and that he should consider himself fortunate that a poly-sci graduate could get as lucrative a paycheck as he did straight out of undergraduate school.

The one element of his childhood notions of the job

that did play out was the part about the hot women. Megan Bobbins was two years older than he, but she started with Security Solutions just a week before he did and it turned out, was equally as frustrated with doing nothing but scut work.

She was as thrilled as he, apparently, when Ms. Bonneville gave them this project to seek out a guy named Frederick Kellner. So far, they'd been able to tease out the fact that he was former military and that his credit sucked, but Ms. Bonneville already knew those details. Their real task was to find the guy and pass that information along. Most thrilling of all was the fact that this request had come directly from Mr. Grave himself.

Now, *there* was a mysterious guy. Cody wasn't sure that he'd actually heard the man speak, but it was clear from all the other employees that he was due a huge amount of respect. And not just because he owned the company and wrote their paychecks. Apparently, he was into a lot of important charities and stuff. And he was worth a bajillion dollars. Rumor had it that he was the wealthiest man in Virginia, but given the number of superwealthy people in Loudoun County, he had a hard time believing that.

But that didn't matter much either way. Cody was a thousandaire and happy for the privilege.

He and Megan stayed late at the office chasing their tails, mostly, and when it finally got to be eight o'clock and he realized that his stomach was ready to consume itself, he announced to Megan that he was going home.

That's when she asked him to come to dinner at her house. It was nearby, she said, and she was a pretty adequate cook. And, let's be honest, she had a ridiculous body. After considering the offer for approximately two seconds, he accepted.

Nearby is always relative, and by Northern Neck standards, where convenience stores may be a half hour away, Megan wasn't too far off. About thirty miles from Fisherman's Cove, but smack on the water.

And what a place it was! About four thousand square feet, he guessed. The whole back A-frame wall was entirely glass, but for the pillars or whatever you had to have to keep the glass in place. At this hour, it was impossible to tell what the view was, but it had to be of the river or one of its tributaries. The apex of the *A* had to be twenty feet tall.

"Holy crap," Cody said as he entered. "How do you afford this? I must have negotiated my salary wrong."

Megan laughed. "No, my daddy negotiated his salary *well*. *Very* well, in fact. He's the CEO of one of the Beltway Bandit companies. He wanted his only daughter to live well."

"Yikes," Cody said. "My dad's a barber, and he's just pleased I didn't flunk out of college."

Megan smiled, then rested her hands on his shoulders. "Since we're partners," she said, "I know you'll take this criticism in good humor."

Even eight hours later, he remembered the unsettled feeling. "Okaaay . . ."

"You stink."

"Excuse me?"

"You smell bad," she said with a big smile. "It's like your deodorant's worn off or something. Did you work out during lunch as usual?"

He winced.

"Well, there you go," she said. "Do us both a favor and take a shower."

And that's how it started. The first-floor guest room off the great room had this terrific, four-head shower, and he had to admit that the shower request could well be code for a good night ahead.

It's when he got out of the shower and saw that she'd taken his clothes that he realized it was going to be an interesting night. The fact that she'd somehow sneaked in and replaced the luxurious towels on the rack with a dish towel confirmed things. After drying himself as best he could, he used the wet rag to drape himself for modesty and stepped into the great room, and there stood Megan, as naked as he.

A lot of career-ruining harassment followed, and Cody learned things about bodies and erogenous zones that he'd remember for the rest of his life. It was exhausting and it was wonderful, but ultimately, dinner turned out to be cold cuts and saltines. Here it was four in the morning, and he needed to do something to replace all those well-spent calories.

As he slid out of bed, Megan stirred only a little, and he realized for the first time that he had no idea where she'd put his clothes.

What the hell? He'd snack naked. There literally wasn't a spot on his body to which she had not acquainted herself very, very closely.

"Eat your heart out, Mannix," he mumbled as he opened the door to the master bedroom and padded out into the great room. As he crossed the main level, past the massive gas fireplace that continued to spout flame and had made the place a little too warm, he said a little prayer that her fridge would have more stuff in it than his.

Now, *that* was not a high bar.

A chilly breeze pulled his attention toward the front door, which looked in the dim light that maybe it was open. Could it have been that way all night? If there was one thing for sure, it was that he didn't give a lot of thought to Megan's security precautions during their sexual Olympics. As he approached the foyer to shut the door, he sensed a shadow moving behind him and he whirled.

Two men stood there, both dressed in black, but with their faces clear. Both had a military bearing about them, and one of them looked familiar.

"Jesus!" Cody nearly shouted. He was vaguely aware that one hand covered his heart while the other covered his junk. "Who the hell are you?"

The taller of the two cocked his head. "You're Cody Johnson, right?"

"Yeah. Who the hell are you?"

The other one said, "We tried to visit you earlier, but when you didn't come home, we came to visit your colleague. What an amazing stroke of luck to find you both here. Your state of dress answers what you've been up to."

Cody's heart raced, but his brain felt frozen. He had no clue what to do. So he circled back to the familiar. "Who *are* you?"

The taller one said, "Seriously, you don't recognize me?"

He stepped forward again, but Cody was already against a wall and had no place to go.

Then he understood. "Kellner?"

The taller man faked a smile. "You'd think when a man goes searching, he'd pay closer attention to who he's searching for."

Cody never saw the knife, but he felt a horrific pain just above his pubic hairline, and then it progressed to his rib cage. Just as he noticed the stuff tumbling out of his gut and he reached to tuck it back in, he felt nothing at all.

Chapter Thirty-one

Technically, this was Irene Rivers's meeting, but because Jonathan had the most to lose, he chose the venue, then didn't advise the others where it was until they were already on the way. The Ritz-Carlton at Mason's Corner was beautiful by any standard, but the Chairman's Suite was truly stunning. Jonathan chose it because of its spaciousness and overall impact. He delayed the announcement so Uncle Sam and his loyal servants wouldn't have time to bug the place.

He'd been there for nearly an hour, napping on the curved living room sofa that overlooked the ho-hum skyline of this new Mecca for tech companies. He didn't realize he'd fallen asleep until the doorbell rang. It was a door chime that toned the sound of Big Ben—or maybe another famous bell tower. He rose, walked through the dining room into the preciously decorated stone foyer and opened the door.

He was greeted by a tall, fine-looking woman in a dark blue business suit who was armed with a briefcase that wasn't big enough to hold more than a couple hours' worth of reading material.

"Ms. Grosvenor?" he asked.

The United States attorney for the Eastern District of Virginia gave an annoyed smile. "Agent Bonner?"

"Indeed," Jonathan said. "Come on in."

Sandra Grosvenor had been a U.S. attorney for less than two years, and Jonathan happened to know that she and Irene had gone to law school together. The FBI director's strong recommendation help shape President Darmond's opinion of his nominee, so Ms. Grosvenor owed Wolverine a big favor.

"I promise that I'm harmless," Jonathan said.

Grosvenor crossed the threshold. "I'm not," she said. "And to tell the truth, you look rather predatory."

Jonathan gestured for her to follow him into the living room. "It's a façade," he said. "I turn it on to scare bad guys while I'm arresting them."

"I did some research on the way," Grosvenor said as she headed for one of the two curved sofas. "I can't find any cases closed by you."

"How about that." He was ready for Irene to arrive.

"Is it safe to assume that you are the collector of entirely unusable evidence in a case that the entire world wants to see closed?" Grosvenor's expression was hard to judge. She had an intense glare, but he couldn't tell if it was anger or merely curiosity.

"I'm afraid I can't speak to that, ma'am," he said.

"Why are you even here?"

"Because Director Rivers asked me to be," Jonathan replied.

"Why?"

"There are some requests to which one simply says yes," Jonathan replied. He knew Irene wanted him there in case she got confused in the details, but he saw no reason why the chief prosecutor in his jurisdiction needed to know that. This whole thing was seeming more and more like a mistake.

"Am I making you nervous?" Grosvenor asked.

"Nervous is the wrong word," Jonathan said. "Let's go for aware."

"But you do know what all of this is about," Grosvenor pressed.

"I'm sure that Director Rivers told you everything she thought you needed to know," Jonathan said.

Her gaze became even more intense. Jonathan didn't crave conflict with this lady, but he wanted to shut their conversation down. He prayed that Wolverine was right when she said that the U.S. attorney was a realist, not a crusader.

Two minutes passed in awkward silence as they avoided each other's gaze. Finally, the doorbell chimed again, and Jonathan nearly jumped off the cushion to answer it.

As expected, Irene was there with her daytime security contingent. They reflexively took up their nutcracker stances against either side of the door.

Before she entered, she said, "Agent Brooks, would you mind standing post inside the door?"

"Not at all ma'am," he said. He looked to Jonathan and something changed behind his eyes. For a second, Digger thought Brooks might rabbit, but he didn't.

Irene followed and closed the door. "Please come in," she said. "We're going to take a seat and have a chat." To Jonathan, she added, "Nice digs."

"You know me. Only the best." He winked.

As Irene ushered Brooks into the living room, she said, "Special Agent Porter Brooks, I'd like to introduce you to Sandra Grosvenor, U.S. attorney for the Eastern District of Virginia."

Brooks looked more and more as if he wanted to bolt. "Nice to meet you," he said. His hand trembled as he shook hello.

"Have a seat," Grosvenor said.

Brooks helped himself to the chair Jonathan had vacated. Jonathan took a position immediately behind Brooks and out of his view. The intent was to make the man as unnerved as possible. From the way he squirmed, the strategy seemed to be working.

"So, tell me, Porter," Grosvenor said. "May I call you Porter?"

"Whatever you'd like," he said. He looked for guidance from his boss, but Irene remained stone-faced.

"Okay, Porter, let's get right down to it. What is your relationship to a person named Iceman, and how did you meet?" It was a deliberate effort to knock him off-balance, and it worked. Color drained from his face.

Grosvenor continued, "And before you get locked into making stuff up to pretend you don't know what I'm talking about, we have incontrovertible evidence that will nail your ass to the wall. I'm not going to lie to you. You're going to prison. The death penalty may or may not be a variable, but you're going to prison."

Jonathan couldn't figure out where she was going with this. If prison was inevitable, what's his incentive to talk?

"So, here's what's in play," Grosvenor continued. "The perp walk. All the media that would surround you, make the Brookses household names for all the wrong reasons. You've got three children, is that right?"

Brooks sat silently.

"Silence is not an answer," she said.

Brooks's jaw muscles twitched. "Why tell you what you already know?"

See? Jonathan thought. *He's already digging in.*

"Interesting point," Grosvenor conceded. "Because the press is going to dig deep into all of them. Maybe not James because he's only eleven, but certainly his big brother, Aaron, and his sister, Jill. It'll be hard for them to live with the fact that Daddy was a traitor to his country. Your record is going to be the first thing that'll pop up in any background investigation for any job they seek."

Jonathan began to understand her strategy, and he was impressed.

"And Jill," Grosvenor continued. She let that phrase hang in the air, then reached for her briefcase.

In the silence, Irene leaned forward. "I'll take your weapon," she said. "Nicely, please, so my friend behind you doesn't have to shoot you in the spine."

Jonathan couldn't tell for sure, but it looked as if Brooks was crying as he reached under his suit jacket and handed over his standard-issue SIG Sauer P226. He handled it with two fingers and passed it to Irene with the muzzle pointed down harmlessly.

"The one on your ankle, too, please," Irene coaxed.

Brooks passed it over with equal gentleness. An old-school snub-nose .38 five-shot revolver. Then, without being asked, he pulled his creds case out of his jacket and unclipped the gold badge from his belt. He handed them both to Irene. "I'm so sorry," he said.

Jonathan wasn't a lawyer, but that sounded a lot like a confession.

"But you have to understand that I can't cooperate with you," Brooks said. "They'd destroy everything."

Irene put on her kind face. Maybe she was genuinely concerned. "How did it get to this, Porter? Why?"

"Money," he said. "Same story you hear over and over. I took the money for something that seemed so inconsequential, a minor breach of security. Then he had his hooks in me. I couldn't get out."

"Tell me who they are," Irene said. "How many of them there are."

"I don't know."

"Tell us what you *do* know."

"I can't."

"You mean you *won't*." The kind face had gone away.

"Fine, if that's what you prefer. I want an attorney."

Grosvenor laughed louder than the moment deserved. "Ah, that's sweet," she said. "If it makes you feel better, I'm a lawyer, and so is Director Rivers."

"I want my *own* lawyer," Brooks said. His sadness had been replaced with belligerence. Everybody knew that a criminal interview ended the instant a suspect requested an attorney.

"Good for you," Grosvenor said. "That's not happening. I want to talk about your daughter, Jill. You do know that she has a drug habit, right?"

Brooks had locked up completely now.

"But did you know that we had her on felony distribution?"

His walls just took a hit.

"Understand, *Mister* Brooks," Grosvenor said, emphasizing the fact that he was no longer part of the Blue Brotherhood, "I have no desire to hurt anyone. I would hate to see poor Jill indicted for crimes that would put her in prison for at least eighty years, likely more." The USA made a show of opening a manila file with a flourish. "Because here's the God's honest truth. A few months ago, when this criminal referral came across my desk and I realized that she was the daughter of an agent, I hesitated. Then I found out you were on the director's security detail, and I *looked* for a reason to sit on the referral. Thankfully, I found out that she was in a treatment facility—no doubt a part of your financial stress—and I put the referral in my drawer."

She leaned closer. "So, here's your incentive. If you cooperate with us, she gets to keep her life. You have my word on that. Now that she's out of treatment, I hope she's truly on the road to recovery. Imagine how awful it will be when I send agents to arrest her in the middle of one of her classes. I'll have her pushed to the floor and handcuffed in front of her friends. And then *she'll* get the perp walk."

This time, there was no hiding the tears.

And Grosvenor went for the kill. "You have my word on this, too, Porter. While she's sitting in jail, I will make it crystal clear to her that she'd be living a normal life if only her daddy—who's already in jail—had loved her enough to cooperate."

The U.S. attorney sat back in her cushion, seemingly satisfied. Jonathan had never seen awfulness served with such smugness. Such glee.

Irene said, "Porter, look at me."

He did.

"I'm really sorry it's gone this way. But you know the stakes. We must stop these Black Friday attacks. We sense that something big is coming. Is it?"

Brooks tried to cast a glance over his shoulder, but Jonathan took care to stay out of his gaze.

Grosvenor said, "Do you have a proprietary phone at your house that is your primary contact with Iceman?" She uttered the name conversationally, as if he were a celebrity.

He sat quietly. Clearly, he did not want to answer.

"Focus, Porter," Grosvenor said.

"Yes, ma'am, I do."

"Is the proprietary phone the means Iceman would use to contact you?"

"Yes, ma'am," Brooks said.

"Yet on the night of the massacre at Capitol Harbor, he contacted you on your home line. Why was that?"

He looked up as it fell into place for him. So, that's how he was caught. "I knew that would bite me in the ass," he said.

No one said anything as they waited for him to connect the rest of the dots. "I ignored the throw-away," he said. "I just wasn't in the mood."

"Yet you talked to him on your landline," Irene said.

It was killing Jonathan that he didn't get to ask any questions.

"I didn't want one of the kids to pick it up," Brooks said. "I mean, my God, it was a huge violation of protocol. I didn't even know that he *had* my home number."

"What did Iceman tell you?" Irene asked.

Brooks gathered himself. "He told me that there'd been a breach in security, that the FBI had intervened and caused their major op to pull the trigger too early. He sent an abort code."

"So, what's the next step?" Grosvenor asked.

"I don't know."

"But there *is* a next step?"

Brooks hesitated.

"This is not a time to hold back," Grosvenor prodded.

Brooks nodded. "Yeah, I think it is."

Jonathan's cell phone buzzed in his pocket, drawing an annoyed look from Irene. He couldn't ignore it. So few people knew the number, and of those who did, they all knew better than to call it unless there was an emergency. "Excuse me," he said the others.

He stepped away toward the windows and lowered his voice. "This is a really bad time," he said.

He'd been expecting Venice's voice, but got Gail's instead. "I have terrible news," she said.

He tightened his gut against the dire tone of her voice. "Wait a second," he said. Then, to the ladies and their prisoner, he said, "I need to take this in the other room. Give me a shout if you need me to shoot the sonofabitch."

He walked back through the foyer and turned right into the master bedroom, whose architect had to be an Arab sheik. No bauble or flash of gold was unwelcome. He walked to the windows and said, "I'm back."

"Megan Bobbins and Cody Johnson are both dead," Gail said.

It took Jonathan two seconds to place them in his head as his new investigators.

"It's beyond terrible," Gail went on. "Doug Kramer told me and showed me a few crime scene photos. Apparently, they were together—apparently, they had a relationship—and they were both murdered. They were disemboweled, Dig."

"Oh, God," Jonathan groaned. "They were the two—"

"Looking into Kellner, yes." She sighed heavily. "There's a detail I hesitate to share with you, given where you are."

He waited. He wasn't going to ask for what he knew would come, anyway.

"The murderer painted the words *YOU WERE WARNED* in blood on the wall."

Jonathan clicked off without a word. There was nothing to say. Not to her.

When he exited back into the living room, he was facing Grosvenor, and what she saw in his face made her jump to her feet. Irene followed suit and pivoted.

"Digger?" she said. He wasn't Agent Bonner anymore.

Brooks tried to respond, too, but he never had a chance. Jonathan grabbed him by his shirt collar between the skin and the fabric and hauled him backward out of his comfy chair, stuffing bits of his flesh under his fingernails as he did.

"Hey!" Brooks yelled, and as he hit the floor, a lamp came with him.

The front door to the suite flew open, and the remaining Tweedle brother entered with his weapon drawn.

"No!" Irene yelled. "You! Back outside!"

The guard looked perplexed.

"Out!" Irene shouted even louder. "None of this is happening, do you understand me? Your only job right now is to do what I say and to get out. And to keep anyone else out."

The guy retreated like a turtle's head returning to its shell.

Once Brooks was on the floor, Jonathan changed his

grip to the knot of the agent's tie. He lifted Brooks about three feet off the floor, then slammed his fist like a sledge hammer into his nose and mouth. He felt teeth shatter.

As he recocked his arm for another punch, Irene Rivers got inside of it and locked her elbow inside of Jonathan's and heaved back. "Stop it!" she yelled in his ear. "Just stop it!"

Grosvenor had retreated back toward the windows. "What the *hell* is going on?"

Jonathan withdrew his punch but retained his hold on Brooks's tie as he pulled him to his feet. "This sonofabitch just got two of my people killed," he said.

"Oh, my God," Irene gasped.

Jonathan slammed Brooks into the wall. The impact dented the drywall and knocked two paintings off their mounts. Blood streamed from the agent's nose and mouth.

"You told Iceman about me, didn't you?"

Brooks's eyes were wild with fear and pain.

Jonathan punched him hard in the liver.

"Digger!" Irene shouted.

"I'm calling the police," Grosvenor said.

Irene turned on her. "You're not doing anything, Sandy!" she snapped. "Set your butt in a seat, and we'll talk all this through."

Jonathan kept Brooks from falling or even doubling over. "I can do this all day, you miserable piece of shit. Yes or no. You're the one who told Iceman about me."

Brooks nodded vigorously. "I had to."

Jonathan slammed his liver again. "Bullshit."

"I don't know anything about killing anybody who works for you."

"What you don't know doesn't matter," Jonathan seethed. "You set it in motion. You caused them to be eviscerated. Gutted alive."

Another liver punch. If that one didn't tear the organ, Jonathan would be surprised. He let go of Brooks and let him slide to the floor.

Jonathan kneeled in front of his face. "What does 'x-ray zebra' mean? And please don't make me start breaking bones."

Grosvenor was on her feet again. "This is outrageous!"

Irene strode over to her old friend. "I'm not telling you again to sit down," she said. "This will make sense when it's over."

"This is your moment, Porter," Jonathan said. "Truth or dare."

"Just stop hurting me," Brooks said. "Yes, I sent a picture of you to Iceman. I didn't tell him who you are because I still don't know who the hell you are."

"X-ray zebra," Jonathan prompted.

Brooks closed his eyes. He didn't want to do this, that was clear. Jonathan gave him time to get his head right. But he wasn't kidding about breaking bones next.

Brooks turned his head to the side and spat a wad of blood and a tooth along with it. "X-ray means abort," he said. He took a huge breath. "Zebra is an alternative plan. It will be broadcast on one of the standard broadcast days. Not later than a day in early November. The third or fourth, I think."

"What is a standard broadcast day?" Irene asked.

"Mondays, Wednesdays and Fridays. In the morning."

"What's the alternative plan?" Jonathan asked. He hoped that the glare he sent to Irene would be justly interpreted as a signal to shut up.

"What's going to happen to me?" Brooks asked.

"I'm going to beat you blind if you don't stay on point and answer my questions," Jonathan said. "Now, what's the alternative plan?"

"He hasn't told us yet. That's what we'll get on the standard broadcast day. I had nothing to do with the operations themselves."

"What *is* your role?" Irene asked. Behind her, it appeared that now that the punches had stopped, Grosvenor was reengaged.

Both of Brooks's eyes were beginning to swell shut. "If I learned that the Bureau knew anything about their plans or if the investigation into them got any traction, I reported it to him." He bowed his head and started to cry again. "I'm sorry about your people."

"Like I care what you're sorry about," Jonathan said. "Where's your burner phone?"

Brooks smiled through the bloody mess that was his mouth. "In my jacket pocket. Not the kind of thing you want to leave around the house or the office."

Jonathan patted him down and found the old-school folder in his inside right-hand pocket. Then he stood and slid the phone into his own pocket.

"That's evidence," Grosvenor said.

"Not yet," Jonathan said. Before stooping back down, he pulled a capped hypodermic needle from his other pocket. He tried to keep it out of Brooks's view. He pulled the cap off, then he jammed the needle into the agent's thigh and depressed the plunger.

Brooks tried to object, but then he was out. He slid sideways onto the polished hardwood floor.

"Night-night," Jonathan said.

"Someone tell me what's happening here," Grosvenor demanded.

Jonathan gestured toward the furniture. "Let's sit down for this."

They all settled into the same seats as before. Jonathan nodded for Irene to take the lead.

Wolverine leaned forward, her elbows on her knees. "First of all, believe me when I tell you I'm sorry to involve you in all of this. Agent Bonner here is a tremendous asset to the United States government."

"That's not his real name, is it?"

"Of course not. He is a *covert* asset. In fact, today notwithstanding, he is as covert as an asset can get."

"One who steals important evidence," Grosvenor said.

"Evidence is only important if it is admissible," Irene countered.

Grosvenor cocked her head. "What aren't you telling me?"

Jonathan said, "She's telling you that my team and I are going to take care of the terrorists, and no one is going to take credit. There'll be no perp walk, there'll be no glory. The attacks will just stop, and society will be safe. For now. Until next time, God forbid."

Grosvenor cast a shocked look to Irene. "Why have I not been informed of this?"

"You *are* being informed," Irene said. "That's part of what this meeting is about."

"This is *not* a meeting," Grosvenor said. "This is a felony."

"Sadly," Irene said, "a felony to which you were a party."

The U.S. attorney's features darkened. "What are you suggesting?"

"I'm suggesting that you stay out of the way," Irene said. "To look away and not ask questions that are bound to occur to you."

Grosvenor wasn't getting it. "So, that incontrovertible evidence I told Agent—excuse me, *Mister* Brooks about—"

"Is all real," Jonathan said.

"Just not usable in court," Irene added.

"Then what's the use of having it?" Grosvenor asked.

The question startled Jonathan. "To solve the problem."

"The problem is not solved as long as the perpetrators go free," Grosvenor insisted. "And from what I'm hearing, you're making it impossible to prosecute. How is that justice?"

Jonathan left that one to Irene.

Irene said nothing, just waited for U.S. Attorney Grosvenor to catch on.

"Oh, my God," she said. "With what did you inject that man?"

Jonathan said, "A sedative. He'll be fine."

"What are you going to do with him?"

Jonathan smiled without humor. "He'll be fine."

Through her horror, she asked, "Irene, why on earth would you involve me in this?"

"Because Brooks is an insider, and he'd consider any prosecutorial threats to be a bluff unless it came from you, and he'd act accordingly. I needed you for . . . believability."

"So, is that what you think of me, Irene? I am merely a pawn in your games?"

Wolverine sat back in the cushion of her sofa and crossed her legs. "We've known each other for years, Sandy. We've been through a lot together, and now we're both presidential appointees in jobs that *mean* things. We make decisions that make life better for people. You certainly know me well enough to know that what I do, I do for good reason."

"So, now that I know, what am I supposed to do with all of this?"

"Try to forget it," Irene said. "Just like you forgot that Grammercy case back when you were an assistant district attorney in New York. You were there for that confession. You watched as those officers beat the confession out of your songbird and did nothing as he died."

Grosvenor wouldn't have looked more shocked if Irene had slapped her. "You bitch," she breathed. "I told you that in confidence. And Grammercy had buried a child alive!"

"Did you get the child back?" Irene said. Her tone had softened, but her eyes had narrowed.

Tears rimmed Grosvenor's eyes.

"That's what I thought," Irene said. "You aided and abetted the killing of that witness, and there's no statute of limitations on murder."

It all appeared to be more than Grosvenor could handle. "Are you *blackmailing* me, Irene?"

"I'm incentivizing you to do what's right. As far as I'm concerned, we never need to speak of this again."

As Irene stood, Jonathan and Grosvenor did likewise.

"My God, Irene, what have you become?"

"A realist," she said. "I think it's time for us to leave. Agent Bonner?"

"I've got this," Jonathan said. He watched as they exited the suite into the hallway, wondering how in the world they were going to explain things to the other Tweedle.

When he heard the door click closed, he walked through the foyer to double-lock it and engaged the chain. "Okay, Big Guy," he called. "They're gone."

Boxers emerged from the second bedroom, his H&K 45 still in his hand. "You okay, Boss?"

Jonathan didn't answer. "Get the trunk and the air set. Let's get out of here."

Packaging Brooks didn't take that long, maybe twenty minutes. They folded the unconscious man into a good-size travel trunk with four manifolded air tanks that would keep him oxygenated for at least twelve hours—plenty of time to get him transferred to Site Juliet. After that, Jonathan didn't give a shit what happened to him.

They called a bellman for a luggage cart, then rolled the trunk down to the Batmobile, and from there, Boxers would take him to the airport, where the ground crew would help load the trunk without asking questions.

Before leaving the hotel himself, Jonathan stopped by the manager's office to apologize for the damage that was caused by a minor disagreement. No police action was required, he said, because the disagreement ended on friendly terms. And, of course, the company that rented the suite, Belfast Properties, Ltd., would be happy to pay for any damages. To prove his commitment up-front, Jonathan handed the manager two thousand dollars in cash.

All was settled, no questions remained.

Chapter Thirty-two

Again, the waiting game was killing Jonathan. It was November third, the last day to expect the message from Iceman to his troops, and the entire team, plus Derek, sat in the War Room with little to do.

"Are you sure you didn't miss it?" Jonathan asked.

"You know, you're free to do something else," Venice said. "There's no need for you to sit there watching us wait."

"This isn't something you could do at your office at the NSA?" Boxers asked.

"I thought you'd be in a hurry to respond after the call is over," Derek said. He looked up over his glasses. "Whatever this call turns out to be, it won't be the kind of thing that I could relay via Puzzle Palace landline."

Jonathan checked his watch. "It's nine forty-five," he said. "And it *is* November third, right?"

"It was a few minutes ago," Boxers said.

"Could it be that *NLT* in the message meant something other than not later than?" Gail asked.

"I guess anything *can* be," Jonathan said.

"Let's not forget that November third runs till midnight through thirty-seven time zones," Derek said. "We're just assuming that the nine-to-ten rule is still in play."

"Twenty-four," Boxers corrected. "There are only twenty-four hours in the day. There are twenty-four time zones."

Derek gave him the kind of look that most people don't dare to give to Boxers until they've known him for a long time. "Given what I do for a living, do you really think this is a good thing to challenge me on?" he said with a knowing smirk.

"You know I could eat you alive, right?" Boxers said.

"I'll keep that in mind when you start looking hungry."

This kid's stock was growing for Jonathan. It took guts to stand up to—

Every computer in the room dinged, and the burner they took from Brooks hummed on the table.

"This is it," Derek and Venice said in unison.

Up on the big screen, the darkness flickered in and out of light, and then a message appeared. It was a random mix of letters and numerals that appeared to Jonathan to be gibberish.

"Can anyone make sense out of that?" he asked the room.

"Let me earn my way into your heart," Derek said. "I'm running it through decryption software. It will run all the possibilities and within a few minutes it'll spit out—"

"I've got it," Venice said. "It's an address."

Derek shot her a look that was equal parts amazed and wounded. "How did you do that?"

"You're not my only source, cowboy," she said. She ran the decrypted address through some mapping software and came up with a location. When she was done, she recoiled from her screen. "That can't be right." She rolled the wheel on her mouse to pull away from the structure and revealed it to be a house, located in the middle of nowhere.

Derek read out the address from his computer. "That's not far from here," he said. "Maybe thirty minutes."

"Twenty," Jonathan corrected.

"Not much of a target," Gail said.

"It's not a target," Jonathan said.

Boxers guessed, "A rally point?"

"That's where I'd put my money," Jonathan said.

Venice's eyes showed fear and anger. "To attack Fisherman's Cove?"

"To follow through on his promise," Jonathan said. "Again."

Derek said, "Percy and Ariana DeWilda are the owners. Mean anything to any of you?"

"Never even heard the name," Jonathan said.

Derek did a lot of clacking on his keys, then made the image on the big screen switch to an image that was much sharper. "Here it is real-time," he said.

An overweight lady in her thirties was spray painting something in the backyard.

"How'd you do that?" Jonathan asked. "That's a hell of an image."

"I told you we have some of the best toys in the

world," Derek said with a smile. "Even this far away from DC, you're still part of the Greater Washington Metro Target Package. That means satellite coverage twenty-four seven."

"That's amazingly sharp," Gail said.

"You ain't seen nothin' yet," Derek said. With dizzying speed, the image zoomed in so close that they could count the woman's eyelashes."

"Holy crap," Boxers said.

"Is that legal for you to do on U.S. soil?" Jonathan asked. "Photographing people in their yards?"

Derek beamed. "It's not our satellite," he said. "It's Chinese. And while I'm not sure, I'd guess it's not legal."

Venice laughed and said, "That is so awesome!"

"Yeah," Jonathan agreed. "It *is* pretty awesome. Can one of you tell me which political jurisdiction that property is in?"

"It's in unincorporated Mattaponi County," Derek said.

Jonathan turned to Gail. "Would Doug Kramer have jurisdiction there?"

Gail shook her head. "I don't think so. Not directly."

"But they don't have a county police," Jonathan said. "Sheriff's office, maybe."

"They've got the State Police," Gail said.

"Ah, shit," Jonathan said. "I don't want them involved."

"Then don't tell them," Boxers said. "What's your plan?"

"I'm not sure I have one yet," Jonathan said.

"Does what you've got so far involve breaking things and making noise?" Boxers asked with a grin. Honest to God, sometimes he looked like a huge puppy who just saw the leash to go out.

Jonathan laughed. "Yeah, that's pretty much a sure thing."

Jonathan took his time meeting the gaze of each man who'd gathered around the massive dining table in his kitchen. Jonathan had always considered himself a gourmet cook—even though others disagreed from time to time—and when he remodeled the firehouse to his needs, he included a gourmet kitchen. It occurred to him as he looked at the gathered faces that maybe he should have cooked something.

Clockwise down the table and around the far end, he observed Chief Doug Kramer, then Rick Hare, Charlie Keeling, and Oscar Thompkins, members of his security team for his office and Resurrection House. He'd already briefed Doug, who'd decided that it was best not to involve his police officers in what was to come. It wasn't that they didn't have the guts. Instead, it was because they couldn't keep themselves away from social media platforms that revealed every move of every day.

Boxers and Gail sat on his left and right, respectively, while he occupied the seat on the near end of the table.

"Okay, here it is," Jonathan said. "Nothing of what follows during this meeting is a mandatory job requirement. It is not an order. I want you to acknowledge that."

The men shrugged and nodded and grinned their general agreement.

"Not like that," Jonathan said. He kept his tone so serious that he hoped that it would infect them. It did. When he had their real attention, he said, "Rick, what I'm about to ask you to do is illegal and could wind up getting you wounded or killed. We will try to create a good cover for it, but if the cover breaks, you'll likely go to prison. Are you willing to do this thing?"

Rick was a combat vet who'd been seriously wounded in the Sandbox. He stood. "Mr. Grave—"

"Call me Jonathan, please. Or Digger."

Rick smiled. "Mr. Grave," he said, "I owe you and this town pretty much everything I've got. You bet on me at a time when I had nobody left. Now, I've got a family and a reason to get up in the morning. If you asked me to crawl through razor blades for you, I'd do it, sir."

Jonathan waved both hands in front of him. "I don't want it to be like that here."

"Well, sir, it is," Rick insisted. Early thirties, blond hair, and handsome, Jonathan supposed, despite the scar on his cheek. He showed no hesitation. "I have one request, though," he went on. "This can't hurt my family. I'm asking you to give your word that if something happens to me, they'll be taken care of. And I mean *taken care of*, sir."

Jonathan stood, as well, because it seemed like the right thing to do. "You have my word."

"Then I'm on board." Rick started to sit.

"There's one more thing," Jonathan said. "And while I'm sure it is completely unnecessary, I feel obligated to say it."

Rick stood straight again.

"If, for any reason *you* were to leak this, or turn on the team—"

"I would never do that, sir."

"I've got to finish this," Jonathan said. "If you betray the team, the repercussions on you and your family would be devastating." To be totally honest, Jonathan didn't know if he could follow through with a threat like that, but it was a nod to Boxers, who didn't trust anyone.

"I understand that, sir," Rick said. "And because I understand you had to say it, I take no offense."

"Thank you," Jonathan said. "Charlie?"

Charlie Keeling was likewise a wounded veteran, and he was New York City through and through. From his accent to his perpetual bitching about never finding a decent pizza in Virginia, he was everything Jonathan had come to expect from a Yankee—brash, opinionated, and funny as hell. A little round in the middle, he was strong as a bull.

"What, I gotta stand up?" he said as he rose. "I heard every word you said, and I'm with every word Rick said. Boss, you tell me jump and I'll say how high? Yeah, I get that it's dangerous. And since I got no wife or kids, I'm gonna go out and marry somebody real quick just so I can make somebody rich if I get off'd."

Jonathan smiled but said nothing.

"That enough?" Charlie said.

"I guess that'll do," Jonathan said. "Oscar?"

Oscar stood as Charlie sat, giving the impression of a human teeter-totter. He looked uncomfortable. Beyond uncomfortable. Five-eight and thin, he was supervisor of the security team at Resurrection House. "Mr. Grave, sir," he said in his thick Tennessee accent. "Please don't think me a coward. I can't do this."

The direct honesty startled Jonathan. "I won't think—"

"I would take a bullet for the boys and girls of Rez House. I hope you know that. I would take a bullet for you."

"You don't have to explain this," Jonathan said.

"When the fight comes to me, I'll fight back to my last breath. But I can't bring the fight to others. I'm too old for that."

"You're forty friggin' years old!" Charlie said.

"Stop!" Jonathan commanded. "I get it, Oscar. I really do. But I have to ask you to leave."

"Will I still have a job for tomorrow?"

"Of course, you will, Oscar. Of course, you will."

The man looked close to tears as he walked past Charlie and Rick and left out the back door.

"Got no time for weasels like that," Boxers grumbled.

"Nobody has an obligation to fight," Jonathan said. And while he knew that was the deal, he couldn't wrap his head around the concept of walking away.

"All right, General," Doug said. "What's the plan?"

Chapter Thirty-three

It was after five when the Batmobile and Doug Kramer's Chevy Suburban pulled into the scrub growth about a half mile through the woods from the target house. In fifteen minutes, it would be full dark, and that was the environment when they would normally have the greatest advantage. Jonathan anticipated, though, that the bad guys would have night vision as well. With that one element equalized, surprise and marksmanship remained their only leg up.

The first step was to get the DeWilda family to safety. Then, Jonathan and his team would surround the house and wait to see what happened. To be on the safe side, Resurrection House was on full lockdown, and Doug Kramer had unilaterally authorized his entire twelve-officer force to remain on Alert One, which meant that they be able to be activated to full duty within fifteen minutes. He'd have to crawl through broken glass for that at the next City Council meeting, but he didn't have time to seek a vote.

They'd divided into two teams, with Jonathan, Gail and Boxers composing Team One, and Doug Kramer,

Rick Hare, and Charlie Keeling composing Team Two. During the mission brief, Jonathan made it clear that if any assault was to be made on the building, Team One would be the door kickers, and Team Two would provide support and cover. The last thing they needed was a circular shooting gallery of good guys when the balloon went up.

As Jonathan and Boxers passed out equipment, Jonathan said, "I know you've used most if not all of this before, so any questions? The only thing that's changed much in the last few years are the NVGs."

Charlie turned the night vision goggles over in his hands. "On-off switch, headband, use your eyes. Is that pretty much it?"

Jonathan smiled. "Yeah, that's pretty much it."

"And how 'bout the rifle? Is that still look-aim-shoot?" Charlie teased.

"Don't be a dickhead," Boxers grumbled with a smile.

Rick Hare asked, "So, what kind of shit *do* you guys do when you disappear for weeks at a time? Why do you have all this gear?"

"Sorry, Rick," Jonathan said. "You're still not cleared for that."

"Can't blame a guy for trying."

Jonathan handed out some armbands. Each of them bore a round Security Solutions logo. "Put these on. They're IR reflective. If things get hyperconfusing, when your infrared lights hit one of these, you'll know he's a good guy."

The guys all took the bands and slid them over their sleeves. "Does this mean if a guy don't have a band, I can shoot him?" Charlie asked with a big grin.

"Not funny," Jonathan said. "I want you guys in full-soldier. No cheating. That means plates in your carriers. Helmets on. We have every reason to believe that the people we're going up against are very good at what they do. Let's make their job as hard as we can. Now, coms check."

Jonathan had issued radios to everyone. Jonathan, Boxers, and Gail—the members of Team One—were designated One-one, One-two, and One-three, respectively. The same pattern was repeated on Team Two for Doug, Rick, and Charlie. Once each of them went through a brief check, Jonathan keyed his mic, and said, "Mother Hen, did you get all that?"

"Affirmative," she said.

"What's the bird's-eye view tell you?"

"Still clear," she said.

"Stay close," he said. To the teams, he said, "Let's go."

The bareness of the trees was less of a problem at night than it would have been during the day, but as they closed in within fifty yards or so of the objective, they'd still be visible to anyone on the other side with night vision.

The biggest tell in their approach would be the recently fallen crunchy leaves on the forest floor. That was one good reason to arrive early and be in place when the meeting convened.

Jonathan was betting—in the absence of any evidence—that the bad guys would arrive sometime tonight, but for all he knew, they could be waiting out here for days.

And then there was the possibility that he and his team had misread every tea leaf. He decided not to think about that one.

As he advanced through the woods, Jonathan struggled with the notion that the root of this mission was to kill. He was not an assassin. He'd killed many people in his time, both for Uncle Sam and for Security Solutions, but those killings had always been in support of a larger mission—and more times than not as a response to people trying to kill *him*.

He told himself that this was a special case, that these terrorists had proven themselves to be morally bankrupt. They had fractured their social contract beyond any possible repair. The fact that they had wrought this havoc for reasons no loftier than a paycheck sickened him.

And they dared to kill two youngsters who had done nothing wrong but to take a job whose full impact was unknown to them.

That would have to be enough motivation, he supposed, because that was all he had.

He worried about Team Two. He knew Doug Kramer to be a good cop, and he knew Rick Hare and Charlie Keeling to be good guys and good security guards, but he'd never seen them in this kind of action, and until they'd been in the shit, you could never know how anyone would respond. That's why they were assigned to cover and support.

At Jonathan's order, the teams spread out laterally, separated by twenty feet, more or less. They approached slowly and without conversation. So far, he liked what he saw.

* * *

In the War Room, Venice and Derek manned their screens. They could verify without equivocation that nothing had changed.

Venice hadn't felt like this about a man in a very, very long time. Thirteen years and nine months ago, give or take the months since Roman's birthday. And while that relationship did not end well at all, this one felt different. They had so much in common, not the least of which were unmatched skills at computer hacking. Imagine! When his TickTock2 outed her Freak Face666, it could have been a disaster. Instead, it turned to this.

"Your boss doesn't like me," Derek said.

"I don't know that that's true," Venice said. "I saw him smile at one of your jokes. That's a higher bar than you might think."

"And Big Guy—"

Venice held up her hand. "Stop right there. Boxers hates everybody. I've known him for years, saved his life more than once, and he barely tolerates me."

"How much influence does he have on Mr. Grave?"

"You've got to stop calling him that," Venice scolded. "If you want his respect, you've got to call him Digger. Or Dig. Call him Jon or Jonathan, though, and you'll be toast." As she heard herself, she laughed. There really were quite a few unspoken rules.

"I think he thinks I'm a pussy," Derek said. "I've got a fifteen-inch neck and a thirty-one-inch waist."

"You're not an operator," Venice said. "He doesn't expect a lot of brawn. You've got to give him more time. You can't be pushy with Dig." She gave a coy smile. "But if I say I want you around, you'll stay around."

Derek smiled back. "Because he's so afraid of you?"

"No, he *respects* me and always lets me get my way," she explained. "Now, if I got Mama involved, then he'd be *terrified*."

Derek sat up suddenly in his chair and tapped some keys. "Uh-oh, there's a change," he said.

The live feed from the Chinese satellite showed a pickup truck pulling into the DeWilda's driveway.

Venice reached for the radio. "Scorpion, Mother Hen. Emergency traffic."

"Whatcha got?"

"Someone just arrived at the target building," she said. "Stand by." She pointed to Derek. "Pull back till we can see the teams and give me a distance between them."

The image fell away.

"Okay, Scorpion," Venice said. "You are less than two hundred yards from the target. Recommend you stay put until we can get you more intel."

After a brief silence, during which she imagined that he consulted with Gunslinger and Big Guy, his voice returned. "Negative, Mother Hen. Appreciate the concern, but we need to get close enough for eyeballs. I promise we won't be reckless."

Venice pointed at Derek again. "Now bring us in close to the truck. How do the Chinese not know you're doing this?"

The non sequitur seemed to startle him. "Huh? Oh. This technology is able to view a gajillion images at the same time. I guess there's a chance someone might stumble on it, but it's not likely."

On the screen, the pickup truck returned. A youngish guy, probably midforties, stepped out of the truck wearing woodland camouflage clothing. When he leaned back into the cab, he withdrew a rifle and what looked to be some kind of equipment vest.

She relayed the information to Jonathan, then said to Derek, "I'm guessing that the ability to tap into what we're looking at was quite an espionage coup for the United States."

"Oh, God, yes. I'm not a field guy, but I believe that the Chinese professor who helped us with this was executed."

"Oh, dear," Venice said.

"Yeah, the ChiComs don't mess around. They're not as sick as the NoKos—they don't smear guys with nerve agent—but they don't put up with any bullshit, either."

Venice felt a flash of guilt that technology that had been purchased at such a high price was being hijacked for something like this.

Then she thought of Cody and Megan, eviscerated by these animals without mercy or second thought.

"Whoa, look at that!" Derek declared. He hit a key to freeze the frame, which slid to the upper right-hand corner of the larger projection. The image showed a very warm welcome.

"It looks like daddy's home," Venice said.

Derek shook his head. "Uh-uh." Another thumbnail appeared on the screen under the first one. The image was clearly a posed one, something from a business brochure. This thin, dark-haired man was clearly different than the one in the truck. "*That* is Percy DeWilda. He's not the guy in the truck."

"Ooh," Venice cooed. "Maybe daddy's away and it's time for mommy to play."

As if on cue, the man who clearly was Percy DeWilda came out of the front door and gave the new guy a warm handshake and a bro hug.

"Kinky," Derek said. He zoomed in on the pickup truck's license plate, clicked another still, and ran the number. "Hel-lo," he said in a cheesy faux-British accent. He tapped as he talked. "Assuming that that truck truly belongs to him—and there are no reports of it being stolen—Mr. Zane Wortham has just arrived." He tapped some more. "And guess what he used to do for a living."

"Special Forces?"

"Ding-ding. You win a prize. And guess what his credit score is like."

"In the toilet," Venice exclaimed.

"Ding-ding again."

Venice keyed her microphone. "Scorpion, Mother Hen."

"We're getting closer, Mother Hen," Jonathan whispered into his mic. "We need to keep radio traffic to a minimum."

"If only I didn't know that after working together for all these years," Venice snipped. "The new arrival is one of the attackers. And it would appear that the DeWildas are part of the plot."

Jonathan transmitted, "Team One, Team Two, keep

track of your lines and halt at that swale you see about fifteen yards ahead. I want to be out of sight for a while. When you're below the sight line, move to the middle. We need to powwow and modify the plan."

As they were taking position, Venice radioed, "Two more just arrived."

Jonathan keyed his mic once to break squelch. *Okay.*

When they reached the dark side of the swale, Jonathan gathered the teams together.

"There's a fundamental change in the plan," Jonathan said. His voice was barely a whisper. "The DeWildas are now part of the bad guy package. We're no longer mounting a rescue for them."

"Just because they're receiving the shooters doesn't mean they're shooters themselves," Doug said.

"Fair point," Jonathan said. "So, if they don't threaten you, don't shoot them."

"Can we go over the assault plan again, now that we're here?" Rick asked.

"You tell me what you think it is," Jonathan said, "and I'll tell you if you're right."

Rick looked silly in his NVGs—well, sillier than most—because of his thin frame and narrow face. "When you get the word, or otherwise think it's time to move, Team Two takes up a defensive position while you and the rest of Team One go forward and make the assault."

"That's it."

"I'm still not clear what a defensive position is," Doug said.

How was it possible that this was just coming up now, rather than in the mission brief back in the office?

"You watch our backs," Jonathan said. "If you see a

threat that we don't, take it out. If you see a bad guy getting away, you stop him. Slinger, Big Guy, and I are going to be primarily focused on the entry. You make it possible for us to do that without having to split our focus to the rear. Just remember to announce your shots as soon as you can and watch your background. If you shoot a terrorist and then your bullet goes on to shoot me, I'll consider that a fail."

He meant that as a lighthearted comment to ease the mood, but it didn't seem to work.

"Another truck," Venice announced. "Oops, and one more. That's a total of five bad guys. Seven if the DeWildas are part of the package."

Off the air, Boxers said, "What's the number we're looking for?"

"Derek said there were a total of eight phone signals," Jonathan said.

"Want us to shoot up their engines while you're inside?" Charlie asked. "That way they can't bolt?"

"That's a damn good idea," Boxers said. "Why didn't you think of that, Boss?"

"Not as a first priority," Jonathan said. "If it looks like they're going to get away, then yes, of course, take out their vehicles, but only if you can't take out the runner first. Does that make sense?"

Doug nodded.

"Please keep communication verbal," Jonathan admonished. "Even with NVGs, gestures are hard to read." He let a few seconds pass. "Any other questions?"

He was answered by a ripple of *negatives*. "Okay, then," Jonathan said. "Spread out like you were before, and when I give the word, we start advancing." He'd arranged the line so that Team One would control the right side of the line, and Team Two would hold the left. Jonathan anchored the line on its far right flank, while Doug Kramer anchored the left. Gail and Charlie Keeling defined the middle. Pulling his infrared flashlight from its pocket on his vest, he watched as the group spread out. Distances were hard to judge in these conditions, so he waited to hear from the others that they thought they were where they belonged.

After all five of the others said that they were ready, Jonathan keyed his radio and said, "Let's advance. Keep it as quiet as we can."

For the second time that night, they stepped forward into the night.

Fred Kellner didn't speak much as Iceman drove them to the rally point. Kellner didn't understand how Iceman had come to think of him as some kind of right-hand man, but it bothered him. Almost as much as he was bothered by the entire notion of bringing all the players of Retribution together in one spot.

"I'm going to try this one more time," Kellner said, despite the futility.

"Don't bother," Evers said. "The plan is already in motion. It can't be recalled."

"But it can be canceled," Kellner insisted. "Clearly the FBI knows—"

"Nothing," Evers interrupted. "The FBI knows nothing."

"Why do you keep saying that? You forget that I was there at the Capital Harbor."

"That was not the FBI," Evers insisted. "That was the asshole who is going to pay tonight for ruining everything."

Kellner slammed his hand on the dashboard. "Goddammit, Iceman, will you listen to reason? This whole thing is wildly misguided. Killing children? Burning them alive? That's beyond wrong. I don't think you'll get the team to go along with it."

Evers glared at his passenger through the dim glow of the dashboard lights. "Are you saying that *you* will not go through with your mission? That you will disobey your orders?"

Kellner started to answer, but Iceman held up his hand for silence. "Before you answer, consider that you have already accepted payment. Al-Faisel has the information on your family, and he is willing to burn *them* alive."

"But this isn't his mission," Kellner insisted. "This is *your* revenge."

"He knows that, too, and he doesn't care. You're too emotional, Fred. This is business. It's a dirty business, but it's one that will make you very wealthy. Wealthy enough to never do this again."

That was the undeniable point, wasn't it? Kellner got into this for the money, and the money came. Al-Faisel may be a monster, but he was a monster who kept his word. And he expected the same from others.

"You swear," Kellner said, "you give me your word that this is the last mission."

"I do."

"Say it."

"I already have."

"Say it again."

"You have my word that this is the last mission."

"And after this I am on my own. I can go back to my life and put my gear away."

Iceman smiled. "All of that, yes. After this you and all of this phase of Retribution will be free to live your lives as you wish."

The choice of words piqued Kellner's attention. "This phase? What does that mean?"

"That is none of your concern."

"You mean Al-Faisel is not finished yet?"

"I can't say that for sure, but he has millions and millions of dollars, and he hates America with a passion that most reserve for Satan."

"He *is* Satan," Kellner said.

Evers laughed. "It just occurred to me that Satan and Sugardaddy start with the same letter."

Thirty seconds passed. "You actually like this, don't you?" Kellner asked. "You *enjoy* it."

Evers laughed harder. "Ah, the self-righteousness of the mass murderer. It's one thing to murder dozens of people as a business arrangement, but God forbid that you take pride in a job well done! Is that how you plan to sleep well with your family in whatever rich man's haven you settle into? You're going to tell mama that you got all of this money through some fantastic stock deal, or from a really terrific day at the track, and she will choose to believe it because, well, the money's in the bank, isn't it? None of that is especially troubling to you so long as you don't enjoy the work."

"Jesus, Iceman, you're going to fire incendiary grenades into an orphanage!"

Iceman gave him a confused look. "Is it the children, Fred? Is that the step too far? Says the man who shot randomly into the crowd at a high school football game. Were those children somehow less worthy of life? Or was it that they weren't sleeping, because killing the sleeping is a step too far?"

Kellner locked up. He knew there was no winning the argument. Hell, he knew that when he brought it up. Again.

"Well, maybe this will help you sleep better," Evers continued. "We're not just going to burn the children. We're going to burn the whole damn town. Our time on target will be fifteen minutes. One-five minutes. With the right ordnance, we should be able to make quite an impression."

Keeping a low profile or low sound signature clearly was not a part of the plan for the gathering members of Retribution. No one was paying attention to the woods surrounding the house. That gave Jonathan's team some options and took some of the pressure off the need for silence.

The trick was in knowing when it was time to pull the trigger. They'd been hunkered in the woods for nearly six hours, yet Jonathan still was not convinced that all of Retribution had arrived. As long as they remained gathered in one place, time was on his side.

But he worried about Team Two. Unaccustomed to long waits, how were they holding up? He guessed he'd find out sooner or later.

Jonathan had settled into a space where a deadfall met the base of an old-growth tree, with a reasonably good view of the red side of the ranch-style house—

the right side, looking from the front. To call his spot comfortable would be an overstatement, but he could stay for an extended period without his back screaming at him.

Boxers settled in about ten yards to his left. Peering through the telescopic sight of his rifle, he said. "I see the electrical meter at the red-black corner."

"Roger." Jonathan saw it, too. When it came time to launch this balloon, the first step would be to kill the electricity.

"Looks like we're missing a heck of a party inside," Gail said. She was on Boxers' left, not as far down as Jonathan would have liked her to be.

As Jonathan watched the shadows moving in the light and listened to the muffled sounds of people having a good time, he began to get concerned.

"Mother Hen, Scorpion," he said into his radio.

"Go ahead."

"Is TickTock there?"

"He is."

"Can he hear me?"

"Affirmative."

"Okay, here's what I want you to do. We seem to have some time here, and the course we're about to take is as severe as it gets. Now that people are in the house, is there any way you guys can take another electronic peek to make sure they're who we think they are?"

"We told you about Wortham." This from Derek. "We've checked the other license plates, and of the ones we can find a match, they all come back with pretty much the same background."

"Listen to the words this time, TickTock," Jonathan said, doing his best to control a sudden surge of anger.

"I'm the one down here who'll be pulling the trigger, and I'm also the guy in charge. I didn't ask for what I already know. I asked if there was a way to know more. There's really no negative to answer that. It's either *Yes, there is, and here's how it's done,* or *Gee, I don't know, let me get back to you.* Are we clear on this point?"

This time it was Venice's voice. "Understood," she said. "Give us a few."

Boxers said, "That's a new language from Mother Hen. The *asshole* was silent."

Okay, he'd earned that one.

Another vehicle—this one an unremarkable sedan—pulled down the drive and headed toward the house, and Jonathan felt vindicated for continuing to wait.

He hunkered down and froze, waiting for the headlights to wash over his hiding space and then to allow darkness to return.

When it felt safe for him to look up, Jonathan exposed as little of his silhouette as possible. Following the pattern of the others, this driver stood from his door, then opened the back door, leaned in, and withdrew what looked like an M4 rifle and a heavy range bag. He closed up the car and headed for the front door.

He was halfway there when he stopped and straightened, like a dog on point. He dropped his equipment bag and brought his rifle to his shoulder. "Who's out there?" he shouted. "Show yourself!"

Chapter Thirty-four

"I'm sorry that Digger is such a jerk to you," Venice said.

Derek was leaning into his computer, typing furiously. Even as his fingers flew, his voice remained the mellow baritone that it always was. "I've think I've figured it out," he said.

"How to get more intel on the house?" Venice gasped. "That was fast."

He stopped typing. "No," he said. "Well, yes, the house too. But I've figured out why Mr.—Digger—doesn't like me."

Venice waited for it.

"Actually, it's pretty obvious when you think about it."

She wasn't going to give him the satisfaction of asking.

"I think he's jealous," Derek said, returning to the work on his screen and keyboard. "Think about it. You said you grew up with him, right? And you had a crush on him, and he knew it."

"Oh, for heaven's sake—"

"Hear me out. It's powerful stuff knowing you're someone's childhood hero. You never had a father in your life, his father was a dickhead, so you had him."

"He's hardly my father," Venice said. "You are *so* off base."

"And he had you. I think he's the dad—or the really big brother—who's going to kill any asshole who might even think about breaking your heart."

Venice just stared from her chair, vaguely aware that her mouth was open. She couldn't find words to form. His theory was so . . . so—

"I'm in," Derek declared. He triumphantly jabbed one final key, and the screen filled with an oddly composed image of one woman and a bunch of well-conditioned men mingling about, snacking and drinking what Venice assumed to be beer.

Derek explained, "The DeWildas left their laptop open and hooked into the internet. I hijacked their camera."

"That's brilliant," Venice gushed. She'd done similar things before, but always when she had some back-door knowledge of either the network or the computer itself. "Is that secret NSA voodoo?"

"I wish it was," Derek said. "I think maybe it started that way, but you know how secrets go. One Army private with a grudge and a laptop can steal everything but the nuclear launch codes."

"And maybe them," Venice said.

"Nope," Derek said with a shake of his head. "Those are still analog. Can't be stolen." He moved his chair. "Come here, and I'll show you the code."

Venice chuckled. He really was a rookie to all of

this. "I think we should tell Scorpion that we've got eyes on the bad guys. Do you have audio, too?"

Derek answered by turning up the volume and filling the War Room's speakers with the sound of a chattering crowd.

"Even he might be impressed with this," she said. She reached for the microphone.

Jonathan's left hand moved by muscle memory to flip the switch on his radio to VOX while he shouldered his M27 carbine with his right. "Everybody stay still," he whispered. "Not a move." A gunfight before all the players were here could be a disaster.

A rattled voice said, "I think he sees me." Jonathan thought it was Rick Hare, but he wasn't sure.

"Silence," Jonathan whispered.

The gunman wasn't backing down. "Whoever's out there step forward or I will shoot!" He yelled it louder this time, and the noise brought another one of the gunmen to the door of the house.

"This is bad, Boss," Boxers said.

Yes, it was. If everybody could just stay cool, this might end quietly. It's pretty much impossible to hit a target you can't see, and this guy was clearly playing a bluff.

"What's going on out there?" the second guy asked. He stepped outside, also with his rifle in his hand.

"I heard a rustle over there," he said, pointing in the general direction of Team Two. "Then I swear to God I heard a voice."

The first guy yelled, "This is your last chance to come out before I shoot!"

"Okay, Big Guy, take out the electricals. NVGs, everybody." He slapped his night vision goggles over his eyes. This was going to shit, and with the targets on alert, night vision was their primary force multiplier. And that advantage would evaporate as soon as the targets grabbed theirs.

Jonathan's words had barely cleared his lips when a gunshot split the night. It came from the left flank of their skirmish line—Team Two's area. The two targets reacted instantly, dropping to their knees and ripping out a fusillade of unaimed automatic weapons fire.

To Jonathan's immediate left, Boxers' 7.62-millimeter shoulder cannon boomed five times, launching a shower of sparks from the rear corner of the house and drenching the scene in darkness.

Two seconds later, Jonathan settled his IR laser sight on the first shooter's left ear and sent a round through his brain. The second shooter was diving back into the house when Jonathan took a shot at him. He was pretty sure it was a hit, but it wasn't a kill. The guy was going to have a hard time sitting down, though.

The front of the DeWildas' house seemed to come alive with muzzle flashes and rifle fire.

"One down, one wounded." Jonathan announced. "Team One, are you ready to advance?"

He looked to Boxers and Gail on his left, and they both gave him a thumbs-up and transmitted an affirmative.

"Team Two, on my command, focus covering fire on the front door and windows. Team One will advance around the right side. When I tell you to cease fire, do so immediately. Two-one, do you understand?"

Doug Kramer said, “Got it. Jesus, there’s a lot of lead coming this way.”

“Two-two, do you understand your orders?”

Charlie Keeling’s voice was half an octave higher as he said, “I got it. You want to give that order soon, please?”

“Two-three?”

“Yes!”

“Okay, it all begins in three . . . two . . . one . . . Now!”

As the tree line erupted in gunfire, Jonathan and Team One dashed out of their cover and moved as one to the cover of the nearest pickup truck. The outgoing fire from the house had diminished or maybe stopped. With Team Two concentrating their fire on the single known target that was the house, the impact of the bullets was something to behold. Pieces and chunks of the structure flew away or were reduced to dust as it gave way to the hundreds of bullets that were chewing up the façade. Jonathan couldn’t yet see the inside of the house, but in his mind it was being reduced to rubble, too.

Jonathan, Boxers, and Gail crouched behind the safety of the wheel well.

“Everybody okay?”

“So far,” they said.

“Haven’t had this much fun with my pants on in a long time,” Charlie Keeling said, reminding Jonathan that he was on VOX.

He switched his radio back to PTT—push to talk. “I want to go in fast and hard through the back,” he said. “Usual procedures. I want to use a GPC on the lock just because, and when we breech, I'll lead with a flashbang. That should leave them buggy. Then we clean up." A GPC—general-purpose charge—was a lump of C4 explosive with a tail of detonating cord that would be initiated with a detonator. Weatherproof and mostly soldier-proof, GPCs were a staple of Security Solutions' covert activities.

"If they surrender?" Gail asked.

"We'll zip tie them and leave them for Doug and Wolfie to deal with."

Boxers said, "If past performance is any indicator, I don't expect a lot of surrendering."

"Here we go," Jonathan said. He switched his radio back to VOX. "Team Two, Team Two, cease fire. Cease fire!"

Jonathan and Team One would be running through Team Two's firing lanes, so he needed them to stop shooting. The sudden silence was startling.

They dashed forward, moving as one entity, running at a low crouch, rifles up and ready to engage any target. When they reached the rear corner of the building, they stacked up on the red side as Jonathan sliced the corner, ready to engage any targets he saw.

"Clear."

They advanced on the back door quickly, aware of the windows and of the fact that these trained warriors were as likely to stream out of the doors to flank their attackers as they were to stay inside. For now, they were donning gear, Jonathan assumed, but they could be kitted up in less than a minute. The last thing Jonathan wanted to engage in was anything close to a fair fight.

Jonathan and Gail held back and covered the left

and the right as Boxers moved to the door and placed a GPC over the lock and the jamb.

Hesitantly, it seemed, the outgoing fire was resuming from the front. The bad guys were finding their footing.

"Fire in the hole," Boxers said, and he pulled the pin on the delayed initiator. He moved off to the side, and five seconds later the charge detonated, shredding the door and a good chunk of the back wall.

Jonathan led the way through the opening and took a knee long enough to pull the pins on two flashbang grenades. He was in the laundry room, which opened up to what appeared to be the kitchen. "Eyes and ears," he said, and then he tossed the grenades through the door.

Jonathan barely got his hands pressed to his ears before the explosions shook the whole structure.

Jonathan hoped the bad guys had had time to don their NVGs because if they had, the enhanced flashes would leave them blind for all the time Jonathan needed.

"Moving," he said, and they were off, again moving at a crouch. The enemy had been staggered, literally and figuratively. Every one of the fighters he saw had had time to sling their weapons, and three that Jonathan could see at first glance had donned NVGs for the darkness.

It was a turkey shoot. The bad guys tried to resist, but they didn't know how or where. And they certainly didn't have the time. Jonathan and his team picked their targets and shot them. They fell and didn't move. The entire battle, such as it was, was over in less than twenty seconds.

"Team Two, Team One," Jonathan said. "Hold your fire, keep an eye out for new arrivals. We're all fine, the tangos are all down. We still need to clear the building."

Then he turned to Gail and Big Guy. "Everybody okay?"

"That wasn't as much fun as I'd hoped," Boxers said.

"They got more warning than their victims did," Gail said.

They toured the carnage, verifying that those who appeared dead were, in fact, still dead. In total, they had killed eight people, seven men and a woman. Jonathan said, "Big Guy, how about you zip these guys up, clear their pockets, and get photos back to Mother Hen, while Gunslinger and I check the bedrooms and basement for more bad guys?"

"Works for me," Boxers said. Just to be on the safe side, Big Guy would roll each of the bodies onto its belly and tie their hands behind their backs with zip ties. That way, if they came to or pulled a Hannibal Lecter fake dead guy trick, they wouldn't be mobile.

Chapter Thirty-five

Arthur Evers was still a half mile out, Fred Kellner riding shotgun, when he heard the unmistakable staccato beat of small arms fire. "Goddammit," he spat. "That's coming from the rally point." The plan was ruined—again. "We're out of here."

As the chatter of gunfire evolved to sustained bursts, he yanked the wheel to the left, sending them onto a road that was marked only by a route number. People had just begun to slip out of their homes to investigate the noise when an explosion pulsed the chilly air. He knew then that they were out of business.

"Shouldn't we be helping them fight?" Kellner asked.

"They're dead," Evers said. "If not yet, then soon. We can't help them." He looked to his passenger. "Did you have anything to do with this?"

Kellner looked both shocked and confused. "Anything to do with what? The gunfire? Hell no."

"A few minutes ago, you were telling me that the attack on Fisherman's Cove was a bad idea," he explained. "And now this."

Kellner looked annoyed. "I had nothing to do with it. I'm a soldier, Iceman. I do what I'm paid to do. That doesn't mean I have to like it. Our real concern is how deeply infiltrated we have become. Somehow the FBI—or this Jonathan fellow you keep talking about—has been able to stay a step ahead."

"I've been thinking about that," Evers said. "Of the operations this man and his team have disrupted, what do they all have in common?"

Kellner shifted uncomfortably in in his seat. "I know what you're going to say," he said. "That I am somehow the common denominator. But that is not true. That first operation—the one the press calls Black Friday. My part of that went perfectly."

"Actually, I *wasn't* going to say that," Evers said. "You know the FBI caught one of the operators that night, right?"

"No," Kellner said. "I never heard anything on the news or anywhere else."

"That was by design," Evers said. "I know this through my FBI contact."

"Well, there it is!" Kellner said. "Whoever they captured revealed secrets."

"He could not have known about tonight," Evers said. "And he could not have known about Capital Harbor, because even I did not know about this rally point until hours before I sent out the alert. As for the Capital Harbor fiasco, someone had to have alerted somebody."

"Your man Steve, then," Kellner said. "It was not me. I am not the problem. I am not one to sign my own death warrant."

Evers listened to the words, and he observed the

man, and he still did not know what to believe. But he knew beyond doubt—even if he didn't have any hard evidence—that the real common denominator to all the disasters was this fool, Jonathan Grave. He didn't understand the nature of his involvement, and he didn't know how he was able to do so much damage, but as he drove away from the rally point—away from Al-Faisel's primary weapons cache for his Northern Virginia cell—he was more determined than ever to ruin the man.

"You're going through with this attack, anyway, aren't you?" Kellner asked.

"*We* are going through with it," Evers corrected. "My handlers have paid for *three* attacks, and we have delivered only two. That aborted disaster of yours does not count."

"How? I thought all the munitions were back there at the rally point."

"We have rifles and ammunition," Evers said. "And limited explosives. Here in the truck."

"There's no way we can do the kind of damage you want to do with so little equipment."

Evers smiled. "It all depends on how we choose our targets," he said. "I no longer care about the children in the school. There's an old lady in that mansion on the hill. Grave calls her Mama, even though she is black. I don't know the relationship, but I know the affection. We're going to kill her."

"That's not an attack," Kellner objected. "That's a murder. A hit. There's nothing tactical in that, and it will not please your handlers, as you say."

"You say you are a soldier," Evers said. "Act like it."

Kellner started to say something, then aborted the effort.

"If you have something on your mind," Evers said, "now is the time to get it *off* your mind."

Another aborted attempt, and then finally, Kellner slapped his thighs. "Okay," he said, apparently to himself. "Remember you asked." When he pivoted in his seat, only half of his face was visible in the glow of the dashboard. "You keep talking about breaking this man. About ruining his will to fight. I don't know where all of that comes from, but has it occurred to you that this will inspire him to devote his life to retribution? And I mean the *real* kind of retribution."

Evers felt himself smirking. "Why, Mr. Kellner, do I sense fear?"

"Not fear," Kellner said. "Recognition. This is not a man to be trifled with. If you declare this kind of war on him, you will never sleep another restful night. I have seen him in action. I have seen the ice in the eyes of his associates."

There it was, Evers thought. There was the cowardice in Kellner. "So, you are saying that we should quit. That we should just let him get away with the murders of so many of your colleagues?"

"Colleagues!" Kellner nearly shouted. "I didn't know a single one of them. At least I don't think I did. I can't know because I've never met them."

"You were colleagues on the same mission."

"Okay, fine." Kellner could not have been more dismissive in his tone. "Use whatever words you want. But I have no attachment to any of them and no driving urge to avenge their deaths."

Kellner fell silent, but Evers sensed that he had more to say, so he remained quiet to give him the chance.

"But I'll tell you what I do have an attachment to," Kellner continued after his pause. "I'm attached to the notion of this being the end of it. Of me getting my life back and of living in peace without fear of you or *Handler* or anybody else trying to hunt me down. So, if you want to do this thing—as misguided as I think it is—I'll go with you and fight at your side. But then you will never see me again. Agreed?"

Evers sensed that he was being insulted, but as he listened to the words, he could find no fault in them. It was not cowardice to do your job and then retire. That was what Kellner was proposing, and at its essence, there was nothing wrong with it. "Agreed," he said.

Jonathan and Gail focused on the main level first, clearing each of the three bedrooms and two bathrooms by the book, checking every corner and under every bit of furniture. It was too easy to lose concentration at moments like this. No matter how hard you tried or how professional you were, it was hard to pretend that there's a credible threat when you knew in your heart that the enemy was already dead. The first floor took all of six minutes.

Moving downstairs, he felt a little more amped. He hated stairwells. They gave the bad guy all the advantage. If a shooter was committed to his cause and willing to die for it, he needed only to wait and keep steady until his enemy showed himself from the feet up.

If this were a true war zone, Jonathan would have led his descent with a fragmentation grenade or two, but these guys had been planning an assault. That meant a good probability of assembled munitions, and he had no desire to visit Mars tonight. On the other hand, basements were also places where people put the kids away to hide them from danger. Ditto the family pets.

He led the way, illuminating the path with an IR flashlight that cast light in his NVGs as bright and shadows as dark as if he were using visible white light.

"Good God," he said as the scene revealed itself. There were enough explosives stocked here to rattle Tokyo if they went off at once.

"Well, there went my last sympathy for the DeWildas," Gail said.

"Stay focused," Jonathan said. "We've still got to clear the rooms."

"This is where we hope there's no gunfight, right?"

"Your lips to God's ear."

The ceiling down here was low, and the place stunk of isocyanates and mildew. The space was mostly one room, but there were doors on the black and white sides. The one on the white side—the front side—was flimsily built and behind it they found a closet full of assorted gardening tools. Across the room, on the black side, the door was substantial and locked.

"Now, right there is a door with a lock that is begging to be picked," Jonathan said. He lifted the Velcro flap on a pouch on the right side of his vest and removed a lock-picking set. "Hold your light on the lock, will you, Slinger?"

"You don't worry about booby traps?" she asked.

He froze. "Well, not until you mentioned it."

Clearly, the DeWildas had secrets worth hiding, and the steps they would take to hide them were a real question. They took the better part of a minute to search for some kind of initiating mechanism but didn't see one.

"Oh, what the hell?" Jonathan said. "If we trigger something, we'll never know it."

"You could leave it for Wolverine and her crime scene experts," Gail said. "There's no point in ruining every bit of evidence they could use."

He paused.

Gail continued, "I vote we contact Wolverine and call it a night."

As Iceman drove past the sign welcoming them to Fisherman's Cove, Virginia, Kellner told himself for the hundredth time since he'd agreed to this foolishness twenty minutes ago that the mission came first. Of the hundreds of battles and skirmishes that he'd fought, both for Uncle Sam and for private contractors, precious few were conflicts that he believed in. He was just a soldier with rentable skills.

And after this one last thing, he'd never have to fight again.

Iceman parked their Suburban facing downhill, about fifty yards up from the mansion they were about to raid. He killed the headlights, and they watched the house in silence. The lights were on throughout the massive home, and two uniformed guards stood out front, each of them armed with a rifle and a sidearm. Beyond the house, in the space between it and the kids' dormitory buildings, Kellner caught sight of shadows moving in the darkness. More guards, he presumed.

"Looks like they're expecting us," Kellner said.

"They're on high alert," he said. "It seems he knows I'd keep my promise."

Kellner felt something jump in his gut. "What promise?"

"Nothing for you to worry about," Iceman said.

"I beg to disagree. It sounds *exactly* like something for me to worry about. You've been in contact with the Grave guy?"

"I told him that he would pay dearly if he didn't stay out of my business."

"Well, holy shit," Kellner said. "They're *expecting* us?"

"They're frightened of us," Iceman corrected. "Let's go."

Iceman dropped the transmission into DRIVE and once again headed down the hill, turning on his headlights as he passed the mansion. He drove down to the end of the street and paused at the stop sign at Water Street, where an elaborate building occupied the corner on the left. It looked like a firehouse, but it wasn't.

Iceman pointed toward the building. "That's his headquarters and his house," he said.

"Whose?"

"Jonathan Grave's."

"Why aren't we attacking that?" Kellner asked.

Iceman flashed a bit of temper. "I've told you before," he said. "Hurting Grave directly doesn't hurt him the way I want to. It has to be the old lady. It has to be Mama."

"Why her?" Kellner asked. "What makes you think they're so close?"

"Start with the fact that she called him Jonny, and

everybody in town calls her Mama. Plus, I could see it in her eyes when she was talking about him."

Iceman turned right onto Water Street, past a restaurant and several slips of the marina. Then he turned right onto a road that paralleled Church Street. Modest houses lined both sides of the street. Up ahead, on the corner, sat a bank with a large parking lot. It was dead at this hour, its lights off, save for the lighted plastic sign on the roof.

Iceman pulled into the parking lot and backed the Suburban into the darkest of the parking spaces, in the back corner of the lot. He threw the transmission into PARK. "Okay, let's go," he said.

Kellner reached across the console and grabbed Iceman's arm. "Let's go do what? We don't have a plan. You just want to stroll up the walkway and start shooting? That will not end well for us."

"Suppressed rifles," Iceman explained. "We can take out the guards from here. When they're down, we can move. Open your door quietly, please."

Kellner thought it through, then opened his door. It wasn't much of a plan, but sometimes, simple worked best. He walked around to the back of the Suburban, where Iceman had opened the gate to reveal his stash of weaponry and gear. The dome light had been disabled, but Kellner was familiar enough with the gear to recognize the silhouettes he could see. Three AR platform rifles, three ballistic vests festooned with spare magazines, and a duffel-like equipment bag that he figured must carry the explosives that Iceman mentioned during the drive.

"Help yourself," Iceman said.

Kellner started with the vest. It was made of Kevlar, but there were no plates. That meant the armor would stop pistol rounds but might as well have been a T-shirt for rifle rounds. The pouches held a lot of extra ammo. He pulled a magazine out of the pouch just to take a look. He knew just from the weight that it was 5.56 millimeter, the standard U.S. load for nearly five decades. Given Iceman's mission parameters, he'd have preferred 7.62-millimeter ammo, but this would work.

"Have you got coms?" Kellner asked, hoping there'd be a way for them to keep track of each other via radio.

"Those were in the rally point," Iceman replied. "We'll try to stay close. If we get separated, just remember it's my job to breech the house and take care of the old lady. You hold security outside."

"How am I going to do that alone?"

"I figure most of the guards will be dead before we get to the house," Iceman explained. "Then we get in, do it, and get out."

Kellner continued to inventory his equipment. A pistol was integral to the vest, a Glock 19 nine-millimeter Velcro'd into a cross-draw holster at belt level, below the M4 mags.

The rifles themselves were unloaded, with their bolts locked open. That's not how Kellner would have—

"Hey!" a voice called from behind, and they were blasted with a bright white light. "What the hell are you two doing?"

Kellner turned to confront a cop. He was young and skinny, but wearing a vest, with his right hand gripping his holstered pistol.

Iceman didn't say anything, so Kellner filled the silence. "Oh, we're just checking some—"

Iceman drew and fired with startling speed. He fired three times, a classic triple-tap, where the first two rounds nailed the officer in his chest, reeling him backward, and then a third bullet drilled him between the eyes. The cop's legs folded, and he dropped straight down, his pistol still in its holster.

"We left a hell of a mess," Boxers said. "How do you think Wolverine and company are going to explain that?" They'd done just as Gail had suggested, left the bodies and munitions where they were, and then they told Irene Rivers via Dom D'Angelo that a mess awaited her troops.

They'd divided between their vehicles as before, with Jonathan, Boxers, and Gail in the Batmobile and the others in Doug's police vehicle.

Jonathan said, "I imagine that they will happily inform the citizenry of the nation that their ever-vigilant Federal Bureau of Investigation has found and killed the perpetrators of the Black Friday terror attacks."

"Good thing we don't do this for the credit for a job well done," Boxers said.

"It may not be done yet," Gail said from the back. "I didn't see Kellner among the dead. This might not be over yet."

"I didn't see Vitale, either," Jonathan said.

"Maybe they pussied out," Boxers said. "Even if they didn't—"

Behind them, Doug Kramer's light bar erupted with flashing strobes.

Their tactical channel broke squelch. "Break, break, break. We've got shots fired in the Cove."

Without dropping a beat, Boxers floored the gas pedal and the Batmobile took off, leaving the accelerating Suburban behind.

"Have you got more details than that?" Jonathan asked over the radio.

A new voice—Keeling, judging from the accent—took over. "The chief is working through stuff on his own channel. Doesn't have time for you. If I overhear anything important, I'll let you know."

After a few seconds of silence, except for the roar of the Hummer's engine, Jonathan said, "I think you're right, Gunslinger. This isn't over yet."

The sound of the gunshots seemed louder than any gunfire Kellner had ever heard. On a quiet night in a quiet town, it was a sound unlike any other.

"There went surprise," Kellner said.

"Not if we move fast," Iceman argued. "Now."

Kellner slid a rifle out of the bed, stuck his arm and head through the single-point sling, and pulled a magazine from his pouch. He slid it into the mag well, thumbed the bolt release, and he was ready to rock.

"Please tell me you've zeroed these sights," he said.

"They're zeroed to a hundred yards," Iceman said.

Iceman's gunshots had created a stir, and Kellner could feel it in the crisp autumn atmosphere. It took a few seconds for the sense of urgency to ignite, but when it did, the night began to erupt with the sounds of sirens. It wouldn't be long until this bank parking lot was filled with cops, and when they found that one of their own was dead, all hell would break loose.

It didn't help at all that their target—and their current location—was only a block and a half away from the police station.

As Kellner picked up his pace, he realized that this was evolving into a suicide mission. Returning to the Suburban was no longer possible, so they'd have to rely on the secondary exfil plan. But getting from the mansion to the marina would be a hell of a firefight. And then what?

"Focus, Fred," he said aloud to himself. *One step at a time.*

They dashed across the rear parking lot, where they encountered a stockade fence dividing this property from the next. It had been a while since Kellner had climbed a fence, but the muscle memory was there.

When they flopped over to the opposite side, they were behind a Mexican restaurant that carried a Church Street address. Kellner intentionally slowed his pace as he crossed the parking lot because he knew that he'd soon be taking a long-range shot, and he didn't want to have the yips when he did.

"The Dumpster," Iceman said, pointing to the big green box that sat angled to the side of the restaurant. "See if we have a shot from there."

The smell of stale salsa and rotting food turned his stomach, but Kellner wasted no time. He shouldered his rifle as he approached the big trash container, leveled the muzzle in the direction of the mansion across the street, and peered through his scope. After dialing in 4× magnification, he had a pretty good view of the two guards flanking the front doors. It was a two-hundred-yard shot, give or take, so he'd have to hold a little high.

"I've got a good sight picture," Kellner said. Iceman

had settled in on the other end of the Dumpster, on his left.

"You take the guy on the right, and I'll take the guy on the left?"

"Good for me."

"On my count," Iceman said. "Three . . . two . . ."

Boxers drove the Batmobile as if it were a jet fighter, his foot pressed to the floor and the engine screaming. From the shotgun seat, Jonathan didn't dare look at the speedometer, but if it hadn't hit the century mark, he'd have been shocked.

The dark countryside flew past in a gray blur.

"Come on, Boxers," Gail said from the backseat. "If we hit a deer—"

"At this speed, with this much weight, we'd barely feel it and the deer would blow apart," Boxers snapped.

Jonathan didn't think the physics would work that way, but that didn't matter. He knew that this was the beginning of the attack he'd been anticipating, and he knew that he was out of position.

"How far out are we?" Jonathan asked.

"I can look at the road or the odometer," Boxers said. "I'm pretty sure we'll get there when we do."

Jonathan turned around to look out the back window. "When did we lose Doug?"

"Long time ago," Boxers said. "He needs a faster chief's buggy."

"Arriving dead is almost like not arriving at all," Gail muttered, loudly enough to be heard.

Jonathan saw the Bender Farm up ahead on the right, sitting on its hill. That made them exactly three miles from the firehouse. And it meant that they'd gone sixteen miles in the last twelve minutes. *Holy shit.*

Boxers slowed from horrifying to merely terrifying as he negotiated the sweeping right turn around the peninsula of land that defined the Bender place, and then sped up again. If anyone had been coming the other way, it would have been instant death for all of them.

The radio popped in Jonathan's ear. Venice sounded nearly hysterical. "Break! Break! Break! The mansion is under attack!"

Boxers pressed the accelerator even harder. "Okay to go faster now, Boss?"

Jonathan keyed his mic. "Mother Hen, what does *under attack* mean?"

There was no answer.

He looked to the driver. "Can't you get any more out of this thing?"

Chapter Thirty-six

Once Jonathan and his team declared the scene to be secure and they were headed home, Venice had relocated to the secondary command center on the third floor of the mansion, and she'd taken Derek with her. Now guards had been shot at the front door and the world was coming undone. The shrieking emergency alarm—a sound she'd never heard—made a bad situation even worse.

After she alerted Jonathan, she jumped up from her chair. She pointed a finger at a very startled Derek. "You monitor the channels," she said.

"Under *attack*?" he said. "What does that mean?"

Venice didn't answer. She had to get Roman and Mama to Zulu—to the safe room. As she exited the command center, commotion bloomed large. People were yelling downstairs, and she heard furniture tipping over and urgent cries for help.

"Call an ambulance!" someone yelled. She recognized Oscar's voice. "Greer and Munson have been shot!"

Instinctively, Venice ran down two and a half flights,

past the second floor, so she could get a better view, and gunfire erupted outside. In the foyer, two injured men were sprawled on the floor, being stripped of their gear and clothing.

Above her, and behind, Derek called, "A police officer has been killed!"

Oscar's head whipped around at the sound of Derek's voice. "You! Ms. Alexander! Get to Zulu! Now!"

JoeDog appeared from somewhere and sprinted down the stairs toward the action in the foyer.

"JoeDog!" Venice shouted. "Come up here!"

The retriever ignored the command.

"Now, Ms. Alexander," Oscar insisted. "If you get hurt, then none of this is worth anything."

"How badly are they hurt?"

"They've been shot, but we don't know!" Oscar said. Then his tone turned pleading. "Please, ma'am. You have your boy and your mother to think about. Set an example. And hurry."

Outside, the rate of fire doubled, and the radio traffic became unintelligible.

"Venice!" Derek said. "He's right. I don't know what your safe room is, but you have a responsibility to your family." He rushed down the remaining steps that separated them, then grabbed her arm. "Where are we going?"

"The safe room is on the third floor," Venice said. "But Mama and Roman . . ." Before she turned to go up, she yelled, "JoeDog! Come!"

If the dog heard, she didn't care.

Venice turned, climbed the half flight to the second floor. "Roman! Mama! Zulu! Zulu! Zulu!" They'd rehearsed this scenario, but not enough. Zulu meant *Stop what you're doing and get to safety. Don't ask questions, just go.*

Yet the hallway remained empty.

She headed across the hallway to the left to get to Roman. When she got to the door, it was locked. "Dammit!" She pounded on it with her fist. "Roman! Roman, wake up and get up! Zulu!"

Derek stepped up from behind. "Get out of the way."

Venice pivoted out from the door and watched as Derek unleashed a huge kick with the sole of his shoe. The doorjamb splintered, and the door exploded inward. Roman was on his bed, dressed in pajama bottoms, a computer on his lap, his head encased in earphones. He slammed the laptop shut and ripped the phones from his ears.

"Hey!" he shouted. "What the hell!" Then, after a couple of seconds: "What is that noise? Is that the Zulu alarm?"

As if to answer his question, the gunfire outside intensified even more.

"Safe room!" Venice ordered. She pulled him off his bed by his arm. His laptop crashed to the floor.

"Hey, stop!" Roman protested. "Jesus, that was my computer!"

"Watch your mouth," Venice scolded.

He pulled his arm away. "I've got to get dressed!"

Venice scooped the back of his neck with the webbing between her thumb and forefinger and propelled the boy out of the room into the hallway. When he looked back, there was real fear in his eyes. Maybe it was about the larger situation, but Venice preferred that he be afraid of *her* tonight.

By the time they returned to the stairway, Mama had wandered out of her bedroom. She looked confused and thoroughly rattled by all the noise. Mama's nightclothes looked like they were stolen from the Victorian era. She liked long "dressing gowns" that stretched all the way to the floor.

"Oh, thank God, Mama," Venice said. "We need to get upstairs to the safe room."

As they started up the stairs to the third floor, Roman pointed at Derek. "He's not coming, too, is he? There's not much room in there."

"Roman!" Venice said.

"I'm just making sure you get there," Derek said.

"You're coming, too," Venice demanded.

"We're not having this argument," Derek said.

It turned out that the safe room was directly across the attic space from the command center.

"I thought that was a closet," Derek said.

Roman got there first and went to the adjacent bookcase, where he dislodged a dusty old book to reveal a keypad. He checked over his shoulder to make sure Derek wasn't watching, and he punched in the code. Something clicked, and then he pulled on the closet door. It opened to reveal what appeared to be a well-furnished bank vault.

Roman helped Mama in, and then turned to Venice. "Come on, Mom," he said. "You're next."

Venice hesitated. Why should she be protected when all these other people were risking their lives and getting hurt? How was that fair?

"I know you want to fight," Derek said. His eyes were soft, knowing. "But you're a mom above all. That's always got to come first."

"But you . . ."

Derek smiled and touched her face. "I'm going to kick some ass and come riding back to you on a black charger."

Venice felt the grin on her face. "The horse type of charger or the car?"

He laughed, then kissed her.

"Mom!"

Derek said, "See you in a few."

As she stepped inside, he helped close the door.

As the scenery flew by at impossible speed, the Batmobile found every bump in the road, and the shitty suspension magnified them all. Jonathan pulled his radio from its spot on his shoulder and shifted from the encrypted tactical channel to Channel 8, the frequency used by the security force at Resurrection House.

"Security Four, this is Security Ten. Situation report, please."

Wilma's Ice Cream Emporium screamed past the window. "That puts us two miles out," Gail said.

"Security Four, Security Four," Jonathan nearly shouted. He had to control that. Speaking louder did not make a radio transmission better. In fact, it made it worse. "Answer up, please."

"Security Four," the voice said. It was Oscar. Whatever bitterness Jonathan had felt that he'd not volunteered for the assault had now evaporated.

"Thank God, you're there," Jonathan said. "Sitrep, please."

"Ten, we're under attack," Oscar said. "Two men are

down, but they were hit in the plates. They'll be okay, but they're out of the fight."

"Where are the attackers?" Jonathan asked.

"I don't know. Everywhere?"

"Are you on lockdown?"

"Affirmative. The family is Zulu."

"Roger," Jonathan said. "We're only a few minutes out."

Boxers hit the brakes hard. "Oh, shit!"

Directly ahead, the police vehicles had blocked the road, their blue strobes painting frantic splashes on the trees.

"Oh, my God," Gail said from the back. "Why aren't they fighting?"

"Want me to run it?" Boxers asked. "There's enough of a gap we can get through with just tearing off a few fenders."

"Do it," Jonathan said. If somebody wanted to prosecute him later, let them.

Boxers leaned on the Batmobile's horn and jammed the accelerator. As Fisherman's Cove police officers dove to the sides, Boxers nailed the sweet spot of the cop cars, executing a modified PIT maneuver, normally used to end hot pursuits. Metal screamed as the armored beast plowed through, with much less felt impact than Jonathan had anticipated. The cop cars pivoted on their own axes to be nearly parallel to the road.

"Hammer it," Jonathan said. "When they get the gravel out of their teeth, I want to be out of range for pistols."

* * *

Venice couldn't stand waiting in safety. It didn't feel right, and she couldn't do it. She turned to Roman. "Baby, listen to me," she said. "I can't stay here. I don't have time to explain it, but I just can't."

Roman's eyes reddened. "You can't go out there."

"I have to."

"But there's shooting! You don't know how to shoot!"

It had been a long, long time since Roman had looked like a little boy. Manhood was coming on strong, but now that he was scared—really, *really* scared—he looked ten years old again. It broke her heart.

"Venny!" Mama gasped. "You can*not* go out there."

She took her baby boy's face in her hands. "Roman, honey, I love you more than anything. I'll be okay. I'll be back, I promise."

"I don't want you to go!" he said.

"I know." She leaned in to kiss him, and he turned his face away. "You take care of Mama."

"I don't need nobody to take care of me!" Mama insisted.

"I'll come with you," Roman said.

"No, you won't," Venice said. She moved to the door and opened it. The cacophony of the attack was deafening. "Be sure the door is locked behind me."

Roman was beginning to sob as she pulled the door closed. When it latched, she pressed her back against it and closed her eyes. "What am I doing?" she asked herself aloud.

This had to happen.

She took a few seconds to arrange a couple of books to make sure that Zulu looked like a closet again, and then she headed for the stairs. As she passed from the third floor to the second, she saw that the men had been moved from the foyer.

"Derek!" she yelled. "Where are you?"

No answer.

She kept moving. "Derek! Where are you?"

She was nearly at the bottom—nearly in the foyer—when Oscar stepped into view. He had blood on his uniform shirt. He was furious. "Ms. Alexander! Get back to Zulu."

"Are you hurt, Oscar?" she asked.

Derek joined him, a rifle in his hands. "What the hell are you doing, Ven?"

"I'm part of the team," she said. "I have to be a part of defending it. What are we doing?"

Derek and Oscar took big breaths to argue with her.

"Don't bother," she said. "I'm not going back upstairs."

"Ah, screw it," Derek said. He grabbed her arm far too roughly had it not been an emergency and pulled her along. The room to the left, just inside the foyer, the space that Venice had grown up knowing as the parlor, had long ago been converted to the reception office for Resurrection House. It now looked like a fortress. The security team had moved the antique reproduction cherry desks together to form a kind of barricade.

"Get behind there," Derek commanded.

Two guards whose names she wasn't sure of lay on the floor, moaning. Blood smeared the hands and face of one, but not the other. They both seemed barely conscious and in a lot of pain.

"Oh, my God," Venice gasped. "Are they okay?"

"Hit in the plates," Oscar said. He'd joined them behind the barricade and kneeled on one knee, using the desks as a rifle rest. "They'll be okay. They're hurtin' though."

Venice stooped to look more closely at the wounded men and instantly felt terrible that she didn't pay more attention to the staff, whose job always seemed so boring to her. She picked up one of the wounded men's rifles, and when she turned back, she was startled to see Derek posed in a posture identical to Oscar's, rifle to his shoulder and aiming at the front door. "How do you know about these things?" she asked.

He broke his intense focus on the front door and looked at the M4 she held in her hand. "It's a rifle," he said. "I know about them because of things I did that you don't know about. See that fire selector lever on the left side next to the trigger? Turn it up to the single bullet icon and it's ready to shoot. Don't touch the trigger till you're ready to kill someone."

Jonathan had taken Venice shooting before, so she wasn't entirely unfamiliar with an M4, but it felt awkward and wrong to shoulder the butt stock this time. She didn't know if she'd be able to kill anyone.

"Do we have a plan?" she asked.

"Far as I know, this is it," Derek said. "Hunker down and wait."

Oscar explained, "We're rolling the dice that the exterior teams and the police will take them out. If they don't and they get through, we fight them in here."

Venice ran her hands over the wood surface of the desk. "Will this stop bullets?"

"Won't even slow 'em down," Oscar said. "That's why you shouldn't be here. Why Mr. Grave is gonna fire me when he finds out you're here. Guess it won't matter all that much if we're all dead."

"Please go back to the safe room," Derek said. This time when he gripped her hand, his touch was gentle.

"No, not now," Oscar said. "That window of opportunity is closed. Pretty soon, that stairway's gonna be a kill zone. It'll be the place not to be. That's a good door with a good lock, and the structure's all reinforced, but this place ain't built for what's happenin' to it."

As if his words had summoned the devil, the wall to their left was pummeled with a fusillade of bullets. The whole structure seemed to vibrate under the assault, and huge spiders erupted in the armored glass of the front windows.

"This could be it," Oscar said.

When Boxers slid the turn onto Church Street and headed down the hill toward the mansion, the night vibrated with gunfire. Jonathan saw a few police officers along the curb, using their engine blocks as cover, and he saw muzzle flashes up on the yard, closer to the mansion.

He knew exactly what was going on. The Fisherman's Cove PD was a small force that was underpaid and undertrained. Their orders in situations like this were to isolate the hazard and wait for backup. Doug might have gotten them fired up for a fight, but he wasn't here yet to lead them.

"Don't even slow down," Jonathan ordered. "See what this beast can do to a fence." He pointed to the nearest corner of the steel fence. It was far enough away from the cops' position that he hoped they wouldn't open fire, and this section of fence was considerably less hardened than the front gate.

Boxers sped up. "I think this is going to righteously suck," he said. "Check your belts."

They had to be doing sixty-five, seventy miles an hour when the Hummer hit the curb, took some air, and then smashed into the gate. Jonathan's world erupted in noise and heat and the stench of powder as the airbags initiated and punched him in the face.

"God*damn*!" Boxers yelled.

"Everybody okay?" Jonathan asked.

He was already pushing his door open before he heard the answers. Hugging his M27 close to his chest, he pulled the door latch and tumbled out onto the ground. He hit hard, squarely on the hunk of steel that was his .45. That was going to leave a mark. He glanced back and up and saw Gail press the back door open, and she came out feet first. She had some blood over her eye, but it didn't seem to be a big deal.

On the far side of the Batmobile, he saw Boxers working his way over the seats to come out Jonathan's door. He was bleeding from his head, too, but seemed similarly unfazed. As for the Batmobile, well, he'd been thinking about getting a new one, anyway.

"Follow me," Jonathan said. He started running toward the house.

"What's the plan?" Gail asked.

Boxers said, "I don't think we have one. Maybe just a general ass-kicking."

Jonathan heard the words, but he didn't look back and he didn't slow. He'd never felt this level of disorganization before. There always had to be a plan. It was suicidal to barge into a gun battle without some organization. Oscar had already informed him that he didn't have time to read Jonathan in on all the shit they were doing, and he wasn't going to interrupt the guys in the yard.

He keyed his mic as he ran. "Security team, this is Security Ten. We are on the property and moving in to join the fight from the northeast side. Don't shoot the friendlies."

No one acknowledged, but from the volume of fire, he figured they had their hands full.

As he sprinted across the yard, he looked back at the Rez House dormitory building and saw that the guards there remained in position, just as they were trained to do. If the attack on the mansion was a feint to draw attention away from an attack on the kids, there probably weren't enough guards to repel it, but they'd be able to slow them down.

Seeing Doug Kramer's troops cowering behind their cruisers launched a swell of anger. How could they stand by and watch others in uniform blast away in a gunfight and not do something?

Jonathan saw one of his guys on the ground. He slowed and ran backward a few steps while pointing to the downed guard. "Gunslinger!" he yelled. "Take care of him."

Then he refocused on getting into the fight.

Finally, as he cleared the last corner, he saw three of his guards and two town cops hunkered down next to the brick as a blast of full-auto fire chewed up the façade.

"Friendlies behind you!" Jonathan yelled, and he also transmitted.

One of them turned at the sound of his voice. It was Danny Palmer, and he looked fully engaged.

"Thank God, sir," he said. "They want the house. State troopers are still ten minutes out, and most of the townies won't come in."

Boxers had joined him, and a few seconds later, Gail was there, too. The simple shake of her head told him that there'd been no medical care to be rendered for the fallen guard.

"We can't just stay here," Jonathan said. "I'm in command now."

"These guys know what they're doing, sir," Danny said. "They're advancing one tree at a time, and their fire is accurate as hell. Half the time, we don't even know where they are."

"Have you tried flanking from the other side?"

"We've got a guy over there already. Stacy Allen. We've kept them slowed down, but they're not giving up."

Jonathan flipped down his NVGs. "Let's see what happens." He started to move out to sprint to a tree for himself, but before he could move, two sustained bursts of fire chewed up their corner of the structure. Jonathan figured thirty rounds each.

The bad guys were covering for something with all that gunfire, and whatever it was, it was bad for the good guys. Jonathan chose the lull after the second fusillade—when the guy was changing mags—to make his move. He shouldered his M27 and sprinted out into the open, charging across the yard to pick a tree of his own. It was massive—a hickory, he thought, but maybe not—and it gave him clear visual access to the front of the mansion.

He pressed his transmit button. "Friendlies in the front yard. Stacy Allen, sorry I don't know your radio handle. Cease fire and take cover."

Peering from behind his tree, he scanned for targets and switched back to VOX. "Hey Danny, should I be the only good guy out here?"

"As far as I know, but I can't say for sure. But stand by for two more."

The corner of the mansion that Jonathan had just left erupted in outgoing gunfire, sending dozens of rounds downrange and chewing up the real estate. As he looked back to see what was going on, he saw Boxers running out to meet him at his tree, closely trailed by Gail.

"We're a team goddammit," Boxers said as they slid behind the cover. "Next time you forget that, I'll beat you to death."

"While this is very intimate," Jonathan said, "We can't—"

The muzzle of a rifle peeked out from behind a tree near the front door, much closer to the door than Jonathan thought they'd be—much, *much* closer than he wanted them to be. Jonathan chewed up the tree with a ten-round rip of his own. He didn't expect to hit the shooter, but he made him jump back.

"I'm gonna flank him," Boxers said, and he was off at a run. He ran past the closest tree to get behind another one in his advance to the shooter. He was three strides away when the ground around him erupted in bullet hits.

Grass and dirt flew, and Boxers fell.

Chapter Thirty-seven

Kellner was surprised by the intensity and competence of the opposition. These guys were better than any rent-a-cop security force he'd encountered in the past. Anywhere else, on any other day, this fight would have been over in seconds, and Iceman would have been in and out with his revenge card filled. But this fight was going on ten minutes old, and they hadn't breached the entrance yet.

As they advanced up the yard, he'd fired ten or twelve rounds at the front door, but they didn't penetrate. That meant they'd have to make an explosive entry, but to do that, they had to get a charge on the door, and these guys wouldn't give them enough room to breathe. It seemed that every ten yards cost them fifty rounds of ammunition, and his pouches were about empty.

This was a loser of an operation. It had been that way from the first seconds when Iceman told him about it, and it was just getting worse. It wouldn't be long before these rubes got their act together, and then the big guns would arrive. SWAT teams, helicopters, and tanks, for all he knew.

But this current plan had legs. He'd just ripped a full thirty-round mag at that far corner of the building to keep the security guys' heads down long enough for Iceman to dash out and slap a GPC on the front door's lock, and then to dash back again.

Predictably, they unloaded in retaliation, but no one was hurt, and the dwindling ammo problem worked both ways.

When his cover got chewed up by shots coming from a new direction, he understood what had happened. They were moving for position.

That thought had just touched his brain when Iceman opened up from his cover behind the porch stairs.

"Saw one, got one!" he shouted. "Cover your ears."

The breaching charge detonated. Damn things were always louder that he thought they'd be.

"I'm fine," Big Guy said before Jonathan had a chance to ask. "Did you see—"

Jonathan saw the flash from the door half a second before the blast made it to him, and he knew instantly that they'd somehow gotten an explosive pack on the door and blown it.

"They breached the front door," he declared on the radio. They'd made their intentions clear, and now he had a target to watch.

Jonathan charged forward, rifle up and ready, sweeping from the door to the trees, searching for targets. He tried to use cover, but he had to get to the house before the assassins did. Once they started shooting up inside, it could be—

A rifle chattered full-auto on his right, and he dove for the dirt as bullets raked everything everywhere. It was covering fire, and Jonathan knew instinctively that the bad guys were entering the mansion.

The instant the shooting stopped, Jonathan was on his feet again and advancing on the source of the fire.

That's when he heard gunfire and screaming from inside the house.

"Oh, shit," Jonathan said. "They're inside."

The explosion at the door filled the foyer and office with shrapnel, wood chips, glass, and an impossible amount of dust. In the same instant, it obliterated Venice's sense of hearing. The power of the overpressure was something she'd never felt before. It knocked her back onto her butt on the floor.

But she could still hear the presence of noise, even though she could not make out what exactly the sounds were.

Boom-boom-boom-boom . . .

Oscar was still on his knee, shooting his rifle into the foyer, and Venice thought just what a mess it was going to be to clean all of this up.

Somebody grabbed her by the back of her shirt and pulled hard. She felt the fabric rip, and then she saw Oscar's jaw rip from his face. It spun sideways, as if anxious to have a conversation with his ear. And then the top of his head came off.

Boom-boom-boom-boom.

Those noises seemed much closer, and then she understood. It was as if her head had cleared, jump-started. Her shirt was tight because Derek was trying to pull her to safety. The incessant booming was him firing his rifle to save her life.

"Where's my rifle?" she said, but her words sounded as if they were coming from the end of a long tube.

When she finally found her feet, she took over as lead. It was her house, after all. She knew where all the doors and rooms were. This next room behind the reception area was the headmistress's office. It was the end of the line. She led Derek to a hard turn to the right, which led them out into a hallway of classrooms, blocked off from the foyer by secure double doors.

The doors on either side led to expanses of chairs and desks and whiteboards—nothing that could be used as a weapon.

"Stay here," Derek said. "Running isn't fighting. I have to—"

His words were cut off by a second explosion, and this one obliterated the security doors.

She seemed to be pulling Derek now, instead of the other way around. Without even looking behind, they dashed in to Room 4, Mrs. Hirsch's first grade classroom, where the walls were decorated with orange Jack-o'-lanterns on black paper.

"No sense hiding!" a man yelled.

She heard that. Her ears were getting better.

"I'm dead, anyway!" the man yelled. "Might as well take you with me!"

"He's got to come through that door, Derek," she whispered. "You can shoot him then."

"Okay," he said. "But I'm going to need your help."

He sounded strained, frightened, maybe. "Anything you need," she said.

When she saw blood on the floor, she turned to look at him. She spun around. "Derek!" she yelled. He was covered in blood, leaking it, but she couldn't tell where it was coming from. "Oh, no, no, no. Derek. Help me!" she cried.

Jonathan had to get inside.

The intensity of the shooting told him that somebody was putting up a fight, and he was stuck outside. Screw that.

As he advanced on the front door, he kept his muzzle focused on the trees where the overzealous shooter had set up shop.

"Slinger and I are advancing with you, Boss," Boxers said.

The shooter peeked out from his tree just enough to expose his elbow. Jonathan planted his feet, settled his red dot, and pressed the trigger. The shooter's arm spun away at a horrifying angle, and as its owner fell, he exposed his whole body. Jonathan shot him two more times.

A second explosion rocked the mansion.

He dropped his half-spent mag and slapped in another as he ran up the steps and through the front door of his old home. As he lifted his NVGs out of the way, the devastation stunned him. The parlor was a splintered wreck, and the walls were smeared and spattered with blood. The double security doors that led to the classrooms had been blown apart, and he could barely see through the dense veil of dust.

"Help me!"

It was Venice's voice, from somewhere beyond the dust. He charged that way. It was madness to enter alone, but sometimes you had to just bet it all.

"Help me! Please, God, help me!"

Five more steps, and there he was. A man dressed in battle gear was raising a rifle to shoot.

Jonathan snapped his M27 to his shoulder, put his finger on the trigger—

JoeDog lunged from a classroom on the left-hand side of the hallway and took the shooter from behind. Her teeth caught him high in the thigh, under his butt cheek, and she brought him down. The sounds that came from her throat were unlike anything Jonathan had heard before. Once down, she jerked her head from side to side, as if to rip the intruder's leg from his body.

Jonathan ran toward the fight.

The attacker howled as he thrashed on the floor. He swung punches at the dog, but the angles were wrong, and nothing landed solidly. It was Vitale, the dickhead who'd threatened him. Jonathan was four feet away from the scrum when Vitale produced a knife. "I'll kill—"

Jonathan shot him in the face.

JoeDog jumped at the noise, then wagged her tail.

"Good girl," Jonathan said.

When he pivoted to look into the classroom on his immediate right, what he saw weakened his knees. He was too late. Venice faced the back wall, hunched over, and the floor around her was wet with blood. "Oh, Jesus," he said. He hurried to her. "Where?" he said. "Where are you hit, Ven?"

She didn't answer.

Then, when he arrived at her side, he saw. She cradled Derek's head in her lap, stroking his face. "You'll be okay," she said. "We just need to get you to a doctor. Just hold on."

Derek's eyes were fixed and dilated. He was gone.

Jonathan kneeled down next to her and put his hands on her shoulders. "Ven," he said. "Oh, Ven, I'm so sorry."

"No," she sobbed. "Don't be sorry. He'll be fine. He has to be fine."

"Please, Ven."

"Get your hands off me!" she shouted. "He'll be fine. Just leave me alone." Her shoulders heaved.

Jonathan jumped when he felt a hand on his own shoulder. He looked up to see Gail looking down on them. "Let me," she said. "Let me."

Outside, the sound of sirens peaked and then wound down. The uniformed cavalry was arriving. "About goddamn time," Jonathan muttered.

He looked back to Venice and Derek and Gail. His heart broke for her, but comforting was not his strong suit. Gail could manage all that better without him.

As he stepped back out into the hall, cops and state troopers were beginning to fill the place in. One of the troopers said to him, "I'm going to need a statement from you."

"Eat shit," Jonathan said.

Another one said, "Put that weapon down, sir. We've got this."

Jonathan didn't hit the son of a bitch.

In the reception office, Doug Kramer, Charlie Keeling and Rick Hare were all tending to the wounded. Doug made eye contact, but Jonathan looked away.

As he stepped back out into the night to survey the rest of the damage, Jonathan was stunned by the amount of help that had finally arrived. Once the scene was secured, everybody wanted a piece of it. Lights of every color, it seemed, painted their patterns on the homes and businesses of Church Street. Residents packed the far side of the fence, three and four deep. More than a few of them held their cell phones aloft, snapping pictures of the scene, taking videos. Such excitement.

Boxers stood over the shooter that Jonathan had taken down out here in the yard. He was watching the man with a strange intensity. "Are you okay?" Jonathan asked.

"Fine," Boxers said, but he didn't turn away. "It's Kellner."

Jonathan joined them. The man lay on his back, eyes open and blinking frantically. The skin around his nose and lips had turned blue, and his tongue lolled in his mouth.

"You must have clipped his spine or something," Boxers said. "Sonofabitch can't breathe. Just wonderin' how long it'll take him to die."

"Huh," Jonathan said. He moved to Kellner's head and took a knee, so they could see each other more clearly. The guy's chest was moving funny, as if trying to pull in air but it wouldn't work.

Jonathan leaned in close and lowered his voice to just over a whisper. "I did this to you," he said. "I can't imagine dying like this. Slowly suffocating. Must be terrifying. I bet it hurts."

"Hey, Dig?" a new voice said. He looked up to see Dom D'Angelo standing with Boxers. "Don't do something you won't be able to live with."

Jonathan studied Dom's face. The priest was doing him a favor here, and Jonathan knew it. There were lines that should never be crossed.

"Okay," Jonathan said. Then he leaned in very close to the shooter—so close that he could smell the death on him. "I got one word for you, asshole. Retribution."

ACKNOWLEDGMENTS

So, here we are, another book in the can, as they say. My eighteenth, if I count correctly. People ask me all the time if this writing thing gets easier over time, and I never have a clear answer because while it's never *easy*, there does come a point when you know there's a dependable team behind you that will keep you from screwing up too badly.

For me, the star of my team is my lovely bride, Joy, without whom the sun could neither rise nor set. This will be our 35th year married, and 37th year together. Wow. The love story continues . . .

Another question that pops up a lot goes something like, "How do you do all of your research on weapons and tactics?" I'm blessed to be able to say that I pretty much make phone calls to people who truly know what they're talking about. Rick McMahan, who recently retired from the Bureau of Alcohol, Tobacco, Firearms & Explosives (officially BATFE, though the E has never looked right to me) has long been a valuable resource and good friend, and this year he doubled down and introduced me to MSGT Roby Lunsford, U.S. Army (Ret.) who's my new sensei for rifle optics. Thanks to both.

U.S. Navy SEAL Jeff Gonzales, president of Trident Concepts, LLC (www.tridentconcepts.com) and director of training for The Range Austin is my go-to resource on tactics and weapons selection. And when it comes to weapons to be selected, there's no better, more reliable brand than Heckler & Koch, where Robbie Reidsma is not only an expert, but is very tolerant of questions from authors. Thanks, guys.

I can't move past the gun-related stuff without thanking C. R. Newlin, owner of Echo Valley Training Center in West Virginia. Sometimes the choreography of a gunfight needs to be tried in person, and C.R. allows me to try things that other ranges simply don't have the resources to do. (And no, Jeff Gonzales, safety is never jeopardized.)

You never know when ancient connections rise to the top to provide important assistance. I went to school with Martin Lovett about a thousand years ago, yet there he was when I need guidance on how electricity moves from the pole to my light socket. The scene he helped me with didn't make it to the final draft, but that doesn't diminish his graciousness and patience in helping me pretend to understand stuff that I don't think I'll ever truly understand.

Jonathan bought Boxers a new fleet of planes in *Total Mayhem*, and when they went shopping, they took my old firehouse buddy and now airline pilot Chris Thomas shopping with them. Not only did they buy the planes he suggested, but they parked them where Chris thought they should be. Boxers is happy now, and when he's happy, we're all thankful.

If you've finished the book, then you know that life gets pretty hard for Frederick Kellner. What you might not know is that there's a real Fred Kellner, and he contributed generously to RiteCare Scottish Rite Childhood Language Program to have a character named after him. Fred is a Masonic brother of mine and a terrific guy, so take my word when I tell you there's not an assassin's bone in his body.

Every month, I have the honor of meeting with four of the most talented and insightful writers I know to critique each other's works. In over eight years, we've never missed a meeting. Thanks to Art Taylor, Donna Andrews, Ellen Crosby and Alan Orloff for being great friends, and for being so good at what you do.

My team at Kensington keeps working overtime to make me look better than I am. My editor, Michaela Hamilton, continues to be a terrific mentor and friend. A thousand thanks to my publisher, Lynn Cully, and to Steve Zacharius, the man in the corner office. Thanks, too, to Vida Engstrand in the marketing department, who, together with Lauren Jernigan, Ann Pryor, and the rest of team, make it possible for my work to somehow rise above the noise of the book industry. And, of course, there's Alexandra Nicolajsen, my real-life Venice, who helps me tame the ones and zeroes of cyberspace.

Finally, thanks to my friend and agent, Anne Hawkins of John Hawkins & Associates in New York, for making this ride a really fun one.

Don't miss the next gripping Jonathan Grave thriller
by John Gilstrap

HELLFIRE

Coming soon from Kensington Publishing Corp.
Keep reading to enjoy a sample excerpt . . .

Chapter One

Ryder Sims had heard every word spoken from the front seat. They thought he was asleep, and like every other adult, they believed that just because a kid's eyes were closed, he'd been struck deaf. He should be so lucky. He hadn't slept more than a few minutes in the past three days. Since the FBI crashed their house and tore his world apart.

Now, everything was ruined. He and his brother Jeff were being driven to some kind of orphanage by a lady driver, who he figured had to be a cop, and a priest named Father Dom. Both were nice enough to their faces, but it was the quiet conversations that revealed their true thoughts. They pitied him and his brother. They felt *sorry* for him.

When the lady driver wondered how *the boys* would ever get past *this kind of trauma,* Father Dom shushed her, said that such things ought not be discussed within ear shot. As if Ryder hadn't already wondered a thousand times how much his life was going to suck from now on. He'd never let it show to these people, but he was freaking *terrified* of all that had gone down.

Mom and Dad had warned him that that trouble was coming. Ryder didn't understand all the details but he wasn't completely surprised when the cops kicked in their door. Okay, he was *terrified* when the SWAT team pulled him out of bed and onto the floor at three in the morning. And the handcuffs hurt. But only for ten or fifteen minutes, until they figured that a thirteen-year-old and his eleven-year-old brother didn't pose any real hazard. After that, the cops were pretty nice. They let him get dressed, but not without a cop with a rifle watching the whole time. He felt better that the lady who watched him seemed as uncomfortable with it all as he did. After that, they walked him and Jeff straight out to a car where they whisked off to a stranger's house.

He never got a chance to say good-bye to his parents. Hell, he didn't even get a chance to *see* them.

Dad wasn't specific about why they'd done the things that got them sideways with the FBI—those were the words he used, *got sideways*—but Ryder was smart enough to know that pissing off the FBI was a big deal. That meant that Mom and Dad had committed a federal crime, not a state crime. Ryder wasn't sure why one was worse than the other, but everybody knew that federal crimes were the worst.

And man, oh man were there a lot of FBI windbreakers among the cops that invaded his house.

"You're going to hear a lot of bad things about me and your mom," Dad told him just hours before the invasion. "I wish I could tell you that they'll be false, but they're not."

"We've done bad things," Mom added. "We've killed people, but you have to know that it was never because we were angry. It was never an emotional thing."

"Sometimes business requires difficult decisions," Dad said, as if that made anything less head-spinning. "You don't need to know the details."

"You don't *want* to know the details," Mom said.

Ryder remained silent during that talk. It was a time to listen and pay attention. Questions never changed bad news, they only slowed it down.

Dad continued, "Of course, when this happens, it will have a huge effect on you and your brother." He said it as if they were planning a family trip. "We've taken steps for you to avoid foster homes. There's a very good school for people like you—"

"Children of people like us," Mom corrected. Again, as if making an important point.

"Yes, exactly," Dad said. "You've done nothing wrong. This is all on us. But there's a school—it's called Resurrection House and it's in Virginia—and it has a wonderful reputation."

"It's an orphanage," Ryder said, cutting to the chase.

"No," his parents said together. Dad expounded, "You're not an orphan."

"But you are going to jail, right?"

"Maybe," Mom said. Then her shoulders sagged. "Probably."

"We're still going to be alive is the point," Dad said. "Orphans don't have parents."

Ryder had no idea what this Resurrection House thing was all about, but that's where they were headed. If it wasn't an orphanage, then maybe it was a workhouse. He'd seen *Oliver!* so he knew what to expect.

For now, he figured that the Resurrection place had to be better than the house of douchebags they'd been staying with the last couple of days. Their whole house smelled like hot dogs and old socks, and the family stared at them all the time. It was weird. *They* were weird.

He was ready to take a gamble on the workhouse.

Ryder had always possessed an uncanny ability to read people. Not their minds—not like one of the Legimens from the Harry Potter stories—but he was great at reading their intentions, their state of ease or the lack thereof. It was like what they called *stranger danger* in school and what Dad called *situational awareness* at home, but not always. Like right now, he knew that the grown-ups in the car were upset about something. They leaned in close to each other and talked quietly. The driver lady kept glancing up into the rearview mirror.

Ryder quietly clicked his seatbelt open and rose from his captain's chair to turn around and look out the back window. He could see only one other car on the road behind them and it was driving way too close, the way Dad would when he was getting ready to pass.

"Please get back in your seat," Father Dom said.

"Are they trying to pass us?" Ryder asked.

The lady driver—her name was Pam—said, "If they were, they've had plenty of time to do it."

The priest repeated, "Ryder, I really want you to be in your seat."

Ryder opened his mouth to argue, but he decided to comply instead. This didn't feel right to him.

He'd just turned back to face front when the follow car's high beams lit up the back window and blue strobe lights painted wild shadows all over the van's interior.

Jeff jumped awake in the chair to his right. "What's happening?"

"Shut up," Ryder snapped. He didn't want to be mean, but if little dickhead was talking, he wouldn't be able to hear what was being said up front.

"I don't like this," Pam said. "I'm not doing anything wrong. There's no legit reason for us to be pulled over."

"Well, we can't just ignore them," Father Dom said.

The cop behind them popped his siren, as if to cast his vote on what they should do.

The driver pushed the button on the dash to turn on the hazard flashers. "I'm slowing down to thirty-five," she said. "Call nine-one-one to see—"

"Tell me what's happening!" Jeff insisted, blocking out the rest of the driver's command.

Ryder would be happy to call 911, but the FBI had taken their phones. And their computers. Hell, they'd taken everything. He and Jeff weren't allowed to take anything with them but underwear, clothes and a jacket.

As the van navigated a curve, another wall of blue lights erupted out front.

"I guess that decides that," the priest said.

The driver had to lean hard on the brakes, making Ryder feel better about his decision to sit back down and belt himself in.

"I'm scared," Jeff whined.

"Shut up," Ryder said. "We're all scared. Saying it doesn't help."

* * *

Very little about this pickup and delivery had felt right to Dom, and now this traffic stop was icing on the cake. He fumbled with his phone as he extracted it from his pocket.

"What do we do now?" he asked.

"We sit," Pam replied. A retired cop, she'd chosen social work as her second career. The same customer base, she'd explained, but nobody wants to shoot the lady with the clipboard and a smile. "Put the phone back in your pocket. You don't want to have anything in your hands. They'll tell us everything we need to know."

Out front, the cop's door opened and a uniformed officer took a position behind his engine block, his hands full of pistol. "Holy shit!" Dom exclaimed out of reflex. It came out much louder than he wanted.

Pam seemed less unnerved. "What the hell?"

Behind them, Ryder and Jeff almost collided heads as they leaned into the center space to see out the front windshield.

"Oh, my God," Jeff blurted. "Are they going to shoot us?"

"Stay in your seats, boys," Dom said. He thought it was damned good question, though. He waited for Pam to explain, but she continued to scowl at the man with the gun.

An electronic loudspeaker popped from behind. "Driver, turn off your engine and drop the keys out the window."

"Remember," Pam said in a clipped tone as she keyed the engine off. "You want your hands to be empty."

"What the hell is going on?" Dom asked.

"Ask me again in five minutes," Pam replied. "They think we're people we're not, and this is a felony stop. Do everything they say. Move slowly and keep your hands visible at all times." She made a show of dangling her keys out the window before dropping them to the pavement.

The cop on the loudspeaker said, "Driver, open your door and step out of the car. Keep your hands visible at all times."

"I told you," she said. Pam moved carefully. With her left hand extended out her window, she reached across her body with her right hand to pull the handle that opened the door. When it was unlatched, she used her foot to push it all the way open.

"Driver, step out, hands at your sides, fingers splayed, and side-step two steps to your left. Leave the door open."

Pam gave Dom a look he wasn't sure how to interpret and went about the business of following directions. She slid off her seat, her feet found the ground, and then she stepped off to the side. She stood with her arms out to her sides, cruciform, in a posture that impressed Dom as one that would quickly become exhausting.

"I'm really scared," said the younger brother. Jeff. Dom owed it to them to remember their names.

"This will all be over in a few minutes," Dom assured.

"Front seat passenger," the guy on the loudspeaker said. "Same drill. Open your door, keep your hands visible . . ." The instructions were pretty much the same as before.

Dom turned so he could see both faces. Adolescents looked so much younger when they were frightened. "Ryder and Jeff, listen to me," he said. "There's been some kind of misunderstanding. I'm sure everything will be fine. After I get out, I want you both to listen carefully and do exactly what the officer tells you to do."

"Are we in trouble, Father?" Ryder asked. His voice trembled.

"I don't know," Dom said. "But if you do what they say, everything will be fine."

Father Dom slid out of the passenger side door and then moved away from the van.

"Hands farther out to the side," the cop commanded. Dom raised his hands higher, splayed his fingers further out. Could they not see his white collar?

"Stay cool, officers," Dom said. "I'm a priest and my driver is a retired police officer."

For a second or two, nothing happened. Maybe longer. This was wrong. All of it seemed unreal. Unearned.

The kids.

Dom turned to look back at the boys, and that's when he heard the gunshot. Pam fell, and then something kicked Dom hard in the chest. As he fell to the street, he wondered how anything could feel so hot and not set him on fire.

He thought, *Please, God, forgive me.* Everything went dark.

The spatter from Pam's exploding head painted the window just inches from Ryder's face. He jumped and screamed something even he didn't understand. Another shot followed an instant later, and Father Dom dropped from view.

"No!" Jeff yelled. "Oh, my God they killed them!"

Ryder didn't say anything. His mouth wouldn't work. Through the smear of gore, he watched the cop from the front racing toward the van. His flashlight beam bounced as he ran. Ryder's stomach churned. He thought he might puke.

Except he didn't have time.

The cop pulled his sliding door open at the same time the other cop opened the slider on Jeff's side. They opened them hard, causing the panels to rebound halfway closed again.

"Get out," the closest cop said.

"What did you do?" Ryder shouted. "You killed them!"

The cop pressed his pistol against Ryder's forehead. "Open that mouth of yours again if you want to join them."

To Ryder's right, Jeff started to yell. "Leave me alone! Ryder! Help!"

The other cop slapped Jeff across the forehead with the barrel of his pistol, and the boy collapsed.

"Jesus!" Ryder yelled. "Jeff! Goddammit, leave him alone!"

The last part of his words sounded clipped and garbled as a rough sack was shoved over his head and tied tight across his neck. Out of reflex, Ryder brought his hands to his throat and pulled at the cinch.

"No!" he yelled, and he punched blindly at his attacker. "Get this thing off—"

A light flashed behind his eyes and there was nothing.

* * *

Dom hurt. His chest felt hot, hollow and numb all at the same time. He thought his eyes were open, but the world was very dark. He thought he could see the outline of trees across the black sky, but he couldn’t be sure.

“I’m alive,” he said aloud. It was a test of his voice. It didn’t sound right, as if coming from someone else and far away. “But I’m dead soon.” The words didn’t frighten him, though maybe they should. What they did was *focus* him.

He needed help, but out here at this hour, he could go undiscovered for longer than it would take for him to bleed out.

Ancient first aid training from back in his Army days tried to form in his mind. Should he raise his legs to counter the onset of shock, or should he try to raise his torso to slow down the bleeding?

Dom winced against anticipated pain as he finger-walked his left hand to his pants pocket where he could find his phone. Moving an arm meant flexing a chest muscle, though, and that brought the fiery agony back in Technicolor.

“Awww, *dammit!*” he grunted as he brought the phone up to his face. He shut his eyes against the brightness of the screen. He pressed the voice command button and said, “Dial Digger on cell.”

The phone replied, “Dialing Digger Grave on cell.” The electronic lady’s voice sounded even bitchier than usual.

As the call connected and he heard the ring tone, he prayed not to hear the voice mailbox message. Dom didn't know if he had that much consciousness left in him.

After the third ring (or was it the thirtieth?) he heard a click, and then the raspy, sleep-addled voice of his old friend. "Jesus, Dom, it's late. What the hell?"

"Dig, I've been shot."

"Are you serious?" Jonathan Grave seemed one hundred percent awake now.

"I'm somewhere on the Cove Road," Dom said. He spoke quickly because he knew he didn't have time. "Trace the cell signal and get me some help. It's bad."

"Oh, holy crap," Jonathan said. "Shit."

"Dig, listen to me," Dom continued. "It was cops. They shot me and the driver."

"The kids, too?"

"I don't know. I think they took them. I need help, brother."

"It's on the way," Jonathan said. "Keep your phone on."

Dom nodded his answer as he lost his grip.